# Amethyst Saga Book 2

# Ametrine: Twists of Fate

## K. L. Dimago

Butterfly Books Publishing

# Want to Learn the Tale Behind Amethyst's Trusty First Mate?

As my way of saying, "Thank you," for getting your copy of *Ametrine*, I'm *giving you* this free novella.
Learn how the fae conquered the mages, enslaved Darien, and how he partnered with Amethyst.

Go to: *kldimago.com/darienstale*
and download *free* today!

The Amethyst Saga

-*-

Book 1
Amethyst: Rise to Piracy

Book 2
Ametrine: Twists of Fate

Book 3
Iolite: A New Era

Book 4
Tourmaline: The Pirate's Daughter

*Ametrine: Twists of Fate*
Copyright © 2015 by K. L. Dimago
Published by Butterfly Books Publishing
4817 43rd St.
Lubbock, TX 79414

Cover Design by Novex Designs
Interior Design and Typesetting by K.L. Dimago
First Edition: Kellan Publishing 2015
Second Edition: Butterfly Books Publishing 2022
Edited and proofread by Jake Waller.

Printed in the United States of America.

ISBN-13 (paperback): 978-1-7353658-3-1
ISBN-13 (hardcover): 979-8-9859165-0-8



Summary: Amethyst finally learns to love, only to have it ripped away in the most tragic way possible, and must overcome a threat like never before if she is to maintain her reputation and free lifestyle on the seas.

www.kldimago.com

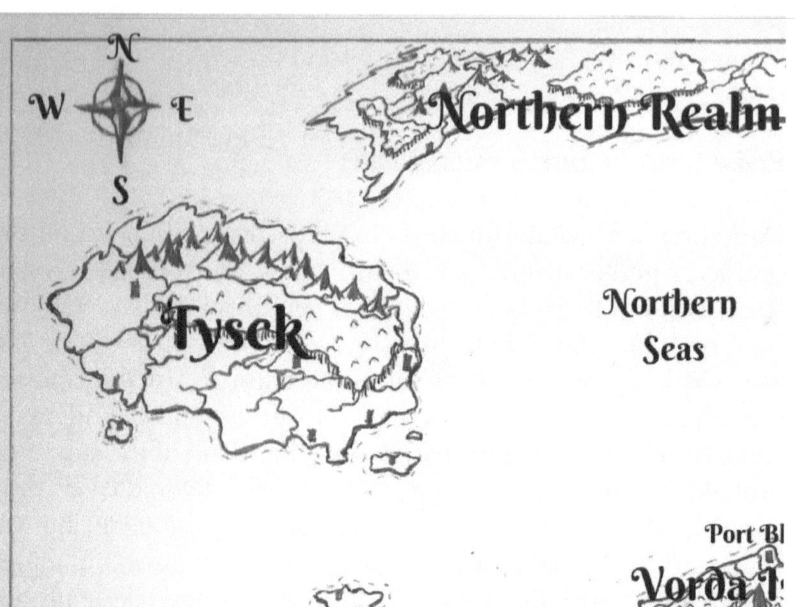

World of Aseath

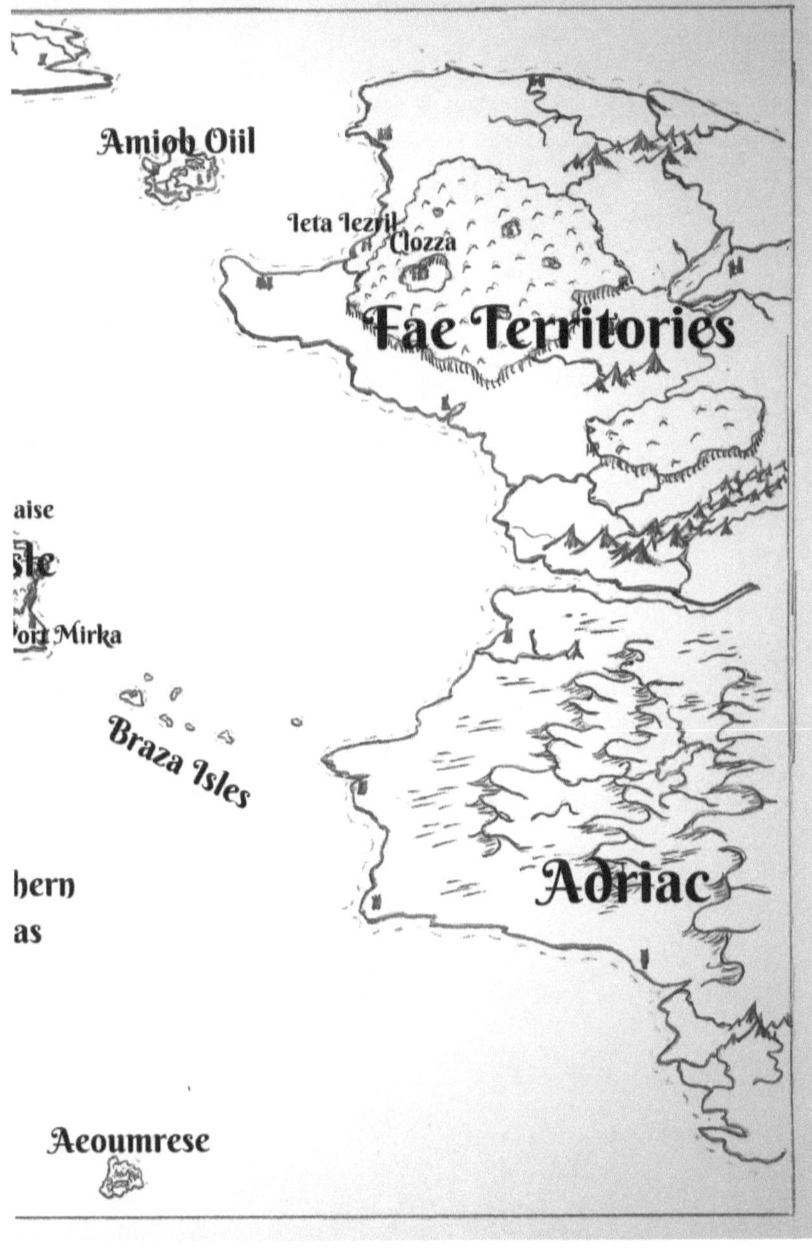

Amioh Oiil
Ieta Iezril
Clozza
Fae Territories
aise
sle
Port Mirka
Braza Isles
hern
as
Adriac
Aeoumrese

# Table of Contents

# Acknowledgments

First and foremost, I'd like to give a special thanks to my husband for all of his encouragement throughout finishing this book. There were definitely difficult times in the process, but I'm very glad he patiently allowed me to bury myself in the story.

I'd also like to thank several friends who supported me and eagerly awaited the finish line. They were with me (sometimes painstakingly) as I talked about each part of the whole process and their excitement for what was to come kept me going.

Finally, a very special note to an old friend of mine without whom much of this story would not exist. She was behind so much and inspired me to make this story into what it is today. Thank you, Azure.

# Pirate Meeting

The day was a gloomy one. Dark clouds in the sky and the scent of rain threatened a vicious storm on the brink of downpour. Already the drizzle that had begun was soaking through the town's old cobblestones.

Though not a large town, Port Drelle was well known amongst pirates and seafarers. Usually Drelle was a wild scene, but today everyone was rushing to get inside somewhere. The streets were mostly empty.

Still, several ships were pulling into the nearby docks and taking anchor. Those just now arriving were late to the urgent pirate meeting that had been called. All captains were expected to attend.

Not long before, a large black frigate had anchored. Its edges and windows were painted silver. The sails were an eerie black, also lined in silver, with the image of a hooded cloak wielding a scythe sewn in red. '*The Reaper's Scythe*' was etched into the sides of the hull near the stern.

The *Reaper's Scythe* was one of many notorious ships at sea, like the *Gargoyle*. The crew were anxious as they carried out their duties on deck. They were discussing the events leading up to the meeting, and what might happen after. Their captain, Cadell, had already gone into town, and now sat calmly in one of the many chairs around a long, rectangular wooden table. The meeting was being held in a large well-known pub, *Skull's Mark*.

Cadell's arms were folded across his chest. He was young, his appearance around late-twenties, and his eyes wandered around the room as he waited for the remaining captains to arrive and settle.

The door opened a few moments later to reveal two rather wet figures standing in the doorway. One was male, the other female. It seemed that the woman at the doorway was one of the only lasses present besides the wenches who served.

All eyes in the room darted to the doorway. The men let their eyes travel across the woman's curved figure. Cadell noted a large scarlet hat with a long peacock feather that drooped to one side of her head. The man accompanying the woman took her hat and long coat, and her tall dark leather boots clicked as she walked across the room. Deep eggplant-colored ringlets tumbled down her back and shoulders, frizzing lightly. Her pale pirate's shirt was tied just under her bosom, revealing her firm, tanned stomach. Not a soul in the room failed to recognize the captain of the *Gargoyle*.

Of course, Cadell couldn't help drinking in Amethyst's figure. But he tried to appear bored and glanced away. Amethyst was stunning. In fact, even with all his education, Cadell could not find a word to describe her beauty. But he kept his opinion to himself. Pirate captains typically kept their distances except in dire circumstances, such as the meeting being held today where alliances would soon be drawn.

Also, Amethyst had a reputation for keeping an especially large distance. She would sometimes let another ship sail beside hers for a brief time, but when she grew sick of them, she would demand they go their way or be sunk to Davy Jones' Locker.

Cadell had decided a long time before that he would respect her desire for distance.

Still, that wasn't to say he could deny the desire she stirred in him.

He glanced toward her again.

A look of disgust crossed her features as she looked around the table at the other captains present. Her eyes moved between Cadell and a large, nasty looking man. Amethyst flipped a piece of hair behind her shoulder as her accompaniment, or rather, her first mate, Darien, pulled the chair next to Cadell out for her and she took a seat. It was very rare that Amethyst was seen anywhere without her first mate.

"Cap'n Amethyst, we 'ere afraid ye weren't goin' t' make it, lass." A man with a rough brogue grinned at her. She raised her eyebrow. "Tha seas 'ere rather rough," the man who had spoken finished.

Some of the other captains present added some teasing comments.

"You speak to me as if I were a common wench, so I will speak to you as if you were a common manservant," Amethyst spat, making a few chuckle. It seemed some were entertained at least while waiting for the remaining captains to arrive.

Cadell on the other hand was not. He was here on business and the matters to be discussed were grim. While perhaps some humor was good, he hoped the others would settle down quickly. Still, at Amethyst's retort, he fought to hold back a small smirk. *'Aye, and the seas'll be stormy once this meeting is over,'* he thought as he caught her pointed look at each of the captains around the table. Amethyst's temper was famous.

Finally, the last members of the group had arrived, though some were still settling. Cadell leaned forward slightly. "Shall we get to the meeting, then?"

A tall, burly man stood after a moment. He was one of the oldest captains present and commanded attention with his muscular build. His name was Xavier, but everyone just called him 'X'.

"All of ye know why we're here. So, I'll get to the point. The seas are on the brink of war, and if ye don't make alliances, many of us will fall." X glanced around, waiting for others to chime in. His gaze settled briefly on Amethyst, as one of the most reputable captains present. A smirk touched the corner of his lip, and his eyes seemed to question if she had anything to say.

Cadell didn't miss X's look toward Amethyst, and a twinge of jealousy touched him. Though one of the youngest captains here, he had already built himself a reputation as one not to be trifled with. The captains present might be poking fun, but he was sure they knew well that Amethyst was no dainty damsel in distress.

Further, if everyone continued toying with her temper, nothing would be accomplished. In fact, the meeting called for the purpose of alliances could instead turn into a pirate brawl! That was perhaps more likely. Still, Cadell remained quiet as others began speaking.

"I've got an alliance as sturdy as I need it," one captain voiced.

"Do ye underestimate us?" said another.

"I've got a strong ship, strong crew. I don't need an alliance."

"Perhaps we do need an alliance. But one how strong?"

"Who knows how strong our opponent is?"

"What're we fightin' anyway?"

Each question came from a different captain around the table.

Amethyst looked up, startled from her reverie of thoughts as Darien set a wine glass filled with rum on the table in front of her. She grasped it and made a point of taking a dainty sip. She resumed listening to the others. Idiots. Pure idiots, the lot of them. She may be a pirate also, but these men were a bunch of broads. She had her dignity, and despite escaping her past, remnants of it remained in her mannerisms.

She looked at X dead in the face and gave him a sugary sweet smile, since he had made a point of looking in her direction. "What does it matter if we make an alliance or not? With you lot, you're all to go down together or alone. It'll only be a matter of time." The tension in the air was palpable. "When you look into the mirror, you see a strapping young man for whom the wenches swoon and who's invincible. But what are you really?" she asked softly, pausing to take another dainty sip, dabbing her mouth lightly. "Fat pigs who have grown lazy with each plunder. Self-absorbed backstabbers." She chuckled lightly. "But that makes a man a pirate, I guess." She waved her hand lazily. "You all may have the brawn, but the brains are certainly lacking."

She glanced at Darien. If it weren't for him, she wouldn't even be here. Why *had* she agreed to come? There were very few people in existence she could tolerate to be around, aside from her own gathered crew. This talk of war on the seas... why should she care? She should just save them all the trouble of fighting and split every cur in the room from head to toe. She cringed at the thought of alliances. She preferred to sail *alone*.

"And what about the ones of us who are like you? As in, we're rather new on the seas, hmm? You group every one of us together like a pack." The response came from the young captain sitting across from Amethyst.

Captain Stephan. Despite being one of the youngest captains present, he already commanded his own fearsome reputation. Someone cunning, fearless and also proper. He had sandy blonde hair and emerald green eyes with skin too fair for someone living at sea. He had sharp, defined features, and an ever-present smirk on his pink lips.

Not much was known of Stephan's past, except that he was the son of a wealthy merchant trader and what time he'd not been at sea he'd spent with a noblewoman mother. He was both arrogant and spoiled.

"Yea, not all of us are as ye say," another man chimed in. With that, the room exploded as others around the table began shouting over each other their own responses to what Amethyst had said.

A loud bang sounded through the room and all eyes shot toward X. His fist was planted firmly on the table and his eyes were sharp. "That'll be enough, Captain Amethyst," X spat out, giving her a cold glare. "This is no joking matter."

As another insult glimmered in Amethyst's eyes, X turned his gaze toward the others. Amethyst exhaled deeply as Darien rested a hand on her shoulder, squeezing it. Yes, she needed to keep her temper in check.

"Now then," X continued, "If anyone has any specifics on the enemy, speak up." He leaned back slightly, eyes moving from each person to the next, commanding and stern. There were a few murmurs in the crowd before Stephan stood. The leader smirked faintly. "Captain Stephan, what could an amateur like ye know?"

Amethyst watched as Stephan's eyes turned cold yet he simply replied with, "Don't underestimate me. I happen to know our enemy isn't just an alliance of ships or some other strong foe. The goal of our enemy is some sort of power. I'm not sure of the details, but I know that already many pirate captains have been enthralled by it. It's evil. I know that much. And this war isn't just between pirate ships. This is a war to see who can get to that power first. This is a war over the very peace of the seas as it is now!"

Stephan's eyes shifted around the room as he seemed to realize he'd gotten excited, and he tried to calm himself as he took his seat again.

"I see. And how, may I ask, do ye know this?" X asked Stephan.

The only answer X got was, "A very close and trusted friend of mine."

Amethyst frowned, though she saw that X seemed to take Stephan's words into thought. She was about to say something, when Cadell's smooth voice reached her ears.

She glanced toward him. This was her chance to assess him more closely and finally get to the bottom of why he created the deep sense of calm and intense curiosity within her. He was the only one in the room who hadn't made advances or expressed a particular interest in her. Yes, she had secretly hoped he would be here. He was the reason she had agreed to come.

"So, then, Stephan. Since ye know so much, how 'bout telling us how to handle this... power. If this 'thing' is so bad, perhaps we must ally together to destroy its source?" asked Cadell.

Captain Stephan remained silent, his lips pursed as he stared at Cadell.

"I don't see why I should have to care about this." Amethyst wrinkled her nose lightly after Captain Stephan gave his little speech. '*An evil power? Leave it to men to get caught up in such matters.*' She was fae, and far more powerful than any of the mere humans in this entire room. In fact, she was *certain* she was more powerful than any of the nonhumans in the room as well.

"Well you should," Stephan responded, "Even if you're a tough captain, you're still a girl, and a pretty one like you shouldn't be so resistant to help. Wouldn't want to lose such a creature as yourself," he added with a smirk.

Amethyst rose and grabbed her weapon in the same instant. The zing of a blade slicing through the air was barely heard before the thud of her dagger stabbing through the wall just past Stephan. "Perhaps you desire for your ship the fate of those who test the captain of the Gargoyle," she hissed, eyes glaring daggers at each of the captains around the room and narrowing further as they settled on Stephan. Darien touched her shoulder lightly and she settled back down, eyes still sharp. Apparently, these new captains needed to learn why she held one of the most fearsome reputations on the seas.

The blast of a gunshot echoed through the room, smoke rising from a rounded pistol in X's hand as it pointed toward the ceiling. "Enough, ye scallywags!" X scolded. He returned to the subject of the meeting. "Captain Stephan, if ye have insight in how to deal with this threat, I suggest ye share it quickly."

"Yes, Captain, what should we do about this *threat?*" Amethyst licked lips that were dry despite the fact she was still drinking from her glass. She glanced up as one of the serving wenches placed a plate of food in front of her. Darien bent close, whispering she needed to eat.

She agreed. If nothing else, it would occupy her focus. She began to eat, stabbing the meat with her fork while pretending it was one of the present captains. Stephan, in particular. A flash of tiny fangs came from her mouth as she chewed, vicious thoughts circling her mind.

Gradually the other captains in the room began to chime in with questions for Stephan about the enemy. Amethyst did not fail to notice the way Stephan seemed to grow tense with all the prodding. His fists clenched and a snarling scowl filled his features. "I don't know anything. I've said all I know. It isn't right to assume anything as if I'm the one responsible for any of this."

Someone else began to speak, and Amethyst noticed a look of relief sweep across Stephan's features.

"I suggest we find out what this evil is. The more we know, the more protection we can have, eh? Stephan, you, if nothing else, know how a person can fall prey to this power, right?" This voice was merely another captain in the room.

With murmurs from the crowd, Stephan scowled again. It was obvious he felt pressured and wasn't handling it well. "Actually, I don't know. But I've heard that coming in contact with someone who's under its influence can have an effect. Just don't be too relaxed. I advise everyone to be watching your backs."

For the first time since this whole thing began, Amethyst intently narrowed on Stephan. She was in touch with her instincts, and something didn't sit right. It felt off. There was more than he was letting on. She frowned, an uneasiness growing in her gut. Why was he so uneasy when he had been the one to bring the information? What was he hiding?

Amethyst glanced briefly at Cadell, and once more, calm swept over her. She closed her eyes, breathing deeply, trying to focus on his scent over everything else in the room.

"...so then we have nothing to worry about! Stop asking daft questions. I–" Amethyst was pulled from her thoughts as Stephan's voice rose in response to demands for specifics from some of the other captains.

All were interrupted by X who retook charge of the situation. "Alright, Captain Stephan. No need to get excited. It's settled. Ye all have been warned and I suggest ye make alliances as ye see fit to fight as you will. The captains won't meet again for some time, so make use of ye chance. Beware of the danger ahead." The last words he said with such fierceness the room tensed.

Stephan only shrugged and rose from his seat. "Fine. Unless Captain Amethyst has something else to add." He flashed a smirk her way, his green eyes daring her to challenge him. As soon as the words left Stephan's mouth, he had to duck to the side to avoid another dagger which buried itself in the wall behind him with a whish of air and a soft zing.

"I have already voiced my opinion and will decide by myself what I shall do, whether or not I go out alone," Amethyst stated, her voice quiet. It sounded so unusual on her that it was almost creepy. Even Darien seemed unsettled. Her eyes lifted to look at Stephan, anger smoldering in their depths. She was a little disappointed her dagger had missed his face. "Stay away from me." Her voice was that same quiet, yet there was an underlying threat. Why was he taunting her?

The room quickly emptied as the captains glanced around and retreated. Afterall, she was sure they were eager to discuss the coming war and their foolish alliances.

Stephan seemed unfazed by her dagger, an infuriating smirk resting on his lips. As much as she hated to admit it, Captain Stephan was a fine thing to look at. He was rather easy on the eyes and his voice had a smooth quality to it. But something about that smooth quality raised the hair on the back of her neck. He gave her bad vibes. She could sense the readiness for a challenge coming off him.

As most retreated, it was soon only Amethyst, Darien, Cadell, Stephan, and a couple others. Amethyst turned to Darien. "Prepare my room." He nodded, heading off. She pushed herself from the table, and immediately regretted it. The movement strengthened the subtle nausea she had ignored before. Her legs wobbled under her.

The room blurred. The lights swirled and noises were staggeringly loud then barely audible. She gripped the table in her hand, cursing as her knees crashed into the cold floor.

Amethyst's vision regained for a moment. Where was Darien? She'd forgotten.

A yelp left her throat and her arms flew across her stomach as sharp pain traveled from her torso outward. Bile rose in her throat and she choked it back, slumping forward. She closed her eyes tightly as her vision blurred again. The pain spoke of poison. Darien must not have detected it in her food. She wondered how long before she might black out.

Then, she felt warmth.

Strong arms grasped her middle and pulled her upward, half carrying her as her legs stumbled. Amethyst barely even registered she was no longer in the pub. Rain hammered at her head and soaked through her clothing. It was then a familiar, soothing voice reached her ears. "Come on, let's get ye to yer ship. Hurry." Cadell.

"L-leave... me... be..." she gasped, pushing weakly against him.

"Lean on me, come on." Over and over, his voice repeated words of comfort.

Stubbornness burned in her halfway conscious mind, but she gave in and leaned into him, fighting to remain conscious.

It was the first time Amethyst had displayed weakness in front of the other captains at sea. Fortunately, it had only been a few. Or perhaps *unfortunately*.

She fought back tears at the pain raging against her stomach and she was glad as they blended in with the rain.

Cadell was glad he had been right beside Amethyst in the pub. As soon as she'd fallen, he'd grasped her. At first, he hadn't known quite what was wrong and had tried to support her in walking back toward the docks. But as soon as they'd gotten outside, he knew it would be better to simply carry her. The rain soaked through both of them. He just hoped that she didn't come out of this with a nasty illness to boot.

He hadn't failed to notice her stubborn attempts to walk herself. But she could hate him for it later.

Soon, the form of the *Gargoyle* was in view and the crewmembers were rushing down the plank toward him. They took her aboard the ship to tend to her. Cadell was baffled. Amethyst hadn't been the only one to eat during the meeting. He turned, assuming that now that she was aboard the *Gargoyle* there was nothing more for him here.

"Captain Cadell, the first mate would like a word."

aboard. Cadell hardly had time to observe anything, especially since it was raining so heavily.

He was led to Amethyst's cabin, where Darien was already taking care of Amethyst. She had been stripped quickly and put into a hot bath filled with both salts and soaps. Cadell had heard of the magic weaved into the *Gargoyle*, but now he saw it was true.

Another crew member was forcing a strange liquid down her throat. In a moment, her body was limp and her head lolling back. Darien sat by Amethyst, cradling her head. He stroked her hair softly, whispering foreign words to her.

Cadell forced himself not to let his eyes linger on Amethyst out of respect for her as a captain. He knew she would be furious if she learned she was in such a state in front of anyone who might damage her reputation. Or at least, he assumed so from their encounters in the past.

Instead, he focused his gaze on Darien. Cadell brushed aside the dark locks of hair that had swept across his eyes. "First Mate Darien. Ye wanted to talk with me?" Cadell asked calmly.

"I wanted to thank you for acting so quickly to help Amethyst. I don't know what was in her food, but I've been able to gather what was left of it to analyze." Darien paused, frowning, then continued. "Anyway, I would like for you to have this."

He gestured toward another crewmember carrying a small box. Darien opened it, retrieving a small dagger with a silver gargoyle etched into the hilt. "It was a prized possession, but nothing is more precious than our captain," he stated softly, looking back at Amethyst, who was fully asleep at this point.

"Oh, it was nothing. I-" Cadell started, but he didn't finish his sentence. He glanced down, eyeing the dagger as it was presented to him. Cadell hesitated, then took the hilt and examined the blade. "Thank you," he said with a smile. He flipped it before sticking it through the leather belt about his waist. Such a gift for his aid seemed exaggerated. Perhaps Darien had something else in mind?

"So, how long do you plan to remain in port?" the first mate asked Cadell.

"Hmm, not quite sure. I was planning to stick around for a few days. Me crew are a bit tired, but more than that, there's much more to be planned on all this war business. Why do ye ask?"

"If you could perhaps, come by tomorrow, when Amethyst is awake, then we could talk more."

Cadell was curious but knew he would learn the answers to his questions soon enough. He was not surprised at the secrecy. Often alliances were drawn in private so as not to draw unwanted attention. Particularly from other captains who might not take so kindly to some other ships joining together.

"Of course. It'll be in the afternoon. I trust she will be feeling up for a meeting by then?" Cadell glanced at Amethyst briefly, still concerned, before returning his gaze to Darien.

"We'll make it an afternoon lunch. I am sure Amethyst will be feeling better. Her body heals quickly," Darien assured Cadell, stroking Amethyst's hair once more. "If she is not, I would still like to speak to you on her behalf," the first mate finished.

"Till tomorrow then. I'll take my leave." Cadell gave a faint nod, turned, and left. He noticed the way Darien cared over Amethyst and wondered what sort of relationship the two had. Not that it was any of his business, but it seemed as though Darien had feelings for her that she may or may not know of. Cadell pushed the thoughts from his mind.

As Cadell walked along the dock back toward his *Reaper*, he twirled his new dagger between his fingers.

Captain Stephan seemed to materialize in front of him.

Cadell's eyes narrowed and turned cold. "What do *you* want?"

Stephan smirked, green eyes burning hatred toward Cadell. "Mark my words, Captain Cadell. I don't care just how powerful you are on the seas, or how good you think you are, stay away from Amethyst. She's mine." With that, he turned and walked off, his face darkening as he did.

Cadell watched Stephan as he left. "She belongs to no one," he said, laughing at the notion. Clearly, this young fool had much to learn.

As Cadell approached his ship, one member of his crew tossed him a rope. He ran forward, grasped the rope, climbed his ship with expertise, and hoisted himself aboard. As he landed on deck, his boots made a dull thud. "Alright, men! We're anchoring for a few days. Karl, Arlo, Dail, come with me. The rest of you, back to work!" With that he headed to his cabin, where he waited for the three men he'd called to report.

Cadell glanced at his desk and sighed, ignoring the various stacks of papers there and simply taking a seat. When his men entered he spoke with each of them, giving them different assignments. Dail to gather a list of weapons, clothes, and provisions, Karl to go with Dail to market in order to gather said supplies, and Arlo to see if there were any young men seeking to join a crew, and if they were worthy enough of the *Reaper's Scythe.*

As soon as they had gone, Cadell settled, his mind sorting through the day's events. He had a feeling he knew what it was Darien had planned for the day ahead.

# *Alliances*

*A*methyst had spent the night in her bathroom, throwing up everything in her stomach. Her face was pale, and she could barely move on her own without support from one of her crew members. But at last, just before sunrise, she had fallen asleep, to the relief of her crew.

As soon as the chance had come, several of her men had moved her sleeping form to the main deck where she could lie under the warm sun and breathe fresh air. The crew then settled into their chores, some swabbing the deck and others inspecting the lines.

Darien barked out orders, insisting everything be clean and in order for the arrival of Captain Cadell later that day. Nothing must go wrong.

The first mate of the *Gargoyle* also watched over Amethyst as she slept. Two of the larger crew members guarded her like hawks should she wake and need something. Or rather if something or *someone* tried to harm her.

Darien hadn't failed to notice Captain Stephan's focus on Amethyst the previous day, and to take precautions, the *Gargoyle*'s first mate had sent a runner with a note earlier in the morning.

It read:

Darien would die before letting anyone else hurt Amethyst. She had been hurt by many men in her past and even when she didn't want it, he would always protect her. He was like an older brother to her, and any man who wanted to get to Amethyst often had to go through Darien first.

Upon return, the runner reported that on receipt of Darien's note, Stephan had laughed, reading it over a few times before voicing his thoughts. "Darien... Darien... how foolish. When did I ever say I would get near the Gargoyle? Don't underestimate me, first mate. I have ways to get what I want... without even coming near the Gargoyle." He spoke to no one in particular.

The runner had been standing behind him on the main deck of *Hell's Serpent*, Stephan's ship. As Stephan turned sharply around, his eyes had been sharp. "Come with me. You are to give Darien a little message in response." The young captain had gone swiftly into a room with a desk and a few papers stacked in the corner and scribbled a response.

The runner went straight back to the *Gargoyle* and Darien read:

*Even so. Don't worry, I won't come within two hundred feet of your precious captain's ship unless with good reason.*
*Captain Stephan*

The runner also reported that Stephan had threatened him, as if not understanding he was a member of the *Gargoyle*'s crew himself. "If you tell him anything besides what is written in this note, I will have your head," he had said while sliding a knife from behind his back.

Darien read the note quickly, nodding at the runner's report and eyes narrowing. He turned in a sharp motion and moved into his cabin, the runner following. Without a word, he snatched another piece of paper and the sound of agitated scribbling echoed. As soon as he was done, he folded the response and placed it in the runner's hands. The runner simply ducked and left.

Upon return to the *Gargoyle* after, the runner once again reported to Darien.

He described how aboard *Hell's Serpent,* Stephan's face had risen in surprise as soon as he saw how quickly a response came. The captain's strides had been long as he moved toward the runner and he took the note and read aloud.

*"Captain Stephan,*
*Perhaps I have not made myself clear. There will be no alliance between the Gargoyle and Hell's Serpent, no alliance ever with Amethyst. I have no intention of meeting with you and no deal will be made. Do not make any attempts at such, or you will be made to regret any thoughts toward our captain."*

Stephan had crumbled the paper and thrown it overboard into the sea. Fury had lined his face, his eyes glimmering. He had told the runner to go, dismissively, and had leaned over the side of his ship, seeming determined and conniving. The runner was sure he was plotting something.

Meanwhile, aboard the *Reaper's Scythe,* Cadell hadn't been able to sleep much the previous night. He was up long before sunrise, and now stood on the main deck, leaning against the railing. He heard the shouts of his crew behind him.

His men were busy taking care of the ship. They stocked and organized provisions, one of which was of course rum, lowered in barrels to the holding deck. They sewed tattered sails and checked the various supporting lines along the stern and the masts.

Cadell moved toward the dock, beginning to aid his crew. There was much to do before they set sail.

As the day carried on, Cadell went to work sharpening some of the weapons and testing them. He finished sharpening a broadsword, flipping it over a couple of times before practicing a few lunges and swings with it briefly. He turned, placing it aside with a pile of other swords, axes, daggers, and knives.

A proud grin filled Cadell's lips, and he wiped his arm across his forehead. As soon as he put away his tools, he moved to upper deck and placed his first mate, Aurek, in charge of the ship. It was time for his meet with Darien and Amethyst.

A little while later, Cadell was on board the *Gargoyle.* The crew welcomed him and pointed him in Darien's direction.

Darien sat at a round table that had been set up on the main deck with three chairs, a pale cloth, rum, and a small meal.

Across the deck, Cadell spied Amethyst's sleeping form and he couldn't help a faint smile. He turned his gaze back to the first mate, reminding himself not to get carried away. "She looks better. Is she?"

"She was very sick until early this morning. Throwing up," Darien said, looking at Amethyst.

"Ah, well, she seems much better now. Did ye ever figure out what was in the food?" Cadell asked.

"Aye. Some spice that is not kind to her fae body. I didn't think to ask about the spices." Darien sighed, looking angry at himself about it. "Luckily, she is strong and her body was able to fight off most of the toxins from the spice. Sometimes, it can be a bit of a pain, but she's very valuable and it's my duty to protect her. Because, let's face it, we both know that she can't protect herself from everything, as much as she thinks it."

The first mate gave a soft chuckle. "If she wakes, she will join us. I do not want to disturb her peace," he said. "Here, take a seat." Darien gestured toward the table.

Cadell took his seat and glanced over the food. He took a bite out of a scone and then grasped one of the goblets. Once they were both seated, Darien started to talk.

"Captain Cadell, I wish to offer an alliance with your ship. And to be completely honest, it's not for this war, but it could come in handy. I wish for you to join us in an alliance to perhaps bring peace to our ship. Amethyst has become even more temperamental in recent times, if you haven't noticed. But we have noticed that she seems a whole lot more relaxed around you.

We would be in your eternal debt if you would just perhaps spend a little time aboard the *Gargoyle* and soothe Amethyst. It would only be for a couple of months." Darien took a brief sip of his rum.

"I believe she wouldn't make any advances toward you, considering she does not like the idea of being tied down with a child at this moment, or even the risk for that matter." Darien paused, his eyes searching Cadell's face.

Cadell had expected the offer. So, this also explained the dagger gift Darien had previously presented. "Ah, I see. A means to keep things calm, eh? Ye'll keep in mind, I won't pretend to be anything I'm not. I'll merely be myself and things will play themselves out. Savvy?" After all, if Amethyst did make advances toward him, he would hardly protest. They would certainly not be unwanted.

"Understandable," Darien responded, "I would have not pressured you, or to be honest, to want you to act as if something was up. I don't want her knowing about this reason for alliance. The only reason that we will give is that we wish to be stronger in case this threat is really worse than it has been made out to be." Darien paused, "Honestly, I would appreciate the extra protection. I have sent a letter off to Mister Stephan, but I doubt that will deter him. I sense ulterior motives in that man, and it does not comfort me."

Cadell mulled this over. "Captain Stephan, huh. Ye're not the only one detecting something off from him. But I'm sure as long as we're in alliance, no harm will come to her."

Darien's voice was still hushed and somewhat quick because he wasn't sure when Amethyst would wake. "Actually, I'd also prefer to offer you payment. We can pay you a very fine penny indeed."

Cadell thought a moment over the offer of money, then shook his head. "It's not important. For now, we'll stick to the alliance."

Darien smiled, leaning back in his seat. "Thank you, Captain Cadell. I must admit, I'm feeling better already about this whole ordeal."

Cadell also smiled and nodded. "As am I, First Mate Darien." Both men's voices quieted as they heard Amethyst stirring, beginning to wake.

Amethyst let out a yawn, pushing herself up. She blinked groggily, pushing her shirt up. She was wearing one of Darien's shirts, and it was just a tad too big. Her eyes focused on the two men and she let out a smile, pushing off the blanket. Long legs were exposed, the soft tan glistening. The shirt was the only thing she was wearing, and it only came down to her lower thighs.

She seemed to pay her appearance little mind as she stood and walked over to the table. "Good afternoon, Darien. You too, Captain Cadell." She smiled brightly. "Are we having a little meeting, and I wasn't invited?" She giggled lightly as she took the last chair. She crossed her legs and picked up one of the goblets, taking a light sip.

Cadell found himself somewhat amused watching her. She was so pleasant at this moment, perhaps because she had first woken up, as opposed to the snarling demeanor she'd had at the meeting the previous day. "Aye, good afternoon, Captain Amethyst," he responded to her greeting.

"Ah, that's good. Tell me, what's this little meeting about?" She quirked a brow, brushing eggplant-colored ringlets from her eyes.

"We were just discussing the details of an alliance between our ships. Feeling better?" Cadell had to keep reminding himself to stay focused on business. And on Amethyst's face.

"Oh, much better." Amethyst smiled lazily, leaning on the table. "My, such pretty weather today, especially after all that rain." She turned her head toward the sun lightly. "A nap in the sun was just what I needed. I was dreadfully sick last night. Oh, it was just horrible!" She started to fix herself a plate, her fingers a bit wobbly. "After we're done, perhaps we should burn that entire pub to the ground!"

Darien helped her with her plate and glanced between herself and Cadell. She thanked him.

Cadell only rose a brow briefly. She had been awfully sick, he knew. But to burn an entire pub for it? Then again, from what he'd known and seen of her in the past it didn't really surprise him.

"An alliance? Darien." Amethyst turned to him, but a smile was on her face. "Oh, very well! I suppose it would've come sooner or later. I'd rather get an alliance with you, Cadell, than one of those other brutes," she scoffed.

Cadell chuckled. "Other brutes? I guess you won't know about any of me other alliances, except when they're needed." Cadell grinned, eyes dancing with mischief. "So, where were we?" he asked, turning to Darien.

"We were just fixing to sign some papers." Darien snapped his fingers, and a crewmember brought a piece of parchment, a quill and a bottle of ink. "If you'll just sign on the dotted line," he instructed. Darien had certainly planned ahead.

Cadell turned his attention toward the paper placed before him and he scanned over it briefly, before nodding and signing his signature. "It's official," he murmured.

"So! That concludes this meeting for the most part. What do ye say? I'm on yer territory. Shall I stay for a bit longer, or return to me own?" Cadell glanced between Amethyst and Darien.

"Well, actually, I was thinking of going into town for a little bit. We'll be leaving port soon and I've got some coins that have been burning a hole in my pocket," Amethyst said. She took another sip from her goblet. "I am assured Darien will man things here on the ship."

Her first mate simply nodded.

"Captain Cadell, would you like to join me in town?" Amethyst asked, tilting her head towards him. She let out a giggle as her shirt started to slip down her shoulder. She pushed it up, then pushed away from the table. "I'll be back in a moment to finish my meal. You can make your decision by then," she said, walking off.

Cadell watched her go. Was this her true person? The one she refused to show to the world? To Darien he said, "I suppose I don't have much choice. I'll go." While he didn't need anything, considering his recent conversation with Darien, if it was to make Amethyst feel more at ease, then he would go.

Darien nodded. "When are you planning on leaving port, Captain Cadell? I will need to send messages out to what other alliances we have."

"I'd planned for tomorrow. But considering some of the other captains, I think it best we leave as soon as possible. Staying here is dangerous. I'm sure ye know the reasons." Cadell paused a moment, unsure if he should bring up the subject of Stephan again or not. "One of them being Captain Stephan," he said briefly.

Cadell didn't know when Amethyst would return, so he spoke softly. "I think we all should keep an eye on him. I've got a feeling his part in the threat of war is greater than he's letting on."

Darien nodded. "Aye, I plan to leave port this evening, under the cover of darkness. The Gargoyle blends in well with the night when all of her lights are extinguished. We hope for cloud cover this evening, so not even the moon will give us away," he glanced toward the sky. "We will wait for you by the cliffs in the north. You have seen them?" Darien asked.

"Yes, I have seen the cliffs. We will meet and leave there. The *Reaper* can be stealthy too." Cadell glanced to where Amethyst had gone. "Tell me, Darien, does the *Gargoyle*'s captain have a girl's spirit when it comes to the market?" he asked after a moment.

Darien seemed to understand. "She won't stay for long. She'll get tired in about an hour or so, I promise you. She's still weak and recovering. And not doubting your abilities as a captain and protector, but I will have some of our crew following. She may notice them and complain, but do not worry about their presence. They are just there for added protection," Darien said.

"Very well. I'll make sure she doesn't wear herself out." He paused, glancing toward some of the crew members tending to the ship. "I'm sure every added hand'll be appreciated."

"What's this now?" Amethyst's voice called out as she approached.

Cadell looked up at the sound of her voice. A soft blue top covered only about half of her middle and a long, black skirt swirled over her legs. The top closed around her arms, leaving her shoulders bare, and like the top she had worn the day before, was tied above her tanned belly.

Amethyst sat down at the table, beginning to eat again.

"Just talking about when we were leaving port, Captain," Darien responded.

She only nodded, her mouth full of food.

"Aye. So, let's be off." Cadell rose slightly in his chair, taking a small piece of bread from the table and nibbling on it. "Thank you, Darien. This alliance won't disappoint you, or Captain Amethyst."

The first mate smiled, nodding his head at Cadell's words. Cadell caught a brief glance Amethyst's way. Darien seemed pleased that Amethyst was clueless, and he even looked a little relieved.

Cadell then turned to Amethyst. "Shall we?"

"Let me grab a quick snack," Amethyst said with a smile, grasping a couple of pastries in one hand and gulping the rest of her drink with the other. As soon as she finished, she caught a small bag from Darien. "We'll be back soon, Darien!" she called out.

"Aye, aye, Captain," Darien said.

"There's this lovely new clothes shop in town, and to be honest, I'm tired of these old rags..." Amethyst was already chatting away as she started down the plank.

Cadell listened and nodded as they went, "Oh? I guess my opinion of those old rags won't matter then, eh?"

At first, Cadell's attention was divided between Amethyst and their surroundings. Yet as time passed, he began to relax and enjoy her company. He knew the crew members Darien had sent behind them would take care of minor trouble. Still, in the back of his mind, he had a feeling he should stay guarded.

Amethyst seemed to be in love with the market. She stopped at nearly every window until finally she seemed to reach a certain destination. In the window hung many garments, and even some hats. "C'mon, in here!" she urged, dashing into the store. Immediately she was drawn to the hats, going through them quickly.

Cadell was amused. Amethyst was far more of a girl than even Darien had suggested. He was glad of it and chuckled every time she stopped in the windows. At times, she asked his opinion, which he also found amusing. Cadell wasn't sure why he had expected anything less. Perhaps because she seemed so vulnerable and innocent all of a sudden. Her fierce reputation seemed to fade. Which also brought about more questions.

Perhaps this was the exact reason Darien had sought him out for an alliance in the first place.

Cadell followed her into the shop she had chosen. "Comin'," he assured her as she gestured for him to hurry.

The poor shopkeep, looking more than a little intimidated by the known pirates, kept quiet and behind the counter.

Amethyst wrinkled her nose as she put on a soft purple hat with peacock feathers sticking out of it. She turned to the shopkeep. "How does this look? Too much purple?"

Cadell looked at Amethyst when she asked about the hat. He couldn't help the tug of a smile on his lips. It was a lot of purple, but somehow it looked good on her anyway. Perhaps it was the other blues and yellows intertwined in the feathers of the hat.

She intrigued him. And despite him reminding himself this was about the alliance, she was already drawing him in.

The shopkeep remained silent, simply staring back and forth between Amethyst and Cadell. Since he didn't answer, Amethyst walked over to the counter and set down the hat. "I want this. But I'm not done yet," she said excitedly, going over to the imported silks.

She held up a pair of silken breeches. "These are nice," she murmured, throwing them to the shopkeep, who was attempting to keep the items she gathered from simply flying around the shop and hitting the floor. He blushed crimson as he barely caught the breeches and noticed as she held up something else: a corset. "What's this?" Amethyst asked, her face scrunching in confusion.

"A corset, ma'am," the shopkeep responded softly.

"What does it do?" Amethyst asked, putting it on her head. "Is it a hat?"

"Er... no, ma'am. Don't you have one on right now?" the poor older man asked her, perplexed.

She stared at the keep, bewildered, and finally she looked down. "I don't think so, let me check."

Up to this point, Cadell had hung back, simply observing and letting Amethyst look around as she pleased. She seemed more amused than he did about how shy and embarrassed the shopkeep was behaving! Cadell couldn't imagine why a man so shy about women's clothing would be working in a clothing shop. Although he wondered if perhaps the man's wife was not about to help at the moment.

Just then, as Amethyst mentioned checking for a corset, she began reaching for her shirt.

Cadell quickly understood what was going on. He clumsily replaced a hat he'd been eyeing and rushed toward Amethyst and the keep.

"Captain Amethyst!" Cadell said, reaching out his fingers and attempting to hold her shirt down. "Sorry, but, Captain, don't forget ye're a woman, and we're men." Even if he was a pirate, Cadell's father had taught him that women were to be respected if there was ever hope of gain with them. He hoped that his mention of her womanhood was all he needed to say, not considering the fact that no one really expected pirates to be decent. Although Darien had pointed out the need for decency anyway.

Amethyst blinked when he grasped her shirt. The back of his fingers brushed hers and she looked dazed for a moment. She shook her head slightly and released her top. "Of course you two are men, silly."

The keep looked as though he wanted to faint from relief.

Cadell was beginning to realize that he didn't know the slightest thing about Amethyst, and that in some areas, she was a bit too naïve – or maybe she just didn't care. After all, he doubted she was completely unaware.

Amethyst tilted her head as she was looking at Cadell and smiled. "You know, I was only going to check. I usually only wear a binding, if anything. They're absolutely dreadful! Why bother with these... things?" she asked, turning her gaze back to the corset. "They must be new. I haven't even encountered them in trades or raiding a merchant's vessel."

Or perhaps she had and simply hadn't known what to make of them. Cadell wasn't sure. He had encountered women who wore them... yet now that he thought of it, it had only been in recent times. Perhaps the shopkeep had also only recently acquired them.

Cadell pulled his hand from her shirt and glanced away, not wanting to be caught staring. "Er... well..." he took a moment and collected himself. She didn't get what he'd meant. He'd explain later, he supposed, not wanting to make the conversation more awkward than it already was. "Never mind about it."

Cadell glanced at the keep. "Ye have dressing rooms in the back?"

The keep nodded quickly. "If you'll follow me," he muttered, scurrying to the back of the store.

Amethyst followed, appearing distracted by the colors and fabrics on the way.

They stopped at a curtain hiding a room behind it. The keep pulled the curtain back, allowing Amethyst to step in. She turned to Cadell. "Are you going to help me put it on?"

Her eyes were searching his face. She must be able to tell he was somewhat uncomfortable. It was then her mouth curved into a slight smirk and her eyes gained a light of mischief. "Or should I just get this one myself?" She reached for the garment.

"Just try it on and see how it feels," Cadell suggested in response to Amethyst. "It won't hurt." Suddenly, he realized he was still holding the corset and his cheeks grew warm.

He quickly handed the thing to Amethyst. As he did, their fingers brushed again. The thought flitted across his mind that in all his life, no other woman had caused his heart to tremor the way she did.

Cadell glanced at the keep, who was still standing there awkwardly. He was becoming irked at this old man. Why were there no women around to help with these matters, Cadell wondered?

Cadell silently hoped he wouldn't have to help Amethyst with the undergarment, but he supposed if he did, he would contain himself. After all, it couldn't be *that* hard to put the thing on. Despite his attempts at self-assurance, he felt his palms grow sweaty.

"Oh all right. I'll try it on. But this thing looks like it would only get in the way, with all the lace and nonsense," Amethyst exclaimed with a huff.

The keep looked at Cadell. "If anything happens, I'll fetch one of the baker's wives. They'll know what to do. Now," he straightened up his shirt. "I believe I'm going to go back to the counter if you've got... everything under control." The mousy old man shook his head, going back towards the front of his shop, muttering something about getting a drink after work.

Cadell frowned at the keep. '*Wormy little one isn't he?*' he thought. He supposed there was no reason to become fierce on the man, but he disliked people who would rather run than face something. He glanced at the closed curtain, hoping Amethyst wouldn't do anything... well foolish. *'Bollocks, I have things under control.'*

A few moments later, the curtain flung back and there was Amethyst, standing there in nothing but the corset and her skirt. "Tell me, Captain Cadell, is this supposed to be some kind of shirt? I must say, I've never tried on a shirt like this."

She had managed to tie the lace in the back, but it was crooked and pushed her bosom upward significantly. "It's somewhat uncomfortable, squeezing my chest like it is,"

Amethyst muttered, looking down. Even the skin that normally lurked under her shirt was flawlessly tanned. "Awful lot of trouble it was, getting this thing figured out." She laughed.

Cadell's body and face grew hot. It was true he was a pirate, but he was still a man who believed in respectability. "Er... no it's not a shirt. It's... supposed to be worn under a shirt. I mean... it's supposed to give support for... I mean, it's supposed to feel comfortable... I mean excuse me, sorry." He turned slightly, shaking his head a bit and taking in a breath.

As he stuttered, he watched as a smile crossed Amethyst's features. She appeared to be enjoying his uncertainty. But her smile fell again when it sank in that she hadn't donned the thing correctly. "But why on earth would you want to wear something with this color if it's not a shirt?" she asked, resting a hand on her hip.

"Well, I don't know. Does color really matter that much?" Cadell had no idea how to explain the reason for wearing it. And why it wasn't a shirt. He wasn't even entirely sure himself. It was a piece of women's fashion... and at times he felt women obsessed over ridiculous notions in the name of fashion.

"But why do I want to wear something over it?" Amethyst asked. "Is it the same as my strap?" She held up the length of flat cloth that she often used to bind her chest. She turned defiantly. "Perhaps I'll wear it as a shirt regardless!" she huffed.

Finally, Cadell had composed himself enough to be able to speak properly and he turned back toward her again. "I don't think I know how to answer your questions. But, aye, it is pretty much the same as your strap, except, it's er, well, it has more fabric I suppose. Anyway, if ye don't like it no one's forcing ye to get it." He paused and then sighed, flustered in trying to explain things to her from his very limited knowledge about it.

"But it's so much fabric! It wouldn't do me any good in a battle. In fact, it would probably hinder me," she protested.

Cadell couldn't tell if it was because she actually liked the thing. "Here, just let me help ye," he said finally, "Just turn around. I'll do the rest." He focused on her eyes, resisting the urge to trace across her skin and brush his fingers against it. Instead, he grasped her shoulders and turned her around to face the back of the changing room where a mirror reflected her front.

Cadell then took her thick, curled purple hair in his hands and hung it over her shoulders. "Mind holding it there for a moment?" he asked.

She only quietly nodded and did as he asked.

He untied the laces and fastened the hooks properly so that the corset would fit properly. "There, does that feel any more comfortable?" he asked after a moment, taking a step back.

She turned toward him at his question, her eyes looking a little dazed again.

"If it feels okay, then ye wear a shirt over it," Cadell used his explanation as an excuse to keep himself busy, moving across the dressing room and grasping the shirt she had been wearing previously. He held it toward her.

She took the shirt and slid it over her torso, looking at herself in the mirror. "Women and their fashions. I'd still rather take my band than this... thing... any day," she muttered. "I guess I could wear it on the outside," she said, turning back to Cadell fully, gaining a stubborn smirk at her final comment.

"Captain Amethyst, I don't know ye completely yet but, since when have ye abided by any normal women's fashion or behavior?" He chuckled lightly, "ye're perfectly fine without it anyway, I'm sure."

"True, I've never been one for following fashions. When you're out at seas for months at a time, no one really cares what you're wearing," she shrugged.

"Aye! Half the time the men stink and no one notices. Or cares," Cadell agreed. At least, that's the way it was aboard most ships. The ones with no magic. Very few had the luxury of baths on their ship like Amethyst did.

"Well, I suppose I could get one," she said finally. "I mean I've already got it on so I might as well buy it. Maybe one day it'll come in handy." Amethyst shook her head, then laughed. "What do you think?" she asked.

"What do I think?" Cadell repeated, "I think, if you really came here to get something new, since ye're sick of those old rags, ye should do so while we're here." Cadell grinned, and then answered her more specifically. "I think you look..." He paused a moment, his teasing fading as he truly gazed at her. Ravishing. But he dared not use that word. "Extravagant." He had once heard this word used to describe fae women.

Their eyes had managed to lock together, and he couldn't pull his away. Perhaps she would save him the trouble? Or the keep would come back for some reason? His breath caught in his throat.

Instead, Amethyst's smile slowly crept back on her face. She leaned a little closer, whispering, "You know, you have the most beautiful black eyes I've ever seen. They're like two onyx stones, or perhaps obsidian." Her fingers tucked a piece of hair behind her ear. "I wish I had eyes that pretty."

He'd hardly noticed how close she was getting. Or perhaps it just wasn't registering in his brain. Cadell was unsure what to do, but somehow he knew that this was his moment. He didn't want it to end. His heart was racing.

He leaned in closer, and before he knew what he was doing he had cupped her elbow in one hand, and his other hand loosely grasped hers. It happened all in an instant. Cadell drew her closer still and softly pressed his lips to hers before pulling back, just slightly, and then lightly kissing her again.

At first, he half thought she might pull away or slap him for such a gesture, but she didn't, much to his relief, surprise, and pleasure. In fact, she encouraged him to go further, at least with the kiss. She kissed him back, eagerly.

He pressed another light kiss to her lips, almost as if to tease her.

She nibbled at his lip, two of her fingers walking up his arm and then tangling in his hair. She began pushing against his head, urging him to kiss her further.

He fulfilled her wish and deepened the kiss.

Cadell had kissed other wenches in the past, but not like this. This was different, sweeter, and more passionate at the same time. There was something about Amethyst that was both like a punch to the gut and the refreshing sweetness of rain.

Now that he was so close to her, her lavender scent filled his nose. As her arm curled around his neck he let his now free hand move about her waist, holding her close to him, and pressing the kiss deeper still.

Up to this point, Amethyst had been toying with Cadell. Never had she met a man, other than Darien, so bent on treating her with dignity. Any other man would be ravishing her with his eyes at this point. Some might have even tried to take her as far as she'd allow. In fact, she *knew* that any other man would have seen her girlish antics that day and lost some respect for her as a pirate captain. It might have even damaged some of her reputation.

But not Cadell.

Everything he did suggested that he could take both sides of her equally. The girl, and the fearsome captain. She felt as though she could reveal her vulnerability without damaging her reputation... at least with him. He drove her wild with curiosity and she hungered after his attention. But it was more than her need for security and reassurance. More than even her insatiable need for control and respect. It was her need for love. Not the brotherly protector type that she got from Darien. Something within her knew that Cadell could give her the love she craved.

Of course, her initial attraction to Cadell only made her want him more.

Each time their skin came in contact, a warm flame tingled through her body from the point of contact. He left her breathless and her heart pounded. But still, she had played it off, amused watching Cadell get flustered.

Then the mood changed. He was so near; he grasped her. The taste of his lips. A hint of rum and the scent of the sea. Never had she tasted a kiss that left her so ravenous for more. She didn't want to stop.

Her whole body trembled and fire burned in her skin at every place their bodies touched. The warmth of his embrace was full of safety and comfort. Her very soul felt serene.

In the back of her mind she knew she must be careful. She didn't know how fast he wanted to dance. How far he wanted to go. But as he deepened the kiss, she sighed and fully closed her eyes, letting herself relax even more.

It was dangerous, letting her guard down. But somehow it felt right. She pushed herself into him as close as physically possible.

Something crashing and hitting the floor resounded from the main part of the little shop and Cadell glanced up sharply, pulling back. He sucked in his breath at the motion. "Interesting timing that keep has," he said with a slight cough. He glanced back at Amethyst and smiled faintly, "Um... sorry..." was all he said before turning yet again.

"Anyway, let's get back to what we were doing." Cadell paused, and then seemed to realize the different meanings his words could have. He smiled sheepishly. "I mean shopping. Got everything ye want or are ye going to be looking around a bit longer?" he asked, beginning to step back toward the rest of the shop.

Amethyst was a little disappointed when he broke the kiss, and a soft pout graced her lips. They were still slightly swollen and tingled from the memory of contact. She blinked slowly, watching his movements. "Cadell," she complained softly, fingers reaching out to grasp his shirt. She wasn't quite done yet. She stopped herself, hesitating. Maybe she should let it be.

A soft sigh escaped her lips, and Amethyst nodded, smiling once more. "Okay. We'll finish up here and stop at one more place," she said, going back to looking at the clothes with now idle interest.

Even if their moment was over, for now, her mind swam with the memory. She desperately desired to grasp him and pull him into another scorching kiss.

Amethyst fingered a crimson fabric with an underlying tone of gold, pulling it back to reveal a strapless dress with the slit about mid-thigh. She grinned and pulled it down. She'd invite Cadell to dinner this evening on the *Gargoyle* after they made it to the cliffs.

After selecting a couple of other things, Amethyst went to the counter to make her purchases, adding the corset that she was wearing underneath her shirt at the moment.

Once she had her items, Amethyst began to leave. She opened the door to the shop and stepped out backward into the street. She looked at Cadell, who was still following her out of the shop. "Hurry up, silly!" she called out with a smile as the sun hit her.

"Aye, aye!" Cadell called back, moving toward her.

Amethyst donned her new hat, beaming. She glanced down the street a bit farther. There was a shop that specialized in perfumes and bath salts.

Then, a chill crawled across her spine as a figure reached out from the shadows of the alleyway between the clothing shop and a few other buildings and a hand grasped Amethyst's arm, pulling her from the street. Shock and panic covered her features. It was none other than Captain Stephan.

Everything happened in an instant. He pushed her against the side of the building and pressed a finger to her lips. His arm held her against the wall, restricting her movement and in his other hand was a small dagger. He didn't hold it close to her person, but she saw the flash of silver in the darkness.

Amethyst's eyes narrowed as she met Stephan's gaze. A satisfied smirk was plastered on his lips and his eyes stared at her with arrogance and determination. A look that told her he would do anything to get what he wanted and that he would bend her to his will.

A low growl rose in her throat and she attempted to thrash beneath his arms. She refused to be handled like this!

"Don't move or scream. One sound, and I swear I'll slit your pretty throat."

Her chest was heaving and she settled with his warning.

"I saw you, after the meeting. And it turns out, the great captain of the *Gargoyle* can be harmed. You're lucky no one else suspects it, or you would no longer be the queen of the seas. I never thought I'd get my chance... but your luck isn't so great, is it?" He chuckled, a sickening sound. "To think the feared captain of the Gargoyle is just the same as any mere wench. You're still a woman."

She was still weak from the spices, and it seemed Stephan knew it as well as she did. Amethyst could feel Stephan's breath on her lips. The feeling of helplessness stole into her heart. She flashed her fangs.

"I'm warning you, you better keep your voice down," Stephan muttered. "You will do exactly as I say," he told her, moving the knife to her throat. His voice was coaxing. She didn't know why he even bothered.

It wouldn't help. Not at all. Her powerlessness in that moment made her feel sick. And then, it happened. Painful memories flooded into her mind and she broke out in a sweat, pupils dilating in fear of the memories, and what Stephan might do to her.

Sharp pain shot up her spine as it had every time her ex-husband had overpowered her. She could still feel the bruises left on her body by the rough, careless hands that had groped her mercilessly. A small whimper started in the back of her throat, tears burning against her eyes and streaming down her face as she slumped, or as much as she could being trapped by Stephan. She started to shake with the threat of an oncoming panic attack.

What was happening to her? The instinct to sink her nails into his throat and spatter his blood crossed her mind but the fear of her memories kept her frozen. Why now? After all this time? Everything she had done to erase that past?

Stephan moved his hand to grasp her chin, though pulled back at the feel of tears on his fingers. "Ts, ts, ts. Ah, don't cry," he said softly, his hand moving to cup her chin and lift her face toward his. He grinned, "I wouldn't hurt you, not yet anyway." His voice grew a bit darker.

As she became more like dead weight, Stephan supported her, one arm about her waist, the other hand grasping one of her arms. "Come, Amethyst, you wouldn't faint so soon, would you?"

Stephan's gaze turned sharply at the sound of screams coming from the crowded streets nearby. Her guards must have noticed she was missing and unsheathed their swords to take on whatever foe had taken her. They must have sent the crowd in the market into a panic. The idea they were coming for her did nothing to ease her as Stephan began dragging her away.

He tugged her further back into the shadows, trying to conceal their bodies. Though her weight made it difficult, and their movements were slow, Stephan managed to reach the other side of the buildings and began pulling her along a dirt road that was the next street. It was empty, and soon he was pulling her into yet another alley. He continuously made turns, as if trying to lose her pursuers.

"Amethyst, darling, you *must* hear me out. When you get out of this, make sure you tell your precious first mate a message for me: 'No matter how strong or powerful you think your captain's ship and crew are, she is still a vulnerable woman, and if you don't watch your back, I will make life a living hell."' Stephan talked as he went.

Another chuckle escaped him, "But even if you don't tell him, it doesn't matter. Because as long as you know this, it's the same." He grinned, a sadistic grin, and his eyes flashed. "This war's about to get a whole lot more interesting," Stephan muttered, seemingly to himself more than her.

"You can't do that to me," Amethyst muttered darkly. "My life has been one continuing nightmare. You're just another phase of it." She spat at his face.

He didn't respond.

"Just stop it, Stephan." Amethyst's voice was a bit of a gasp as he dragged her further along. She tried to struggle again, but her vision was starting to flicker. She really should burn down that pub. Using such spices was unforgiveable! "Why do you want me? You can have any woman you want, yet you persist in trying to hurt me more than I already have been hurt!"

She wondered... could he possibly know her secret? She shoved the thought from her mind. No. She had guarded it too closely.

Stephan shrugged, "No, I won't stop. There's no good reason. Why want you? Because other woman are worthless. You, my dear, Amethyst, are different." He said no more, only continued moving. There was another corner ahead of him.

Perhaps a normal woman would have passed out at that point. But not Amethyst. She may have been weakened, but she still had some strength about her.

Stephan stopped and she peered past him. It was a dead-end street off the alleyway, and it was crowded with old crates and barrels. He pushed her back against the crates, knife held in hand, threatening.

Amethyst hiccupped lightly. In that moment, she was no longer Amethyst, merciless captain of the *Gargoyle*. She was Amethyst, a scared young woman in an older body with scars that would last her several lifetimes. She wanted nothing more than to run into the arms of someone trusted, a crew member, Darien. Cadell.

"Cadell." Her voice was soft at first, but then she tried to raise her voice, unheeding of Stephan's threat. "Cadell," she screamed, "Cadell!" Her voice was begging as she began to try to struggle once more. She snapped at Stephan, tiny fangs flashing. Her nails were lengthening and curling, trying to scratch at his wrists and hands that kept her captive.

She hated that she had so readily succumbed to Stephan's threat. '*What is wrong with me?*' Since when did she *ever* show such weakness? Not since the days before she had taken the *Gargoyle* and become its captain. So what was it about Stephan that had caused such behavior to rear its ugly head?

Stephan glared down at her. The coolness of his blade against her neck made her flinch. His lips curled into a snarl. She wondered why it was he didn't kill her. Perhaps he had been bluffing. "Shut your mouth. I warned you before, didn't I? You-"

She looked up at Stephan, her eyes glistening. "I may be vulnerable, but who isn't when you look deep enough?" Amethyst growled, starting to get her captain spirit back. "And when this is all done and over with, your head will decorate my ship and your bones will adorn my neck and wrists. Your skin will become a blanket, and your meat a hearty stew. I will make an example of you. An example of what happens when you mess with me!" She was pushing the memories back.

Stephan laughed at her threat. "Only a petty wench would say something like that. I only have a little bit of business left with you, and you'll be free to run wherever you wish." He pressed the dagger though not enough to draw blood. "Don't think I won't do it," he whispered.

"You wouldn't do it," Amethyst spat again at him with a smirk. "There wouldn't be much pleasure for you if I were dead, unless you're into that kind of stuff. And at this rate, I wouldn't be surprised," she hissed, fangs flashing once more.

"I would. I would rather slit your throat than have you with anyone else." He paused, pulling the knife back slightly, "But that is not what I'm here for now. You will be mine, however long it takes." He licked his lips, and she felt sick at the look in his eyes. "But first, you will swear an alliance to me. I only wanted to get your attention long enough to present it, and the gods know I couldn't have done it any other way. The *Gargoyle* would do well sailing aside *Hell's Serpent*, and you would be glad of having me near." Stephan paused again, his eyes staring into hers. "Swear it to me, or you will regret the day you turned me away." His face was so close she could tear into it with her fangs if not for his knife at her throat.

Once more, helplessness clutched at her chest and a pounding in her head clouded her focus. She couldn't think straight. "Cadell," she screamed in one last attempt. Maybe she should accept Stephan's demand for her own safety, she thought, as his hand closed over her mouth.

The smooth baritone of Cadell's voice cut through her haze. "Ye've gone too far from the start, Stephan. Back away from her, now! Back away, or I swear ye won't live to see another day."

Amethyst groaned as Stephan's weight was lifted and she rolled off the crates, landing with a bit of a dull thud. The cold dirt felt good and with another slow breath, everything went black.

Right then, Cadell could care less if Stephan died and was left there to rot. He didn't care if all of Stephan's allies came after him. He could only imagine the fury which would ensue once Amethyst was returned to the *Gargoyle* at everyone's carelessness letting this happen, himself in particular.

Before Stephan could react, Cadell gripped his arm, pressing the vein in his wrist until he writhed, releasing Amethyst and turning fiercely toward him.

"I told you to stay away from her. I told you she was mine! Back off, Cadell. I-"

But Stephan couldn't say another word because there was a dagger pressed to his gut. Cadell had no facial expression, but his dark eyes burned. "Get out of here," he murmured.

Rage swelled in Cadell's chest, and it took everything within him not to beat Stephan to a bloody pulp. It was clear Amethyst needed attention and for all he knew, the time spent on Stephan would put her at even more risk. The pounding of steps alerted him to the approach of the rest of the crew and he hoped they would take care of Stephan instead.

As Stephan tried to stab Cadell with the dagger he had used to threaten Amethyst, Cadell gripped the collar of his shirt and threw him to the side, slicing a long cut in his face. "Let that be a warning," he growled before moving past him.

Stephan cursed, his eyes sharp but he turned and vanished just as Amethyst's crew were arriving.

"Amethyst, did he hurt you? Are you okay? I'm so sorry," Cadell said as he lifted her from the dirt.

It was only then he realized she was out.

Cadell sighed, stroking her gently, pushing locks of hair from her face. He silently cursed Stephan but was even angrier at himself. He was glad to see that Amethyst didn't appear to have any physical injuries.

He lifted her into his arms and began carrying her toward the marketplace which was also on the main road back to the docks.

The crew had questioning looks. "She's safe, don't worry. But Stephan is probably back on his ship, or almost there." Relief seemed to lighten their faces and they followed him.

As they walked, Amethyst was coming to. As soon as she became conscious, she began to flail in Cadell's arms, screaming his name. She opened her eyes, and the light came into them as she took in Cadell's face. "Cadell," she whispered, blinking back tears, her eyes still slightly dazed. She let the tears fall, her body beginning to shake. Her breath was rigid.

"It's me," Cadell whispered. "You're safe."

She closed her eyes and whatever she was thinking made her sob harder and harder. She clutched desperately onto Cadell's shirt and turned her face into the cloth.

"Don't leave me." Amethyst hiccupped softly. "Please, don't leave me." She was still shaking.

Her request evoked that part of him that naturally wanted to protect. Cadell wanted now to hold her forever and never let go – not for anyone, or anything. Ever. His fingers gently stroked her arm. "I won't leave you. I promise." He paused, glancing at the sky. It was going to rain again.

Cadell glanced back down at Amethyst, not sure if he could hold her any tighter without making her uncomfortable. "I'll never leave you," he repeated softly. And at that moment, he made a silent vow to himself to always keep that promise no matter what happened. Somehow, though unintentional, this fae woman had managed to draw him into a place he had never gone with any other.

Amethyst was silent for the most part after she had calmed down, fingers still clutching his shirt. Her eyes were drooping lightly, and she came in and out of consciousness. His words seemed to calm her, at least for the moment. She blinked slightly as a small drop hit her head and she looked up at the darkening clouds. A shudder ran through her.

# Sparks

Soon, they were approaching the docks. It was nearing sunset, though the sky was already dark with the storm clouds above. The group was soaked as they approached the *Gargoyle.* Despite all the commotion, Cadell hadn't forgotten about Amethyst's purchases while in the market. He'd made sure her crew grabbed the clothing and brought it with them back to the ship.

"I'm just becoming a regular damsel in distress, aren't I?" Amethyst asked softly. Her words sounded oddly bitter as she spoke. And she was bitter. As much as she liked the feeling of Cadell holding her, she felt ashamed.

Cadell shook his head, "No, Captain. There are some things ye can't do anything about. Ye're still every bit the *Gargoyle*'s captain I'm sure." He gave her a light squeeze in comfort.

Unfortunately, Cadell's words fell on deaf ears. She still felt awful, and her drooping ears showed it as well as her crestfallen expression.

What had happened to her tough exterior? Her ability to survive without a man helping her? And further, why hadn't Stephan been afraid? He must know she hadn't been lying. She would hunt him down and make good on her promise.

Did he believe he had something that would prevent the *Gargoyle* from taking him down? Since her initial escape and rise to piracy, she had been strong, firm, ruthless. Especially in the face of others. Her vulnerability had only been shown when alone... or with Darien. Yet Stephan's actions had resurfaced buried memories from her already weakened mind.

The fears of her past had returned once more. And in her heart, she knew Darien had seen it coming and it was for that reason he had reached out to Cadell. Still, she knew Darien wanted to think he protected her secretly and so she let him.

Her head bowed, eyes focusing on anything besides Cadell or her crew as they made their way up the plank. She suspected he didn't mind, but this was the second time within two days that she had had to rely on Cadell completely. It didn't sit well with her.

She just turned her face into his shirt once more, breathing in his scent and grasping for that sense of calm he always brought her.

The rest of the crew on the ship were eager to help, but once they'd done all they could, they were bustling with questions of what had happened. Cadell ignored them, for the most part. He moved across the main deck toward Darien.

"Amethyst! Cadell! What happened?" Darien came towards them not long after they boarded. He looked at Amethyst's disheveled form, then at Cadell, a scowl on his face.

Amethyst murmured something nearly inaudibly. "What was that, Captain?" Darien asked gently.

"It was Stephan," she said, bringing her eyes up to meet his. "He tried to... he tried to..." She couldn't bear to say it. Her past still burned in her mind.

But Darien instantly understood. Anger smoldered in his eyes. "I warned him to stay away. Now he's going to die," he growled.

At Darien's words, the promise she had given Stephan flickered through Amethyst's mind. Yes, she would make him pay.

Darien turned back to Cadell. "We are ready to leave port. Do you wish for me to send a runner, or will you be returning to your ship for a time?"

Cadell cursed to no one in particular. "Send the runner. I'm not leaving." With that said, he turned slightly. "My first mate, Aurek, will take care of everything. Just tell him I have important matters to tend to and will be back with the ship when we meet at the cliffs. And Darien, thanks."

"Aye, aye, Captain," Darien said with a nod before disappearing. It seemed that even if he was first mate of another ship, Darien was content being under Cadell's orders for now.

Cadell did not hesitate to carry Amethyst off to her room, some of the crewmembers already having gone there to prepare it for her. He gently laid her on her bed. He glanced toward the door as a few of the *Gargoyle*'s men entered in order to leave their captain's purchases. They left quickly, though not without looking over their captain with a blend of fury and concern.

Cadell sat down on the bed beside Amethyst. "Need anything? Or do ye only wish to rest for now?" he asked after a moment.

"Rum," Amethyst replied softly. Her face was turned away from him, eyes looking out the window. "And some food," she murmured, "But give me the rum first." She wanted something to numb her body and feelings, and rum tended to do that.

Cadell was silent a moment, gazing softly at her. There was a slight frown on his lips and his brows were wrinkled with worry. Finally, he nodded. "Rum it is then!"

Amethyst laid there for a moment before pushing herself up. She looked at Cadell, and suddenly threw her arms around him and gave him a hug and a kiss on the cheek. "Thank you," she murmured, her eyes burning with the tears threatening to fall once more. She got up and pulled a silken gown from her wardrobe.

After slipping into her bathroom to change, she then emerged wearing the gown. It was long enough to rest on the back of her knees and her hair was pinned up, showing a long, graceful neck. It was clear she felt more comfortable as she flopped on her bed once more, staring up at the ceiling.

Not but a few moments later, Darien entered, looking toward Cadell. "What happened?" Amethyst cringed. She didn't really want to talk about it, but she knew Darien needed to know. Once more, Cadell came to her rescue.

"I'm not sure exactly, but he appeared to be kissing her." Cadell spoke angrily. "He didn't beat her; I wonder what he was after." He glanced briefly at Amethyst. "I'll be back shortly." Cadell rose and with a brief nod, he left.

Amethyst had never considered what Cadell's perspective must have been when he had arrived on the scene. But the way Stephan had been bent over her... Besides, even if Stephan hadn't actually done anything sexual, he may as well have tried. He took advantage of her and tried to bend her to his will. It was basically the same.

Darien nodded back to Cadell and then sat down next to Amethyst, scooting closer. He inspected her neck, where his brow furrowed as he saw the line Amethyst was certain remained from Stephan's dagger. "Amethyst... when you are ready..." He didn't finish, for she nodded her understanding and glanced away. Darien was silent a moment. "I'm going to prepare the ship for our trip to the cliffs," he said.

She nodded again and gave her first mate a small smile.

As Darien left, Cadell returned, a bottle of rum in one hand and a plate of food in the other: some grapes, meat, and vegetables. "When she is asleep, I would like to talk to you," Darien murmured to Cadell in passing.

Cadell merely nodded in recognition of Darien's words and continued his movements toward Amethyst, displaying the food before her with a sweeping gesture and putting on a playful smile. After placing the food on her nightstand, he then produced a deep wine glass which he filled with rum and placed the bottle near the food.

Amethyst gave a lopsided grin as Cadell brought what she had requested. Rather than taking the glass, she grasped the rum bottle. Popping the cork with a fingernail, she tipped the bottle to her lips, gulping down the contents rapidly.

After a moment, she gave a soft giggle and looked at Cadell. It was obvious that she was a lightweight. "Want some?" she asked. As she spoke, two fingers crawled up Cadell's body and she rested her hand on his chest.

He leaned toward her until he was bent down, one hand resting on the bed beside her to support himself. "Ye sure?" he asked.

"Of course I am!" she laughed softly, pushing the bottle into his hand. "You'd better get this offer while it lasts, because normally I never share the good rum." She grinned wickedly, licking her lips. Her ears had perked back up and jingled lightly from her earrings. Her curls were falling down into her face, but she didn't care. Her cheeks were already flushed, but at least she was smiling.

"Ah. Well then, don't want to pass up such a rare chance!" With that he took the bottle from her fingers and pressed it to his lips, grinning before tipping his head back slightly and drinking.

"Drink, Cadell, drink!" she encouraged. "Drink to our alliance, to our futures," she murmured, hiccupping slightly with another giggle. "To Captain Stephan's death. May his bones adorn my body and his skin adorn my ship."

Cadell brought his head back down and dangled the bottle above her head, moving it around with a chuckle. "To Captain Stephan's death. And the sinking of his ship." He pulled the bottle back away slightly, gazing at her. "May ye get yer revenge, Captain." Cadell took another sip of the rum before placing it on the bed beside her, though keeping his hand on it so it wouldn't spill.

Amethyst noticed when he stopped, and she insisted he drink some more.

He chuckled again, "Trying to get me drunk, are ye?" Cadell asked, resuming his playful demeanor and tapping her nose lightly with his finger.

She gave an innocent gasp, "Why, I wouldn't dream of it!" She laughed softly afterward, seeming to have forgotten her gloom.

He grinned, his dark eyes full of mischief. "Of course ye would! Just wait until we're out at seas a bit. I have to sail a ship later, ye know."

Cadell's gaze turned toward the falling sun on the horizon out of the window. The rain that had drenched them on their way to the docks had been short. Even though some clouds remained, the sun shone through. They were already sailing toward the cliffs.

Amethyst noticed the way the sun's glow softened Cadell's skin. The memory of his kisses filled her mind again. "Has anyone ever told you how beautiful you are?" Amethyst's question was soft as a whisper, and it seemed she paid no mind to the oddity of the statement.

He was silent a moment before shaking his head slightly. "No, I don't believe I've ever had someone tell me I'm beautiful." He paused. "But I am sure ye've often heard those words about yerself." Cadell gently traced a finger up her arm before he let two fingers walk on her shoulder.

She blinked, idly reaching up to brush back a strand of hair. "And that you're a very, very good kisser?" Her eyes were slightly smoky from the rum and other feelings. "Because you are," she finished, reaching toward him.

"Really? I've got an infinity of those, y' know," he said softly, the hand that had been keeping a hold on the rum loosening a bit as she leaned toward him. He paused briefly, then gave in and pressed his lips to hers, letting the fingers on her shoulder trail back down her arm.

Amethyst shivered lightly as his fingers made their ascent then descent on her arm. The taste of her favorite strong rum was ever-present in his mouth. She tried to nip gently at his lip. Or perhaps, true to her kind, he brought out the blood desire in her, not like a vampire, but simply in the sensual pleasures. And she was curious. What would his taste like?

Cadell paused, as if thinking of something, then quickly became more aggressive. His mouth captured hers and he pushed back against her, demanding she fall back on the bed.

Normally, Amethyst was not the submissive type. But somehow, she felt safe with him. For once, she wasn't worried or afraid of not being in control. She welcomed his kisses and the feel of his body against hers. Despite every past experience, there was something new about this with Cadell. Something... desperately irresistible. For the first time in her life, she could totally let go and just be. He made her feel like a woman in the most powerful and glorious way.

The spot where she had nibbled at his lip drew blood and it trickled slowly down her tongue. His blood had a sweetness to it that tempted her. As she licked it, sucking his lip between kisses, she felt a warmth spread from her stomach into the rest of her body, and she wasn't sure if it was the kisses or the rum, but she figured both.

Either way, she was determined to find out. At that moment, the oddest thought crossed her mind. Perhaps... perhaps she had found a man worthy to become hers.

Cadell didn't want to frighten Amethyst, not after what she had just been through. He was fighting to contain himself.

She was so warm against him; her taste alluring; he wanted to have her forever.

Yet before they passed a point of no return, she needed to know of his other bloodline. He was less than half, yet it drew out a darkness in him he fought to keep suppressed.

Already, fangs had grown where usually normal teeth were in his mouth. They weren't large yet but they were there, tempting him. Amethyst was there, tempting him. The taste of blood on his tongue tempted him. He knew, that if he dared taste Amethyst's blood, it would become nearly impossible to hold back.

As much as he didn't want to, Cadell paused and pulled away, breathing heavily. He was still so close to her. He could feel her breath. He could still taste her lips.

She let out a soft groan as he pulled back. "Cadell," she grumbled, brows furrowing and breath coming light, "You've got to stop doing that."

He knew what she meant. Her eyes blinked lazily.

"Sorry," he said after a moment, eyes opening slightly to gaze into hers. "There's something I need to tell you. I'm half-vampire. I don't want to hurt you." He knew that the fae had their own taste for blood. Amethyst especially had a reputation. Yet, he hoped she knew he meant he could overpower her and lose himself.

Either way, her response was nonchalant.

"Is that it?" she muttered, dismissing the fact as if he were talking about the weather. "You aren't going to hurt me, silly." She laughed softly, arm reaching to wrap around his neck. "Now, let's get back to what we were doing!" she urged, batting her eyes and pouting.

Cadell gazed at her a moment before smiling back at her, "Aye, that's it," he whispered. Rather than capture her mouth again, he began a trail of kisses, first down her jaw, then down her neck. No more holding back. His instincts reigned and his fangs sank into her neck, his tongue indulging.

He paused only for a moment, letting the blood trail down enough to color her chest. He smirked, meeting her gaze with mischief as he then pushed her all the way back, gathering the blood trail with his fingertip and bringing it to his lips.

"You won't clean that up?" she asked with a giggle, pushing his face toward her chest.

Cadell shook his head until she brought him to her, and let his tongue trace the line up to her neck where he tenderly circled the pinpricks.

He grasped her mouth with his again, now nipping her lip as she had his. Their blood began to mix as their kisses resumed. His fingers traced down her side, fingering the fabric of her silken gown. How he desired her.

"Cadell," she gasped, pulling apart from his kisses long enough to say it.

He paused, gauging her, suddenly wondering if he should wait until their judgment wasn't impaired by alcohol and blood.

"No... don't stop," she whined, lacing her fingers through his hair and drawing him back to her lips.

"Cap'n Amethyst...?" A light male voice came from across the room.

Amethyst turned her head sharply to the doorway, cheeks turning red with embarrassment and anger as one of their younger crew members walked in, eyes wide and jaw hanging open.

"What do you want?" she snapped.

"I – I – I..." he stammered, cheeks flushing red. He turned around, a hand over his eyes. "Cap'n, Darien want'd me ta tell ye we 're at the cliffs and that he was waitin' for Cap'n Cadell." He spoke so quickly his words ran together. He shut the door and dashed out of the hallway that led to her room.

Amethyst rolled her eyes, trying to push herself back up. "He should learn how to knock," she said, growling in frustration and brushing a hand through her hair.

Cadell somehow managed to understand most of what the man said, and he scowled. "Young lads," he muttered under his breath.

He touched Amethyst gently. "I should be at that meeting then." In a way, he was relieved, but the real truth was, if it hadn't been for the fact they'd reached the cliffs...

Cadell pushed that thought aside. "Before I go, I should wash a bit," he said with a faint smile. He stood from her bed and went to her washroom. He splashed water on himself and scrubbed with the bar of soap she kept on the side of her sink.

Amethyst followed Cadell toward the washroom and leaned against the doorway. "You know, I could have simply licked that off for you."

He glanced toward her and grinned. "Of course ye could've. But that would probably set us off again." Cadell leaned down toward her, then pulled back, brushing past and moving toward the door.

When he leaned down, she closed her eyes. She paused, and when she realized he'd moved past her, she opened an eye and stared at him. "Tease," she hissed lightly.

Amethyst turned, watching him go. "Wait... come back to me... when you both are done talking."

Before he left, Cadell nodded, answering with, "Aye, aye. I'll be with ye again soon."

"Before you come back though, bring any personal items you wish over tonight. You'll put them in here." She grinned.

He winked and then the door closed behind him.

Cadell moved out on the main deck, eyes searching for Darien. He found him leaning against the railing, sipping on a glass of rum. Cadell slowly released his breath, letting everything of the moments before out and he moved toward the first mate.

"Thanks again, for taking care of me ship," Cadell said on approach, glancing off slightly to see the form the *Reaper's Scythe* close by. The black hull of the ship was difficult to make out against the shadow of the cliffs, even so close. Dark clouds above covered what light might have illuminated them from the night sky.

"Of course." Darien gestured to another glass beside him. "I'm guessing Amethyst took longer to fall asleep? I figured with a bottle of rum in her system, she'd be passed out." He chuckled, looking also toward the other ship encased by darkness.

Cadell smiled and shrugged. "I suppose." He didn't say much more on that. He didn't want to explain anything and he'd come to talk business. Cadell was silent a moment, turning slightly so he could also lean against the railing, letting the sea breeze blow about his face.

"Another storm will be coming soon," Darien murmured faintly. "And I doubt it will bring rain. And if it does, it will be crimson droplets."

Cadell nodded and frowned. "Aye, this war is about to become a nightmare on the waves," he murmured. "It'll bring about more adventure though. Something I can't resist. Especially the heat of battle." Cadell smiled then at the thought of it.

"I don't think any of us can resist adventure," Darien thought aloud, tilting his chin up. "I mean, it wouldn't be much fun if we just sat on our ships all day, twiddling our thumbs."

"Of course not! But that's what makes us pirates, and good ones at that! Hmm. But it is harder to rest easy in the heat of war. At least we'll enjoy every minute of it we can," he finished with a chuckle.

Cadell wondered just what sort of war this would be: whether it would be long and fierce leaving a scar on pirates in later times, or if it would be short. From what he'd heard at the previous meeting, things weren't looking toward the short route.

"Well, there's nothing like the rush of battle. The pounding of your heart, being soaked in sweat and blood, the straining of muscles as you drive your sword into another's chest," Darien said, shaking his head before straightening his hair out by pushing a hand through it.

"Except," he continued, "Have you ever just wanted to put down your weapon and just truly enjoy the seas? Without the worry of who you're going to chop up next, or where you're going to plunder in order to get a decent meal?" Darien tilted his head lightly toward Cadell. "Perhaps it's just me." He shrugged, stretching lightly.

Cadell watched Darien for a moment before smiling, "No, it's not just you. Life without worries just to enjoy what ye love most: the sea breeze on yer face and the feel of freedom. Of course I know the feeling. And I'm glad of it. Times like those happen and they're to be taken full advantage of, as ye probably know."

Darien nodded his understanding.

Cadell went silent, thinking of how he might enjoy such times if he had them. He reached a hand up to briefly touch his neck and the action turned his mind toward recent events with Amethyst. Perhaps they would simply sail together, an unstoppable force to do as they pleased.

As Cadell went silent, so did Darien. Idly, he took a seat on the rails, looking down where there was splashing below.

It seemed both men were caught up in their thoughts, perhaps a moment too long. "Everything alright, Captain?" he asked Cadell.

Darien's voice broke Cadell from his thoughts, "Hmm? Oh, it's nothing. Just a thought crossed me mind."

"Down to business," Darien said finally, "I'm curious why Stephan did not beat Amethyst when he so clearly had the opportunity. Even though I know that he too wishes to come to her bed, most would take the opportunity to hurt her, to weaken her and perhaps get a little revenge. But the only thing he left was a fine line from a dagger. Tell me, do you know anything else about Stephan? Like his history?"

"I'm not really sure. In fact, I find myself asking similar questions. Stephan is a newer captain, and... I'm not sure if anyone really knows all that much about him. I think he likes it that way. But I'm sure he has his reasons. The main thing I'm wondering is what his intentions are."

Darien listened to Cadell quietly, taking a sip from his glass. His eyes briefly closed, inhaling deeply. Finally, his brow wrinkled. "Aye. I'm sure he has his reasons to hide whatever he has to hide. And I do not think it is the regular skeletons in the closet that most pirate captains seem to harbor."

Cadell understood what Darien meant. Pirates often had some sort of past, and usually, that past had a way of influencing their decision to become pirates. Cadell wondered what Amethyst's were. For him, it was the profitability and the fact he was mostly left alone. As a merchant trader, he had constantly dealt with pirate raids or disputes in the markets. As a pirate, his life was somewhat more peaceful. Ironically.

As Darien mentioned Stephan's secrets, Cadell found himself excited by a sudden idea. Though he didn't know Stephan's past, he was thinking of a way they could learn it. If he sent a spy, perhaps they could finally unravel the scallywag's secrets. "Aye, but that's not for long. Whatever he is keeping behind doors, whether it be common skeletons or cursed sails, we will find out." Cadell's eyes sparkled at those words.

Darien smiled. "True. And the sooner we figure it out, the sooner I'll be able to rest easy at night once more."

Cadell turned back to Darien. "Actually, I have plenty of spies that I could have infiltrate his ship, as well as a few connections. I'm sure I could get someone who'd be able to get information about Stephan." He paused, considering his idea. "Perhaps you had similar things in mind?" he asked after a moment.

"Of course, Captain. I would love to meet with your sources, if you wouldn't mind, sometime soon." Darien took another sip. "My theory came to me rather out of the blue. I believe Stephan has some ultimate aim with Amethyst, specific to her. She is, after all, one of the only female pirate captains on the seas and furthermore, holds nobility in the fae mainland. It's not common knowledge, but Stephan may have his own sources." He paused. "Perhaps he has another reason. I want to know all the information from your spies."

Amethyst was... *nobility?* Cadell was silent, partially shocked, and yet part of him was not surprised at all. So much about her suddenly made perfect sense. He quickly regained his focus. "If ye wish to meet my sources soon, ye will. And as we spoke of the war before, they will probably be joining us at certain points as allies. However, there is one lass I had in mind." Cadell paused, grasping the glass Darien had gestured toward earlier and taking a sip. It was wine. He was glad that Darien tended to prepare something when a meeting or discussion was in order.

Cadell continued. "She isn't far from here. Unless she's moved along, she should be at the next port. Quite a piece of work in a lot of ways, but she's perfect for this job. She'll get to Stephan faster than most. Whatever his intentions are with Amethyst, I assure ye, we'll know soon."

Darien was perfectly silent until Cadell mentioned another woman. The first mate became alert. "She can't come on the ship. She can't even be remotely close to the ship. Amethyst will not have it."

Cadell knew well that most fae women were extremely territorial. They treated other grown women as potential rivals. There were few exceptions. Of course, this was only grown women. They usually didn't mind younger girls. Given Amethyst's position, and her bloody reputation, Cadell assumed that Amethyst was one of the more extreme of the fae women. No wench ever captured by Amethyst had ever survived.

Cadell sighed patiently. "I wasn't suggesting that she be on the ship. I was merely saying that she is the perfect person for this job. Don't get me wrong, Darien. I would never allow Amethyst to get the wrong idea. I'm more than aware of how territorial the fae women can be."

"I just want to make it clear that this woman cannot even be remotely near the ship or Amethyst will have a fit. And after she finished the girl off, we'd be next for letting her get near the ship, and I don't think you want to be strung up by your essentials so soon," insisted Darien.

The first mate smirked, but his voice emphasized that this was no laughing matter. "We will discuss this further when we are closer to the port. Until then, let us not speak a word of it around the captain, nor even hint at such a thing, lest she suspect mutiny," he said more quietly. "I hate to keep things secret, but I think it would be best if they were for the moment."

Cadell frowned. "Aye, I agree. Better not to risk it. She won't hear a thing from me 'til the right time." He hoped they could leave this discussion at that. Cadell needed to return to his ship briefly. And he knew Amethyst was still expecting him.

Cadell continued, "Speaking of the next port, I was hoping we wouldn't stay long. We should get there and then leave as fast as possible. Perhaps we could set up a meeting."

"We'll have to set it up on shore then, with just this girl, Amethyst, you and I. Amethyst will not take kindly to me or you if we bring another woman aboard. She'll get the thought in her mind that we want to overthrow her and put this girl in charge. This will have to be a very delicate process."

Cadell nodded, moving away from the rail. "Aye. She shouldn't be that busy now. I'll send some of my crew ahead to find her. They know her well enough. Just keep in mind she's... a bit of a character. Er... a handful more like." Much like Amethyst he supposed.

"Headstrong, eh? Well, I've got plenty of practice with Amethyst and her stubborn ways, so I guess this woman can't be all that bad. Sending your men ahead's a good idea. Still, I would like to send a couple of my own crew along, just to scope her out and relay back to me. I'm sure you wouldn't mind." Darien looked at Cadell, his eyes flickering. "That way, I can determine how long we should wait in order to introduce Captain Amethyst to this female. I don't want to just introduce them and hope everything goes well. That would be like trying to wash a cat." Darien wrinkled his nose, as if having done that.

"No, I wouldn't mind. Bring a couple members o' the Gargoyle's crew. Probably will prove to be best."

Darien was silent a moment, and then seemed to change his mind about keeping everything secret. "Perhaps we should discuss things with Amethyst, but let's take things slowly. I will talk to Amethyst tomorrow at breakfast. We both can," Darien said. "I will get us moving as soon as you are settled in for the night. If you have no problem with it, I will give the instructions to your first mate, so that we will all be on the same page and course, so to speak."

"Alright, that's settled then." Cadell drank more of the wine.

"Well, if that is everything, I am ready to shove off when you are comfortable. Would you like for me to show you to the room we've prepared?" Darien asked.

"Actually, no. I was heading back to me ship for a bit anyway before we set sail again. Don't worry about me. Ye look tired, Darien. Ye're no good to Amethyst with only half yer strength. Get some rest." Cadell grinned. "I can find me way around. See you in the morning." He drained his cup.

Darien looked a little relieved and gave a small laugh. "Very well. Goodnight, Cadell."

Cadell answered Darien with a short, "G'night." With that, Cadell set off, heading back toward his ship as Darien was shouting orders to his crew.

# Love

As soon as Cadell landed on the deck of his *Reaper*, he called together his men. They were aware of the alliance with the *Gargoyle*, but Cadell gave them more of the specifics, particularly concerning Stephan and the war.

Above, the moon barely shone through the dark clouds, and Cadell briefly felt a sense of foreboding about the war to come. He shrugged it off as he turned to thoughts of Amethyst and the night at hand. Up to that point, he had not felt very tired, but suddenly his exhaustion hit him like a wave.

He gathered a few of his belongings from his quarters and slipped back to the *Gargoyle*, moving effortlessly down the short stairway from the main deck and toward the captain's cabin.

Amethyst was already half asleep in her bed, curls unpinned. Her nightshirt had been carelessly tossed on the floor, and her full body was exposed. Apparently, she wasn't one to wear clothes to bed. Either that or she had plans.

She murmured something and turned toward her stomach. Her ears were drooping lightly, the many rings jingling and her eyes partially opened. The moonlight reflecting on her skin gave her a soft gleam and her curls cascaded around her freely.

Cadell approached her, leaning down and speaking softly, his lips not far from her ear. "Ye haven't waited too long have ye?" A faint grin graced his lips as he moved away to sit beside her.

"No," she replied, looking up at him with a sleepy smile. She lifted herself until she leaned against her elbow.

Silence ensued for a few moments, each alone with their thoughts.

Perhaps she was taking things a bit fast with him, but Amethyst didn't care. She remembered when she was a little girl talking with her grandmother about how there was a perfect fit for each person somewhere in the world.

Amethyst had taken heart when the old woman had assured her it didn't have to be from her species, considering she hated most of the males of her own kind. Of course, it didn't hurt that in lieu of recent events she desired someone comforting. Safe.

And she believed Cadell was. Not just someone comforting, but someone that fit her perfectly. A part of her was fearful... that he would be like so many other men she had allowed to get close. But her heart told her otherwise, and she trusted her heart was right.

She lightly trailed a finger down his arm, desiring touch, and she gazed at him, her guard completely down.

"Ye look tired," he murmured softly.

"I'm a little."

Cadell reached back, pulling the tie and letting his dark hair fall about his face, tousled faintly by the breeze coming in through the window.

She reached a hand up and toyed with his hair, running her fingers through it and finally sat up, letting her finger trail down his cheek, his neck, his chest. Her gaze remained steady with his own. Amethyst pushed her hands under his shirt, and he removed it, casting it lazily aside along with his boots.

"Well, I did have other plans in mind," she responded, grinning mischievously. She snuggled into his arm. "Though I am in dire need of sleep," she finished.

He moved to lie beside her, gently stroking her back. "We both should rest then..."

Amethyst curled her body against his, wrapping her arms around him. "For tonight..." Her words drifted off, her tone still somewhat mischievous. She tilted her chin toward his face.

Cadell smiled faintly, then kissed her. Despite her exhaustion, passion kindled. Every time he kissed her, waves of desire coursed through her. She could sense that it was the same for him. She didn't want to stop. And this time, she knew they wouldn't be interrupted. She felt him curl a leg around one of hers.

Amethyst giggled, still sleepy but also becoming more alert. If he wanted this, she would not protest. Instead, her hands slipped toward the tie of his pants, demanding it be undone.

Cadell chuckled through his kisses, and finally assisted her, all clothing now entirely forsaken. He shifted, pushing himself upward until he held himself above her. His lips moved from hers down her chin, seeking the taste of her once more in his mouth.

But he paused, again.

She grew annoyed. "What?" she gasped softly.

"I know the ways of your kind. The taste we had before was only that. But this..." He paused. She saw the two, pointed fangs behind his lip. He didn't need to finish. She knew. If he took her, marked her, there was no going back. Not for her. Not for him. She wondered if she were the first nonhuman woman he'd been with.

There could be no other after this. In all of her romping, she had never permanently marked another. Even her ex-husband she had refused to return a mark. She had even used magic to remove any physical traces. No other man had stirred her heart like this. She desired him, but more than that. She wanted Cadell to be hers forever. She needed him. She *had* to have him. She didn't want him to be with anyone else. Ever. And neither did she want to be with anyone besides him.

If they continued, according to the ways of her kind, they would be wed.

"Stop. Doing. That." She knew. She had decided. And she could see it in his eyes that even if he wasn't aware yet, he knew too.

She pulled him back toward her, slowly tracing his lip with her tongue. Then, pushing her hands against his chest, she forced him back. Lying over him, she laced one hand through his and proceeded to trace kisses down his jaw, his chest, then upwards to his neck. She sank her fangs into his skin. He was hers.

Cadell released his breath. "Amethyst..." he whispered, his hands grasping at her body.

She giggled as she drank his blood, not to harm him, but to have him. It was only for a few moments, but the marks she left in his skin would be permanent. Magic helped a little with that too.

Finally, she sat back, tilting her head to one side, tantalizing. The smirk still rested on her lips, inviting him. She didn't care if this was too soon. It was too late now. No one, besides Darien, had ever made her feel this safe, this warm, this protected, this loved. She didn't know if he meant to do it, or if it was simply his personality. But she couldn't let him go.

For once, Cadell didn't hesitate. His arms were wrapped around her and as she moved back, he moved with her. He was seeking her lips, but she shook her head. Certainly he knew what she wanted.

His lips traced down her neck and finally, his fangs sank into her skin too. She couldn't help the satisfaction that spread warmth as the binding coursed through her. She wasn't sure if it was because of the magic or the way he made her feel. Maybe both. Now she was his.

Cadell grunted, indulging himself. He pulled back, forcefully, as if it took much effort for him not to devour her. He captured her mouth again, pushing her back into the pillows. She moved with him, urging him onward.

At last, she knew what it was to truly have him.

Amethyst let out a groan as she shifted, the sun's rays shining on her closed eyes. She turned away from the sun and towards the warm body beside her, cuddling close as one eye opened, being met with a tanned chest.

She let out a soft sigh as she heard the splashing of the waves, beckoning her to come out and play. Later, she thought, as she rested a hand on the chest in front of her, smoothing the skin lightly. Waking up like this wasn't half bad, she thought as a yawn escaped her.

Amethyst moved away from Cadell. She immediately missed his warmth, but a grumbling in her stomach insisted she get up. She pushed herself into a sitting position, purple curls falling everywhere as she shook her head to try to wake herself from her sleepiness. She pushed a hand through her hair, stretching out her neck. It felt sore. Why?

"Oh, that's right," she giggled, recollecting the night's events. She looked to her side at Cadell, merely wanting to watch him sleep.

A gentle groan escaped Cadell's lips as he shifted, eyes opening slightly. He looked a little confused for a moment, then his eyes opened more and the light of recognition filled them. Cadell smiled as soon as he laid eyes on Amethyst. "Mornin'," he said softly, his voice low and rough.

"Morning," Amethyst murmured, letting out another yawn and tucking a loose curl behind her ear. She was still groggy herself and blinked lightly as she looked down at him, the smile still on her face. Yet her stomach gave another angry rumble and she moved to stand.

She paused as he grasped her arm and give it a gentle tug. "Wait, just a little longer?" he asked, his eyes pleading.

Amethyst complied, leaning toward him.

Cadell grinned, moving closer to plant kisses on her lips.

Amethyst welcomed them, grasping his arm. She could get used to waking up to his kisses every morning. It then occurred to her she had slept the whole night without any disturbance from her dreams.

Usually, nightmares of her past haunted her mind, tormenting her, and it was a rare night she slept in peace. She silently prayed it was not simply a coincidence and that every night from now on would be as serene.

As if on cue, Cadell pulled back slightly and toyed with one of her stray curls. "Sleep well?"

"Very. You?" she asked, lacing a hand through his free one.

"Perfectly," he said with a smile.

The breakfast bell sounded.

"We should get going soon. They'll be looking for us," Cadell remarked.

Amethyst sighed softly, a faint nod coming with it in agreement. She was after all, very hungry. She leaned toward him, demanding more kisses as her lips met his. "Perhaps I could have you for breakfast," she teased.

Laughter escaped him and he went toward the mark he had made in her neck, only lightly teasing it with pointed teeth and tracing it with his tongue. But just as he pressed his lips to her skin, his stomach rumbled loudly. "I guess my stomach has a mind of its own. Personally, I don't want to listen to its complaining." He grinned, eyes sparkling.

Her eyes were half-lidded when he finally pulled away, and a soft laugh escaped her. "They just don't understand," she said.

Cadell shifted, releasing her slowly and rather reluctantly from his embrace. "Come on," he said, placing his feet on the floor and reaching for his shirt. As he donned it, he reached for hers. "Shall I dress ye?"

She blinked, then smiled. Perhaps if any other man had asked, she may have been insulted. Just because *she* had let him in her bed didn't mean she suddenly was a damsel to be tended to. But with Cadell...

As he leaned toward her to put it on, he paused, as if expecting her to kiss him.

Instead, she pulled back a little, grinning.

"Ah, I see. I tease ye, ye tease me, so now we're even. Next time, no teasing," he muttered.

"That's how the game is played," she cooed, fluttering her lashes. Her hand rested lightly on her hip. "I'll think about it... next time. You sound so certain."

"Aye," he said, "I've got no reason not to be." The marks they now shared permanently erased any possible uncertainty. It was the same as wedding bands for common folk.

"And to think, it has only just begun." Amethyst's eyes sparkled mischievously. "I like confidence. I think it's rather... how do you say, sexy?" she purred. Amethyst prided herself in confidence, having started out in the very beginning of her pirate career, and life really, without much of it.

"Ugh... I'm getting pale again," she suddenly commented, looking down at herself. "I don't think I'll be putting any clothes on today. I need the sun. I hope your crew, if they happen to look over, don't mind."

"Well, I hope they don't look over then," Cadell muttered. "I don't want to have to go snapping them back in place." He chuckled at the thought.

Amethyst headed toward the bathroom.

When she came back out, her hair was pinned up and all loose curls were put back. She smirked. "I hope *you* don't mind me going around without any clothes on, then." She raised a brow. "If you would prefer, I'll put some on, but I doubt they'll stay on very long." Amethyst waited to see his reaction.

"Well, I don't really like the idea of anyone else eyeing ye like pigs. Then again, yer crew are probably used to it. I don't mind, but," he stepped closer to her, poking her playfully and then placing a hand on her upper arm. "Am I expected to keep off ye when we're not alone?" he asked with a grin.

"To be honest, I don't care if they stare. I got over the shyness problem quite a while ago. In fact, I would much like to see you in action. Well, pirate action." She smiled and headed back to the bathroom. Once more, she emerged, this time with her face and body glimmering with wet droplets from rinsing off in her bathtub.

A chuckle escaped Cadell, "I might've noticed ye don't have a shyness problem. But I get the feeling ye like a lot of attention."

"I always do as I wish, on my ship and at my port." Amethyst continued talking, simultaneously rubbing a fluffy towel about her skin to dry off. "My men are used to it. In fact, if it's a particularly lazy day and it's hot, most of us will go for a swim and then dry up on the deck." She laughed and then tilted her head slightly. "I doubt they very much care what you do, as long as it doesn't consist of a blade in my flesh or you forcing yourself on me."

He tried to appear semi-serious, though she knew he wasn't as he whispered, "And what if I do?" He paused, watching her face.

She gazed between his eyes as he partially teased. "If you did, you'd find yourself being dragged across the ship to attract the sharks before they devour you." Her voice was also a partial whisper, only semi-serious.

Cadell added, "I'm sure yer crew have nothing to worry about. I would never."

"I know you wouldn't," she said with a soft smile.

"Well I guess I'd deserve it..." he muttered.

"You know, I would very much like a tour of your ship," she said suddenly.

"A tour? That could be arranged. Would ye want to go after breakfast or a bit later in the day?" Cadell asked.

"After breakfast, if you wouldn't mind. I plan to tan later on in the day as we sail. You are more than welcome to join me." She nuzzled against his shoulder, pushing past some of the cloth that covered his skin. "Thank you, oh honorable Captain Cadell." Amethyst teased him again.

"Then I guess we're stuck together, for at least until after ye've seen my ship," Cadell said. Finally, as he heard footsteps approaching the room, he moved toward the door, reaching for the handle. "Let's not torture our stomachs any further, shall we?"

# Strategy

$\mathcal{A}$s they climbed from below onto the main deck, Cadell breathed in deeply. The scents of the ocean and of freshly made breakfast filled the air. The *Gargoyle*'s crew were going about their duties and their laughter resounded. "Ah, nothing like the morning on a pirate ship," Cadell said pleasantly.

"Almost better than battle." Amethyst grinned, her head tilting back as the sun flooded her face.

"Aye," Cadell murmured.

As she had said, the crew members did not stop and ogle but rather gave enthusiastic waves and greetings. She waved also, searching for Darien.

Cadell watched Amethyst for a moment before being bumped by a crew member hurrying by. As they looked for Darien, it occurred to Cadell... he hoped Amethyst wouldn't feel like he had cheated her in any way when she learned about the girl they were going to meet, Akaisha.

Cadell hadn't specified her name to Darien. The fact was, she was a well-known lass, an information source. Anyone could pay a fine penny to learn almost anything about someone else from Akaisha.

Cadell knew her for different reasons. He supposed worst-case scenario he simply could suggest a few of his crew go to find her so the *Gargoyle* wouldn't be anywhere near her.

As he spotted Darien, Cadell pushed his thoughts aside and moved toward the *Gargoyle*'s first mate.

The two captains approached a round table on the upper deck where breakfast had already been prepared. Darien was bent over it, scrutinizing all the objects. Cadell assumed he was preparing for Amethyst's reaction and double-checking there wasn't anything sharp.

"Good morning!" Amethyst called excitedly.

Darien looked up, and as soon as his eyes fell on them, his jaw dropped. His eyes glanced between Cadell and Amethyst for a moment, before he noticed their hands, laced together, and gathered himself. The first mate cleared his throat. "Good morning, Captain Amethyst, Captain Cadell."

Darien's eyes continued tracing over them. They settled on the mark in Amethyst's neck, and his face scrunched in a bit of confusion. He was scrutinizing. "Late night last night?" Darien asked. Of course, Darien would have no way of knowing about Cadell's vampiric blood.

"I had a wonderful night last night. Had the best sleep in a while," Amethyst stated, which seemed to bring Darien's focus away from the situation and on the conversation. She took a sip from her goblet and leaned forward.

Darien began preparing Amethyst a plate and while she waited, she crossed her legs and rested her elbows on the table. When he was done, she ate peacefully, eyes drifting off. Her gaze was slightly dazed, and her face seemed to glow.

Cadell couldn't help tracing over her features. He noticed her every movement, pleased with the merriment gleaming from her face.

"Fine morning it is," Amethyst stated. "I plan on catching me a tan today." A pause. "So as soon as breakfast is over, if Cadell and I don't go over to his ship, I am going to lie out and soak up some sun. If you would be a dear, have the men lay out my favorite book, and don't forget the rum!"

"Aye, aye." Darien nodded before looking at Cadell pointedly.

At the nod from Darien, Cadell finished his plate. The longer he waited the worse it was, so there was no beating around it. If he played it right, perhaps Amethyst wouldn't become as upset as Darien had suggested she would.

"Amethyst," Cadell paused, uncertain exactly how to change the subject so suddenly. He didn't want to open a fresh wound too quickly, or harshly. "Darien and I have discussed the matter of Stephan. That man is up to something, probably significant to the war. Darien and I want nothing less than to make sure he won't ever come near you or your ship again. And also that he won't hurt anyone else. If it can be helped, this war could have one less leader of sorts."

Amethyst was looking calmly at Cadell, but when he mentioned Stephan, she became rigid. "Yes, I know that son of a whore is up to something. And he won't come near my ship unless his bones are decorating it," she spat.

Cadell nodded in agreement with her. "Aye, I was thinking of sending in a spy to learn his intentions."

"I do not mind sending in a spy, but I will be the one to finish him off and that is final," Amethyst snarled. She was silent again to let Cadell finish.

"Aye! You can have him and do as you wish with his bloody neck," Cadell agreed. "I've an idea in mind, and I'm pretty confident it will work. A mere crew member as a spy would perhaps learn a great deal, but we need someone who would learn everything and dispose of anything he has. So, perhaps I am dead wrong, but I was thinking a woman who would gain his trust, know him intimately. It would have to be one who could entirely handle the situation. I need to know what you think, because if you disagree, we'll find some other way."

Amethyst stiffened further when the subject of a woman filling in as a spy was mentioned. She was silent, contemplating everything Cadell had suggested. Her lips pursed and her brow furrowed.

Rather than wait for her response, Cadell continued. "The woman in mind, her name is Akaisha. And she's on the next port. Or should be. So, whether we stop there or not, is up to you."

Cadell fell silent, eyes firm. He hoped she would be able to see there was no trickery from him, only care for her.

Amethyst looked hesitantly between Cadell and Darien, then down toward the table. "But, could we trust her?" she asked, lifting her gaze to meet Cadell's. "I don't want her to lure us into thinking we can trust her and then steal everything I have worked so hard for right from under my nose," she murmured, looking down once more. Once again, only for a moment, her vulnerable interior showed.

Cadell felt a wave of relief. He placed his hand on hers gently. "I promise, Captain Amethyst, you have nothing to fear from her. She won't touch anything of yours or be around it. Trust me, and Darien. We won't let anything happen." He knew she wouldn't trust Akaisha, no matter what. And that perhaps would be too much to ask.

"How close are we to this port where she is located?" Amethyst asked.

"Well, if we continue sailing, we're about another day and a half away from the port. So, you have plenty of time to think over it," Cadell responded reassuringly.

"I will sleep on it tonight," Amethyst finally stated. Cadell assumed that if she wouldn't trust him, she would trust Darien. Though he hoped especially after recent events, that she trusted him equally if not more.

"That sounds like a good idea, Captain Amethyst," Darien nodded, chewing on his breakfast. "I will make sure she is never within range of your ship. But I would suggest a meeting, between the three of us and her. And if you do not like the feel of her then, we will come up with another way of destroying Stephan."

"Yes, he will die at my hands." Amethyst seemed to say it to herself as reassurance.

Cadell nodded his agreement. "So, I suppose we'll get our answer in the morning? Until then, we shall continue sailing toward port."

"Yes. We will continue sailing to the port," she said finally, seeming now to be immersed in thought.

Cadell took a sip from his glass as if to finalize and confirm the agreement, and as he set it down, he picked up a piece of bread and a few grapes and began to eat them. As the end of their meal approached, he sought to lighten the mood. "So, ready for that tour?"

It seemed Cadell easily moved on from the discussion back to lighter matters. He was asking her something. What was it? The tour...

"Oh, yes, sure..." She wasn't entirely sure what she was answering to, but she figured 'yes' would suffice for right now. They were still sitting at the table for breakfast, but her mind was drifting.

Despite the clear skies, she felt wary. She had not noticed it before, but within the last few moments, a strange feeling of something approaching had come over her. She tried not to show her unease, other than the slight tilting of her ears. She was trying to catch any sort of sound waves, indicating someone else's approach.

But alas, she only heard the call of the birds, the waves of the sea, and the breeze which wafted across the ship. She blinked lightly.

"Amethyst, are you alright?" Cadell asked slowly, his brows folding in concern.

"Oh, I'm fine," Amethyst smiled. One of her strengths had always been trusting her instincts. They never steered her wrong. Something was off but without any further indicators, there was no use alarming anyone. Surely, whatever it was would become evident soon. Yes, the tour. She sighed softly, the breeze ruffling her hair once more. She finished off her plate and stood, stretching and resting her hand on the back of her chair.

"Well, shall we be off? Would you rather me stop by and get my own clothes or just use your shirt?" She was pretty sure he didn't want her going around naked on his ship. She could care less, but it was *his* ship, after all.

Cadell nodded, still looking concerned. "As long as you don't mind, just wear mine. It's easier," he said, easily pulling his shirt over his head and making a notion to slip it over her.

Amethyst breathed in deeply, inhaling his scent, and smiled. Somehow, it made her feel better, if only for a moment. Still... something was tugging at the pit of her stomach. Perhaps it had been the discussion of that other woman.

No, it was something different.

Amethyst closed her eyes, tilting her head back and taking in another deep breath. Perhaps it was just the effects of yesterday still lingering.

Curse Captain Stephan, she thought.

# The Phoenix

"Sail ho!" cried the lookout from the crow's nest above.

Immediately men rushed to the sides, peering over to see what ship could be approaching. It was hardly difficult, even from a distance, and was unmistakable. The hull was colored in bursts of yellow, orange, and red, and its sails were like tongues of fire. It was a brig, a ship with two square-rigged masts and a small fore and aft sail. The type was common among pirates who either couldn't afford a larger one or didn't have enough deckhands to pillage one.

The captain of the approaching ship had not been at the meeting a few days before, but everyone suspected they knew why he was approaching: in search of an alliance.

"It's the Phoenix," Cadell muttered, mostly to himself. All focus was now on the flame-colored ship. "Do ye still want that tour or do ye want to wait and see what the Phoenix's captain is up to?" Cadell asked Amethyst, whose eyes were fixed on the *Phoenix.*

Amethyst licked her lips and remained quiet. This had been the source of her uneasiness.

"I'd rather have ye touring my ship naked than let the crew of the Phoenix set their eyes on ye," Cadell said quietly to her.

"I won't let him see me that way," Amethyst said, turning her gaze toward Cadell finally. When she looked at him, she smiled, but her eyes betrayed her anxiety. She looked away again. "Anyway, the tour will have to wait, I'm afraid," she said softly to Cadell. Amethyst turned to Darien. "Darien, bring my pants, would you?"

Her first mate nodded and went to do as she requested. "Don't worry," she said as she patted Cadell's shoulder gently.

"Raise the sails," Amethyst shouted to her crew, who immediately jumped into action. "Let them approach," she said.

Darien returned with her pants and she donned them, reaching for her glass from the table as they waited for the *Phoenix* to draw closer.

It would be at least a couple of hours before the *Phoenix* would be fully broadside the *Gargoyle* with the wind being light as it was. However, Amethyst desired to be present immediately upon the other ship's arrival, regardless of her desire to be anywhere else.

"Go easy on him, Cadell," Amethyst said, meeting his eyes and searching. Cadell nodded his agreement, smiling at her.

All of her memories from the last time she had seen Mikhail came flooding back. How long had it been again? Not to mention that their parting hadn't exactly been smooth.

She wondered how Cadell was feeling on the matter. Mikhail had been a member of Cadell's crew first and had abruptly abandoned the *Reaper's Scythe* in lieu of joining the *Gargoyle*. In fact, as she recalled, he hadn't even told Cadell he was leaving. He had just disappeared.

Whatever Cadell was feeling, she couldn't read him. His dark eyes were focused on the fiery-colored ship which was now fully in view. She wanted to ask, but maybe it was better not to.

Her crew busied themselves with duties around the deck, and she continued to breathe in Cadell's scent from his shirt, shifting her focus to the rippling waves around the ship.

It wouldn't be much longer now.

Finally, after what felt like much longer than the short couple of hours from the initial spying of the ship, a white flag raised in surrender became clear and at last, the two ships drew broadside each other. Captain Mikhail stood at the prow of his ship, orange-red hair flying everywhere. He was shirtless, a tattoo in the color of a phoenix in flight shining proudly against his skin, flames bursting around its feathers. A boyish smile was on his lips and his eyes were shining.

"Let's get this over with," Cadell muttered.

"Permission to board, Captain Amethyst?" Mikhail gave a smile. His eyes were completely focused on Amethyst. At least at first.

Amethyst nodded her approval and the *Phoenix*'s plank landed across.

Mikhail calmly walked across the plank. It was then that his gaze met Cadell's and a frown crossed his features. "Captain Cadell. What a surprise," the *Phoenix*'s captain said.

Cadell nodded. "Aye, I could say the same to ye, Captain Mikhail. Coming along well, I see." Mikhail was no longer the boy he remembered. He had grown some, and his features were toned and distinguished. His jaw was set and angular, with high cheekbones, and it was clear he was as able as any old seadog.

"Aye, I am," Mikhail stated. "In no time I'll be in the same ranks as ye, Captain Cadell." The words were nearly a challenge instead of an agreement.

"I'm sure ye will," Cadell told Mikhail.

"I just hope ye don't regret not hiring me on as a part of yer crew. I would've done yer ship well. But now, I've got me own ship." Mikhail seemed quite proud of that fact.

Cadell bit his tongue as he briefly remembered it was not he that had rejected Mikhail. Rather, Mikhail had discovered the *Gargoyle* and her captain and decided the *Reaper's Scythe* was not good enough. "Aye, and a good one at that," Cadell said, referring to Mikhail's ship.

Cadell watched as Mikhail's eyes traced down Amethyst's figure and narrowed slightly. The fiery ship's captain then glanced sharply toward Darien. "It's been a while, Darien, hasn't it? Ten years?"

Darien nodded silently.

Cadell glanced at Darien. Ten years? So then, his stay aboard the *Gargoyle* had been short-lived. While Mikhail had only gotten his own ship and crew within the past few years, it left a lot of questions as to what had happened in between.

Mikhail approached Amethyst, taking her hand and kissing it. She blushed softly and looked away. "It's been too long since we've seen each other last." He looked briefly at Cadell. "I 'as hoping for a more... private conversation with ye." Mikhail looked back at Amethyst, demanding her eyes with his own as he said the last words.

Cadell controlled himself, knowing it would only upset Amethyst to react badly. He did, however, press his hand against her lower back. Beneath his fingertips, he could feel her tension. She was nervous. She seemed to relax slightly for a moment, then tensed again.

"Perhaps a meeting could be arranged later on this afternoon. You see, Captain Cadell was about to take me on a tour of his ship," Amethyst stated.

Mikhail's features fell in disappointment.

"Well, Captain Mikhail, I'm afraid ye were just a tad bit off in timing. But I assure ye ye'll have yer meeting." Cadell glanced at Amethyst, looking for signs of disagreement with him. He was glad she had mentioned the tour. Clearly, she was growing more uncomfortable and wanted a chance to breathe and gather her thoughts.

Plus, Cadell could tell there was something else that was bothering her. Everything about the way Mikhail looked at Amethyst indicated a past relationship. He suspected such a relationship would be the reason Amethyst was not being more strong-headed and aggressive. Cadell hoped she would tell him, though a part of him suspected she would rather not.

"That makes me remember something," Mikhail said. "Captain Amethyst, ye be invited to dinner on me ship tonight." He paused. "Ye may come as well, if ye wish, Captain Cadell." It was stated as more of an afterthought.

"Oh, well, I'd be honored to have dinner on your ship, Captain Mikhail." Amethyst smiled lightly. Cadell could still feel her tension. "And I'm sure Captain Cadell would love to join us."

Cadell suspected Mikhail had only invited him to get in Amethyst's good graces. He didn't miss the pointed look from Mikhail in his direction. "Aye. It'll also be good to see your accomplishment." He smiled.

Cadell was serious; he really did want to see Mikhail's ship, but he had deeper intentions. He wanted to see just how much of a potential threat Mikhail might be if he decided to change his tune in the near future. Even if Mikhail got an alliance with Amethyst, Cadell had a feeling he shouldn't trust the younger captain anytime soon.

"Well, wonderful," Mikhail said simply. Silence ensued, and Cadell moved to curl his arm around Amethyst's middle. Afterall, it wasn't hard to read the situation and whether Mikhail liked it or not, Amethyst was no longer available outside of strictly alliances.

As soon as Cadell's hand became visible on the other side of Amethyst, Mikhail's eyes narrowed further. Amethyst squirmed, and there was a nasty sort of anger emanating from Mikhail's person.

Amethyst began toying with the hem of Cadell's shirt. It was big on her, and one of the shoulders slipped, revealing her skin. She quickly covered it, fidgeting.

Mikhail smiled again, his eyes unconsciously drifting to the bare skin that was soon covered up by the shirt. His tongue slowly licked at his lips.

Cadell reluctantly let his arm drop, giving Amethyst the freedom she was struggling for. As soon as she was free, Amethyst stepped away from both he and Mikhail, moving closer to Darien. She visibly relaxed.

Cadell knew he was part of the source of her nerves, but he was no simpleton. He could tell there was history between Amethyst and Mikhail and clearly, Mikhail was disregarding how much time had passed since then. Well, Mikhail may have physically grown up, but had he emotionally? It wasn't like Amethyst was going to wait around for a boy... surely Mikhail must have known Amethyst would move on.

Cadell caught Amethyst's gaze as she glanced toward him, her eyes searching his face.

Finally, Mikhail broke the silence. "Well, tonight is fine then. But before, perhaps five minutes won't matter?" Mikhail peered at Amethyst, who was nibbling on her lips, her ears twitching lightly.

She let out another soft sigh, frowning.

"Please, Captain Amethyst, if ye allow me a brief meet now, ye won't have to worry about such matters with me later. Ye are very busy, I'm sure, and I wish to keep..."

"Ye'll just have to wait, Mikhail. Clearly, now isn't a good time, especially for her alone. Ye're dismissed." With that, Cadell stepped between Mikhail and Amethyst, eyes commanding. Whether Mikhail liked it or not, captain or not, he was on board a stronger ship. If he was truly sincere about alliances, he would have to submit to requests made of him for the time being.

Yellow eyes turned dark as Cadell spoke. His eyes screamed, '*Who do you think you are, on Amethyst's ship, to tell me what to do?*' Mikhail didn't budge. Clearly, he was waiting on Amethyst to be the one to tell him something.

Amethyst was still fidgeting lightly, and she looked at Cadell before turning to her first mate, as if pleading for him to do something. Sweat had broken out on her forehead and she absentmindedly wiped it with the shirt that covered her. As she did so, she looked at the clothing with disdain. Perhaps she didn't feel comfortable turning away Mikhail so harshly.

At last, she dropped her fidgeting hands as Darien stepped forward. "Captain Amethyst, may I borrow you for a moment?" Darien asked her with a brief smile at Mikhail. At this point, there was no need to take over and force anyone to leave. The *Phoenix*'s captain was still on good terms and Cadell now saw perhaps he'd been too abrupt. It was up to Darien now to ease Amethyst's nerves. He seemed to recognize his task.

At Darien's request, Amethyst nodded, turned and followed her first mate. She was approaching her cabin and once she was out of view, Amethyst breathed in Cadell's scent from his shirt, letting it calm her. '*What are Mikhail's intentions?*' she wondered.

She knew that one of her greatest weaknesses as a captain was her emotions. She could gut any wench without so much as a moment's hesitation. She could slit the throats of other captains and all of their crew and smile while doing it. But a past lover and a tangle of feelings threw her into disarray.

Amethyst knew she needed to confront Mikhail and be honest with him at some point. She honestly hadn't thought she'd ever see him again.

This evening. Yes. Over dinner. Perhaps she could make it clear that he was more than welcome to aid her in battle so long as their alliance was nothing more. She knew what he wanted. And she'd just have to put her foot down. Past or not.

It was time to face him fully, not like the way she'd simply abandoned him before.

# Lured

$\mathcal{C}$adell's thoughts had been drifting in every which way all day. In fact, he had almost forgotten the dinner plans on the *Phoenix*.

Thoughts of Stephan and the approaching war plagued him. Further, he thought of Akaisha and how with Mikhail's arrival, the whole plan would be put on temporary hold.

Even if they continued sailing toward the port, Amethyst would have her mind preoccupied. He was admittedly upset about the timing of Mikhail's arrival.

As the sun began to fall toward the horizon, Cadell gazed toward the *Gargoyle* with rising frequency, remembering the night before. He let a sigh escape his lips and handed the *Reaper* over to Aurek once again. It was time to get ready for dinner.

Cadell had half a mind to go as he was, but despite those urges, he moved to his cabin and donned his nicer clothing, a dark vest over a pristine shirt and dark pants. He even combed back his hair in a pleasant fashion.

He stepped aboard the *Gargoyle* near sunset, just as Amethyst was leaving her cabin and moving toward the *Phoenix*. He smiled as she smoothed the fabric of the crimson dress she had bought on their shopping venture and drank in her curves, accentuated by the way the dress hugged her figure and the slit to her thigh on one side, perfectly balanced with the single shoulder strap on the opposite side. Her eggplant ringlets were pinned up, though a few rebelliously danced about her neck. A splash of makeup shone against her cheekbones and drew him to her lips, painted red. He casually stepped behind her, walking alongside Darien, and lightly tapped her shoulder.

As she turned, Amethyst's eyes lit up with delight when they met his.

Amethyst looked at Darien, who released her arm and stepped away. "Would you like to escort me to dinner?" she asked Cadell, holding out her arm in an offering.

Cadell nodded faintly with a smile toward Darien before taking Amethyst's arm, "Aye. No lad in his right mind would miss out on such an opportunity."

"You clean up nicely," she said with a smirk. She seemed more calm and resolute. Had she determined what she would do?

Cadell's grin widened. "Well I guess I could've just boarded the Phoenix looking like a dirty, worked-up pirate captain, but that wouldn't go too well."

"I'm sure Mikhail wouldn't have cared too much." Amethyst shrugged, looking ahead at their destination as they strolled there.

Cadell chuckled, "Well then, I guess I really have no reason after all. What's yer reasoning then?" he asked, poking her playfully. He glanced around, taking in the *Phoenix* and its features and qualities as they finally stepped aboard the fiery-colored ship. It was a fine piece of craft, not that he had expected any less.

"I thought you might like this outfit; I got it while we were in port the other day," she explained, answering his previous question.

"Mmm, ye were right," Cadell murmured, bending toward her ear so as to keep those words between just the two of them. "I might have to ask ye to wear it more often."

"You compliment me too much," Amethyst responded, eyebrows raising gently at him. A blush coated her cheeks. "But, you can ask anytime," she said.

"Trying to seduce me?" Cadell asked playfully.

"You'll never know," Amethyst said with a smug face, shaking her head to rearrange her curls. "I missed you today," Amethyst admitted toward Cadell. "But it was best I keep my distance from both of you. Mikhail's temper's worse than mine and it could've proven disastrous. I hope you understand," she finished, her eyes soft as she sought his face. A breeze swept over her, ruffling her dress and hair.

The look in Cadell's eyes was gentle. "Ye don't have to explain to me, Captain. I understand." Finally, they reached the table Mikhail had prepared and they turned their attention to their host, who was almost green with jealousy. Cadell hardly cared. Amethyst was his, and not in any way Mikhail could ever come between. He would neither rub it in the other captain's face nor would he allow the other to make any sort of attempts.

Still, pleasantries were in order. "Captain Mikhail, I presume your day went well?"

Mikhail was standing by the table, sipping on a glass of wine as he watched them, doing a terrible job of attempting to appear casual. As they approached, he pulled out Amethyst's seat, waiting.

Amethyst unlinked her arm from Cadell's.

Mikhail turned slightly to Cadell, "Aye," was his short answer before he focused on Amethyst again. "My, ye look extremely lovely tonight, Captain Amethyst. Please, take a seat and I'll get some wine."

"Perhaps," she said at first, then, "I would love a glass of wine, Captain Mikhail." She smirked once more, smoothing down her dress. Mikhail's eyes followed her hand as it caressed over her side and hip. He was utterly mesmerized by the simple motion. As Amethyst fully sat down, Mikhail gave her a kiss on her hand and commented once again on how gorgeous she looked.

Cadell kept his composure, holding himself back with each of Mikhail's gestures. For Amethyst's sake. Aye, this would be a long evening.

"Crimson is truly your color, my dear," Mikhail said.

Cadell disagreed. While she was certainly dressed to kill in crimson, he felt there were other colors far more suited. Still, he couldn't help the soft smirk, knowing Amethyst had not only dressed for him, but had specifically bought the dress for him to enjoy her in it. It didn't even bother him that Mikhail was privileged enough to see it too.

Once she was seated, Cadell, at last, took his own seat. "So then, Captain, I see ye have a fine ship. Never really got a look at her features 'til now. I like her." His tone was sincere. What Cadell didn't let on was that he was secretly testing Mikhail. What kind of man had he become these last ten years? How would he handle the situation with the fact he hadn't gotten away with just Amethyst alone?

"Thank you, Captain Cadell. That means a lot coming from *you*." There was a bit of a sarcastic edge to Mikhail's voice. His eyes danced with wisps of hair floating in and out of his vision.

Cadell simply smiled warmly at Mikhail. '*It should,*' he thought, considering he definitely knew what he was talking about. After all, he was no amateur.

Mikhail turned his full attention to Amethyst, fussing lightly over her and making sure that she was comfortable and asked if she wanted anything special. The food had not been brought out yet.

"Well, would ye pass the bottle?" Cadell asked pleasantly. He was doing his best to keep things casual. The last thing he wanted was to stir up the nervousness and tension from Amethyst again.

Mikhail grudgingly eyed Cadell as instead of passing the bottle, he poured him a glass. He was the host for the evening, and Cadell assumed he meant to put on a good face for Amethyst.

Still, the constant fussing over her was irritating. Why was he trying *so hard?* Cadell wondered if Mikhail were attempting to win back Amethyst's affections. Hadn't he noticed the mark on her neck? Or perhaps he was in denial.

Amethyst took a sip of her wine and smiled delightfully. "Mikhail, this is such a fine wine! Tell me, where did you get it?" she asked, taking another sip.

Mikhail looked pleased. "It is a wine made from your homeland." Her lips thinned a little bit, but still seemed pleased. She swirled the liquid around. "The fae always did make good wine. Of course, it was always laced with a hint of magic."

"The food is almost done, I'm sure. That will allow me to speak with you a bit, Captain Amethyst."

She quirked a brow as Mikhail addressed her but smiled again. "Let me guess. You would like to propose an alliance?"

He leaned forward on the table, chuckling softly. "You read my mind, Captain."

Cadell didn't miss a beat. "Well, Captain Mikhail, you'd be making a very wise choice in alliances, siding with two of the greatest ships at sea." His focus was turned from Amethyst for only a moment. "All three of us together would be nearly unbeatable as some of the greatest captains on the seas." He grinned at Amethyst, having meant it as a compliment to her.

Mikhail was quick to correct Cadell when he spoke of the alliance encompassing all of them. "I never said I was offering an alliance to *you.*" His smile turned dark. "My alliance will lie with Captain Amethyst only." He spoke very clearly.

Cadell merely shrugged and gave a faint nod to let Mikhail know he understood the picture. Cadell didn't press the matter. He could see that no matter what he did, this subject was a rather tense and touchy one. It would be impossible for Amethyst to be completely and entirely relaxed.

Amethyst let out a soft sigh. "Mikhail," she murmured softly, "you aren't interested in an alliance with Captain Cadell as well?"

Cadell wasn't sure why Amethyst asked such a pointless question after Mikhail had already specified. Though it made him glad she was making it clear where her heart truly lied.

"Listen, Mikhail–" Amethyst started, clearly intending to say something important.

Just then the food was brought out. Darien reached for Amethyst's glass and filled it with water. She pouted, but he made no move to change it. "You need to keep a clear head, Captain," Darien reminded her.

Mikhail looked disappointed. "Ye're first mate's a smart man, Captain Amethyst," Mikhail said gently, taking another sip of his own wine.

"That he is. But now, let's eat." Amethyst grinned, picking up a piece of meat and putting it in her mouth.

Ignoring the question concerning an alliance with Cadell, and whatever Amethyst had started to say, Mikhail continued, "So, Captain Amethyst, I have also heard some rumors that Captain Stephan's after ye."

Cadell nearly choked on a bite of meat, and casually took a sip of wine, trying to appear unfazed.

Amethyst showed no outward reaction as she ate. She swallowed, looking at him with a smirk. "Aye, he is."

"Well, I come to offer protection as well," Mikhail told her.

She gave a haughty laugh. "I can handle myself."

"Captain Amethyst, wouldn't ye rather be safer than sorry?"

She paused as if to think about it. "We'll discuss it later, all right, Captain Mikhail?" Her tone put an end to the discussion.

Cadell was glad. Mikhail could've waited to bring up *that* topic and Cadell eyed him.

Amethyst was silent as she ate, even though Mikhail tried to make idle chatter. The food was delicious. Cadell noticed she seemed to grow more distant the further she got through her meal. She seemed to snap out of a dazed reverie when she drank her water, then zoned out again. When spoken to, Amethyst gazed between Cadell and Mikhail appearing disengaged. Her eyes, normally alert with a touch of mischief, were glazed. She looked as though she were under a spell.

Cadell frowned, a bad feeling settling in his gut and he looked at Mikhail, now certain the other man had done something. "Amethyst... what was it you started to say earlier?" he asked.

Amethyst glanced at him, her gaze somewhat clouded. "Hmm? Did I start something? I can't remember," she said with a giggle.

Mikhail seized the opportunity. "Well, now that our meal is over, we were about to discuss the details of our alliance."

"Oh, yes, I think that would be wonderful," Amethyst said, her tone completely different than before.

Darien and Cadell's eyes met immediately.

Amethyst refused dessert, and Darien moved closer to his captain. Amethyst, no matter what, never refused a sweet treat. She insisted she was full. Her pupils were large.

Calmly, Darien laid a hand on her shoulder. He began talking to her in her native tongue. He asked her how she felt, and she said that she felt like she was floating on a cloud.

Cadell was surprised he had understood them. The fae tongue was familiar, but he didn't know it fluently. It was like a distant language from the past. Still, knowledge of it had seemed to be enough.

"Excuse me, gentlemen, but I think Amethyst needs to go lay down for a bit," Darien murmured, pulling her up. "Let's finish this conversation later, Captain Mikhail."

Amethyst stumbled a bit, gripping onto her first mate's shirt lightly. "I'm fine, Darien." Her words were soft, and a hiccup escaped her. She giggled lightly. "Honestly." She pouted and tried to sit back down. He let her, but he stood directly above her.

Cadell's concern intensified as Amethyst resisted Darien's advice. True, she could handle herself, but from what he knew about their relationship, Amethyst trusted Darien like no other, and if he thought she should rest, she would normally comply, unless the situation pertained directly to a decision for her to make as a captain.

Cadell glanced at Mikhail only briefly. He wasn't sure if that was trickery of the light or not, but he swore he saw a look of satisfaction on the other man's face. Amethyst may not have been sick, but she definitely wasn't all right.

Amethyst turned her head towards Mikhail. "So, why do you want an alliance with me?" she asked.

"Well there be so many things I could say, Captain Amethyst." Mikhail smiled gently. "But I think ye are the best ship a pirate like me could be aligned to. We could help each other in numerous ways."

Cadell didn't like the look Amethyst's eyes had taken on. She gazed over Mikhail's figure pleasantly like she would a dear lover. Cadell grew tense. He knew better than to be jealous, recognizing the look Amethyst was now giving Mikhail, though also recognizing she wasn't entirely herself.

Darien looked at Cadell once again. She was in no condition to talk about alliances. Darien grabbed Amethyst's dinner plate, a scowl filling his features as he sniffed and then turned to Mikhail sharply. His normally pale skin was red and he grasped the collar of Mikhail's shirt, yanking him forward. "I don't know what you've done, Mikhail, but I will find out." His other hand was curled into a fist.

While Darien focused on Mikhail, Cadell moved toward Amethyst. Perhaps he could get through to her where Darien had not. "Amethyst, don't be fooled by these suggestions. Ye already have everything ye desire."

She turned toward Cadell slightly, seeming to focus for a brief moment.

In that moment, he kissed her, the touch of his lips as soft as he dared, and after only the touch of their lips, he pulled back, eyes searching hers.

Amethyst blinked, seeming confused for a moment and then looking around. She seemed to regain herself. Her eyebrows furrowed and her fingers reached up to grasp Cadell's shirt. "Cadell," she mumbled, "I don't feel so good."

Cadell didn't fail to note Mikhail's desperation as he attempted to push past Darien, eyes flashing with envy. "Captain Amethyst, please, ye can rest here if need be," his voice was coaxing.

If not for the fact he respected Amethyst's firm desire to handle things herself, Cadell would have already taken her to her own ship, as far from Mikhail as she could be at that moment. He attempted to stare Mikhail down. '*One more word and you'll wish you hadn't been born,*' he thought.

Amethyst blinked again, turning her head to look at Mikhail. "Thank you, Mikhail, but I believe I want to retire to my own room tonight." She still remained polite. Cadell wondered if Amethyst still wished to let him down easy. What exactly had happened in the past, he wondered?

Despite Mikhail's ignoring Darien's first threat, he pushed him backward forcefully. "I want you on your way and as far as possible from this ship as soon as we're off your deck," Darien said.

Finally, Mikhail grew pale and nodded. If only Darien would give him a nice beating. However, as they *were* still aboard *his* ship...

Cadell turned back to Amethyst, glad she was semi-thinking straight and he grasped her hand in his own, letting her curl herself into him. As she shut her eyes, he tried to scoop her into his arms.

"No," she insisted, shaking her head.

He frowned but let her lean on him instead and walk on her own two feet back to her ship.

As Cadell helped Amethyst aboard her ship, her head lay back against his arm, and her eyes focused on the stars above. It was a pretty night. Another hiccup came and bile rose in her throat, the taste filling her mouth. She winced. How disgusting.

Amethyst began to think about how weak she was becoming. Ever since the pirate meeting, Cadell had constantly been rescuing her. What was happening to her? Fear swelled. She didn't want to become some weak, man-dependent woman! No! She swallowed her fear and frowned to herself.

Cadell's movements were fluid. He didn't stop until he had safely reached Amethyst's cabin. He paused, halfway between her bed and the bathroom. "Amethyst, do ye need to take a shower first?"

"Yes," she answered, hoping it would quickly clear her thoughts.

Cadell simply nodded and released her. "Alright." He lingered for a moment, then left.

Once he was gone, Amethyst immediately turned on the water to cold and just sat in the shower, letting the water rush over her. The water hit her face and cleared her mind of all the fogginess and cobwebs that decorated it. She hiccupped again and the bile finally escaped her mouth, spilling onto the floor of the shower. She gagged but let the water wash it away.

Amethyst continued to simply sit in the shower; for how long she didn't know. Her mind raced. What was she going to do? She really couldn't remember much right at the moment, only the fact that she was being weak.

She hated how often she had been rescued by Darien and Cadell recently. What was happening? She had risen in the ranks all by herself, through coldness and bloodthirsty tactics, creating a reputation of fear and respect.

She thought back to when she had first encountered Cadell. There had been something about him even then that stirred her inner desire for safety and security.

But that was just it. She had created that on her own just fine. Amethyst could rescue herself. She was a pirate captain, one of the best there was out on the sea. What would it do to her reputation if the others saw her being carted off by someone after chipping a bloody nail?

The thought irked her.

As Cadell stepped out of Amethyst's room, Darien was waiting outside the doorway. He was fidgeting anxiously, pacing. Darien briefly turned back to see Mikhail's ship drifting a little further behind, a few yards away, just as he had ordered.

Cadell scowled as he also caught sight of the *Phoenix*. Hatred rose within him. Regardless of what relationships had happened in the past, there was no way he could settle for an alliance between him and Amethyst. Of course, he recognized Amethyst wouldn't necessarily be agreeing to one now anyway. He just wished instead of keeping a distance, Mikhail would give up and sail away.

As soon as the first mate noticed Cadell, he asked, "Cadell, is everything all right with her?"

"She'll be fine. She's in the bath." Then, Cadell got straight to the point. "What exactly was it?" Now that he had a moment to focus on something besides Amethyst, his mind immediately returned to the incident.

"A spice from some fae islands." Darien said. "It's kept aboard many ships for different purposes. We keep it aboard our ship to help Amethyst calm when she needs it. It's great in low doses when she has an episode and needs to relax for a while, but I suspect her food was sprinkled with it heavily." He frowned. "I will certainly be discussing this matter further with Mikhail," he muttered.

Cadell frowned and nodded. It was probably a good thing Darien would be handling the matter instead of himself.

"We'll be reaching port soon." Cadell paused a moment, glancing at the closed door and then back at Darien. "Amethyst won't be leaving the ship 'til after sunrise, even if we reach port before midnight."

"Aye, I'll handle matters after our meeting with your friend." Darien sighed. "Just make sure she gets some sleep. She'll be cranky in the morning. I'm sure of it."

'*Great*', Cadell thought. '*All we need is a cranky fae captain.*' Out loud, he said, "Very well then. When we reach port, I'll send someone ahead to talk to Akaisha." Cadell paused.

Regardless of how cranky Amethyst was, and despite Mikhail's troublemaking, Stephan was worse, and no one knew when the balance would tip and the sea would host the bloodthirsty chaos of war among pirates. So, unless Darien or Amethyst called it off, Cadell was determined to carry out this meeting.

"I'll make sure to send some of my men with you as well. Amethyst will want the opinions of her own crew," Darien stated, shifting from foot to foot.

Once again, Cadell noticed the heaviness of his shoulders.

After a moment of silence, the first mate looked toward Amethyst's door. "Don't be too angry with Mikhail. He is still in love with her, I imagine. So go easy on the kid." He gave a crooked smile. "His intentions were not to hurt her, but I'm assuming to make her more receptive to him. He misses her, and a man's grief will make him do crazy things." Darien turned to leave.

Cadell was silent a moment, considering Darien's words, "Perhaps ye're right. He won't get what Stephan has coming. But I hope he's learned his lesson. 'Cause if he does try something like that again, he's not getting off so easy." He paused. "Anyway, don't worry. I'll make sure she recuperates." Even as he said the words, he thought of how he desired to be on board his *Reaper*. He hadn't been able to spend much time there as of late.

"Thank you, Cadell. You make my job so much easier." Darien nodded appreciatively. "Goodnight, Captain."

Cadell watched as the first mate of the *Gargoyle* turned to leave. "It's nothing. Good night, Darien."

As the other man left, Cadell returned to Amethyst's room and let his eyes wander a moment, at first around the room, and then out one of the windows. It was dark outside, yet the room was filled with soft moonlight. Cadell thought of how he loved Amethyst and how he could never abandon her. She had become precious to him.

Yet what would that come to once the war was over and the alliance was no longer needed? It was true they were united, but he wondered if she would desire to settle or not. Cadell fell back on the bed, staring upward.

Amethyst entered the room a few moments later, water still glistening off her body. She reached for a garment draped over her desk and donned it, then rubbed her nose lightly on the sleeve of her garment as she shifted over to sit on the bed.

Cadell looked toward her. "Feeling better?" he asked.

She briefly nodded, moving toward him. "I'm fine," she said, forcing a smile.

"What happened between ye and Mikhail?" he asked.

She frowned, looking away. Why must he ask? She imagined him saying he had marked her and thus she owed him an explanation. She wasn't owned by anyone, would be her stubborn response.

Instead, he said, "Amethyst, do ye trust me?"

She looked toward him again, sucking in her breath softly. "Of course I do!"

"As much as yer first mate?" he pressed.

She bit her lip. It had truly been hard for her to open up and Cadell had been the only other she had ever met besides Darien to have proven truly trustworthy.

"Well if I didn't, you would never have seen me so... *weak*," she said stubbornly and filled with frustration that he would question her.

"That doesn't answer my question," he murmured.

"Mikhail is a former lover. He joined my crew and eventually wormed his way toward me. But he was young, immature, and couldn't be trusted. I left him drinking with some friend before he even had a chance to return to the ship. I never gave him an explanation or a goodbye."

She frowned as Cadell smiled. "Ah, so that's it. Ye left him ruthlessly and now ye can't do it again?"

She scowled. "I wasn't sure how to deal with him so unexpectedly. I needed to collect my thoughts and before I could give him his answer, I wasn't thinking straight."

"And yet ye still have heart for him even after he tried to–"

"No," she said firmly. "I no longer love him. I never did. He's still the same boy as he was then, even if he looks older. I'll deal with him on my own."

Cadell nodded. She saw both concern and relief in his eyes, and he reached toward her, fingers barely coming in contact with her skin.

Just as he began the gesture, a familiar sound reached their ears.

They both glanced sharply out the window just in time to see a large splash and she knew. The boom of cannon fire echoed in the distance. Cadell needed to return to his ship.

Cadell's eyes snapped back to Amethyst's. Already they could hear the shouts outside from the crews of the *Reaper*, the

*Gargoyle*, and the *Phoenix*. The war was beginning, and they were under attack.

There was no more time for regret or fickle emotions.

Cadell didn't hesitate any longer. "Amethyst."

She didn't let him finish. "I know," she said.

"Good luck, Cap'n," he said with a small smile. He paused a moment, before another large splash burst in the air sending a jolt through the ship. The cannonball had fallen just short of the hull. At that, he turned and left, the night breeze whipping over his face.

Immediately Amethyst was up and moving around, throwing on clothes and gathering her weapons, just in case they were boarded. Now was her chance. No more letting Cadell and Darien save her. A battle was just what she needed.

As soon as Cadell had gone, she gave a faint smile. Now there was a man after her own heart. Hang it all. That was part of why he had captivated her. His perfect balance between genuine care and being a pirate through and through.

She quickly tied her long hair back, a sheathed dagger resting between her teeth. With the utmost care, she slipped it in between her cleavage, a lovely little hiding spot if she thought so herself.

# And Then Came Fire

 adell moved almost noiselessly. As he arrived on board the *Reaper's Scythe*, Aurek was already shouting orders but looked relieved to see his captain.

"Aurek, go below deck and ready the cannons. I'll handle things here," Cadell ordered.

"Aye, aye!" was Aurek's response, immediately moving into action.

Cadell raced up to the stern where he took the wheel. He could feel the blood pumping through his veins, his heart racing. It was not from fear, but adrenaline and anticipation. He bellowed orders to his crew members as they raced around deck, taking stations, grabbing guns. The spray of the sea wet his face as a cannonball missed Amethyst's ship and met the water near his own.

Only every now and then Cadell glanced around him to where the *Phoenix* and the *Gargoyle* sailed. Whether they liked it or not, by circumstance, they now sailed together united against a foe.

The opposing ships were drawing closer, dark silhouettes lining the horizon. Closer. Closer. Cadell's muscles were tense, waiting. Already his men had fired their guns many times, and by now they were close enough he could see the men on the other ships and hear their shouts as well. Aye, the battle had begun!

As soon as she was on the *Gargoyle*'s main deck, Amethyst was trying to assess the situation. Darien was at the helm, driving the ship forward and shouting orders to the crew. Amethyst spoke with him quickly in her native tongue, finding it faster to speak than the common tongue.

The first mate nodded quickly and dashed off, grabbing the nearest crew member and pointing toward Mikhail's ship. Despite recent events, Amethyst knew they needed Mikhail's help, and Darien was sure the *Phoenix*'s captain would give it.

As soon as the cannonballs had struck, Mikhail was seen emerging from his cabin and barking out orders to his crew. He stopped as the crew member from the *Gargoyle* approached. Mikhail's yellow eyes glanced toward the *Gargoyle* and settled on Amethyst. A smile crossed his features. It was brief, though. Soon he ran to take control of the wheel as his crew was getting the cannons ready.

The *Gargoyle* sailed ahead, trying to get in front of the *Reaper's Scythe* and the *Phoenix*. Amethyst turned her ship in order to have a good firing range and her battle flag was hoisted up. It had been with her for ages and was soaked with the blood of many. Patches where cannonballs had gone through were sewn up with pride.

Amethyst left the steering in charge of Darien while she made her way on the main deck. She picked up a gun and held it at eye level before firing it at the attacking ships. It was the way she fought that she was truly known for. They wanted a fight? She'd give them a fight.

The *Reaper's Scythe* was gaining speed, now almost level with Amethyst's *Gargoyle*. As the enemy ships came into range, Cadell swung the wheel and turned the ship. "Fire!" echoed from the crew followed by the boom of the cannons.

As soon as Cadell was sure his ship was steady, he summoned Aurek back to the helm.

Cadell then leaped from the upper deck to the main deck, firing his pistol at an enemy pirate trying to board. He turned, shouting to a member of his crew who knocked yet another boarding attacker to the seas below. He whirled, eyes searching. More booms of cannons resounded and clouds of smoke billowed into the skies. The stench of blood reached his nostrils.

Cadell winced slightly as a shred of wood whizzed by, slicing his cheek and leaving blood to flow freely down his face. Despite what small damage his ship had taken, already cannonballs had sunk holes into the sides of several enemy ships. This battle would be swift.

From the corner of his eyes, he caught a flash of purple moving in a blur.

Cadell looked toward the *Gargoyle*. Amethyst had tossed her gun aside and was sprinting along the edge of her ship. She dove straight into the water. Apparently, she had decided not to wait for the next approaching ship, but rather to go to the enemies! Several of her men dove in after her.

"Amethyst!" Mikhail shouted from his ship nearby. It was then the *Phoenix* lurched forward, trying to follow the *Gargoyle*'s captain.

Cadell was a little worried as cannonballs flew downward into the waves around his allies, but she surfaced, a wicked grin spreading on her lips.

Cadell also grinned in turn. This was the feared captain of the *Gargoyle*.

Soon, she pulled a dagger from her chest and began climbing up the side of the enemy hull, her nails and the dagger digging into and destroying the wood. In no time she and the hands from her crew that had followed crawled onto the enemy deck and attacked the pirates there.

The captain of the *Reaper's Scythe* turned his attention once more on the battle as the crack of splintering wood reached his ears and they narrowly avoided the falling mast from a nearby enemy ship.

If it weren't for the enemies trying to board the *Reaper*, Cadell would probably have dove in himself. One invader was trying to climb over the rail of his ship and Cadell twirled a dagger and sliced it across the attacker's throat before leaping to the next foe and shoving him over the side and into the sea below.

Another invader had successfully boarded and was charging toward Cadell. He turned and met daggers with his enemy, pushing him back and cutting him down. "Aurek! Bring us closer to the ship!" Cadell bellowed.

As Aurek followed orders, Cadell swung from his main deck to that of his opponent. Another round of cannonballs and a nearby ship began to go down. Many of the *Reaper*'s crew followed their captain. They boarded enemy ships and attacked their enemies head-on, quickly taking more and more ships.

Those who remained on the *Reaper* kept invaders trying to board it at bay. "Find the one behind this! Find their leader!" Cadell yelled to his men. Shouts of excitement followed and clangs of swords and daggers, as well as the explosions of gunfire, echoed through the night air.

The stench of blood grew stronger and fires licked at the skies.

As Amethyst let another body drop, licking the blood from her dagger as a kitten would cream, her eyes narrowed. A bad feeling entered her stomach and she immediately called out to halt her crew members.

They finished killing whoever they were tied up with and turned their attention to Amethyst.

"Head back to the ship!" she ordered.

They looked at her a little confused, but nodded and swung over as Darien pulled the ship up broadside to the one they were on.

Amethyst followed, quickly going to Darien and shoving him out of the way to take hold of the wheel.

"Captain Amethyst, what are you doing?" Darien demanded.

"Getting us out of here," she snarled.

"What?" Darien blinked.

She knew why he was confused. Amethyst almost *never* ran away from a fight.

"I don't have a good feeling about this, Darien. Trust me," she said, making a full turn. Her ship rammed into the nearest enemy ship but sustained only minor damage thanks to the magic that surrounded it.

Somewhere, in her gut, she knew her biggest enemy lurked nearby. And she knew that she was not ready to face him now. She would be... soon. But not now. She needed space and more time to prepare. Part of her success in building her reputation was taking on ships at the right moment... when she knew she could defeat them. And then doing so.

"What about Cadell and Mikhail?" Darien asked.

Amethyst paused for a second before answering, "They can handle themselves." She began to head away from the ships, attempting to escape despite the cannon fire and chaos of battle.

Cadell dropped yet another enemy pirate. Another ship was overtaken and sweat dripped down the side of his face.

In his gut, Cadell felt it. He just knew it was *Hell's Serpent* behind this attack. He searched the ship's remains, but the roaring flames and thick smoke blocked both his view and his senses. The stench of blood made it harder also. He could hardly distinguish the living from the dead.

Still, he was determined to find the ship he knew was behind it all. He became still, ears twitching. There were only two or three ships remaining that weren't severely damaged or already sunk and they were already fleeing. The battle was won, and yet...

He licked his lips where blood had splattered from a few previous victims. For a moment Cadell's eyes flashed with blood lust. But he shook his head, clearing it.

No, now was definitely the wrong time. As he cleared his thoughts, he suddenly caught sight of the *Gargoyle*, sailing off. Cadell released his breath. Obviously Amethyst had sensed the same danger he did and had reacted to it.

"Back to the ship!" Cadell ordered to his crew, and they moved quickly. He hesitated, itching to continue and face the one he *knew* was behind this head-on.

Finally, he made his decision. He didn't blame Amethyst for trying to get away as fast as possible. But if he could get his chance in now, Cadell was going to take it. Right now, taking down Stephan was the most important thing.

His eyes scanned the sight of the battle. Smoke was stealing the oxygen and blurring his vision. Bodies and blood stained the waters of the usually blue-green ocean. Any usual human would probably be sickened by the sight, but not Cadell.

Once everyone was aboard the *Reaper,* they sailed ahead. Soon, the form of *Hell's Serpent* became clear in the distance.

Cadell raced toward the helm and took control of the wheel. Soon, he was driving his great black ship straight for Stephan. Everything else seemed to fade from his mind.

Until he was sailing past the *Phoenix.*

Cadell glanced toward the fiery ship and Mikhail's crew. '*I wonder,*' he thought as he returned his gaze toward his goal. Was it possible Mikhail, or one of his crew, had betrayed them? It was strange, after all. Mikhail had arrived so suddenly and pulled his stunt on Amethyst the previous day. And then a sudden attack?

Amethyst had barely recovered from the spice in her food in time to fight the oncoming threat.

While Cadell loved the taste of battle and was glad that it had brought Amethyst back to normal, the coincidence was too close.

Despite his thoughts, Cadell thought he should find out more concerning the *Phoenix* later. For now, he continued to sail through the fog toward *Hell's Serpent.* Almost there. '*Stephan, this night ye'll regret ye were born.*'

"Captain Cadell!" Mikhail's voice reached the *Reaper*'s captain and Cadell turned his gaze.

Mikhail's hair had burst into flames and two wings of fire had burst from his back. He took a running leap from his ship and he flew quickly across the gap between them. "Ye be a bloody blaggard of a man! It was ye who brought on this attack in hopes of destroying me!" His wings burned brighter as he spoke.

Cadell knew that the *Phoenix* had been specifically named for its captain who was rumored to have phoenix in his bloodline, though had never before witnessed Mikhail's true power. It was only brought on by intense emotion, and in this case, he suspected it was rage.

As he heard Mikhail shout his own thoughts to him, Cadell shook his head. The irony. He glanced at Aurek, and Aurek understood, taking the wheel. Cadell whirled, facing Mikhail head-on.

He almost felt a wave of relief and excitement as he let the vampire bursting within take over his body. The scent of blood and the sight of dead and a victim heading straight for him. It took only a matter of seconds for his fingernails to elongate to sharp claws and fangs to grow so that they hung over his bottom lip, waiting.

"Me, Mikhail? Ye're one to talk, trying to lure Amethyst by tainting her food! Ha! I'd say ye were the one underhanded. But funny, that ye dare attack me! Bring it on, flame-boy!" Cadell chuckled at these words, spreading his arms, waiting for the impact as Mikhail plunged toward him.

Without averting his gaze Cadell shouted to Aurek, "Turn the ship! Forget the others for now! I'm showing this amateur his place!"

Aurek turned toward the *Phoenix*. "Load the cannons!" he bellowed to a man who then passed the message below deck.

The clanging of cannons being loaded on both ships resounded as well as the scraping of swords against scabbards.

Mikhail smirked. Instead of attacking Cadell, he soared onto the mast, or what was left of it, perching on it like a bird. He spread his wings, letting them curl around the wood. A fierce call erupted from his mouth, and the booming of cannons filled the air as the *Phoenix* fired at the *Reaper*.

As soon as Mikhail landed on one of the *Reaper*'s masts, Cadell began to climb it. "Boy, get off my ship and back where ye belong," he shouted to Mikhail. "Ye're just an ignorant brat!" Cadell slipped a dagger between his teeth and climbed the rest of the way up the mast.

The flames that were engulfing the mast of the *Reaper* were falling swiftly. Because of the dry air, they licked at his ship greedily. Cadell knew he didn't have much time before the mast would fall and lead to a much larger fire on his ship. He couldn't have that.

Below, the men were shouting orders and scrambling around in their fight now directed toward the *Phoenix*. Cannon fire echoed as did the crackling of wood being blasted apart and the whoosh of water exploding in huge bursts.

Cadell trusted his crew. Already many of them were focused on trying to put out the fire that threatened to destroy everything Cadell had worked for and loved most: his precious *Reaper.* The ship held strong, and the crew were depending on their captain. As he was also depending on them.

At last, Cadell reached the top of the mast, wincing slightly at the heat of the flames that were cackling toward the sky. "Ye picked the wrong person to mess with," he muttered before leaping toward Mikhail.

Mikhail smirked. "And what do ye think that makes ye? Ye're a fool who messed with *my* woman," Mikhail snarled, his orange, yellow and red wings turning a soft blue, then white.

As Cadell moved closer, he watched as Mikhail's feet turned into talons, his fingers doing the same. He was ready to fight and only moments away from turning into a full-fledged phoenix.

"Oh really? Well *yer woman* ditched you, and now she is mine," Cadell said, almost mockingly.

"I didn't have to leave anything physical to mark her mine," Mikhail sneered, standing neatly on the wood beneath him, "But I'll make sure to do that next time." His eyes, which had turned a beady sort of black, narrowed onto his opponent.

Cadell merely laughed. "What, ye think ye being one in her long line of lovers had any significance? Poor phoenix-lad, longing for love that'll never be fulfilled!"

"I'm sure if she'd upped and left ye the way she did me, ye'd be just as angry." There was bitterness, depression, and longing all at once in Mikhail's tone.

Cadell ignored these words. He used the phoenix's distraction as a chance to get close. He twirled his dagger in his fingers before drawing back and attempting to stab the dagger through Mikhail's chest. It was fortunate for Cadell that Mikhail's torso was not full of fiery feathers yet.

Mikhail managed to dodge Cadell's attack, though did get a long slice down his side. He let out another ear-piercing cry and launched himself at Cadell, striking at him with his talons. He even batted his wings at Cadell, the heat licking at his clothing.

Cadell winced as he dodged out of the way, narrowly avoiding being set ablaze. He stepped backward, poising himself on the mast, watching Mikhail carefully. One more step back and his heel hit the edge of the mast. He didn't dare glance back and give Mikhail an opening.

He let his face remain calm, his eyes relaxed, impenetrable. It was that comfortable look he knew infuriated Mikhail. He didn't care that it would only further provoke an already infuriated phoenix. Cadell wasn't afraid of death – he simply felt he had a few things left before he went.

He glanced to the side, watching Mikhail from the corner of his eye and acting as though he really were stupid enough to give Mikhail an opening. Would the phoenix fall for it? "Aurek! When we get back, remind me to hire a water sprite," he called down to his first mate with a laugh.

As Cadell had suspected, Mikhail lunged when he saw Cadell look away. He was ready for it. His muscles were tense, waiting like a tiger ready to spring on a hunt.

As Mikhail attacked him, Cadell sprang a second dagger from his belt and sliced both the daggers through Mikhail once again before leaping backward with a taunting grin on his lips.

The crew knew their captain well and as he fell, they tossed a rope his way. After tucking the daggers back through his belt, he grasped the rope and swung around to the upper deck.

Mikhail's face almost didn't register that a blade had gone right through his belly. It was only until the warm blood started to run down his skin that he seemed to realize he'd been wounded, and he looked down. He hunched over, reeling from the impact. The half-turned phoenix began to cough up blood.

In a mere moment, he went from a half-human to a great flaming bird, lighting up the evening sky like the sun. The stars almost seemed to disappear as he let out another terrible screech and made a swoop for Cadell if only to burn him and the rest of his ship. It seemed he just couldn't give up without one last attempt.

Cadell stood his ground alongside Aurek, who had to keep a hand on the ship to make sure it didn't veer off course. The rest of his crew scattered, many men wincing and grunting as the heat from the flame scorched their clothes and left burns on their skin. But nevertheless, they were loyal to Cadell, who had never failed them, and they continued to put out the fires that lit up the skies and filled the air with further billows of rising smoke and debris.

The *Reaper* had taken a lot of damage. But she wasn't defeated yet.

Cadell let out a loud cry as he raised his sword, "Not had enough, eh? Ye scurvy bilge rat!" And with that, he plunged his sword toward the oncoming phoenix.

Mikhail only swooped away and circled the ship swiftly, making the water beneath him boil angrily as he brushed his wingtips against the hull. However, everywhere he went, blood sprayed from his stomach wound. His one chance had failed, and soon he was flapping away from the ship, lighting up the night sky. A great crash echoed as he landed on his ship's deck, changing back and fainting from exertion.

"Bloody fool," Cadell muttered to himself. To Mikhail, he shouted, "Go back to yer ship and recover! Challenge me when ye're worthy!" Cadell didn't yet put his sword away, not wanting to leave himself open. Already much of the firing had ceased from his own ship, and he didn't know if Mikhail's had taken any damage or not.

As soon as Mikhail's flames had gone, the ocean cooled.

Still, Cadell's ship was hanging on between destruction and survival with victory not so near in sight, despite pushing Mikhail back where he belonged. The sooner they could dock at port, the better.

Cadell was engulfed in the smell of the blood that was splattered all over his body, partially from Mikhail. He licked his lips as he scrutinized the situation. He sprinted to where Aurek stood, taking the wheel once more and turning his ship. Besides getting out of the mess with Mikhail, he had one other goal.

A bad feeling was a knot in the pit of his stomach, and it was wrenching at him. He had to deal with it, and there was only one way to do so. The ship sprang forward, leaving the battle wreckage behind.

As the battle had erupted, there was one man who stood calmly on the bow of his ship a small distance off and hidden by the smoke and fog. His fair skin glimmered in the moonlight above, and the sea breeze caused his sandy blonde hair to whip about his face, but his piercing, cold green eyes stared forward, arms folded over his chest.

"Cadell, Amethyst. What happened before was only the beginning. I will crush you both before this war is over," Stephan chuckled faintly, his voice carried away by the other noises of battle.

He glanced back as a strong, entrancing voice echoed behind him. Even though he didn't need to look to know who it was, he looked anyway.

Akaisha's wavy dark hair whipped about her face. A faint smirk rested on her red lips and her icy blue eyes gleamed. Her pale hand rested on his shoulder, her other hand gripping the long blanket draped over her figure. "Stephan, you have plenty of time. Toy with them; play with them. Let them beg for mercy and death. Let them think they've won. This first battle is just to test them. Will they win this one?"

"Silly girl you are. Repeating my own thoughts into my mind. But of course, killing them too quickly takes all the fun out of it."

She slipped her hand down his arm and around his waist. "Must you be so adamant on Amethyst? Am I not good enough?" she asked, toying with him.

Stephan gently stroked a finger down her cheek. "You misunderstand me. My business with her is much different. Or must I question your intentions of being here?" He watched her with a slight smirk, surprised when she only laughed and rested her forehead against his shoulder.

"Fine, fine, I'll leave you alone about it," she said.

Stephan had actually been a bit worried. Akaisha was proving more troublesome than he wanted. In fact, he'd prefer that she stayed aboard when they reached the *Gargoyle*. But she knew the rules with fae women, especially since she was one. What she did was her choice. Stephan had already warned her and saw no point in doing so again.

He turned slightly, pressing his lips to hers and sliding his hand inside the blanket.

Akaisha let out a light squeal before grinning. "Now's not the time to play with me!"

Stephan only laughed and turned away, moving toward mid-deck and barking orders to his crew.

He approached a gangly man leaning back against the rail of the deck. "This is interesting," the man said.

"Indeed," Stephan responded mildly, eyes glimmering.

Mikhail's flames brilliantly lit up the night sky and the flashes of light from cannon fire blasts illuminated the ships' silhouettes against the smoke rising from all the other fallen ships. From their distance, the details weren't clear, but thanks to the phoenix fire, Stephan could just make out the battle between the captains of the *Phoenix* and the *Reaper's Scythe*.

They were atop the *Reaper's* mast, and fire already licked at the sky and was roaring across the hull of the ship. He hoped they utterly destroyed each other and were permanently removed so he could move in on the *Gargoyle*, which he had also seen fleeing the scene.

How unlike her, he thought of Amethyst. A smirk filled his lips. Perhaps he truly had gotten to her in the marketplace.

Then, the shadow of Cadell's form leaped from the mast followed by the phoenix swooping, and Stephan was certain it was over. He whirled and shouted orders to his crew and at once *Hell's Serpent* began to move after Amethyst's ship at an amazing speed as it moved through the waters.

As soon as they were in motion, Stephan slapped the gangly man who had also been watching the battle on the back in a friendly manner. "Much thanks to you. Your pay is waiting for you. Go to my first mate." The man scampered off eagerly. He had apparently grown sick of Mikhail and decided to give him a bit of trouble. Stephan had been all too eager to oblige, given Mikhail's obsession with Amethyst.

"Greedy fools," Stephan muttered. "Yet what would I do without them?" His eyes narrowed as they approached the *Gargoyle*. There was no one to stop him now.

Amethyst, meanwhile, had tried to put as much distance as possible between herself and the battle. In her flight, she had looked back long enough to see something alight on Cadell's ship and she winced when she heard Mikhail's phoenix cry. She should've known.

But instincts had taken over and she knew she needed to protect herself for now. Amethyst silently prayed Cadell would be alright and forgive her for running. He could handle himself. He wasn't captain of the *Reaper's Scythe* for nothing.

As soon as she felt she had gained enough distance, Amethyst slowed down. The knot in her stomach began to ease. She went to the edge of her ship, watching as flames licked at Cadell's ship in the distance. A terrible pain burned in her heart, but she shut it away. That was the way of pirate life. Plus, there was no way of knowing quite yet if Cadell was done in. Sighing, she took a seat on the deck, having a bottle of rum brought to her.

Darien joined her a few moments later. "Everything all right, Captain?"

Amethyst gave a nod. "I want to bypass the port. We'll go back to my resting spot for a bit, make plans there."

Darien nodded lightly, starting to shout out orders.

"Come, Captain, I'll have a bath drawn for you," Darien murmured, helping her up and leading her downstairs.

Already, her men were starting to recuperate. Some went below deck, while others lounged around on the upper deck, passing a bottle of rum in between them.

As Amethyst was sinking into her bath, she was startled by shouting and the clash of swords. *'What now?'* she thought desperately.

Quickly, she got out of the bath, grabbed a towel, and ran for the door. But before she could open it, she heard the lock click in place from the outside. Darien must have locked her in.

Which only meant one thing: Stephan was attacking.

A low growl escaped her throat. How dare he prevent her from fighting for her own ship! Even if Darien *was* her protector.

She hastily looked around for her clothes but realized they must be in her main room. Amethyst cursed under her breath. Well, if she must fight in a towel, so be it!

Amethyst tried to unravel the door lock. Then she remembered Darien had instilled some of the locks with magic. She pounded on the door, screaming to be let out. Did her first mate really believe she was this weak?

She shook the thought from her mind. He would pay for this as soon as everything was over, she noted. He would pay. But the one who had caused these attacks would pay first – that was, if she could even get out...

Stephan stood at the edge of *Hell's Serpent*'s main deck as his crew swept over the *Gargoyle* in full attack. Shouts of battle rose in the air as blood was spilt once more and the battle became focused on Amethyst's ship.

At first, Stephan hung back, as usual, merely shouting orders. He didn't often directly get his hands dirty.

Darien was coming for him.

Instead of allowing the other man aboard his ship, Stephan leaped across to the *Gargoyle* and drew his weapon, preparing to fight. A smirk rested on his lips. "How interesting," Stephan murmured before his sword clashed with Darien's. "Ah, Darien! Good to see you! Where is Captain Amethyst? Or is she afraid of me?" Stephan's eyes glimmered as he spoke.

"I should've snapped your neck when I had the chance," Darien snarled, taking a firm stance between Stephan and the stairs that led below deck. "I'll make sure not to make that same mistake again!" He lunged at Stephan, his sword glowing.

"Perhaps! Let's test just how close you can come, eh?" Stephan taunted, blocking Darien's sword once more. The cold from Darien's blade seeped toward his body. That Amethyst's most trusted dog had magic was something his allies had failed to mention. Or perhaps it wasn't known. But Stephan figured it out quickly enough.

Stephan tried to ignore it. His purpose here wasn't with Darien. This fight was only a brief distraction. As he whirled, blocking another hack toward him, he caught a flash of purple and he changed his focus from the fight. Amethyst was bursting in a rage toward his ship.

He hesitated, contemplating whether to slip out of this fight with Darien and engage in his business with Amethyst.

The cold sting of Darien's blade slicing across his chest startled him back to the fight at present and Stephan gasped sharply. Blood splattered from his body and across Darien.

Stephan grimaced, glaring daggers at Darien, yet after a moment, pulled his sword across on the defense, a slow smirk coming to his lips once more. He'd been careless; he refused to admit underestimation of anyone.

Darien smirked. "Had enough yet? Ready to die quietly? If not, I've always enjoyed a good torture session," he said.

Stephan just shrugged, feigning boredom. "Mm, torture. Sounds interesting. You sound a bit like me, Darien. Funny, two people so alike fighting. I must ask: just how good is your captain? Has she ever met her match?" Stephan shifted, keeping his eyes on Darien at all times. He couldn't leave himself open again. He lunged, bringing his sword down and across in a vengeful attack. Stephan was injured, but he was determined not to die. Not yet.

"Me, be like you? Hardly. I'm not lower than dirt. And as for meeting her match, she's way out of your league, so don't even try," Darien sneered.

Stephan chuckled. "I wonder then, if she's so great, just who could be in her league?"

Darien growled, rushing forward again and swooping down to get at Stephan's legs. He continued the motion and thrust upwards.

Stephan made a counterattack, managing to block Darien's sword and metal sparks flew. As their blades broke apart, Stephan lunged again, tearing open Darien's shirt and drawing blood from his shoulder.

Darien jumped back further, eyes narrowing, then lunged forward and repeated his previous attack.

Stephan leaped backward, Darien's sword slicing upward and ripping his pants, leaving a shallow cut up his leg. Stephan could still move around as he pleased, though somewhat painfully. "Taking the same move twice, eh? You just got lucky!" And with that, he sidestepped and brought his sword across.

Stephan's eyes were calculating. Despite his lack of hardened days at sea, he had been trained with a sword and each move was with expert skill. Darien's brow glistened and his breathing was already coming shorter. His opponent was older and would probably soon be defeated. Still, Darien fought back with some unknown, driven force.

Instead of trying to outsmart him, Stephan began attacking at random, lunging in and out in a whirl and striking constantly. Darien growled, struggling in defense.

A burst of pale flames erupted up Darien's sword.

Stephan had forgotten for a moment that Darien was not fighting with strength alone.

# Fae Women

$\mathcal{A}$s Darien fought to protect the *Gargoyle* and his captain from Stephan, Amethyst let out a scream of frustration as she rested against the door, sweating and cursing. She scratched the door and then stopped, scratching again. A smirk fell across her face as she lengthened her nails and began to claw at the door. Within moments, the wood was in shreds. She wasted no time gathering up some clothes, slipping a dagger under her shirt and in her boot, grabbing a sword, and rushing upstairs.

Everything was in chaos. Her men were fighting against others and for a brief moment, she began heading toward Stephan and Darien.

But it was then her eyes fell on the deck of *Hell's Serpent* where low and behold, another fae woman stood, merely watching the battle idly. Furious instincts began racing through her, all rational thought cast aside. How dare another woman be so near, especially fae. And on Stephan's ship! Certainly, this other woman hoped Stephan would defeat the *Gargoyle* so she could take everything Amethyst had worked for!

Never.

Amethyst's fangs grew and her nails lengthened further. She was going to skin the other woman alive. Her eyes grew larger and brighter, and with a small yell, she sprinted toward the other damned fae, her focus narrowing only on the wench. Everything else blurred around her.

As soon as Amethyst's eyes locked with the other woman's, the wretched thing quickly went on defense. The blanket around her dropped to the deck. The other woman was dressed scantily, with dark blue silk about her bosom and shoulders, a long slit blue skirt, and only a pale partially opaque cloth rippling over her stomach. Her skin was as fair as snow.

Amethyst smirked to herself. It would not be difficult to mar this girl's pretty body and rip past her pathetic excuse for clothing.

Amethyst was in a blind rage, especially after a cut landed on her back from a missed blow in the fighting around her. As Amethyst approached the other fae woman, she whipped her blade through the air, hoping to cut the other woman in half.

The female spun and unsheathed her own sword, blocking Amethyst's initial attack. However, her next blow cut through one of the shoulder sleeves and the fae wench growled, eyes glaring daggers as if to say, '*How dare you harm my perfect skin.*'

Amethyst only laughed, fueled on all the more.

For Cadell, a ways off from the battle taking place aboard the *Gargoyle*, already the winds of the sea were shifting the smoke. Soon, it was clearing, and he was sailing away from it. If only his ship would hold out a bit longer. His thoughts drifted once more to Mikhail. The fool was probably trying to heal back on his ship. He wondered if he had seen the last of him, but even if not, he had learned the grave lesson to be better guarded. He pushed that from his mind. How much time had passed?

Finally, Cadell saw it, the familiar form of the *Gargoyle* in the distance. He was getting closer, and he caught his breath. There was the form of another ship alongside it, and a growl rose in his throat. Cadell hadn't yet transformed back to his human self, and this new rage made the chance of that happening quite slim for the moment. If only he could get there.

At last, Cadell was near enough to make out details, and if it were possible, his face grew paler yet. He cursed, slowing his ship to turn it as he drew broadside *Hell's Serpent*. As he took in the battle that was going on, Cadell's eyes fell on Stephan and Darien, and slowly he smirked. He had arrived in time to see Stephan's blood splatter everywhere. That's right. He hoped Darien chopped him up nicely. But his attention was instantly pulled elsewhere. "Oh, bloody hell," he said.

Cadell turned, giving the wheel to Aurek, and dashed toward the edge of his ship, swinging over and soon landing on the deck of *Hell's Serpent*. He knew it was perhaps both foolish and pointless to do so, but this couldn't have been worse! He'd gotten what he'd wanted. Amethyst had met with Akaisha. But this was the absolute farthest thing from how he'd pictured it in his mind.

At this point in the battle, Amethyst had tossed her sword aside and lunged straight in for Akaisha's body. Her fangs bared, she tackled the other and was even throwing punches.

Of course, Akaisha had responded in kind, tossing away her own sword. She had met Amethyst head on, taking a blow to the side and landing another into Amethyst's gut.

Cadell groaned and cursed under his breath in frustration. "This is all Stephan's fault." Afterward, he bellowed, "Akaisha! What are you doing on this accursed ship?" Running toward the two fae women, he had hollered the question without even thinking.

This was Stephan's ship. What the bloody hell *was* she doing here? Cadell shook his head, his gaze falling on Amethyst. Breaking them up wasn't going to be easy. But he had to try.

Running forward again, Cadell tried to come between the two fae women. "Amethyst! You've-" he stopped as Akaisha's nails sliced through his shirt and into his back. He gritted his teeth. He should have known they wouldn't even notice him, too focused on their fight and each other.

Cadell paused. Part of him wanted to stand back and see which one would come out the winner. But the further this battle went, the higher the chance of one of them ending up dead! He actually loved Akaisha, as a very close friend, perhaps almost like a sister in some ways. Not like he loved Amethyst.

But he didn't want either of them dead. And if it were Amethyst, he'd never hear the end of it from Darien. He leapt forward. The two fighting women had managed to push each other apart long enough for Cadell to come between. He intercepted Amethyst as she was once again lunging back into the fight.

Cadell grasped her wrists and then pressed his forehead to her own, breathing heavily from the struggle. He acted completely on instinct, and as her momentum continued toward him, he pulled her into a kiss, nibbling at her lips.

At first, she struggled and then seemed to recognize what happened. She turned whatever adrenaline was coursing through her into fierce passion as she bit down forcefully on his lip. She pushed into him, fingers grasping at his shirt and hair, a low growl in her throat.

Cadell's grip on Amethyst's wrists loosened to more of an affectionate touch as he slid his fingers up her arms and finally around her waist and shoulders to hold her close to him. He was satisfied. It had worked. He couldn't help the sense of relief that poured over him, but with the passion Amethyst now was putting into it, the vampire within him began to react wildly.

Blood was drawn from his lips and mingled with Amethyst's and he pressed the kiss further. His mind reeled with desire and he was startled as the sounds of cannon and gun fire reentered into his conscious.

Cadell pushed Amethyst backward gradually, starting to lessen their physical contact until he could manage to pull away and gain control of himself. "Amethyst," he whispered for her ears alone, "don't fight pointless battles. Ye will lose nothing to her. Trust me, I love you. Ye have bigger things to worry about."

He was trying to make her go against her instincts and not fight the other fae female. And it was working. Amethyst's eyes drifted down slightly as he whispered to her. He could tell she was trying to resist the urge to attack his mouth again. A slight smile spread across her lips as Cadell whispered that he loved her. He noticed the way her eyes briefly looked at Akaisha and she smirked, as if saying, '*Look what I have.*'

Cadell grasped Amethyst's shoulders and spun her slightly so that she could see the fight going on, particularly between Darien and Stephan. He grinned slowly, "Let's kick bilge rat booty, and then we can celebrate another victory, hmm?"

"Stephan's mine," Amethyst stated, her eyes glowering as she watched. Stephan was probably trying to weaken Darien. Immediately, she moved to get away from Cadell and sprinted toward Stephan, crashing into him and knocking him away from Darien.

Cadell started to move toward her, though he could tell she was far from the helpless person Stephan had threatened at Port Drelle.

He paused as Akaisha's eyes snapped on him and her pail fingers gripped his shoulder. "What is wrong with you? You just jumped into a fight between *fae women.*"

Cadell grinned. "Nice to see ye too. I was imagining more of a friendly hug or a, 'Hey, Cadell, haven't seen ye in a long time.'"

He laughed as she scowled and muttered, "We're in a war and he expects me to be so cordial."

Cadell moved toward her. "Who cares. I know ye don't want to fight her that badly. Let's discuss more when this is over."

At that, he moved toward the battle Amethyst had now engaged Stephan in. The other fighting had diminished already as the crewmen began to realize their captains were settling the score.

Amethyst barreled into Stephan.

He grunted and fell off balance. Darien's blade slid across his arm and Stephan stumbled again, wiping a hand across his mouth. His eyes flashed and he regained himself, glaring at Amethyst. Finally, his features relaxed somewhat and his brow settled. Stephan held his sword out in front of him, a smirk coming back to his lips. "Ooh, she finally gets what she's wanted. Come on, Amethyst, let's see what you can do." He watched her, waiting for her to attack.

"Such a coward, Stephan. Hiding behind your sword," Amethyst snarled, sharp nails flexing lightly. "I didn't expect any more." As much as she wished to fight him at the moment, she wasn't going to give it to him.

Instead, she straightened herself, her fangs and nails going back to normal and she shook her hair, tying it back sloppily as she looked at Darien, who was standing there, confused. "Darien, you're dismissed for the moment." Darien didn't look like he was going to move, but he did anyways, moving to help fight back Stephan's men. Amethyst turned her gaze back to the blond-haired man.

At first Stephan scoffed. He watched Darien warily and then returned his attention to Amethyst.

"Call them off, Stephan." Her voice was soft, and her gaze became alluring. "I'll call mine off, and Cadell will call his off. They're tired." Her eyes tried to connect with his, wanting his focus to be only on her. She gently trailed her hands down her sides, smoothing out her clothes. "We're tired of fighting."

This time, she was ready. She knew exactly what she was doing. And *she* would be in control. Why bother taking the fun out of killing him by killing him quickly?

Stephan stiffened, eyes narrowing as he hesitated.

Good, she was confusing him. At first, he seemed more on guard. But then, he seemed to relax. His sword lowered, moving to the side, though his muscles still appeared tense.

Finally, his eyes softened and he seemed to give in. Stephan nodded slowly raising a thumb and forefinger together. "Hmm. Perhaps a good idea. But I won't call mine off and have you go back on your word." He paused and stepped toward her slightly. He snapped his fingers and his voice billowed over his ship. "Men! Gather!"

Instantly, though reluctantly, Stephan's crew stopped fighting, now only blocking attacks as they moved toward Stephan until they had gathered behind him in a ring of themselves. Their swords were still raised in defense and they eyed Stephan questioningly.

"Mmm, I wouldn't expect any less," Amethyst said. As soon as Stephan called his men, she waved a hand and with a sharp whistle, her men gathered around her also. Darien was just a few steps behind her, still holding his sword tightly in his hands. "There, now that we're no longer battling, I suggest a meeting."

Amethyst snapped her fingers and instantly, a table and two chairs were brought and set in the middle between Amethyst and Stephan. She shot Cadell a warning look to stay out of her activities before taking a seat and twirling a piece of hair around her finger.

Amethyst had briefly debated attacking Stephan, but she knew that would only bring up the battle again and she truly was curious why Stephan wanted her so badly. Why was he after her with such intent?

She was wary of him despite the dreamy look which masked her eyes. She wondered if he just wanted to dispose of her... or if there was something else. She suspected something deeper, especially after the day in the market. So she was using her fae magic on him. There were very few who could resist it, and though it was not often Amethyst used her magic on others, since it risked revealing her most guarded secrets, with Stephan, she hoped it was her one chance to get him to spill his own secrets.

She thanked a crewmember as he set a bottle of wine and two glasses on the table. She popped the cork and poured half a glass, finally swirling the liquid around lightly. "Don't worry, it's not poisoned," Amethyst smirked.

Stephan lazily leaned forward after he had taken a seat and placed his chin in his palm. As soon as the wine was brought, he also helped himself, taking a sip. "Oh, I wouldn't be worried about that." Though he tried to do it sneakily, she noticed his hand slide behind his back and a few of his crew members at a time begin to disappear below deck, though most of them remained. Clearly, he wasn't as entirely under her spell as she had thought.

Could he merely be playing along with her game?

"So, a meeting indeed. Obviously, I came for purposes involving you, and obviously you were protecting yourself. But tell me, honestly, that you weren't hunting me, plotting against me with your little-" Stephan paused, glancing at Cadell and then back before adding a bit dramatically, "allies." He chuckled lightly, "But that could be expected, I suppose." He took another few sips from his glass of wine. "So, what do you propose since you called this meeting, hmm? Or perhaps we could make better decisions without so many... distractions."

"I won't lie. I have been hunting you down like the scum you are," Amethyst's lips twisted at this statement. She tilted her head, a few curls falling over her shoulders. "What your true intentions are is what I would really *love* to know." Her ear twitched and behind her, some of her crew members began sneaking off as well as Stephan's. Perhaps Amethyst and Stephan thought somewhat on the same level. Pirates.

"Scum, eh? Tsk, tsk. Well maybe I was simply seeking a night with you. I've heard rumors about the ease of getting into your bed." He smirked.

Amethyst frowned and continued with her point. "I know it can't be all about power and eliminating your rivals. You want something else. Tell me Stephan, what is your true desire that concerns me?" Her voice was a seductive purr as her eyes moved over him suggestively, her lips forming a pout. "I think discussing it right here is just fine."

She leaned over a bit, her shirt dipping low to reveal some tanned cleavage. Perhaps using her womanly charms as well as her fae magic would draw out the information she sought.

Then, she resisted a growl of frustration when out of the corner of her eye, she spotted several flags and immediately knew what they were. Her focus was broken. The flags bore the emblem of the Fae Royal Navy. They were coming after her, no doubt.

Why were they here right now and at such an inopportune time? Perhaps they had received wind of the pirate war brewing and had seen the enormous billows of smoke from the recent battle?

Or worse, somehow, they had received notice of her location. Whatever the case, the only upside she could think of would be that Stephan would be captured along with them. The bad thing was that Cadell would be captured as well. Amethyst knew what fate would await them.

But it could wait, at least for another moment. She stared at Stephan, the same look in her eyes though impatience circled in her mind. Perhaps her nerves were the reason why the magic wasn't working as well as it should be on her enemy.

Stephan replied casually, "What is it I want? What could be greater than conquering my rivals at sea and ruling them to let everyone know just who I am? Or are you still convinced I'm a traitor like the scum who managed to get themselves cursed by greed and led the seas to these dark times so dark they called for a meeting at Skull's Mark. Or do you not remember that wonderful day?" His facial expression didn't change except for a faint hint of another smirk. After a few moments, he shifted his position slightly. "And what if I were to propose an alliance? It would be incredibly beneficial for the both of us."

The Fae Navy was ever a concern with Amethyst and they would be here within the hour, she suspected. They would have to start moving soon. Forget Stephan for the moment. It was then she noticed that his eyes had taken on the same alluring look and she wondered if he had been exposed to this sort of spell before. Only someone trained mentally could resist it. Or someone being protected. The fae woman she had been fighting flashed in her mind. Was it *her* fault then? Despite his resistance, she continued to try. Even the smallest hint of something could clue her in.

Amethyst groaned inside. Perhaps he thought he could beat her at her own game? Hardly. A part of her felt bad for trying to seduce Stephan in front of Cadell. She would just have to show Cadell how much she loved him later.

Her eyes darkened, but still feigned desire. "I'm assured that you do want something else besides the power. You want a little something... softer." She whispered the last word with such a tone that a few of Stephan's crewmen seemed to blush. "And yes, I still am convinced that you're a traitor corrupted by greed. In fact, you could almost be Davy Jones himself," she said, her tone as alluring as she would dare.

Stephan's ears twitched lightly as she spoke again, "Softer. Yes," he echoed. "Yet, if it were only something softer I wanted, there are plenty of girls that would play into my charms easily enough." His eyes gained a look of mischief. A chuckle came from his lips. "Amethyst, darling, even your magnificent ship would be no match for Davy Jones." He paused, finishing his glass of wine and setting it aside.

'*If you wanted any woman, then why would you come after me?*' Amethyst thought, frustrated. "Well then, that's why I said you could *almost* be Davy Jones," she told him, finishing her glass as well.

Then, her voice changed, becoming more serious. She could see that despite her efforts, he wasn't being affected for whatever reason and she was getting nowhere closer to discovering his true intentions. Perhaps she hadn't thought through the information she already had well enough. "Perhaps I do want something." '*Your death*,' she thought. "But that's for another day. As for an alliance, you have a better chance staying cool in hell."

She finally pushed away from the table. "Leave my ship, Stephan, before your sorry bum is captured and placed behind bars. I want nothing to do with you. An alliance with you would do both of us no good." She leaned across the table, her face almost too close to his. "And don't think that I can't see that desire in your eyes. The only way you'll get me in your bed is when I'm dead and cold."

He stroked a finger up her jaw to her chin, "Mmm, perhaps such beauty is wasted on you," he whispered to her.

She snarled, and at that moment, cannons fired from her ship towards Stephan's.

Neither of them flinched. Instead, Stephan used the distraction to grasp her arm and steal a kiss, short but fierce, then pushed her away. "Very well. Your foolish mind will cost you."

"I could probably say the same about you," she murmured. She wasn't going to lie. Stephan, as black as his soul and heart might be, was still quite attractive. She showed nothing except a small smile which curled across her lips. "You only wish." She let him push her back and used it for momentum.

"Indeed, I do..." she heard Stephan murmur.

As soon as Amethyst seemingly finished her game, the men rushed forward to rid the *Gargoyle* of Stephan's crew. Already Amethyst's ship was starting to move. She was going to try to outrun the Fae Navy.

The task was not difficult as most of Stephan's men moved back to *Hell's Serpent* anyway. They fired off a few good shots toward the *Gargoyle* as they were also heading away. Stephan caught a rope tossed him from one of his men and easily swung over, standing over the rail with a sly grin on his face.

Amethyst had a feeling that this wasn't the last she would see of Stephan. This was hardly over. As the two ships parted, her eyes fell on Stephan like a cat watching a cornered mouse. She leaned against the railing, watching him sail away.

Clearly, there had been no more need for hand-to-hand fighting since Stephan obviously wanted her for something besides to kill her. And he hadn't been able to capture her then. She was furious the Fae Navy had come before she could learn what it was. She was certain that despite his resistance, she would have eventually gotten through.

Amethyst only moved when Darien pulled her away as the parts near her exploded from the cannons. She knew that soon peace would resume as they distanced themselves and thus there was no more need for her further commands.

She retired to her room, shedding her clothes and sprawling across her bed. Her body still rushed with adrenaline and her wrath against Stephan seethed beneath the surface. She buried her face in her blanket, trying to rid her mind of everything that had just happened.

About halfway through Amethyst's meet with Stephan, Cadell had figured out what she was doing. Trying to lure the scum's secrets from him. *'Bloody blaggard bilge rat filth,'* he thought. But still, watching Stephan steal a kiss from Amethyst made his blood boil. There was no time to dwell on it, though, as everything plunged into chaos once more.

Cadell swung back to his own ship, which was in quite poor condition from his battle with Mikhail. The *Reaper* was firing cannons in attempt to damage *Hell's Serpent* before they got too far away. Wood and steel from Cadell's ship exploded into the air, as did some parts from Stephan's ship, and all the while the ships were sailing away from where they had been, away from the Fae Royal Navy.

The *Reaper's Scythe* would not hold out much longer under this strain. Her captain just hoped they made it to the next port before it fell completely apart. The repairs the deckhands had been able to make were helping but were not quite good enough. "Just hold a bit longer my beauty," Cadell murmured to his ship. Even now, the hull quaked as the *Reaper* tried to keep up with the *Gargoyle.*

Cadell left the ship in his first mate's hands and slipped toward Amethyst's ship once again. Just as he landed on upper deck of the *Gargoyle,* Akaisha stopped him. In the midst of battle, Amethyst must not have noticed the other fae woman boarding her ship from *Hell's Serpent.* Apparently, Akaisha had abandoned Stephan.

Cadell frowned, "What were you doing on Stephan's ship?" he asked bluntly. He always made an effort to speak properly when he was with her. Ever since they were children, playing along the fae shores.

Akaisha grinned slowly. "What, did you think I was *actually* his lover? As soon as I heard the news about everything going on out on the seas, I figured you might come looking for me. You do way too often, you know. I fished around and gathered what I could, and I figured Stephan would be someone I could get quite a bit of information from. I see that might come in handier than I'd expected."

Cadell sighed. "Two steps ahead of me. Am I that predictable?" When she nodded, he pretended to scowl and scold himself, before he attempted to move past her.

She stared at Cadell expectantly, blocking his path. "You know, you could pay me a little mind. I'm not sticking with you blokes for nothing. I'm sure you want the information in my brain." Akaisha grinned mischievously, standing with her arms crossed and her hip slightly protruding.

Cadell sighed. "Not now, Akaisha. But later, once things have calmed down a bit. Besides, we'll need to hold a meeting anyway and discuss all of this. I suggest you give us our information then."

"But I don't trust anyone else with the in-" she started to protest but stopped when Cadell raised a hand.

He smiled. "You trust me. I trust them. So, you can trust them. Now stay here." With that, he walked past her and toward Amethyst's quarters below deck.

Cadell looked back long enough to see an exchange between Akaisha and Darien.

Darien approached Akaisha, glaring down at her. "If you're going to stay with us, you stay on Cadell's ship. I don't have the time or patience to watch after another fae woman. And you're rather unwelcome here."

Akaisha stuck her tongue out childishly at Darien and turned away sharply, flicking her thick, black hair in the process. "You'll think better once you hear my secrets," she muttered indignantly. She then disappeared amongst those on Cadell's ship and began helping the men on deck with repairs and work.

At least it was something to do to keep her mind and body busy, Cadell thought. It didn't hurt that she possessed some magic of her own and was able to use it to advance the repairs. All in all, he was glad she was here.

# Aftermath

Cadell descended the steps to Amethyst's cabin and stepped inside. He gazed over her figure, glowing in the light filtering in from the window. He crossed the room in three long strides and curled his arm around her before bending to brush his lips against her neck. How he longed to erase Stephan's filthy touches from her skin! Yet he knew he must wait a bit longer. "Well done, Captain," he murmured.

"I'm sorry," she whispered as she turned towards him. She wrapped her arms around his neck and pulled him close for a long, scorching kiss.

Apparently, no words about the meeting were needed.

"Cadell," Amethyst whimpered softly, moving to nuzzle his neck and push herself into him. "I need you right now." Her fingers slid down his arms and then his sides before resting at the hem of his shirt. There was no hesitation as she slipped her hands beneath the cloth to grasp at his skin.

Cadell trembled as she kissed him, kissing her back deeply. His skin warmed under her fingers and he pulled back long enough to remove his shirt and toss it aside. "I thought you'd never say that," he whispered.

He rolled, pushing her back against the bed and captured her mouth again with his own. He sucked gently at her lip, nipping, then kissed her deeply once more. Her moans drove him further and soon all clothing was lying on the floor.

He was going to make this a night she would *never* forget.

Meanwhile, aboard Stephan's ship far from the *Gargoyle* and the *Reaper's Scythe*, one of *Hell's Serpent's* crewmembers ran up to its captain, panting lightly. "Captain Stephan! We've spotted another ship, the Bloody Rose, commanded by Captain Zyara."

Stephan looked off to the distance where he could now see the other ship. Captain Zyara had managed to pillage a deadly frigate some years before and the sight of it often was enough to scare off any enemies.

Her ship, like many others, was a true piece of art. Blood red roses were carved into the dark hull along with stark white skulls. The black flag flying above depicted a skull emerging from a blooming flower. The guns alone rivaled the *Gargoyle* and the black sails topped off the square-rigged masts and massive decks. The ship was ominous.

Zyara stood at the helm, grasping a rope to steady herself. She had thick red locks, tied behind her, and eyes as black as night.

Stephan glanced lazily at the man that brought him the news of Zyara. He grinned slyly and nodded. '*This should be interesting.*' He signaled to one of his men and *Hell's Serpent* slowed her speed and waited for the *Bloody Rose* to draw even.

As she pulled alongside Stephan's ship, Zyara pushed back some strands of her dark red hair, flashing a white smile. "Permission to board, Captain Stephan?" Her voice was a caress.

"Permission granted," Stephan replied slowly, watching her with interest and faint curiosity. He drank in her figure, idly licking his lips.

"Not bad, not bad," Zyara said first. "I've heard o' what ye're doing." She leaped from her perch and landed on *Hell's Serpent's* deck. "I came as soon as I could. I'm willin' to partner with anyone interested in ending the *Gargoyle.*"

"Glad to know I have another ally, at least for the time being. Come, make yourself comfortable. I believe we have a few things to discuss." With that Stephan turned, leading her toward a table on his deck which his crew had prepared with wine and a few treats, though he doubted Zyara would pay them any mind. Instead of sitting, he leaned backward against the table. "Now, tell me, what is it you desire?"

Zyara smirked. "Well, Captain Stephan," she murmured, "I desire a lot o' things. But maybe ye could fulfill one o' me desires right now?" She raised a brow.

Stephan leaned toward her with a smirk. "Perhaps."

She stepped closer to him and pushed her hands through his hair, curling her fingers around his head and drawing him closer for a burning kiss. Zyara was notorious as the type of woman to do as she wanted and ask questions later. She was straightforward and usually demanded intimacy before politics. "Maybe we could move to yer quarters?" she asked.

Zyara was definitely his kind of woman, Stephan thought. He slid one hand down her back and the other through her hair. "With pleasure, luv," he said. He would play her game. She often tried to use bedding a man to manipulate him. But she would soon learn he was not so easily put on puppet strings. He couldn't wait to discuss matters with Zyara, who he knew would help him bring Amethyst to her knees.

A while later, Stephan stood idly on the upper deck of his ship. He could still taste Zyara's lips on his and his skin tingled with the lingering memory of hers against him. She certainly knew what she was doing, he thought.

"Captain, orders?" One of his crew members broke him of his thoughts.

Stephan glanced toward the man and finally turned from his position. "None. The sooner we get there the better. And remind the crew that once we reach our destination, we will sink the *Reaper's Scythe* and her crew, once and for all." The man nodded and scampered off. Stephan's thoughts shifted away from his intimate pleasures.

Oh yes, how Stephan hated Cadell. How he would make the captain pay for what he'd done. Amethyst *would* be his.

The clanging of hammers hitting nails echoed over the peaceful ocean air. The crew of the *Reaper's Scythe* were using what materials they could to make repairs.

Cadell stirred, slowly lifting his eyelids and smiling as he breathed in Amethyst's scent. Sunlight shone in through one of the windows, reflecting off her perfectly tanned skin. She was so beautiful... truly, he was fortunate. He traced a finger along her cheek, with barely enough pressure to feel its warmth and then pushed away from the bed, donning his clothes.

As he stepped out into the morning sun, Cadell blinked, dark eyes adjusting to the light. He glanced toward his ship and sighed. She was a terrible mess. Sails and wooden beams hung low in a depressing fashion and the hull creaked with every sway of the ocean. His men were hard at work, but unfortunately, they didn't have time to dock at a port and stay. They would just have to make do.

Scanning the deck, Cadell easily found Darien. The *Gargoyle*'s first mate was leaning against the railing on the upper deck, the sea wind tangling through his dark hair. Cadell ran his fingers through his own locks and approached the other man. "Morning, Darien," he said, his voice rumbling.

Darien glanced at him and gave a brief nod before returning his gaze toward the distant sea.

Cadell was silent a moment, debating how to bring up the present business. On one hand, at least Darien had met Akaisha. On the other, it was under less-than-ideal circumstances. "I think it's time for the meeting with Akaisha. She has valuable information from her time with Stephan. It could prove extremely useful to us."

Darien glanced toward Amethyst's cabin. "Perhaps. But as I warned you..."

Cadell nodded. "Ye needn't explain. I'm well aware of the ferocity between fae women." Briefly, he thought of the scratches Akaisha had left on his back. "I'll do my best to keep peace. I was hoping that my actions will've proven I'm Amethyst's alone. But then, considering last night..."

Darien nodded. "Yes, she'll be especially sensitive after her battle with Stephan and a night spent intimately. I suggest we hold the meeting on your *Reaper*. Amethyst isn't going to like this. But she definitely won't hear anything out if another fae woman steps one toe aboard her ship."

Cadell chuckled lightly, knowing every word was true. At that, Darien moved to speak with Amethyst.

With ease, Cadell swung over to his ship. He helped his men set up and prepare a small table on the main deck with various fruits, some bread, and some drink.

A few moments later, Amethyst swaggered toward the *Reaper's Scythe* with exaggerated movements and a beaming smile lighting up her face. As soon as she locked eyes with Cadell, she waved and swung aboard the *Reaper*. Wasting no time, she threw her arms around his neck, drawing him in to capture his mouth. He gripped her, pressing the kiss deeper as desire coursed through him from her touch. She grinned as she pulled away, pushed back a chair, kicked up her feet, and popped a few grapes in her mouth. "So, what are you discussing without me?" she asked.

Cadell smiled at her carefree movements. "Good morning, Captain. Yer sleep was well?"

Amethyst smiled and nodded, yet almost immediately her gaze turned sharp and her features scowled as she caught sight of Akasiah. The other fae woman was not far off from them helping one of Cadell's crew with mending a sail. Amethyst glanced sharply at her two most valued men, demanding an explanation.

"Akaisha has important information concerning Hell's Serpent and its captain. She spent much time aboard and learned several of his plans and some secrets. This information could be essential in our attack and bringing him down," Darien said to Amethyst's unspoken question, then paused.

Amethyst glanced back and forth between the two men, and finally at Akaisha once more. "Very well," she said sharply, her good mood ruined.

At that, Cadell rose and motioned for Akaisha to join them. As soon as she was seated, Amethyst spoke again, impatiently. "Well? Proceed," she demanded.

Akaisha glared at Amethyst. Cadell could only imagine her indignation about taking orders from the other fae woman, however, she kept her thoughts to herself, much to Cadell's relief. She was across from Amethyst and glanced at each person in turn.

Finally, Akaisha spoke. "I will make this as brief and yet informative as possible. First, you need to know that the tale Stephan gave at the meeting at Skull's Mark was only partially true. He was trying to distract everyone from his true purpose. There are many who have become enamored with the power of which he spoke. The power is very real. But it is not as Stephan presented it. It is simply a magic source which can be used by its wielder for either good or for evil." She paused.

"The source can be either given or taken, though I was not able to learn where the source is located for certain. The island which he indicated may only be a location where he has set a trap in order to draw those in his way to their doom."

"He is a power-hungry brat, probably seeking control he otherwise would never have, and that power is his only true goal. He wants nothing more than to be the greatest captain possessing whatever he wishes and having all others do as he commands without question."

After another brief silence, Akaisha's eyes fell on Amethyst somewhat pointedly.

Cadell spoke first. "Akaisha, how exactly does Amethyst tie into this? Are ye sayin' Stephan is after her 'cause she has somethin' to do with this goal he has to capture an' use this... magic source?"

Amethyst said nothing. Nor did her gaze waver from Akaisha. Her face grew tense.

Finally, Akaisha spoke again. "Well, Stephan would never release the true intent or secrets to me surrounding his purpose with you. Perhaps because I am also fae. But I do know this: it has something to do with his ultimate gains and he truly believes you have something to do with the magic source. He sails for the isle of Amioh Oiil where he has led his allies to believe the magic stems from." She turned her gaze to Cadell. "That is all I know."

They were all silent as Akaisha spoke, though Amethyst looked like she was constantly resisting the urge to lunge across the table and slit the other woman's throat with her claws.

Amethyst stood, her face twisting with anxiety. "Darien..." was all she said.

Her first mate nodded and stood as well. "I will meet with you later, Cadell," he stated, before he and Amethyst departed swiftly, going to his quarters aboard the *Gargoyle*.

Cadell remained with Akaisha, munching on some more of the food which had been prepared. He was curious what had come up all of a sudden, but since Darien had assured him he would know later, he saw no point in dwelling.

Instead, Cadell turned to Akaisha. "While they're busy, do you want to tell me, now, the rest of your story?"

Akaisha gave him a mischievous grin and responded, "Wouldn't you like to know? Nosy."

It was not that Cadell felt lighthearted at all. In fact, his heart was very grave. A pit was in his stomach and he knew that at this point, Stephan had the advantage, and it would take a lot for them to defeat him. Still, he was hopeful. After all, was this not one of the greatest alliances currently possible?

Despite recent events, Akaisha always brought out the playful side of him, much as Amethyst did when she was in the right mood. Cadell just couldn't help it. They had grown up together, and at times they acted as though they were still children with no worries at all. He shrugged at her comment, and she knew that he was only curious – and concerned for her wellbeing.

Giving in, Akaisha leaned forward, finally eating some of the food herself. "After the meeting at Skull's Mark, word got around to me of all that had happened. I figured you would be needing help in the near future, and I began investigating with the other captains more of the details. It wasn't hard to figure out the main culprit behind all the stories and finally, I found myself on Stephan's ship."

She paused. Cadell had figured out that much, and he simply stared at her, waiting.

"You know I keep up with you... just to make sure you're alright." Akaisha smiled at him teasingly.

Cadell glared at her, though somewhat playfully as well. "Aye, well, it's a good thing that's never gotten out. Think how it would look if everyone thought I was secretly protected by a *woman.* I would hardly be taken seriously as a captain."

Akaisha laughed and punched his arm. "Anyone who thinks you are unworthy is free to find out for themselves." With that, she stood, stretching her arms upward and finally leaving the table. "I'm going to help your men with repairs," she told him as she descended to the lower deck.

Cadell nodded, knowing he should help as well, but curious about what Amethyst and Darien were discussing. He assumed Darien would send a crewmember to fetch him when he was ready, but he felt it was important he be let in on whatever they were hiding. Cadell returned to the *Gargoyle* once again, heading toward Darien's quarters. Reaching the cabin, he knocked softly before opening the door.

Amethyst and Darien were talking fervently. "...I don't know! Only those of my family's house and the priests and priestesses know." Amethyst stopped and grew very pale, though her eyes were fierce.

"That bastard," she murmured, her words hardly audible. "Of course, he would do this to me. He just couldn't let me go my way!" Her voice rose as she became more and more certain of whatever it was she was thinking.

It seemed Darien agreed with her and he looked sharply toward Cadell. Apparently, they just noticed his entrance. Darien hesitated a moment and then motioned with two fingers for Cadell to proceed forward.

Cadell remained quiet, simply moving toward them. His eyes were steady, though questioning, glancing between the two of them.

They knew what Cadell was here for. But Amethyst was not quite ready to tell him. Maybe after this was all over, then. But now, no matter how essential it was toward Stephan, she just couldn't. It was too guarded a secret and for all her trust in him, she feared anyone knowing that didn't already. She pushed past Darien and sat down in one of the chairs by his desk.

How they proceeded next was critical and Amethyst knew in her gut that if they went to meet him in battle, it was very likely Stephan would get everything he was striving for.

It had always been in her instincts to stay far away from any situation which was this dangerous towards her. Particularly after everything that had happened with her ex-husband. But she knew that Stephan would pursue her forever and she would never be rid of him. She stared at Cadell, searching his face and then something swelled within her.

Amethyst was not the same woman she had been back then, either. Back when she had still lived in the fae lands. She had sworn to defeat Stephan and decorate her ship with his bones. No, even if it was a trap, there was only one way to deal with this. And that was exterminating the threat.

Furthermore, she drew confidence from the captain standing before her. With the *Reaper's Scythe* sailing beside her, she knew that they could win. They had to. "Cadell... come with me," Amethyst stated finally.

She knew Darien wished to discuss some things with him, but he was only first mate, and whatever they discussed was privy to her as well. She was captain of this ship, and *she* would lead her crew to victory.

Cadell glanced briefly at Darien, who simply stepped back and allowed the two to leave towards Amethyst's room.

Once in her room, Amethyst moved towards her bed, throwing herself down on her stomach across the mattress. She was silent, only for a moment. "I know you must have questions. But I can't answer them right now." She paused, staring out the window. Finally, she looked toward him, eyes meeting his. "Until I can... Are you with me?"

At Amethyst's response, Cadell felt frustrated but knew he shouldn't press his questions. If she couldn't tell him now, then so be it. Her words implied she wanted to, but something held her back. When her eyes met his, he could read her easily.

There was conflict, yet determination, and something else. Uncertainty?

He finally moved toward her, sitting beside her on the bed and placing a hand on her back. "Always."

Amethyst rolled over, staring up at the ceiling now. She took in a deep breath and let it out, seeming pleased at his response. "Let's talk strategy. Stephan will be expecting the two of us. From the fleet we witnessed on his last attack, it seems he has spent his time until now conquering much of the seas and forcing what ships he can to sail behind him. Because neither of us really spent much time developing alliances, we will be outnumbered."

Cadell listened silently, though at the last statement, he answered, "But not necessarily outmatched."

She smirked slightly at this comment and resumed what she was saying. "I say we have our first mates take half of our men and meet them head-on while you and I take the other half and create a surprise attack for Stephan." One of Amethyst's signature moves was to swim through the sea in order to overcome an enemy ship. If they could kill Stephan and sink his ship, the rest of the ships would surely retreat.

Cadell mulled over her words. He liked the idea, but there was something nagging in the pit of his stomach. He couldn't pin it though. There were so many things that could go wrong. "I know there isn't time to make port to gather more men or even get supplies. But perhaps we should take what time we can to at least give ourselves a chance. If we sail now, I know for sure the Reaper will fall apart."

"We will take three days. If we wait any longer, we may lose our chance entirely." Stephan would only wait so long before he would hunt them down himself.

Cadell nodded, leaning down and placing a gentle kiss on her face. "I'll see you tonight, then," he murmured before he rose and left. He needed to help his crew with repairs; the more hands the better.

# War

Over the course of the next three days, the crewmen of the *Reaper* and the *Gargoyle* spent most of their time repairing damages and discussing the details of the upcoming battles. As the men worked, the captains sent out letters to their other allies, any who had not been overtaken by Stephan. They needed their own fleet if they were going to win this battle. Darien used his magic to send each letter with haste so that the respective captains received them nearly instantaneously.

Fortunately, most of those allies were not too far as word of Stephan's handiwork had spread quickly. It soon became clear just who was fond of Amethyst and who loathed her. Among those who had come was Leo, captain of the *Golden Lion*. Somewhat reluctantly, Mikhail had decided to help as well.

The allies soon were gathered, and Amethyst filled them in on the details they still needed. Finally, it was time to meet their enemy in battle, and they set sail. The *Reaper's* condition was much better overall; it was the best they could do to give themselves some sort of fighting chance.

The journey to Amioh Oiil was long. But everyone was determined to reach the place where they knew Stephan was waiting. Before they had been sailing long, they saw enemy ships approaching in the distance. Stephan must have sent them ahead to weaken them.

But they would not be so easily defeated.

Amethyst stood on the main deck of her ship, eyes fierce as they stared ahead. She knew they would have to make it through the hoard of others before she even came close to reaching Stephan, but somehow, in her gut, she just knew it was on Stephan's ship where she would face her enemy.

As they neared, Darien's cry filled the air, "All hands on deck! Prepare for battle!" The clatter of swords and knives being drawn, as well as cannons being loaded, resounded. The days ahead would be long.

With the whoosh of the sea, the ships met the first wave of enemies, shouts of battle rising. Blades clashed and cannons boomed, splinters of wood and parts of bodies flying in all directions, splashing into the water below.

There were so many, yet the allied ships moved forward boldly and with fire in their eyes. Amethyst and Cadell, as well as many of those gathered, had seen their share of battles similar to this with foes two to one.

Amethyst began to shout orders to her men, Darien echoing her own words from the upper deck as she began swinging onto enemy ships and taking the men there head-on.

"Follow the captain! Let's send these filthy dogs to ocean's bottom!" Darien called. Shouts of agreement echoed, and some men followed Amethyst's lead, not waiting for their ship to be boarded but preventing it from harm by taking out the enemies on other ships.

As they plunged forward, the ships rocked, creaking beneath the weight of the bodies which moved around so quickly.

Cadell was on his own path of death, revealing exactly what his ship's name meant as he and his men cut down their enemies like those faced with death and unable to escape. He was fierce, focused, and steady, guiding his crew with his orders.

To some, he instructed, "Remain on the ship! Send anyone who tries to board into the sea!" To those with him, he called,

"With me! Flank me left!" The men hardly needed the instructions. They knew what to do and Cadell was glad as one of his tenured members sliced through one man who had been trying to sneak up on Cadell.

Already, smoke was rising into the air along with the scent of blood. Fire ripped across some of the ships, consuming those that had not already been defeated by the blade. Several of the enemy ships had taken significant damage, though more than the structures, much of the enemy men had already been defeated.

The quickest way to stop a ship was to destroy its crew. Part of the success of both the *Reaper's Scythe* and the *Gargoyle* was the sheer fighting skill of those in their crew – easily overcoming most of the enemy ships.

Cadell did not hold back, but rather released all of his vampiric instincts, moving with speed and agility and drawing more blood as he thrust his blades into a body and yanked it toward himself. He drew strength from those he defeated, letting them press him onward. Already the blue of the ocean was tainted.

After disposing of one of the captains among the many present, Cadell grasped a rope and fell back, swinging once more aboard his own ship, which was taking some damage of its own. His men were doing well at keeping the enemies off it, but he knew eventually with how many ships were present, some would successfully board.

The battle dragged on. Hours had passed and the sun was falling lower in the sky. It seemed many of the other ships at sea had aligned themselves with Stephan and his crusade against whatever magic he had convinced them was a threat. Stephan had told them that they must subdue the *Gargoyle* and anyone who aided it or else the danger would become more rampant and the magic more powerful.

They defeated the first wave of enemy ships and sailed onward through seemingly clear waters. Soon, however, the next wave of Stephan's allies came into view in the distance. The crew members attempted to make small repairs and recuperate some, but ultimately there was not much time before they were under attack once more.

Each battle was similar, the enemies coming in wave after wave, some by day, and some by night. The crews of Cadell and Amethyst's ships and their allies had little time for rest. They slept with sword in hand and guns by their bedside, ready for the call from the lookout. Amidst it all, Cadell was surprised at how many ships came in waves to defeat them under Stephan's orders. Had he truly deceived so many of the other captains?

Weeks passed in a similar fashion. As time went on, they lost friends and allies, but the ranks of fallen enemies grew faster. They were exhausted already, unsure when they would reach the isle where Stephan was waiting. Still, they held out, praying they were close to their planned battle with Stephan. If they were going down, they were at the least bringing the wretched *Hell's Serpent* and her crew down with them.

Darkness had fallen once more, and Amethyst and Cadell knew they must retreat for the night this time. They had not slept in days and needed to recoup for the battle to come. They began to fall back, now their men only fighting to keep the enemies away.

The ships they had already defeated served as a wall, or at least an obstacle, against the enemies that were oncoming. For the time being, the gathered allies were able to keep the enemy at bay and off their ships.

Finally, it seemed there was a break.

They weren't sure when the next wave would strike, so Amethyst moved to her quarters to rest and recuperate. She needed to regain strength and she trusted her men and her allies.

Amethyst moved slowly across her quarters, dropping her clothes as she went. Her skin was raw from the fires on the ships surrounding them and the way she pushed through the flames toward those who challenged her. She threw herself across her bed, suddenly longing for Cadell's presence.

She didn't have to wait long as Cadell entered, eyes tracing her figure before he grasped a bottle of lotion on her desk and began rubbing it as gently as he could across her scorched skin. She sighed into the feel of his hands. "Thank you, Cadell. You make me feel so much better." She hurt all over, but she knew it was only part of the current war.

Cadell looked out the window, the fires still roaring across the sky and shouts resounding in the air. How much longer would this go on? After a few more moments, he went to wash a bit.

While he was gone, Amethyst let her mind wander, thinking of how she was glad to be sailing alongside this man, glad to be sharing this with him. She knew they would be victorious, together, and she briefly considered how after this, she would discuss a more permanent arrangement for them.

Cadell was the one and only man she had dared allow herself to love, she finally admitted to herself, given everything in her past. With him, she felt she could truly love, for once, without fear. She felt safe with him. Trusted him. And she knew he would never use her for any of his own gain. Things were so different now than they had been with the disgusting man who had called himself her husband.

Cadell emerged from the bathroom, sitting once more beside her and she grasped the lotion, beginning to tend to his body as well. "Perhaps we could take a break for tonight," she whispered softly.

Cadell agreed. "Darien and Aurek can handle it for now."

"They are good men."

"We should rest and regain our strength. It will only get harder and we still have *Hell's Serpent* to face." Cadell traced a finger across her skin, finally moving to lie beside her, and pressed his lips to her neck.

She nodded in agreement that they should rest, shivering lightly at his touch. She suspected she knew what he wanted, but she turned, nuzzling into his chest. "Let's just cuddle..." It was more effective for preserving energy anyway.

He smiled softly, wrapping an arm around her. "I could do this with ye forever."

Amethyst was silent a moment, mulling over his words in her mind. Forever. "When the war is over, what do you want to do?"

"I haven't thought so much of it," a pause, "but I suppose spend more time with ye, Amethyst..." Cadell whispered. There was silence, then, "and ye?"

"I will be the number one female captain. I will be feared and respected and no one will contest me. I will be better than any male captain on the seas," Amethyst said with a fiery grin.

"Then I'll stand by ye, though not so much that anyone might say, 'She was helped by a man,'" he teased with a light chuckle. "I'm sure ye'll achieve yer goal," were his final words as they drifted to sleep.

They awoke early to the boom of cannon fire. Cadell bolted awake and threw his clothes on with haste. The sky was yet dark outside though was lit up by the fires which continued to consume man and wood.

He moved swiftly, leaving the *Gargoyle* and returning to his own ship, getting an update from Aurek. The current wave had struck only moments before, though they had been fortunate to have a few hours of peace for most of the night.

It seemed rather than getting less numerous, the enemy ships were coming in larger and larger quantities with each battle. Cadell was beginning to seriously wonder if they were going to actually end up facing *Hell's Serpent,* and if they did, if they would be strong enough to defeat it.

He was certain that Stephan was enjoying himself idly and would be well-rested and fed before their battle with him. Meanwhile he and Amethyst, and their allies, would be drained from so much time already in battle. He shoved the thoughts from his mind. They *had* to defeat him.

Cadell whipped around, eyes fierce at the shouts from a fellow man. One of the enemy captains was boarding his ship, and he grasped a rope, swinging down from upper deck and landing on the main deck, thrusting his knife forward through the other man's heart. He shoved him overboard and turned, his crew drawing strength from seeing their captain and giving similar deaths to oncoming opponents. "The end is near! Look!"

At last, in the distance, the unmistakable enormous stones of Amioh Oiil became visible, jutting upward into the sky. They were still a good distance from the isle, but now he knew... the battle with Stephan would be soon.

Shouts echoed across both the *Gargoyle* and the *Reaper's Scythe* as the men were spurred onward with newfound strength, more bodies falling to the ocean as this wave of ships was defeated. New confidence grew within them, certain that if they had defeated what had come so far, they could defeat the likes of Stephan.

"Save the last of the cannon fire! We take these bastards down ourselves this night. And tomorrow, we'll sink Hell's Serpent to the bottom of the sea!" Cadell's voice echoed across all the ships present.

A similar battle was going on aboard Amethyst's ship. The *Gargoyle's* captain smirked as Cadell's bellowed words echoed in her men's ears as well. Certainly, this had been the best choice of alliances she and Darien could have made.

In not much time, this final wave of ships was defeated, surprisingly smaller than they had expected, and it was nothing but clear seas between them and a small group of ships much nearer the island shore.

The waves crashed against the giant stones, white foam spraying the air.

The men panted with exhaustion, sweat gleaning on their faces. But victory was near.

# Showdown

Cadell disregarded the damage their ships already had.

Of course, it was nothing near perfection, but the repairs they had been able to make here and there in between battles helped and he was certain it was at least what they needed to get through.

Stephan was an arrogant fool – and Cadell was all too eager for him to be put in his place. *Hell's Serpent*'s captain needed to know exactly who he was dealing with.

Of course, all the men present knew ultimately, Stephan would be Amethyst's to kill. But that didn't mean they couldn't each get their own blow in along the way. The remainder of the night they prepared: sharpening weapons, tending to their ships and to wounds, and once more going over their strategies.

Adrenaline pumped through their systems, and once again they rested where they could in shifts, if only for a few hours. Thunder rumbled in the distance, promising a storm, but they paid it no mind.

At last, they neared the shore, careful not to get too close lest the tide sweep them against the stones and tear their ships to shreds.

"Stephan, for all the wrongs you have done, you will pay." The words rolled off Amethyst's tongue, eyes as bloodthirsty as they had ever been. How she longed to see him on his knees before her, begging her for mercy, for his life. Time seemed to drag as the ships sailed closer, each and every one of the men anxious for this final battle ahead of them. They hoped it would be over quickly.

They were in range and with a shout of, "Fire!", the boom of cannons exploding roared, response shots and cannonballs flying from *Hell's Serpent.*

As the battle begun, Stephan was relaxed. "Come to me, my pet. Come and be mine at last." His gaze turned toward his crew as they busied themselves readying for battle.

When the ships finally collided, he hardly flinched. Cannonballs rocked the ship and even sent parts of it flying into the water below.

Of course, he had expected some damage. But he could see that the faces of his opponents were weary, and he hardly cared that they had defeated so many already sent. It had only managed to give them hope. Hope he was all too eager to crush within his grasp.

Within moments, *Hell's Serpent* became flooded with enemy men. The crew of the *Reaper's Scythe* and the *Gargoyle* seemed to eagerly swing aboard Stephan's ship. Those who remained aboard their own ships were already pushing back Stephan's men as well.

Stephan scanned the scene for Amethyst. She was nowhere in sight. Not on Cadell's ship or hers.

It was then Stephan caught sight of her and a smirk filled his lips. The sneaky wench. So, she thought she could pull a surprise attack on him from two fronts. He watched as several of Amethyst's men emerged from the sea and climbed up the side of *Hell's Serpent*'s hull with their captain. They leaped aboard and immediately started taking out many of Stephan's and

Zyara's men. Apparently, they had hidden knives all over themselves.

At first, Stephan simply stood back and let her reach the main deck. Now that she was on board, there would be no way out.

Stephan glanced at Zyara. Her brow was furrowed and a snarl crept onto her lips. She had finally noticed Amethyst's presence. Stephan belted out orders and Zyara joined him. The battle had become heavily condensed aboard the main deck of *Hell's Serpent* and soon, Zyara's men began pushing their enemies back to their own ships.

Along with the sounds of the battle, thunder boomed above their heads and thick droplets of rain began to fall. The storm which had whispered its presence the night before now had reached them and began its downpour on their bodies. It whipped the sea into a rage.

While most of the men were occupied, Stephan noticed Cadell seemed to focus on his ship all of a sudden. It was now Stephan noticed the *Reaper's Scythe* quaking under the pressure of the already violent waves. Cadell had taken hold of the wheel and was fighting the storm to keep his ship afloat.

For a moment, Stephan had wondered if maybe he had underestimated his opponents. Their determination was incredible and together, they made a powerful force. But perhaps things were in his favor after all. It seemed the *Reaper* had taken on more damage than even her captain was willing to admit. Cadell had been a fool to think he could take his precious ship into battle. Stephan would see to it she met her demise.

With a motion of Stephan's hand, a small number of his men led by his own and Zyara's first mates boarded the *Reaper's Scythe.*

While the battle centered aboard *Hell's Serpent,* Cadell stood at the helm of his ship, his hands firmly gripping the wheel. His hair clung to his face and he gritted his teeth, his muscles straining against the waves. He watched as some of the enemy boarded his ship. Cadell tried to shout a warning and orders to his crew, but his voice was carried away as thunder boomed overhead. Soon, the enemies were moving below deck and reappearing with the prisoners that had been there.

He knew the crew members below deck were already exhausted. It must have been easy for Stephan's men to take them out, free the prisoners, and then add them to their group. Even weak, those prisoners would help the enemies. There weren't many left on the *Reaper* at this point since most of his men were engaged elsewhere in battle.

The *Reaper's Scythe* was struggling. She wouldn't hold out much longer if this storm kept up. Gradually, the attackers were getting closer and closer to the ship's captain. Cadell was giving all he had to take care of his ship while his crew fought. At least by the time the attackers had returned to the main deck, the crew had caught on.

Normally, Cadell would leave the ship in Aurek's hands and be in the front of the battle, but as the storm grew more violent, he diverted his focus. This was his ship, and he was going to do everything he could. Though it seemed that wasn't much. Even with all of his enhanced abilities, it didn't stand a chance.

The cannon fire from the *Reaper* had ceased now. Were none of his crew left? Or perhaps they had already abandoned ship. She was falling apart. The wood cracked and part of the foremast fell, piercing through the main deck and the hull.

Cadell cursed, knowing that he could not release the wheel. If he did, there was a chance his body would be tossed like a child's doll. He scanned quickly, and finally with a shout, beckoned some of his men back to his ship. They returned swiftly, blades clashing as they met with those who had boarded from *Hell's Serpent.*

But time was running out.

More explosions rang and Cadell glanced up sharply as a cannonball burst through the main mast of his ship, the wood creaking and cracking. Shreds of wood fell to the already raging sea. More cannonballs burst from both *Hell's Serpent* and the *Bloody Rose* and it was only then Cadell realized that this whole time, they had been only aimed at his ship. Gradually, they had taken out chunks until now, when he knew it was almost over.

There was nothing more he could do.

Cadell looked toward *Hell's Serpent,* where Amethyst and her men plunged onward, fighting through the men which blocked her path to Stephan, standing with that smug look on his face as he watched the battle. The cowardly bastard. Not once had he gotten involved save for belting out orders and instructions. Perhaps he was simply saving it for his battle with Amethyst to come. But Cadell's focus was not there for long. Would she even notice?

Cadell looked up once more as another round of cannonballs blasted holes through his ship. He was going down with her, and he knew it. Perhaps he had gotten his hopes too high and the repairs from his battle with Mikhail hadn't been enough.

Something knocked into him and his grip on the wheel weakened. He didn't even have a chance to try and regain himself as the ship rocked beneath his feet. He stumbled, struggling to stand. His ship quivered as waves knocked her back and forth. Perhaps he could swing aboard the *Gargoyle.*

The chance never came.

Another cannonball exploded near him, tearing apart more of his beloved ship. He fell, the slap of his body hitting the water hardly noticed above the roars of battle and the thundering storm. "Amethyst!"

She stopped, ears twitching, a snarl on her face, fangs bared. Amethyst's eyes had settled finally on Stephan, and just as she was about to swing herself up and face him, Cadell's voice echoed in her ears.

She whirled, eyes searching but not finding him. It was then she saw the flames which were engulfing the *Reaper*. She watched some of the men working hard to put out the flames and throw out the water which was already threatening to cover what was left of the ship.

With a slice through one man's throat, Amethyst shoved his body aside, running toward the edge of *Hell's Serpent* and finally spotting Cadell amongst the writhing waves. "Cadell!" she screamed.

Amethyst fought her instincts and her bloodlust.

Her mind was blank except for one thought. To rescue Cadell. This was entirely foreign to her. She was missing her maybe one and only chance to rip apart the man she had come to kill. But would she kill him at the loss of the man she had finally allowed herself to love?

Before she could even try, strong hands grasped her.

Amethyst was bleeding, badly. The adrenaline rushing through her and her focus on the heat of battle had prevented her from feeling the blows she received. She had hardly noticed. She fought against the hands grasping her arms.

It was Stephan. His men had managed to restrain Darien, and the others stopped as they saw the sandy-haired man gripping their captain. Amethyst's crew knew she would hate them if they hesitated even briefly in destroying him if it was to release her. But already his warning that he would slit her throat and send her to the bottom of the sea held them at bay.

"Drop your weapons!" Stephan ordered, the men having no choice, though their faces burned with hatred. Stephan held Amethyst firmly, facing the same way she was as she watched Cadell fight against the stormy ocean. Amethyst screamed as gunpowder exploded, Stephan's men attempting to kill the *Reaper's* captain where he swam. She knew Stephan wanted her to watch him fall, wanted to break her so that at last, she would do as he told her.

With a motion from his hand, one by one his men began to slaughter the remainder of her and Cadell's crew, along with the allies aboard that had not already escaped. Amethyst heard everything, but she focused on Cadell, her eyes locked with his. "No! No! Cadell!"

Stephan pulled Amethyst against him, his face so near her own.

Cadell watched, a snarl on his face. But he could not fight the waves for much longer. Nature was stronger than he. He was quickly losing strength. He watched as Stephan began pulling her away from the edge. "No!" '*Amethyst...*' Her name was only a movement on his lips, a whisper drowned out by the sea. He had failed her. Cadell wasn't sure if it were only rain running down her face, or tears. As she tried to reach for him, a wave crashed over his body. Then, his consciousness faded.

Amethyst began to fight against Stephan's grasp violently, shaking her head. Sobs erupted from her and her chest heaved with rage. No. He had to resurface. "Cadell! *Cadell!*" But there was no sign of him. She knew they were defeated.

'*How?*' As Stephan pulled her around, she caught sight of Darien. A dagger was pressed to his throat, Zyara the one who held it. She had been laughing at Amethyst's antics. "Poor little girl. How does it feel to be completely helpless and at someone else's mercy, hmm?"

Amethyst fell to her knees, surrounded by the bodies of her crew members, their deaths also finally hitting her like a punch to the gut.

She grasped Stephan, her heart completely broken into pieces, tears streaming down her face and mixing with the blood from her wounds. "Please! Don't take Darien from me. He is all I have left. Stephan, I must remain with him. Please!" Amethyst begged, her voice shaky.

Stephan smirked, toying with the idea of slaughtering Darien. Yet it seemed, finally, that he was satisfied with giving her back her first mate since her lover and crew were all dead.

How she hated the smug look of satisfaction on his face and in his eyes. She could only imagine the satisfaction he was feeling watching her beg for Darien's life.

Stephan shrugged, nodding to Zyara to release the *Gargoyle*'s first mate. "Come, Amethyst, get off your knees. You won't be so weak, will you? Clearly you put your faith in the wrong man. Cadell was not worthy of you. Look how easily he fell. How weak he really was. When it came time to be tested, he failed you." He paused. "He even abandoned his men in the battle so as to return to his ship. Come now, you must be exhausted."

Stephan took her hand, and Amethyst did not fight him as he led her to his quarters. She whimpered as he pushed her onto his bed and then he left. She curled into a ball and wept, Stephan's words echoing in her ears. Her body shook uncontrollably and at last, exhaustion overcame her.

# Broken

Amethyst was out for two days, though when she awoke,
they were nowhere near the island where they had been headed
before. She sat up slowly, groaning. On the table beside the bed
was a tall glass of liquid and a plate of food. She was ravenous
and she ate it, sniffing at the liquid. Rum. She gulped it down
without question, eyes suddenly searching frantically for more.
At last, she spotted it, the bottle atop a dresser across the room.
She darted toward it, beginning to drink straight from the bottle,
a warm feeling soon overcoming her.

Afterward, Amethyst emerged from the room, a glazed look
over her eyes. She looked around. There was only the endless
ocean. No other ships were present, and even animals seemed
to have chosen other waters to swim in. She slowly walked to the
edge of the ship, staring out, bottle in hand. Cadell... briefly the
memories of before flashed through her mind. She hiccupped
and began gulping more of the rum as pangs ripped at her heart.

She jumped at the sound of Stephan's voice. "It's good to
see you awake."

Amethyst turned her gaze sharply to him, but his face was
unreadable. It almost looked... sympathetic. That had to be
wrong. But she couldn't think straight with the alcohol that had
already overtaken her system. "What do you want?" she asked
softly.

"You, my dear. You to realize that you have been running to all the wrong places and that I will never abandon you."

She stared off, ignoring him, sipping on more rum. Where was Darien? Slowly, she sank, and finally passed out once again on the deck.

For months she followed this pattern, each time believing Stephan a little more. After all, he hadn't ever given up in pursuing her. He hadn't ever actually taken her by force or specifically *done* anything to her. He had only ever tried to persuade her. She did not believe that Cadell had intentionally hurt her. But clearly, he had failed her. And of course, Darien was kept below deck, far from her, so that he could not clear her mind of the poison Stephan was putting into it.

Finally, they neared a lesser-known port. By this point, Stephan had weaved the idea into Amethyst's mind that he truly did love her and that he would always care for her and keep her close. He had convinced her she needed him, and that he would love her as no other man had – or could.

Stephan told her once they reached port he had a surprise for her. Amethyst was curious, and she proceeded to prepare herself, bathing and caring for her body.

Soon, she met Stephan on the main deck, and he led her into the market. Many who had not seen her since she was with Cadell could not help but stare, wondering what had happened. Of course, they knew a little, since Zyara had gone ahead of Stephan and spread a story of his victory and how Cadell had fallen, though she had made it sound as though it had been Cadell who was the enemy all along and Stephan had rescued Amethyst in the nick of time from Cadell's clutches.

After the market, Stephan took Amethyst to dinner, telling her she needed a proper meal after so much time at sea. She obliged him, and he humored her, pampering her. Finally, he grasped her hand, saying, "Marry me, Amethyst."

She was conflicted. Somewhere within her was screaming against this. But already he had confused her mind and brainwashed her. And so, she agreed, feeling so broken and lost that she had no choice.

They married according to human customs and settled in a house on the shore of a place called Tysck. It was there Stephan began to build his new place on the seas.

Without Cadell to oppose him, he rose quickly, particularly with Amethyst at his side, and easily took over as top captain on the seas. There were few who opposed him now.

Several years passed, and Amethyst became pregnant. There were occasions over the years when she relapsed, remembering Cadell and becoming overcome with grief. She lashed out against Stephan, demanding to know what he had done, but soon would be sedated and convinced that all was well.

As she became farther along in her pregnancy, Cadell weighed heavier and heavier on her mind. She had never properly grieved his death, and the hormones from the pregnancy were not helping. Night after night she dreamed, each night the dream becoming more vivid.

*She was crying, body flung halfway over the side of Stephan's ship, watching as Cadell's ship sank to the watery depths. Amethyst could hear voices surrounding her, rough hands touching her, trying to drag her away. She clung onto the side, gold eyes filled to the brim with tears, blood streaming down her face like tiny rivers.*

*She was faintly aware of a pain in her side, but she was so focused on the fact that she had lost Cadell, lost the only man who was anything to her. She could hear a woman laughing, and she was getting pulled further away from the side of the ship. "No! No! Cadell!" She continued to scream as her vision started to fade.*

Amethyst jerked awake in her sleep, panting gently as sweat rolled down her bare back. She held the pale covers up to her chest, fingers clutching the fabric as if it were her lifeline. Hastily she looked around, breath still harsh.

She slowly took in the plush room, furnished with a large mahogany dresser and a luxurious vanity. Her bed was against the far wall opposite the door and opaque curtains waved gently from the breeze flowing through the open window.

The room was so serene, colored in soft neutral tones. Amethyst breathed in slowly, taking in the fresh morning sea air. It was beautiful outside today. It was always beautiful near these shores. They had been docked off the coast of Tysck for several months now. Stephan said it would be better if they stayed near a coastal city, especially since she was so close to her due date.

Those words shimmered in her head. Due date.

Amethyst peered down at herself, seeing the swell underneath the blanket. She was at least eight months along, and she felt like she would pop if she grew anymore. Of course, there was no way to know exactly when she had conceived. Still, the doctors had told her she should expect her child within weeks.

She flung off the blankets, looking down at her now bare stomach, hands moving over the taught skin. A bitter chuckle left her. Amethyst had never wanted children and had always made sure to stay away from men during that time of the season. But Stephan had more or less forced her submission to him and here she was, five years after the sinking of Cadell's ship, married to Stephan and pregnant with his child.

She just hoped Stephan was happy now, and that he would enjoy a screaming brat running around the ship. He'd probably throw it overboard once it started to move around, and Amethyst wasn't quite sure if she would stop him. After all, that little brat would be a constant reminder of how she was a failure.

With a groan, Amethyst stood, waddling over to the vanity. Easing on a silk robe, she sat down and began the day like any other. She ran a brush through her long purple hair, gently untangling the curls. She leaned over slightly, frowning at a few wrinkles on her face. Amethyst realized she had aged more in the last few years than throughout her entire life combined.

Despite her age, she had always looked like someone in their mid-twenties. Now, she guessed mid-thirties perhaps. She added a touch of blush to her cheeks so she wouldn't look so washed out. She had been having nightmares for at least two weeks, and lately she had hardly any strength to even move about without wanting to fall over.

But she refused to become just the useless wife of the marvelous Captain Stephan. Amethyst still considered herself a high-ranking captain, but at the moment, it was nothing more than a flashy title for Stephan to throw around at pirate meetings, such as the one he had tonight.

Anger burned inside of her and she bowed her head. Before she could stop herself, she folded her arms, gentle sobs escaping. Amethyst had never cried so much as she had in the last five years. Between the pregnancy and mourning the loss of Cadell, she was nothing but an emotional wreck.

Across the house, Stephan sat back as he set a glass roughly down on the top of the hearth. He ran a hand through his hair and gazed around the room. He and Amethyst lived in a large house, complete with two stories and several rooms.

The main room was tall and spacious and well furnished. It was colored with white, black, and blue. It was brightly lit from the large windows on most of the walls.

After defeating Cadell and forcing Amethyst to submit to his will, it had been all too easy to rise to the top for Stephan. No one stood in his way or questioned him any longer. Any attempts were easily snuffed out, for indeed, Amethyst was key to the power he had sought before.

Ah yes, Stephan had it all. Except perhaps the child in his lover's belly. He didn't understand why he'd been with so many women yet the one he had wanted more so for his ambitions had gotten pregnant. He hadn't really wanted a child, except perhaps to raise it as a form of himself. He was convinced it would be a boy who would take up his ambitions when he passed on.

Stephan sighed and licked the last drops of his drink from his lips as he stood and began walking toward the hall. What was his *dear* Amethyst doing, he wondered? Perhaps she would actually attend the party tonight for a change. She had done so at random times, especially recently, and he loved walking around with her on his arm. She was his prize, his trophy, and well deserved too, he thought.

He moved down the hall and before long he reached the door to her room, which he opened and peeked inside, an innocent expression on his handsome face. "Amethyst, darling, how are you doing?" Stephan asked, his voice coated with honey despite its poisonous intentions.

Stephan knew all too well that if it weren't for her circumstances, Amethyst wouldn't stand him. He looked over her figure, curled up on itself. He sighed once more and stepped in, leaving the door cracked as he moved swiftly and easily across the floor to the bed where she sat. He curled an arm around her and pulled her toward him comfortingly. Stephan then kissed her head and whispered words to her that she would be alright. "Don't cry, love. Say, would going out tonight help?"

Her entire frame tensed against him as he spoke. Her ears tilted back, the rings in them jingling gently and she flinched away but did not refuse his kiss. "No. But you want me to go anyways, don't you? So you can trot me around like some prize."

There had been a time when she had clung to him like a lifeline, right after the death of her beloved Cadell. It was then that he had taken advantage of her weak mind, convincing her that she needed him and that he loved her dearly and would never hurt her. She had believed every sweet word he had uttered, and he knew it.

"Oh, don't be silly, Angel, you're more to me than that." Stephan's vocals were husky yet velvety as he spoke, ever watching her.

"It is doubtful," Amethyst muttered sullenly. "I hate you so much." Today was obviously one of her days where she would relapse, her hatred burning strong for Stephan when most nights she tolerated him, or actually seemed to love him back.

"If you say so," Stephan murmured, stroking her hair while he had the chance.

Stephan considered the fact that in a way, he did love Amethyst. But she was so different from before. He hated the fact that Cadell could still take her from him even in death. He knew on some level that Amethyst wasn't entirely fooled.

Still, he had won. Amethyst was his, no matter what anyone said. That victory forever shone in his eyes.

She sharply pushed away from him, "Don't touch me right now. I don't feel like having your slimy hands on me." Amethyst stood hastily, clutching her robe tightly around her. She glared down at him, though there was a mixture of need and sorrow in them. She held her face in her hands, trying to stifle the sobs that still wished to escape. "I'll go, but I won't like it," she managed between sniffles, clearly conflicted between memories and her current situation. She raised her head, rubbing her eyes slightly.

He chuckled softly. '*Women and their moods,*' he thought. "Very well... as you wish, darling." He didn't hide his satisfaction when Amethyst consented to go after all.

Amethyst just stood there, staring at Stephan. She was fighting an internal battle on whether to go to him and let him comfort her or go to him and snap his neck. She caught the look of satisfaction and she looked away, biting her cheek until she felt a copper taste flood her mouth.

It just wasn't fair. Cadell would have never treated her as if she were some sort of trophy wife like Stephan did. She paused momentarily to reflect over her thoughts. She had been thinking about Cadell more often than not lately, and it brought about more mixed emotions. How had things ever come to this in the first place?

Had she been in her right state of mind, Amethyst would have used her closeness to Stephan for a chance to do as she had promised, watching the life drain from his eyes and then returning to the seas, victorious. Now, fully pregnant, it seemed more a far-off notion.

There was a knock on the door, and Darien entered. His expression was sullen, and when he gazed on Stephan, fire smoldered in his eyes. "I heard crying," he muttered gruffly.

Darien had never once left her side, especially when she had managed to be convinced by Stephan to marry him. Luckily, she had still been in her right mind enough to demand for Stephan to keep him around. Amethyst needed him, needed him more than any other in her life. He was her protector and would always be. "Is everything all right, Captain?" He looked at Stephan before looking more interestedly at Amethyst.

Stephan glanced toward the door when Darien stepped in, his eyes glimmering. "Oh, everything's perfectly fine," he said casually. "Thanks for the concern," Stephan grinned slyly, his eyes glimmering in the dim light of the room. "But do accommodate the lovely girl, she certainly needs it."

Darien scowled at Stephan. Both his hatred and his helplessness were evident.

Amethyst raised her head slightly. "I need something to drink."

"My Captain, you cannot. You would risk your child's life?" Darien asked.

"Well if it's his child, then it can very well die!" In a flurry of anger, she grabbed the vase off her vanity and slammed it into the wall. Amethyst had not been able to touch a bottle of rum in several months, once she had learned she was with child, and it was driving her absolutely insane to be sober all the time.

Perhaps that was why the  memories of Cadell increasingly plagued her.

Stephan paused at Amethyst's words and her outburst. "Ts, ts, ts," he murmured, shaking his head. "Temper, temper, luv. He is yours also. You wouldn't want a drunken baby now, would you?" Stephan glanced toward Darien, seeming to indicate he was waiting for the other to do something.

For a moment, Amethyst let herself relax at the words from Stephan's lips. But a prompt kick to her stomach by a little foot jerked her out of that reverie. She turned her head away from Stephan, not wanting to see his face, her temper flaring again.

What was it about this man that could bring out the worst of her? Amethyst's eyes began to burn, especially thinking of how Stephan tried to coax emotions from her in reminding her the child was hers also. She very well knew that. But she had felt no emotional attachment to this child since the beginning. If it had not been for Darien and Stephan, she would have rid her body of the growing thing inside of her already.

"I could care less if the baby was drunk," she sniffed slightly.

Amethyst drifted back to the early years of her marriage to Stephan. Her relapses had been frequent and during those times, Amethyst had fought Stephan tooth and nail and any attempt to be intimate became a battle of wills and domination. Everything about it reminded her of her first marriage in the fae territories, the one she had fled.

After those first two years, she had settled down considerably after realizing that Cadell was never coming to her aid, and she realized how weak she really was. She had become too compliant with Stephan. Now it was like the early years all over again, except she didn't know why she was fighting. Surely it could not be solely because of the pregnancy.

Stephan stood and began to leave. "Well, I shall leave you then. Be sure you're ready." He glanced toward the window on the far side of the room from which the sea and the docks could be seen. Afterward he left, winking at her briefly before closing the door behind him. It seemed Stephan tried to remain as cool as ever. It only irked her all the more.

"Wait, don't leave." Amethyst moved after Stephan, Darien stepping aside. She caught Stephan's hand, searching for some answer. "What have you done to me, Stephan?" she whispered. When she had her relapses like this, she often asked this question. She did so because every time she went back to Stephan's compliant, loving, wife, she forgot these little episodes.

Stephan looked down at her, then leaned so close she could feel his breath on her face. "Amethyst, luv, honestly, I have done nothing." He cupped her chin with his finger and thumb, tracing her skin lightly. He then whispered, "You know I love you." He moved back, a slight chuckle coming from his throat. "Don't look that way. With that pout... it's irresistible." Stephan attempted to take his leave at that time. He would often leave and return at night in time to pick her up and take her with him.

Amethyst felt like she was suffering through her first marriage again when she had been a young fae before she had run to the seas. Except this time, it was worse because she couldn't bring to tear herself away from Stephan.

She had sometimes thought of leaving him. But that thought of leaving made her heart beat fast in panic. Oh, Stephan had woven something tight around her and she couldn't escape it. Never had she felt such an overwhelming desire to slam her head into the nearest blunt object in order to escape the pain. "I don't love you." She shook her head. "Stephan, you have done something to me. I know it." She closed her eyes and pulled back away from him. She needed to get ready.

# A Change of Plans

$\mathcal{A}$methyst spent the next few hours bathing and readying herself for the meeting that night. She would essentially be going as a wife and nothing else. After all, what use was she anymore without a ship or crew? Not to mention she was at the mercy of one of the most powerful, if not the most powerful, captain on the seas now.

She had to put her make up on several times, considering each time she put it on, she began to cry, which would wash everything off. Darien had come in to check on her throughout the day, but each time she just shooed him out.

Now Amethyst was sitting at her vanity, putting on the last touches. Her long hair was pulled into a high ponytail, the curls straightened and falling down like a waterfall. She had only a few pairs of earrings in her long ears rather than having her ears lined with silver like usual.

Her face had the slightest hints of blush on it. She had not been able to tan for a while, and her skin had become pale again, almost an ivory pale. Her eyes were painted with silver eye shadow, dark liner around them to bring out the gold in her irises. Her lips were a deep red, making her feel young as she once had. Slowly she stood, her back already aching.

She wore a long flowing dress of silver that prominently showed off her rounded belly. Amethyst figured Stephan would love to show off his pregnant wife, though the thought was bitter. It fit snugly around her belly, with long sleeves that draped off the shoulder and covered her hands. It had a low back, showing off her old crest tattoo.

She had seen the image earlier in the mirror, and it had brought back a whole slew of memories. Just thinking about it made her eyes water. But she would not cry again. Instead, she moved to slide into her silver slippers – heels would be unacceptable with this stomach. Hopefully Stephan would be coming soon, and they could get to this party and have it done with.

Stephan strode up casually, dressed as always for such parties with his hair tidied a bit and knocked on Amethyst's open door. She didn't need to see him to know. When she approached, he leaned close and murmured how lovely she looked, just as he always did.

Sometime later, Stephan and Amethyst entered an old tavern worn from common use. A sign hung from the outside with a great bull carved into the wood and 'The Drunken Bull' was etched below the figure.

Inside was spacious, with countless round tables set around the main room and barely enough space between them for all of the chairs. The air was loud with shouts and laughter and the bartenders were overwhelmed handing out mugs brimming with ale.

As always, Stephan was greeted warmly, giving a grin as he passed by others with Amethyst on his arm.

Amethyst remained silent and passive as Stephan trotted around, smiling that stupid little grin that she hated. She kept her face turned away for the most part, though it lingered on the group of female pirates.

Five years ago, she would have been standing near them, an icon for them to look up to. But now they were looking at her with confusion and some with betrayal. She didn't blame them. After all, she had once said that no man, pirate or otherwise, would ever own her completely in body, soul, and mind. In a way, by marrying Stephan, her status had diminished among her peers. And it upset her terribly.

"Why, Captain Stephan, what a pleasure it is ta see ye here."

Amethyst's neck snapped up as the tall, red headed woman came striding towards them. She gritted her teeth in annoyance. Zyara. If there was anyone she might hate more than Stephan, it was this woman right here.

"And ye've brought yer wife, tha lovely as always Amethyst. My, my, Amethyst, ye look as if ye might pop any day now."

"Indeed it is, Captain. You look stunning as always," Stephan said to Zyara.

Amethyst snarled lightly as Zyara reached out to touch her stomach. Immediately Zyara stepped back. Amethyst might be pregnant, but if she wanted to, she could still make someone lose a finger or two, perhaps even a hand. And she knew Zyara knew it too.

As he seemed to notice the interaction between Zyara and Amethyst, Stephan said, "Ah, ah, be careful." Amethyst recognized the disguised words for the thought of, *'You know how fae women are.'* She knew it, but he didn't say it out loud. "Wouldn't want anyone upset," Stephan murmured instead.

"Anyways," Zyara continued, dismissing Amethyst lightly with a wave of her hand, "might I steal ye away fer a moment, Captain Stephan, before tha little meetin' gets underway?"

Amethyst at once tried to move away from Stephan. "Please, take him," Amethyst muttered. She wanted to sit down due to the pain in her back.

She made her way painstakingly over to the bar, and with a soft stiff groan she sat down, tempted by all the liquor sitting on that shelf. "Just some water," she sighed, bypassing the ale and the rum. Darien would kill her if she got drunk. Stephan probably wouldn't even care.

Once Amethyst was away, Zyara pulled Stephan toward the stairwell at the back of the tavern for a more private conversation out of view. He didn't resist. She gently ran a finger up his shoulder, a light smile touching the corner of her lips. "It's been a while," she murmured, moving to lean close to him. "I've missed ye terribly." She gave him a light kiss. "I don' see why ye keep her around," she frowned. "She's just hinderin' ye."

Stephan knew no one was watching him or Zyara. No one really cared. He chuckled at Zyara's words, and abruptly pushed his hands against the wall behind her, attempting to trap her between his arms. "It has, hasn't it." He allowed her to touch his arms, his lips. He even moved to kiss her back a bit more intensely than she had anticipated.

Stephan smirked as he pulled away, crossing his arms. "Oh, Zyara, jealous? You know the reason I keep her around. All will be as it was in time." He paused, leaning closer to the other captain once more. "You of all others know my secrets. Was her destruction not part of our alliance? Don't worry, luv. She will soon be of no concern." Of course, Zyara didn't know *all* his secrets. She didn't know that for Stephan to remain as powerful as he was, he must keep Amethyst close. But he played it out well.

"What about tha child she carries?" Zyara murmured, stroking his hair slightly. "Ye'll dispose of her an' the child?" She tilted her head.

Stephan listened silently as Zyara spoke and at last he gave her a look that said, *'Don't worry, everything's under control.'* "Ah, yes, the child. I have special intentions even for the little one." He paused.

"I thought ye would do more with her rather than just tote her around as a trophy. After all, trophies begin ta lose their luster after a while," Zyara continued. "I daresay she was more entertainin' when she was allowed ta run the seas amuck an' with ye chasing after her." Zyara chuckled. "At least gave me some entertainment."

If there was one thing Stephan had to admit, it was that Amethyst had certainly deserved her place as top female captain. Zyara now did for several reasons, but Amethyst certainly had been more entertaining. And far more intelligent. "Perhaps you worry too much."

Zyara scowled. "Ye should have just come alone."

Stephan traced a finger up Zyara's side, a bit of huskiness rising in his voice. "Do you need a bit of a reminder to calm your anxieties?" It would be all too easy for them to slip up the stairs to a room and disappear for a bit to return later. His typical smirk returned as he pulled his hand away from her.

Zyara squirmed lightly under his touch. "Perhaps," she murmured, glancing up the stairs herself. "But later, the meetin'll be starting soon." She winked at him.

"I still can't wait 'til ye decide to reveal yer plans." Zyara licked her lips slightly. "Surely you won't disappoint?" She raised an eyebrow towards him. "Tell me again of yer plans with that little wifey of yers? It's been too long." She leaned against the wall, moving to weave a leg around his.

He gripped a lock of her hair and gently drew it to his lips. "All will be revealed in due time," Stephan murmured.

Amethyst wasn't stupid. She knew that on those long nights Stephan spent in port he was undoubtedly with another woman. And then he had the audacity to come back and try to be with her with another woman's scent on him.

It drove her absolutely insane, and she was beginning to think he was doing this all on purpose, just to get her riled up and ill to the point where she would be on the brink of killing him, only to schmooze his way back into her mind and keep her from wiping that smug little look off his face.

Amethyst slowly rose after a moment of sitting in the bar, angered by thoughts of Stephan with Zyara. They were out of view, and in her opinion, they had been off for too long. If he was her husband, then he didn't need to be fooling around with any other women!

A sudden pain hit her in her stomach as she walked, and she almost toppled over. Her eyes shut in a wince as her hands gripped her stomach. Something wet slipped down her legs and at once her eyes opened in horror. She was having this baby tonight. "Stephan!" she cried out shrilly, halting all conversations in the bar. It was then Amethyst turned towards the bar.

She stopped, the warmth draining away from her face. Cadell. There was Cadell. He was sitting right there. No. No way. He must be a ghost. "Cadell," she whispered, fingers reaching out to touch his knee, though they retracted instantly as another wave of mind-blowing pain swept through her.

Earlier that day, Cadell had arrived in port at Tysck.

A few years before, he had woken aboard a passing merchant ship with no memory of anything from the previous five years. The merchant ship's crew had saved his life. They had found him washed up on the beach of Amioh Oiil Isle, halfway across Aseath from Orlesce, and barely alive. All he had on were tattered britches and two rings, one on each index finger. One ring featured a simple dagger, surrounded by a circle on a gold band. It was the symbol of his father's ship. The other ring bore a hooded figure wielding a scythe.

Aboard the ship they had given him a loose pale sailor's shirt and a new pair of dark pants. Once he had been nursed back to health with a full stomach and plenty of water, Cadell had been able to talk with the captain, who had told him he recognized the symbol of his father and had saved him only because of a debt he had owed his father before his passing. The captain otherwise had little interest in helping a pirate. Which was fair, perhaps. Upon learning of his amnesia, the captain had been less than forthcoming on any information he *did* know, if there was any. Instead, he said, "Let the past be. You've got a new chance at life, don't ye?"

Still, Cadell had been grateful and decided to focus on doing just that – living life as a merchant sailor. When they docked at ports, he often remained aboard the ship, in part due to the captain's orders, and otherwise spent his time carrying out duties on deck.

He had made friends with another on board the merchant vessel, named Sahen, and the two had come to the tavern that night to enjoy themselves and take a break.

Sahen teased him that he should try and woo one of the gathered female pirate captains at the far end of the tavern. He needed a lady friend. Perhaps it would be entertaining for the night.

Cadell left his glass on the bar, turning with every intention to walk over to the group of female captains and begin conversation. Yet just as he turned, a lass with eggplant colored hair was before him, shrieking in pain.

As his eyes fell over her figure, a strange sensation rose in his chest. Yet due to his amnesia, for all he tried, he could not figure out why this woman created this feeling in him. Or rather, this tangle of emotions clashing.

It was then she looked at him, and their eyes locked, and his breath caught in his throat, and then she whispered his name and reached toward him.

As her hand jerked back in pain, Cadell moved fluidly toward her, putting a hand on her back to steady her.

Who was this woman?

Another was approaching her. She had cried out another name before. Stephan. Another feeling rose in Cadell's chest at the sight of the captain. These emotions were less tangled and more distinct. Anger and the urge to fight. But still, he didn't know why.

This Stephan grasped her from Cadell's hands. "Step back, I've got her," he said, then, "Get the midwife." The words were an authoritative command. The man looked at him sharply, emerald green eyes full of arrogance and power. Then the blood drain from the other man's face, but just as quickly he snapped out of whatever he had been thinking. "Now, hurry!" he urged, as the woman shrieked once again.

As the other man scooped the woman into his arms and began to carry her toward the stairwell, she became frantic. She stared straight at Cadell. "Cadell! Cadell!" Her voice was desperate.

She was writhing in the other man's arms, sweating and clearly struggling against the pain her body was suffering. She gripped at the one she had called Stephan.

Cadell simply stood, baffled.

The tavern had grown quiet, everyone looking around at each other nervously, and more so staring intently at Cadell. He looked at Sahen, who only nodded and scurried off. Someone still needed to fetch the midwife!

Rather than being asked questions he didn't know the answers to, Cadell followed the woman and man upstairs. He couldn't help himself. Instinct drove him forward. He needed to know... who was she?

Amethyst was hysterical. She gripped at Stephan's shoulder, sobbing and then screaming. "Cadell," she said over and over again, her words now a bare whisper when she could manage to say anything at all.

Stephan's movements were the gentlest she'd known from him as he carried her and set her down on one of the beds. He stroked a finger across her forehead, watching her.

She turned away from him, flinching under his touch. Stephan was a thing of the past now for her. She had seen him. He had looked straight at her, he had even touched her, proving to her that he was no thing of the past. Not lost to the seas. Not dead.

Cadell. Her mind raced with confusion and questions.

The midwife burst into the room, approaching the bed swiftly. Amethyst barely heard as the midwife asked Stephan a series of questions and he answered.

Amethyst turned toward the doorway, breathing heavily. Cadell was standing there, his eyes a mixture of emotions and concern etched on his face. But he stayed back.

Her ears twitched as Stephan's voice reached them. It was cold and sharp. "Out. She doesn't need more stress to deal with..." Amethyst knew he was talking to Cadell.

"No! Wait!" Amethyst gasped, barely able to talk. "Cadell! Don't leave me, Cadell," she begged, demanded. She clutched at her stomach, moving forward. Pain racked her body again. She wasn't sure how much time passed. She suddenly longed for Cadell to be by her side and Stephan to leave her. But she couldn't even vocalize it.

The midwife began shooing everyone out into the hallway anyway. Men did not attend births, she insisted. As soon as the door was shut, she was speaking to Amethyst, guiding her through the pain. Amethyst was vaguely aware of time passing. How long had it been? Minutes? Hours? The midwife was urging Amethyst to push and then was holding a screaming infant and smiling. "A healthy little girl," she said.

It wasn't over yet.

More pain continued to ram through Amethyst and she was breathing heavily. The midwife turned back to her and after some more time, was holding up another baby. "My, a beautiful little boy too," said the midwife.

No wonder she'd been so large, Amethyst thought. She was torn. Part of her desired to hold her babies, bond with them. But part of her hated the fact they were Stephan's. They never should have been. Cadell was alive. He was here. And she had abandoned him at sea. She wept, her tears mixing with the sweat of child labor and she felt trapped.

The midwife tended to the babies, and finally, they were bundled and presentable.

Amethyst looked over, watching as the midwife presented her the babies. The human woman helped her to begin nursing them. They were hungry, after all.

Amethyst observed the boy. He was bald, so she had no idea what color his hair might be. She briefly looked over the girl. Tufts of blue hung about her head and she gazed upward with innocent trust.

Part of Amethyst was wary. A girl did not bode well, especially for a fae woman in her state at the moment. But the thing was still innocent. Perhaps she could find a good place for her. It would not be looked on well, but she didn't care. What did it matter at this point?

Tears surfaced in her eyes again and she sharply looked down at the boy again.

For Stephan, standing out in the hallway while the birth took place, everything had been swept into a blur. He had barely been able to keep himself together long enough to wrap his head around the situation and react. Questions and thoughts raced through him faster than he could process them.

Usually, Stephan was cool, calm, collected. Completely in control. But control had been ripped from him and sent into a realm of chaos. At least for the time being until he could regain himself. His thoughts echoed Amethyst's voice. *Cadell. Cadell.* But not in her desperate manner. His was a snarl, vengeance. *'How?'*

Eyes burned with emotions as Stephan stood in the hallway. He knew that he should return to the main room of the tavern below. The pirate meeting would already be starting without him.

He let his thoughts drift back to moments before, when Amethyst had been begging for the man he had once known. His lips remained a fixed snarl of disgust. He glanced from the corner of his eye toward the larger man standing across the doorway from him.

As he traced over Cadell's face, he realized there was nothing but confusion written all across it. Stephan studied the other. Certainly, the man had stayed here since Amethyst had requested it. What else could he do against the demands of a screaming woman in pain?

But Stephan saw that Cadell's face held no love, passion, longing. It held concern and confusion. Slowly, his mind began to pull itself back into sanity and new thoughts began forming.

Well, well, perhaps Cadell was not just brought back from the dead after all. Of course, there was always more to it.

His thoughts were drawn away with the sounds of whoops and hollers downstairs. Yes, there was business to attend to. He could check on Amethyst afterward. She would need to rest. And Cadell wouldn't be as much of a problem as he had first thought.

Stephan moved toward Cadell, standing silently for a moment. "So, Cadell. Long time no see. Attending the meeting in a bit?" he asked casually.

Clearly, Cadell had been lost in his own world of thoughts, but he glanced at Stephan, staring at him for a moment. "Er, what meeting?" Cadell asked.

Stephan shifted. All pirates would know about it. Was Cadell no longer a pirate? "The one everyone's gathered for," he said. "I'm sure it would bore you..."

Cadell was clearly mulling over something. "So, obviously ye know me name. Why don't ye inform me with yers?"

"Stephan, captain of Hell's Serpent and one of the top on the seas." He studied Cadell for another moment, then turned and moved down the stairs to the tavern below. So, it appeared Cadell retained no memory of them. A new plan was coming together. He leaned against the wall by the stairwell, at last having a chance to think about all that had just happened. Soon, he spotted Zyara and attempted to catch her gaze.

Zyara approached him swiftly, having been waiting for him. "Any word?" she asked softly.

Stephan knew what she meant and shook his head. He didn't yet know anything about the child.

"Well aside from that, I'm surprised ta see Cadell here. I thought he was dead," Zyara stated.

Stephan ordered an ale from the counter, feeling the need for a drink. "So did everyone else on this planet. It is of no matter though. Cadell has no memories of what happened. As far as he's concerned, we're just more strangers along his way." Stephan didn't know if this was entirely true, but he said it nonetheless.

"Does Amethyst know this? His lack o' memories, I mean," Zyara asked, twirling a piece of hair around her finger and licking her lips. She leaned against the bar, looking at him intently.

Stephan gazed at Zyara a moment, contemplating just what her thoughts were. He finally shook his head lightly. "No, but I'm sure she'll learn it soon enough. For the time being, I'll let her believe it's too good to be true." He paused, sipping at his drink.

Stephan looked up as another man approached, giving a notion the meeting had started. He glanced at the stairwell, briefly, and then nodded. He took his drink with him and he, along with the other pirate captains present, and a few others, shuffled into one of the rooms to the side.

It was similar to the meeting rooms at *Skull's Mark* with a long, oval table and many chairs. Stephan took a seat near one end. He instantly noticed Cadell's presence at the opposite end of the table and regretted asking Cadell about the meeting before, though he hadn't yet known of his memory loss. Stephan grimaced, but as Cadell remembered nothing, perhaps he had nothing to be anxious about.

One man had been appointed to oversee the meeting and prevent any brawls. He announced a few minor details and finally sat back.

"Fer those of ye who haven't yet sensed it, tha world on tha seas is changin'. Many of ye have spent more time on land than in pas' times an' there's a growin' number of tha governmental patrols, 'specially from tha fae. Tha trade routes are not as safe for tha likes of ye, an' tha's not jus' tha' merchant trades." Although the man didn't say it, it was implied.

Over the last few years, the trafficking of fae women had grown rampant. Other trafficking remained prevalent, but without Amethyst ruling the seas and demanding respect for her kind, many of the pirates and others on the human trade market had seized the chance. Fae women fetched a massive sum. Thanks to Stephan, Amethyst was subdued, and he had taken control of the seas in numerous ways, including various trades.

The Fae had focused on their own territories of late, though the Fae Royal Navy had increased its patrols in an attempt to squelch the trafficking. Money and power were enough for Stephan not to care.

It was not surprising that Zyara didn't hesitate to voice her opinions. "I think we should really discuss tha traffickin' issue." She looked around. "An' no one play stupid. This really should stop. Or at least be more controlled. Tha traffickin' is the reason tha fae patrols have increased. And we all don' need that. Tha fae need ta keep ta themselves. They only spread violence." She jerked her thumb towards the stairs. "We should all know from experience o' dealin' with Amethyst."

She paused, letting *that* sink in. Stephan knew it. Amethyst may have been off the seas for a few years now, but there was no way everyone had already forgotten her time as both a feared and respected captain. Or perhaps they now remembered it differently. Stephan had tried to paint a specific picture for everyone that fae women were things to be subdued in order to gain power.

After all, most everyone knew that the fae were one of the races in this world which could access the flow of magic.

"For once, I say we work with tha authorities an' at least control what we can," Zyara continued. "Ther's money ta be made even returnin' tha fae. Besides, if we keep this up, then we'll suddenly find ourselves overrun by tha fae people. Soon they'll be controllin' our trade routes, our materials, and us. Do we really want them ta be over us, that lot of temperamental curs?" She looked around. "Who knows. The fae ye've bought might even decide to take over yer ships."

"Ye men were threatened by Amethyst, and I'm quickly rising in tha ranks," Zyara said. "Yet we 'ere only two women an' we caused terror ta seep into yer bellies. Just think 'bout this. A hundred, or even just a dozen, of the likes of me and Amethyst out here on tha seas. Ye'll be grounded to land and used as nothin' more than a cheap workforce. Do ye really want that? I don' think so."

Stephan smirked, listening to Zyara.

"'Though I've extreme dislike for Captain Zyara, she brings up a valid point, lads." Mikhail sighed. "I've engaged in a few bouts of trafficking, I'll admit. But now I've basically sworn off fae women. And we're basically letting them loose into our world. And now the fae government is gettin' involved. If we're not careful, we'll unleash unspeakable horrors on the world with the fae army focused on conquering all our territories. Think wisely captains. If ye hold a female fae in yer ship right now, release her or take her back home. I promise ye, ye'll regret the decision if ye do not."

A few murmurs of agreement echoed around the table.

Finally, Stephan spoke. "You lot are right. The whole thing has grown out of control." Not everyone could weave a spell on their minds as well as Stephan had with Amethyst. Though granted, he had had to wait for the opportune moment to do so. "Trafficking of them makes them spread and while those who are sold as such are under control for a time, eventually they retaliate. And spreading them has invited their patrols into our lives. Nevertheless–" Stephan stopped as Cadell stood up, interrupting him. Maybe his lack of concern around Cadell's presence had been premature...

As soon as Stephan had returned to the downstairs of the tavern, Cadell had followed. Once below, he had been approached by yet another face which caused him a mixture of emotions. How he wished he could remember! The other certainly caught his attention with his fiery colored hair and confident demeanor. "Cadell, we all thought ye'd drowned. Please, forgive me for our last encounter. I was... a fool. Where have ye been all this time anyway?"

"Er, pardon, but... I don' remember ye," Cadell said, frowning. How he wished the merchant captain hadn't kept him so... in the dark.

The fiery individual gawked, staring at him for a moment, and then finally seemed to recollect himself. "I see. I'm Captain Mikhail, of the Phoenix. A pleasure." The man seemed a bit relieved at his lack of memory. Had this Mikhail done something terrible? "Well, anyhow, join me? Since ye're here, ye may as well learn what all tha fuss is about."

Cadell looked around, and not finding Sahen, decided Mikhail was right. It seemed this meeting was of importance, even if he had previously no clue about it, and perhaps by attending he could gain some insight into this blasted amnesia he carried. He nodded to Mikhail. "Aye, then." He followed Mikhail into the meeting room, sitting beside him.

As he looked around, it sank in that everyone present were pirates. Many of the faces were vaguely familiar to him, somehow, but none stirred his memories or struck any emotions the way Stephan and Mikhail had upon first glance. The fact they were all pirates, he realized, was why he hadn't known about the meeting.

Once the conversation was started, he carefully listened, paying close attention to what everyone was saying. Yet, something didn't connect for him. What exactly was it that had caused such a hatred – or fear – of fae women? Clearly, this Amethyst they spoke of had been a force to be reckoned with on the seas.

Regardless of his amnesia, Cadell retained the memories of his childhood and he was fond of the fae. True, they were bloodthirsty and lusted after conquest. They were proud, and powerful. But he disagreed: the fae certainly weren't the ones at fault.

Cadell had no idea what was really going on, of course. But to him, he didn't think that these fae women were about to create some sort of violent revolt and overtake the whole world from whatever edges they had been spread to. They had been sold, probably beaten, and subdued. True, they were violent and vengeful. But they would probably wait for their moment and try to return home.

"Captain, forgive me interruption, but I feel ye all are going too far. I don't know of this Amethyst, but I'm sure if she is a fae woman, she would say what I'm about to. Ye all bring up a point. The fae women are possessive and powerful." He paused only long enough to take another breath.

"But I'll say this: if terror has seeped into yer bellies of these fae women, isn't it true ye've allowed it? Isn't it true that if fae women take over the seas, it is because ye've allowed it, or perhaps caused it? Isn't it true that ye choose what alliances ye make, what battles ye fight, what beds ye take? This has not as much to do with the will of fae women as how ye as men have allowed yerselves to become weak, and probably given reason for terrors to happen. Or perhaps it has to do with the violence which ye have brought on yerselves through the trafficking. Fae women act only in response to wrongs done, not out of inner viciousness and hatred toward others for no reason. The women who have been sold have probably been abused, beaten, who knows what else. Perhaps ye should simply free them."

Cadell watched the others, eyes steady. He wasn't sure why he felt so confident to speak up when he wasn't even a captain anymore. There was something about being around the others in the room... it was like he was driven to speak up.

He finally looked at Captain Stephan, who was silent, but his eyes burned with something that stirred deep anger within Cadell.

"Thank you, Cadell," Stephan said. "What you have said only enhances the point." He seemed to ignore the idea of simply freeing the women. "If we as captains don't rise up and do something about it, but rather sit back and allow it, the fae will probably take over our ships and what Zyara and Mikhail pointed out will happen. We'll be under the control of the fae and horrors will reign over our world."

Stephan continued, "Just be aware of one thing, captains. Many of you know that if you are hiding a fae and are caught by the patrols, you will be taken prisoner as one allied with a criminal by their laws. The way to work with them is for us to travel toward their shores. But still, remain aware of fae women's power."

Cadell frowned. He knew better than what Stephan was spouting. Anyone caught by the fae holding one of their women captive would be taken and held accountable to their own laws for violating them.

Stephan continued, "We will aid the patrols, and I suggest handing over the fae. Present yourselves as having caught the fae women and wanting to return them. There is perhaps money to be gained. And ye will then go unnoticed by the patrols in the future for other trades."

The room was full of nods of agreement and a few murmurs of ideas. Stephan then spoke once more, "For any information, report it back to me and we will move from here."

Cadell was beginning to see just what sort of man this Captain Stephan was. 'The top on the seas' he had said when introducing himself upstairs. Was that in terms of respect or fear, he wondered? He also began to understand the real scheme. They didn't want the fae trafficking to end. They only wanted to mask themselves temporarily until the fae patrols decreased and they could resume, undetected, as normal. A sick feeling churned in his gut.

For the time being, however, Cadell said nothing more, though inwardly cursed his amnesia. He had been a fool to simply listen to the merchant captain and live life carefree the last few years. He wondered if the others on deck had also kept silent under orders of the captain.

Had he been someone terrible, just like these men present? Had they kept him in the dark out of fear that he would slaughter them? If only he could remember the truth.

Certainly, now that he was among those who recognized him from before, he could find someone who was an ally. Someone who wasn't aligned with everything Stephan was saying. He need only wait for the room to clear and then to learn more.

# Escape

Sometime later, the pirate meeting had ended, and the captains emerged into the main room of the tavern, which was just as animated as before, if not more so. Usually, Stephan stayed late drinking and partying with the others, but tonight was different.

He took Amethyst and the newborns home.

Meanwhile, Cadell had spent the night enjoying the party and getting to know other captains, although they seemed to already know him rather well.

As soon as the meeting had ended, several of them flocked to him flabbergasted and excited. He noticed Captain Mikhail left immediately after the meeting.

"Captain Cadell! Ye ol' bloke. You're alive!" one of the captains that had gathered said.

"So, ye cheated Davy Jones himself, did ye?" said another.

"Eh, there's a reason he was cap'n of tha Reaper's Scythe, gents. He's tha reaper 'imself!" Bellows of laughter followed.

"But honestly, how are ye alive, Cadell?" yet another of them asked finally.

Cadell was somewhat at a loss for words. "Of course I am," he said. "Why shouldn' I be?"

"Why shouldn't ye be? Cadell, what's tha las' thing ye remember?"

Cadell thought for a moment. "Securing me ship an' crew when I first became a pirate captain, I suppose," he said a bit hesitantly.

The men all looked at each other. "So ye don' remember tha war?" one asked him.

"What war?" Cadell asked.

Suddenly, the men's faces grew quite grave. "Cadell, that bilge rat Stephan is the one who started the war, sank yer ship..." one of them said finally.

Cadell could tell there was more. What weren't they telling him?

The men all exchanged glances. "Well, let's not talk about such depressing matters! Surely ye want ta know tales of yer' days as cap'n of tha Reaper?"

Cadell grinned. "Tell me," he said.

As the night wore on, he learned tales of his adventures and his reputation. He even learned a few things about himself that he was uncertain had been true. It was much to his relief when he learned he had been quite the respectable pirate captain with a reputation of honor and a distaste for spilling the blood of those aboard any ships he pillaged, unless they truly deserved it.

"So, Cadell, will ye be joinin' a crew and takin' to tha seas as a pirate again?" one of them asked.

Cadell mulled it over. He had truly enjoyed his life as a merchant sailor these past years. It had been different than before under his father's ship. Yet he now saw that it had been a life of naivety. He couldn't return to it knowing what he did now. Even if the memories themselves hadn't yet returned.

"Perhaps," he said.

"Well, if ye do, wait until all this traffickin' business is sorted out," one of the older captains told him.

After that, they shared with him tales of other adventures, the reputations of the different pirate captains, and how he should go about joining a crew, whenever he chose to do so.

The next day, the pirate captains returned to their ships. Cadell, on the other hand, chose to walk along the beach, breathing in the ocean air. He couldn't go back to the merchant ship. Not now.

At last, he chose a spot in the sand and sat. Even after everything he had learned from the previous night, his mind was a web of confusion. He grasped a handful of sand and let the grains slide slowly through his fingers. What should he do now?

Amethyst woke to the cries of an infant. She slowly sat up, her mind buzzing through the last twenty-four hours. The light coming in through her window indicated mid-afternoon. An annoyed growl left her. She supposed the little thing wanted to be fed. With stiff joints, she slowly got up, snagging a robe from the back of a chair and sliding it around her.

Perhaps she would not be so edgy if her mind were more at ease. The children were in the next room over, a nursery prepared for them long before. She moved from her room to the children's. Approaching the crib, she looked at the girl with disdain. She bent over, picking up her son and nestling him close. She couldn't help it. Part of her still recognized the girl's innocence. But two children... let alone Stephan's...

She was glad Stephan could afford a nursing mother. Normally, she would be fiercely territorial. But she had long given up with Stephan. He did as he pleased, and her natural instincts were subdued. Besides, she really had nothing left to fight for. Or at least she hadn't all this time.

The other woman had entered the room shortly after her and scooped up the girl, taking her to the rocking chair on the opposite end of the room and rocking her gently. Amethyst ignored her and left.

She paused, briefly, as she began walking back toward her room. She heard Stephan in his study, writing something. The scratching of the pen was frantic as it scribbled across the parchment. She scowled and moved back toward her room, trying to ease the soreness remaining from labor. As a fae, she would heal more swiftly than any human woman. But, especially after having twins, it would still take some time.

Finally, Amethyst settled on the ledge of her large window, peering out across the beach toward the sea.

There was a figure sitting on the beach. Her eyes narrowed. Cadell? Cadell was out there. Uncaring of her appearance, she slowly slid her legs over the windowsill and moved out through the window, landing in the sand below.

Still holding her newborn close, Amethyst began to move towards the figure she saw seated on the beach. "Cadell! Cadell!" she breathed, her eyes alight with emotion. Her hair was wild and her makeup smudged from the tears of pain from childbirth.

She looked awful, but she didn't care.

Once she reached him, Amethyst stood there in a joyful horror. "I knew you were real," she whispered. "What happened, Cadell? Why didn't you come find me?" She had to keep remembering that she was holding her son to her so she would not drop him in the sand. Her son.

Amethyst looked down and was greeted with Stephan's eyes. Immediately she held distaste for the boy, like his sister. Her mind was made up. Somehow, she must leave Stephan. She must break free. Somehow... she and Cadell would be together again.

She had startled him, and he rose quickly, turning toward her. His eyes seemed an array of emotions when they met hers. She wondered what he was thinking. At first, he remained silent, staring at her a while longer. Didn't he recognize her?

Then he coughed. "Perhaps, miss, ye have me confused with someone else? Cadell is me name, but..." He paused. "Well, tell me yer name. If it isn't too much. Sit with me here, tell me what's happened." His eyes showed that he was honestly concerned and also quite curious.

Within a few seconds of opening his mouth, Cadell had completely crushed her. He did not remember her. Did not remember the love that they had had, the plans that they had made to destroy Stephan, the plans to rule the seas side by side. He remembered none of it. In that instant, a gaping hole tore its way through her heart. It was like she had been punched in the stomach. She had been suspecting it. But denying it. His words confirmed it.

Amethyst swallowed deeply and her eyes glanced back at the home that she had just left, figuring that she would only have a little time to try to make things right before going back to that *husband* of hers. "I confuse you not." She straightened herself, still holding her infant close, guarding him from the intense sun.

"You are Cadell, previous captain of the Reaper. You are the only man that I loved and the only man that I mourned." She paused, tracing down his face to where the mark she had given him still lingered on his neck. Hadn't he noticed it? Didn't he wonder about it? She couldn't move her hair to show him the one he had given her without risking dropping her baby. She took a step back. "I can't stay and talk. Stephan will certainly know if I am gone too long." She licked her lips.

It was silent again for a few moments. Cadell stared at her a moment, clearly trying to think of something. But still he did not speak. His brow furrowed and then he looked toward her house and back at her. How she wished she knew what he was thinking. The silent question of what had happened seemed to hang unspoken between them.

Finally, she broke the silence. "Go to the other captains; ask what the name Amethyst meant to you." She stared at him intently.

Amethyst suddenly looked down at her son. This should not have been Stephan's son. This should have been Cadell's son. The thought made her hate Stephan even more. "Goodbye,

Cadell." At last she gave a watery smile before turning back around, hoping to return to her home before Stephan noticed her absence.

She hesitated as his voice reached her ears. "Wait." The word was not a command, more a request.

She turned slightly to look at him. "Yes?" Her voice was soft as once more, their eyes met. She took a step towards him, unable to resist the hope rising in her chest. Her son shifted in her arms.

His lips parted and shut for a moment. "Can you meet me tonight on the docks?" he asked finally.

"Not today or tonight," Amethyst murmured. "Perhaps I will send you a message." She started backing away. "For now, I need to go." She closed her eyes briefly. "Go find Captain Mikhail. Go find any of the captains. They will tell you what you need to know."

She opened her eyes again. Cadell was biting his lip, clearly conflicted. He nodded slowly. She once again told him about speaking with the other captains, and all he could do was nod again, telling her he understood. There were no other words for him to say and so he watched her go silently, finally going his own way also.

While Amethyst was on the beach, the sound of a wailing infant was flooding the house. Stephan was busy scrawling at scattered papers on the desk in his study. He glanced up sharply as Darien entered.

"Stephan, the nursing mother is missing, and Amethyst will not tend to your daughter. Perhaps you could take time to care for your child. I'm not a babysitter."

Stephan was silent a moment, seething with anger. How dare this man interrupt him in such a bold fashion. The only reason Darien was even still alive was because Stephan dared not risk Amethyst's reaction should he kill him. Darien should be grateful. Or at least recognize the fact that he wasn't the one in power. Stephan had won.

And still, Darien seemed to lie in waiting, ignoring Stephan's victory. In fact, Darien was the only one who seemed to think Amethyst might someday snap out of it.

Finally, not being able to stand the screams of the baby any longer, Stephan moved toward Darien, taking the child in his arms. "Of course," he muttered softly. Normally, Stephan might say something or even strike Darien for his insolence. But with Amethyst's moods lately, he knew he must keep the peace as well as he could. He bit his tongue, thinking Darien would not be spared so lightly again.

Instead of Darien, Stephan turned his thoughts toward Zyara. She had once told him that if the child were a girl, she would want to adopt it. It wasn't unheard of, especially for the fae. Certainly, Zyara had some purpose for the child and while normally, the fae mother would work out an agreement, Stephan hardly cared what Amethyst thought of the matter.

Stephan waved a hand, dismissing Darien. He then started to soothe the infant. She began to quiet down once she was in his arms.

"Captain Stephan, you have a visitor." One of his crew members was at the doorway.

Stephan looked up, annoyance crossing his features. What now?

"Oh, move out of the way!" There was the slight scuffle of a struggle before a scraggly looking man shoved the crewmember aside and stepped into the study. A long stringy beard dangled from his chin though it did not hide the youth in his face. He was not much older than Stephan. His hair was long and pulled back into a ratty ponytail, but his eyes were glimmering with eagerness.

The man stared at Stephan a moment, before looking at the infant. "Well, well, I woulda ne'er pinned ye fer tha fatherly type," he said, sauntering forward and plopping himself down in one of the chairs. "Oh, I bet ye don' recognize me." The man smirked a deadly sort of smile. "Ye amember, yer ol' ally, Captain Dovian, don' ye? We used ta terrorize tha seas tagether, before I got sent ta prison and ye got off scot-free."

Stephan had not failed to recognize the man, though the greasy scragginess did make Dovian look different. "Yes, I remember. How could I ever forget those years?" He sighed briefly.

Stephan's mind briefly returned to several years before, when he had ravaged the seas despite his youth. He hadn't really tried to remember any specifics about his allies, only that they followed him like dogs. But, of course, there were always the close few.

Dovian had remained silent, and finally, Stephan grew impatient. "Get to your point. What is it that you want?" he asked.

"I wanted ta see ye, ol' man." Dovian grinned towards Stephan. "I heard ye were in port, an' I thought it migh' be nice ta pop in an' say hi." He fell silent again.

Stephan ignored this. He knew that Dovian had another purpose, and he simply stared at him indicating he would not ask again.

"I've been hearin' a lot o' other rumors too, Captain. I've heard of yer little marriage wit' Amethyst – ye must've done somethin' really underhanded ta achieve that. An' that ye're thinkin' 'bout stoppin' yer traffickin' o' fae women." At this Dovian's face drew back slightly. "I'm afraid tha's not in everyone's best interest. Ye see, men are willin' to pay a fine penny fer those women, regardless o' how things turn out between 'em. An' I meself 'ave acome quite wealthy doin' it. So tell me, Stephan, why exactly are ye tryin' ta halt tha process?"

Stephan didn't like the way Dovian was addressing him. He slowly moved to lean back against his desk. He was still holding his daughter and she had fallen asleep. He didn't want to wake her.

Completely ignoring Dovian's mention of Amethyst, Stephan cut straight to the question of the trafficking.

*'Aye, the trafficking issue,'* Stephan thought. *'This fool. Of course, there is conflict. Always has been, always will be. That's the world of business, isn't it?'* He was still studying Dovian.

Finally, Stephan spoke, his voice soft, and his tone authoritative. "If you'll remember, my friend, I make decisions only in the best interest of the majority of the captains, not with random individuals who have issues. It's just business."

Stephan continued, "Remember I am first and foremost a pirate captain, and I have worked diligently to attain the position among the other captains that I have. Now, having said that, I am fully aware of the profit in trafficking fae women. But, Captain, do you really know me so little?"

Stephan paused, gauging Dovian's reaction. "How could you think I would just all of a sudden stop something such as fae women trafficking without some sort of plan? I have other motives, and in truth, the trafficking will not cease." He paused once again, his eyes steady. "Do you wish to know of my scheme, Dovian? Perhaps become allies as we once were?" Stephan could read this slimy cur like a book.

He thought of just slicing his throat and being done with it, but he also knew that Dovian could prove to be a resourceful ally. And besides, he didn't feel like cleaning up a soiled rug.

Dovian seemed satisfied, for his smirk grew and he closed the door, returning to his seat and looking at Stephan expectantly.

Amethyst crept quietly back through the window, listening. She heard the muffled voices of Stephan and another man. Seeing Cadell had given her new focus, for though he didn't remember, she did. Everything. Hatred for Stephan was steadily increasing within her soul, and a single thought was constantly replaying in her mind. She had to get back on the seas.

She slipped down the hall to the nursery, placing her son in his crib and hoping he did not awake any time soon. Returning to her room, Amethyst began going through her things, picking out trinkets of value as well as essential items. The creek of the door caused her to start and she looked up, eyes fierce, only to calm when she recognized Darien's face. "Oh..." she breathed softly.

Darien took a brief look and seemed to quickly assess the situation. Before he could even ask, she began to explain.

"I am leaving this hell. He has kept me bound for far too long and it's time we take back what is ours."

A smile touched his lips and he turned, leaving as quickly as he had come.

Amethyst remained busy, stuffing the things she was taking into a pile and folding a blanket around the items. She tied the blanket into a makeshift sack and shoved it under her bed. She prayed Stephan would not suspect anything.

She turned once more at the sound of the door, once more breathing a sigh of relief as Darien entered again. He was holding a small purse. "What is that?" she asked.

Darien smirked. "It is such a shame we won't be around to see Stephan's face red with rage at the sight of missing funds."

Amethyst frowned. She didn't want any of Stephan's money. But she could see that it would be pointless to argue with Darien at the moment. Probably a waste of time she could be spending preparing. Perhaps she could wait and use the money to shove down Stephan's throat in the future.

After a moment of silence, Amethyst turned and resumed checking her things. She wanted to be absolutely sure she wasn't forgetting anything and that nothing looked suspicious, in case Stephan visited her room before she left.

"We'll wait," she told Darien.

He nodded, pushing another sack under the bed beside hers.

With that, Amethyst left her room, moving toward the nursery. She slowly looked around at the decorated walls, the blankets, and the toys prepared for her children.

A pang gripped her heart. Part of her desired to remain, but she remembered it should have been Cadell giving her this life. No, she had already wasted too much time.

Hours later, Stephan entered her room. Amethyst was sitting idly on her bed, staring out the window. She glanced toward him, disgusted as his eyes trailed across her figure.

"Dinner is prepared," Stephan said.

Amethyst wondered if he could see the old fire rekindled in her eyes. She prayed he would not.

She slowly nodded and stood, following him down the hallway and toward their dining hall. Soon, they were seated, and he began to talk.

"I got a visit from an old ally today. Captain Dovian."

Amethyst had to keep herself from choking on her bite. She remembered the name, and it was hard to keep a snarl from her lip and bile from her throat at the thought. "Oh? What did he want?" She tried to sound nonchalant.

"He shared some valuable information with me in return for a renewed alliance."

Amethyst wasn't stupid. She thought briefly of what Stephan had been up to lately. She knew his wealth came from more than common pirate trades. Darien had kept her quite up to date. She had simply been too broken to care.

But now, now was different. She was not entirely her old self. Too much time with Stephan, convinced Cadell was dead had taken its toll. Perhaps some might even think she had gone a little mad. But she was still the same woman, and she cared passionately about her kind. Perhaps even in a different way than her kind's national pride. "I see," was all she said in reply.

Stephan smirked, remaining silent for a moment. She longed to reach across the table even now and snap his neck. But it was not the time. She must wait. She wished she could read his thoughts. She recognized that look in his eyes. He saw her as a trophy, a shadow of her former glory. She had to resist the urge to smirk herself. He had no idea that she had snapped out of his spell. He probably thought she would begin groveling before him now that the children were born.

"I just thought you should know that I will be busier in the times to come. But don't worry, I will always be around for you," Stephan said. Pretending to be the ever-loving husband, she thought with a mental scoff.

Amethyst knew what he really meant. Just because he would be around less, it was an implied warning for her to stay put and not try to escape.

Perhaps on some level, he suspected Cadell had had influence over his grip on her. But it didn't matter. Or perhaps deep down, Stephan's instincts were telling him that she would still yet prove the greatest threat to his operation.

She knew there would be a very narrow window for her escape, and even now she resisted the instincts coursing through her to simply up and run as fast as she could. Amethyst knew that if she did so, she wouldn't get far.

Amethyst silently bit her tongue, staring at her food so that she wouldn't gaze at him with hating eyes. She couldn't have him become suspicious. He would lock her in, and she wouldn't ever escape.

She had been silent too long. "Of course," she said, finally looking up at him. She had managed to gather herself enough to smile faintly. "The babies will need both of us." She hoped this might secure her opportunity. Surely Stephan would leave her alone if he felt she was bound by her children.

Her thoughts drifted to memories of her beloved *Gargoyle*, rage and grief welling up at the thought of it at ocean's bottom. Yet, perhaps she could secure herself a new ship. Her fingers itched to grip the familiar wood of the wheel. Time was dragging and she ached for this meal to be over. Night could not come quickly enough.

They finished in silence, though she felt Stephan looked pleased.

At last, Amethyst stood, dabbing a napkin at her mouth. "Excuse me," she said softly, retreating to the nursery. She breathed slowly. Her heart was racing with her hatred.

Amethyst prayed Stephan would return to his study soon. She listened carefully, her ears twitching. As she waited, she fed both of the babies. They had fallen fast asleep, and she gently trailed a finger across their faces.

In the silence, tears slowly fell down her cheeks. This wasn't how it should have been. She couldn't be the mother these babies needed. And ultimately, she couldn't stay. *'Please forgive me, my little ones.'*

She heard the door to Stephan's study close across the house. He would no longer see where she came or went.

Amethyst slipped to her room, curling up in her bed. She needed to rest as much as she could, and she trusted Darien would wake her when the house was quiet.

Amethyst awoke with a start. She was breathing heavily. Cadell had filled her dreams again.

She looked around the room until her eyes fell on the figure of her first mate. The moonlight shining through the window reflected off his navy hair.

"Ready?" Darien asked softly.

Amethyst nodded, grabbing the sack from beneath her bed, not even bothering to make the sheets to cover her tracks. It occurred to her that Stephan would realize she was missing at some point, and by then, she would be long gone.

She was dressed in a plain white pirate's shirt and brown pants. It felt good to wear her black leather boots and her skull cap was tucked into her belt. It flapped softly in the breeze coming off the sea as she slipped out of the window.

Amethyst and Darien made their way down the beach and toward the docks. There, a merchant ship was leaving for Orlesce to the south. She steered clear of the pub they had gone to previously for Stephan's pirate meeting. Amethyst had a feeling those loyal to Stephan would be at the *Drunken Bull.*

Instead, they boarded a merchant ship. She demanded they leave immediately, and the entire voyage she spent staring harshly in the distance.

The voyage to Orlesce was not long, and as soon as they made port, she visited a nearby pub which brought back many old memories for her. *Skull's Mark.* She was hoping she could find some old allies there. The tavern hadn't changed much, and she and Darien took a seat, eyes scanning the room.

"Well, if it isn't Amethyst. Strange to see you here, away from Captain Stephan and dressed like that. It's been a long time."

Amethyst looked up, pointed ears twitching at the sound of the familiar voice. Leonard... Leo. Captain of the *Golden Lion.* "I didn't know I had any remaining allies," she said softly.

She stared at him a moment, taking in his light brown eyes and thickly curled hair. So dirty blonde it was sometimes mistaken for brown. His skin was lightly tanned, and his strong frame made for a warm impression. His white teeth always showed when he smiled, she noted.

"There are far more who have waited for you to break away than you realize," Leo told her.

"I'm looking to gather a crew and take myself another ship." Amethyst got straight to the point.

"Oh. You hadn't heard then?" Leo asked, brows raising in surprise.

"Heard what?" Amethyst asked.

"Your ship, the Gargoyle. Stephan's held it under guard this entire time."

She stared at him, blinking slowly.

"He ordered some of his crew to sail it to port after the battle. Once you were captured and Cadell and the Reaper sank, the rest of us were lucky to escape," Leo explained.

Amethyst's fangs bared. "That bastard," she whispered. Stephan had kept her this whole time, making her believe she had nothing left but him. Making her believe her ship was gone. Making her believe she had nothing left to fight for.

Slowly, she smirked. "Well then I'm looking to take back my ship."

"Sounds like a bit of a fight coming up. Just the fun I've been needing..." Leo seemed excited.

She smiled back at him finally, standing up.

Stephan would notice her absence soon. Even though the journey to Orlesce from Tysck was not far, morning would still be coming. It had been several hours since leaving Stephan's mansion behind.

She wanted to strike the guard before Stephan had a chance to prepare them. "I assume you know where my ship is being held?" Amethyst asked Leo.

Leo nodded, glancing at Darien, who was seated across from Amethyst.

"I found papers on Stephan's desk some time back," Darien said softly. "I made copies and gave them to Leo for safekeeping when I had the chance."

Amethyst nodded. She understood why Darien hadn't told her sooner. She would have been in no state to try and do anything about it being pregnant. Not to mention the fact that she would have had little motivation since she had believed Cadell was dead.

As soon as they had made a plan and agreed on a meeting place not far from the *Gargoyle,* they parted.

Within a few more hours, Amethyst, Darien, and Leo met on the beach not far from where her ship was being guarded. It was off Bohai Island, a mass of land about halfway between Tysck and Orlesce where travelers could rest if sailing toward the eastern end of the world from either region.

Amethyst was surprised by how many accompanied Leo. She had thought Stephan and Zyara had massacred all of her crew members. But some had escaped aboard allied ships and some others had joined them since. They had sailed below the flags of other captains since then, but now they were ready to unite under her helm.

Their loyalty had not faltered.

The hint of early morning was in the air as they turned their focus on the docks, all eyes falling on the dark, old, familiar form of the *Gargoyle.* The first touches of light were on the horizon and the sky was turning a lighter shade of blue in the distance.

Their window was getting smaller for surprise, and they knew they needed to attack now.

The gathered group moved forward with ease, daggers and swords drawn. The guard was light, perhaps because Stephan had not yet had time to strengthen it after learning Cadell was alive. Or he doubted Amethyst would escape having just given birth. And now he didn't know she knew the *Gargoyle* was well.

Whatever the case, she was glad the capture would not prove difficult.

Soon, the guards on the docks were fallen, their blood already beginning to stain the dark waters below. The group crept forward. The takeover was easy. Within moments after slaying the dock-guards, they were boarding the ship and tossing overboard the bodies present.

Despite their stealth and speed, they failed to prevent one guard from escaping. Perhaps he had been specifically stationed to report if anything happened. But he was sailing away in a rower, and swiftly, for the opposite shore.

They saw him, but Amethyst did not think it was worth it to send someone to dispose of him. Let him go. A smirk filled her lips as she thought of Stephan's face filling with rage. Yes, let him find out. Let him try and stop her. He would be too late.

Stephan had been in a deep sleep and he awoke with a start at the sound of pounding on his door. With a growl, he got up, dressed loosely in a pirate shirt and plain pants. "Better have a good reason disturbing me at this hour," he grumbled, eyes fierce. He opened the door angrily, somewhat surprised to see one of the *Gargoyle*'s guards before him. "What?" he snapped.

"It's Amethyst. She's acquired a crew and taken back her ship." The man was quaking.

Stephan grimaced and nodded. "Go. You will be paid later. Alert *Hell's Serpent* to prepare for battle. I will arrive shortly, and we will send the *Gargoyle* to ocean's bottom once and for all."

The runner nodded and was off.

Stephan cursed. He should have sunk the *Gargoyle* long ago when he had had the chance. In truth, he had kept it in hope of using it as leverage against Amethyst at some point. But now, he regretted that decision.

It did not take long for Stephan to dress and head for the docks. The night wind whipped his clothes and hair as he took charge of his ship and set sail for Bohai Isle. He would rather see Amethyst dead than going against him again. Although he had worse plans.

He was not yet planning to kill her. Instead, he would kill Darien once and for all, and tie Amethyst up. She would never see the light of day again.

Stephan and his men were soon combing the seas looking for any indication whatsoever of the *Gargoyle.*

Meanwhile, Amethyst was busy with her crew trying to get away as fast as possible. She needed to get somewhere safe where she could recuperate and return her ship to its former glory.

She waved to Leo, who was returning to his own ship not far away.

Darien approached Amethyst, and touching her elbow, he pulled her into her quarters. "*Hell's Serpent* will not be so far behind, especially given the guard that escaped. We must mask the ship until we have reached the strength to combat our enemy sails."

Amethyst stared at Darien harshly a moment. She knew he was right, but she was stubborn and did not want to admit they could not match Stephan at this very moment. But Darien was the only one on whom she would not release her temper. "I thought we agreed never to speak of my magic."

Her first mate was silent. "Your escape will be futile unless we have time to recoup."

Amethyst nodded hesitantly. "Prepare the crew."

"Aye, aye, Captain," he said softly and left.

Amethyst sat for a moment. She knew she didn't really have time to dwell on it or to embrace her emotions, but just being alone in her cabin, everything the same after all this time, was surreal. She closed her eyes, breathing in deeply. Amethyst let her thoughts drift toward what Darien had said.

Most knew that the fae could use magic. It wasn't a well-hidden secret. But the true secret was why. Certain members of the fae race were guardians of magic itself. They were called sources. Only a select few of the fae folk possessed the gift as a source and it was passed down to each generation by birthright, the firstborn. Those who were a source were blessed with abilities greater than any of their fellow people but were held responsible for protecting the magic for all fae folk to use and share.

Amethyst was one such source. Something she had thought no soul knew of except her kind and a few of her crew. While her ship had always been laced with magic, no one had found out more than that she was a fae. Anything out of the ordinary had always been attributed to small fae spells but she had never done or spoken of anything more.

As a young fae, Amethyst had run. It was true that she had done it to escape from her abusive husband. But she knew then she had denied her responsibility as a guardian. Her parents had always thrust her duties on her.

She wanted to live her life as she pleased, answering to no one. She would still protect the magic, she had promised, by keeping it a secret. But she chose a life on the seas. A life where she could control her own fate.

Or so she had thought.

There were a few other races with access to the magic, though none as powerful as the fae. Mages were one such race, though the fae saw them as lesser and had long ago dominated them and made them servants. That was the reason Darien had served Amethyst so wholly. He had been assigned as her personal servant when she had resided in the fae lands and she had freed him, giving him the title of first mate and allowing him true freedom.

Outside of those privy to magic, there were few ways the other races could access magic. One was through a direct relationship with a source. There were two possibilities. If one were to force or manipulate the source, they could bend the magic to their will. But those who desired the magic for evil were tainted by it and it cursed them.

Or the source could choose to give his or her heart away and to wholly love and trust another. If a source chose to do so, that other could then also control magic as well. A source only bestowed such a blessing on another if they found them truly worthy.

Now that she thought of it, Amethyst now realized that Stephan must have found out somehow. It all made sense now. Him hunting her down relentlessly, manipulating her, controlling her, twisting her mind. Trying to keep her close. He had only wanted her for access to magic. That was how he had overtaken the seas so quickly, once he had overpowered and manipulated her.

She knew he had never truly loved her. But the realization stung regardless. She had spent five years with him. A part of her had caved to his seduction. Against her better judgment no less. It drove her mad with fury both with herself and at Stephan.

This was the power which Stephan had craved and started a war over. His hunger for control of that power had taken everything from her.

She had known while she stayed with him that Stephan had sought to destroy the fae. He knew the race in general was far more powerful than him. Amethyst knew of the fae trafficking. How Stephan spread the fae, broke them. It all made sense. He wanted to singlehandedly possess the remaining source.

Well not anymore.

Darien was right. She needed to recoup. And end this. But to do that, perhaps she needed to turn to the thing she had tried to ignore for so long.

Amethyst took a deep breath. They needed to do this quickly. First so as not to draw too much attention. And second, because time was running out.

Finally, Amethyst stood, moving fluidly out of her room and onto the upper deck. Darien had already prepared the men and they now looked to her. "Let's do this," she said, her voice clear and ringing over her ship.

Amethyst closed her eyes, breathing slowly. When she opened her eyes again, the gold emitted a soft glow. She spoke, the language of her people rolling off her tongue.

*"Ihm mala aalo bh uiiecht miolzam*
*Ksiu hohulha tesc eot oselo heha*
*Osimhum ue Zeszieih, osimhum ue ushy*
*Mlii yh esh aekh eot ueo shohy!"*

Amethyst cried the words in rhythm, and those with magic in her crew echoed it. There was a slight pulse from her chest and she winced but held herself, spreading her arms as the spell took effect.

Soon not one soul would be able to see the form of her ship, save those who were already on board. Light spread in a globe from the helm to the bow, encasing the whole ship.

As soon as the spell was complete, Amethyst breathed a sigh and closed her eyes once more. When she opened them, the glow was still evident – and it would be as long as the spell lasted – but now it pulsed softly with a faint light. She looked toward Darien and he nodded at her. Now they must focus on recuperation.

The same night after his encounter with Amethyst on the beach, Cadell had returned to the pub. Was this what the captains had been hiding when they avoided telling him of his demise?

He saw some of the captains who had shared tales of his days as a captain and joined them for a drink.

They must have recognized his state of mind by his expression, because immediately they turned from their own conversations and focused on him.

"Oy! Cadell, are ye ill, mate?" one of them asked.

He shook his head. "Nay, but I've been commanded to inquire about... Amethyst," he said.

The captains immediately exchanged glances.

"What does... did... she mean to me?" he asked, his eyes pleading. He had to know.

"Listen, Cadell," one of the older captains started, shifting in his seat. "It's best ye jest forget about it an' let it go. It'll bring ye nothin' but heartache and misery."

"Is there anyone who *will* tell me?" Cadell implored.

The older captain shrugged. "Mayhap, but ye'd best leave it be. Here, I'll get ye an ale... on me," he added with a toothy grin.

Cadell remained for a while, listening to their lively talk, but his mind was far off.

A few nights afterward, he sat quietly in a different small nameless pub. A flask was in his hand with a strong ale from which he drank sporadically. He stared against the distant wall, brows furrowed in thought. He was extremely confused by recent events.

He started at the touch of someone and turned. Cadell was surprised to see Mikhail's pale face with red hair and startling orange eyes.

"Cadell." There was a brief silence.

"Ah, Captain Mikhail, was it?" he asked, recalling the pirate meeting.

The other man grinned widely and nodded. "An' don' forget it!"

Since the pirate meeting, Cadell had had time to think and he realized the last time he had seen Mikhail, he had been a boy. Cadell hardly recognized him. He was truly a man now, with defined features and a strong demeanor. "What do ye want, Captain Mikhail?"

"Let's just say I owe a friend a favor and I'm repaying a debt." The captain fell quiet again for a moment.

Cadell was still slightly confused. What did this have to do with him, he wondered? Although the clue could be in his lost memories, of course.

Mikhail must have recognized his confusion, for he explained only slightly more. "I feel partially responsible for this whole ordeal, and helping ye clears me conscience." He paused again, and finally said, "Come on."

Cadell hesitated, but his instincts told him to listen. He got an odd feeling with this man which he couldn't put his finger on, but at the same time a vague familiarity was present. He stood, chugging the last of his ale and followed the captain out of the building.

In the years since Stephan had taken over, those who had once aligned themselves with Amethyst had begun meeting in secret, waiting for their chance. It wasn't that they would do this for anyone in particular. But as much trouble as she caused, somehow none of them were pleased to see her in the clutches of Captain Stephan and had all agreed to work together to get her back where she belonged: on the seas.

With Cadell's return, the distraction would have thrown a kink in Stephan's constant foresight and it was the best chance they had seen in a while. Finally, they might be able to get Stephan where they needed him.

The captains had gotten together and decided on a course of action. Mikhail had been the one given charge of making Cadell someone of importance once again... someone worthy of the seas, ironically. Everyone knew Leo would have the best luck helping Amethyst directly. Mikhail had been worried she would blame him for her loss of the battle... and Cadell... since it was the battle with him before which weakened his crew and ship before Stephan had attacked. It was true that nothing brought people together more than a common enemy.

However, Mikhail did not speak to Cadell of the past. He only helped him gain status.

After many more weeks, Cadell had set up a nice home in Orlesce, trading with merchants, travelers, and pirates. Mikhail had advised him to get to know the world again, and from there join a crew. Once Cadell was confidently running his trade, Mikhail had set sail in his fiery-colored ship.

Cadell grew comfortable. He received offers to join various crews, but none felt right. As time passed, he eventually forgot about all the events that had happened in Tysck, with the mysterious woman. He assumed he wouldn't see her again, and even if he did, he probably wouldn't recognize her.

Cadell focused on the future, and on regaining himself in society. He knew it was the sea where he belonged, and he hoped he would still have a place there after all he had lost. But for the time being, he trusted the right opportunity would present itself.

# Return

For two years, Amethyst stayed on Aeoumrese: her own personal sanctuary, named in the fae tongue. The island she had discovered and hidden away from the world for her and her crew alone.

There, she trained to regain her strength as well as make repairs which had long been neglected.

Her crew could tell she had changed.

Amethyst felt it too. Deep inside remained the woman she had always been, but on the surface she was overtaken with rage and a thirst for blood.

On the first nights, she had barely slept. When she did, nightmares plagued her sleep: constant reminders of the night when everything had been ripped from her.

Finally, unable to bear emotional torment any longer, and exhausted from her sleepless nights, Amethyst cast a spell which buried those memories to the deepest parts of her mind. A spell that made her forget her love and passion for the only man on the planet who had truly captured her heart in that manner. Only Cadell himself could reawaken the memories. Before casting it, she had a secret hope that fate would reunite them and all would be made right. Until then, she needed to be able to move forward, not trapped in despair.

Her focus was placed on Stephan and all the wrong he had done her. She wanted to make him pay. Everything in her body during all that time was completely focused on her revenge. Every waking moment, every ounce of energy.

The first year, she physically strengthened her body, tirelessly climbing the inner rock walls of the island, and sparring with her crew. It was good practice, for herself and for them also.

Further, it helped keep her mind away from the children she had left behind. When visions of them flashed in her mind, it tore into her heart. But there was no going back. Not until she could end the monster who had enslaved her once and for all. She only prayed a better fate had awaited them than the one she had lived for so long.

It wasn't long before she was every bit in body the captain she once had been, wielding her blade with expert skill and easily overtaking whoever challenged her.

In the second year, she began to become reacquainted with using her magic. Not that she had lessened in her abilities. Rather, since leaving the fae territory before she ever became a pirate, she had used her magic sparingly, only when absolutely necessary, relying on others around her who had magic instead. She feared should she use it, the Fae Navy would find her.

But she was taking no chances ever again with Stephan. She had vowed to do whatever it took to make good on the promise she had made so many years before now. If that meant using magic to strengthen her attack when she faced him, so be it.

In that time, her crew had left the isle and returned, cloaking the *Gargoyle* using their own magic, anytime they needed supplies, but otherwise stayed about to practice with her and continually train.

As it was entering the months of the third year since her escape, Amethyst sat by the fire after a day of sparring, staring into the flames. The sun had set, and her crew was mostly asleep, sprawled out around the camp. The island was always warm, yet they still lit a fire each night in part for cooking and in part for light.

"Amethyst."

She turned at the familiar soft rumble of Darien's voice. "It's time," she said. "I'm ready. That bastard has had far more time than he ever should have, and I've already been gone longer than I wanted."

Darien smiled. "You needed the time, Captain," he said softly.

"Yes," she answered. "You're right, Darien. But no more waiting. We'll leave tomorrow."

Despite her isolation, Amethyst had been able to keep up with Stephan's activities. When her crew had left to gain supplies during their stay, they had been able to also gather information.

A short while after her escape, Stephan had given up on his search and had instead turned his focus back on fae trafficking. Perhaps he had thought he would lure Amethyst back. But she knew until now she had not been ready.

Amethyst also knew that Stephan's spies lurked everywhere. As soon as word reached him of her presence on the seas, she knew he would hunt her down. It was only a matter of time before their battle would take place.

The next morning, the crew busied themselves making sure the *Gargoyle* was well-stocked from the goods on the island and that all was prepared. By midday, they set sail northward.

At last, she had returned to the seas. Captain of the *Gargoyle* once more. She stood with her hands on the wheel, reveling in the feeling as she stared forward.

She knew she wasn't the same captain she had been before. Tragedy and cruelty had buried that side of her for the foreseeable future. She was bent on revenge and she could feel the coldness of emotionlessness emanating from her heart throughout her entire being. She knew that it would be also evident in her face.

Stephan was about to reap his reward.

She would show him just why she had a reputation not to be trifled with.

After two more months of sailing, she finally tracked him down.

In the distance, the familiar sails of *Hell's Serpent* whipped about as the ship surged forward. Amethyst's eyes narrowed, her fangs flashing in the sunlight. She could already imagine herself slicing her blade through his flesh and tasting his blood in her mouth. Darien was shouting orders in the background.

"Ready the cannons!"

Swords against scabbards filled the air as the ships drew closer together and then broadside. Shouts of "Fire!" echoed along with cannon explosions and wood splintering.

As soon as they were close enough, Amethyst drew her sword. She searched across *Hell's Serpent,* until she spied Stephan.

He stood on upper deck of his ship, pail hands gripping the railing as he watched Amethyst and her crew. His face was set in a terrible grimace, but that arrogant glimmer remained in his eyes.

Amethyst wanted nothing more than to squeeze that ever-present smirk off his face. Even when it wasn't on his lips, she could see it in his eyes, his soul. How it enraged her.

Stephan had won before. Had taken her. Had taken over the seas. Had caused enough pain. And never truly fighting his own battles.

Amethyst grasped a rope and swung aboard the enemy ship, bypassing the planks which her men used to run across. She ran straight for Stephan, untouchable to his crew. She blocked or dodged each swing of a sword that came her way and as soon as her eyes locked with Stephan's, she screamed, "Stephan! Come and fight you bastard!"

With a loud grunt, she swung at those defending Stephan from her and pushed them back, some of them falling overboard and others stumbling away to be dealt with by her crew. Amethyst was unstoppable and a force to be reckoned with. This time, nothing could stop her from taking down Stephan.

At last, Stephan drew his sword, that smirk tugging at his lips. He probably still thought he would win. That he would be sinking her and her ship to the depths this time. Perhaps he was thinking of watching her blood stain the waters below. She hated his arrogance.

Amethyst leaped forward, throwing her weight and momentum into her first attack. Just moments before reaching Stephan, she had muttered a spell in her native tongue into her sword.

*"Ilzam ebioh klii ue bieth*
*Blot mah tescohaa bhkish ue*
*Ahsh eot oiy yh ylii bh aeoht*
*Mala ursah oi uish ylii bh!"*

Despite her practice on the island, this was the first time Amethyst had *ever* used magic in a battle. She had always believed that her kind using magic in its conquests in times past had been wrong. She was against the wars her kind raged in the name of power and domination.

But she made an exception. Stephan already knew about her connection to the magic of her people, so there was no use continuing to hide it now.

As her blade clashed with Stephan's, an immense light exploded outward, pale blue at first, though as it rippled outward it changed slowly to a golden core and it crackled with energy. The force was like a wave which pushed back Stephan's crew, many of them startled and wondering what had just happened.

Amethyst watch Stephan tense, falling backward slightly himself though pushed his blade forward, unwilling to be put down so easily. With a loud cry, he sliced his blade upward and brought it around in a side swipe.

She met him equally, bringing their blades upward once more before they broke, clashing again. Both their faces were a snarl, her lips revealing her pointed fangs and his eyes glinting.

Her blade pulsed with each strike, slowly absorbing Stephan's energy. She smirked. Her spell was working.

Sweat broke on Stephan's brow, and Amethyst could see his muscles straining. She knew he would refuse to admit it.

Stepping to the side, Amethyst was slowly pushing Stephan toward the bow of his ship. Stephan seemed to notice as he lunged forward, shouting another battle cry. He shoved his blade toward her stomach and pulled back, slicing toward her neck. She could tell he was trying to gain the advantage. Perhaps he sensed that she had the battle.

Amethyst defended his strikes without blinking, and she seized her chance as she saw a break in his step, breaking her sword with his and lunging low, her elbow catching his stomach.

Stephan coughed, but raised his arm, bringing his hilt down. He was trying to clobber her head, maybe to confuse her long enough to take the advantage.

Amethyst twisted her arm, her wrist catching his as it was coming down and she pushed against his body, using it as a boost to propel herself off him to land squarely on her feet.

Without hesitation, she lunged once more, this time grasping a knife from her belt and with a flick of her wrist she threw it, bringing her hand back up to grasp the hilt of her sword and meet his downward swing.

Stephan's face paled and twisted as her knife met its mark, the blade sinking into his gut and red staining his shirt.

Amethyst forced him to his knees, pushing him down with her blade on his until he gazed up at her, his eyes filled with loathing.

Then, his gaze narrowed, a spark of realization lighting in them. "So, it was you all along." His voice was raspy, and his breath heavy.

"What?" She snarled. Was he trying to throw her off?

"You... you're the source... of the magic I've hunted..." Stephan gasped. "I don't know how you kept it hidden. I suspected it, but now I know... for sure..." He panted now, struggling. "The curse... I spoke of at the beginning... I understand now... because I forced the magic... now it cannot be satiated, right?" His lips curled into a sick grin and he chuckled. "I will have it yet. I've subdued it already... I owned the seas... I will own you!" Arms shaking, he pushed back against her with renewed force.

He'd succeeded, if only for a moment, in throwing her off. She had been wrong, only slightly. He had been hunting the magic and had forced it. But he hadn't known for certain that it had been her. And now she'd given herself away.

But it didn't matter, because despite all the time spent keeping it hidden, now that it was out, those who knew were about to die. Stephan. And his entire crew with him. She also now had renewed vigor. How dare he! She regained focus. She would not be subdued by such lowly scum again.

Amethyst could see that victory was near. With the blows she had already landed, Stephan was weak. She suspected he would try to win still; she knew him too well. Without a moment's hesitation, Amethyst ripped the knife from Stephan's gut and plunged it into his heart. She wanted to watch him bleed.

Stephan gasped, his blade clattering to the floor of his ship. Amethyst grasped his arm, preventing him from falling backwards. She watched as blood pooled and stained his ship. She leaned forward, her lips close to his ear. "Those who have joined you will also suffer your fate. Feel the pain which you have caused and know that victory will never be in your grasp."

Hatred flashed through his eyes, and he tried one last time to strike her. Amethyst had to admit she was amazed at his persistence. As Stephan attempted to strike her, Darien appeared and caught his fist in his palm. With his boot, Amethyst's first mate pushed Stephan on his back.

Darien looked at Amethyst. She was a little surprised since she hadn't even noticed him approaching, or the fact that Stephan's crew had already been defeated. "She is ours," Darien said.

Amethyst nodded and made a motion with her hand for Darien to leave her. He paused, then turned and commanded their men to tie Stephan's crew to the masts of *Hell's Serpent.*

While they were busy, Amethyst knelt, placing her lips to Stephan's neck. She thought of all the times she had wanted to taste his blood, not in pleasure, but in hearing him scream and beg for his life. She sank her fangs into the flesh, not gently, but harshly, the wounds deep as the main artery was penetrated. His blood filled her mouth and dripped from her lips, her eyes filling with satisfaction as he writhed, finally laying still beneath her.

Stephan's body was soaked in his own blood, the sticky liquid leaking below deck and staining the ocean waters. It was human blood which could replenish her magic as easily as rest or gaining strength from fellow fae folk, and she could feel energy ripple within her, even more than the energy she had stolen from Stephan in the battle.

Amethyst stood, a red trail trickling down to her chin which she wiped across her sleeve, a smirk coming to her face and a glint in her eyes.

Bloodlust had taken hold.

She turned, gazing at the men of Stephan's crew as they struggled against their bonds. They pleaded in protest, but she barely heard them. She had half a mind to slit all their throats. But the thought of their screams as they burned seemed equally pleasant to her.

Amethyst's crew had already returned to the *Gargoyle* and were now only waiting for their captain's orders. Grasping another rope, she swung aboard her ship. Her crew stood with torches already in hand. She looked at *Hell's Serpent.* "Kill them. And let their ship of rotting bodies sail away for anyone who sees it to know that I have returned."

She paused, then looked to where Stephan's warm body remained. "Bring the bastard's body to me, though. That I may keep my word. His bones will decorate my ship and my neck as a reminder of what happens when *anyone* tries to mess with me."

The men stared at her a moment, and finally nodded. Amethyst smirked at the screams of Stephan's crew as her men ran them through. They pulled in the planks, disconnecting the ships, and with no direction whatsoever, *Hell's Serpent* sailed away, full of rotting corpses as a warning to passersby.

The *Gargoyle* had taken significant damage itself from all of *Hell's Serpent*'s cannon fire and it looked ragged. It would need significant repairs if Amethyst didn't want it to sink to ocean's bottom. With a brief word to Darien, she slipped into her cabin and retrieved a bottle of rum, falling back on her bed and sipping it.

Amethyst felt satisfied, yet exhausted... and yet somehow, she felt empty. Once she had downed much of the bottle, she passed out with a sleepy smile on her lips.

After that point, Amethyst lost herself. For the first few weeks, she kept to her room. She ate only when Darien insisted and waited for the repairs she knew her crew would take care of. She began to wonder who she had once been. She felt lost, vague, a shadow.

Blood lust ravaged her heart. It was insatiable, and she knew she must feed it soon or go mad. Amethyst began to wonder if perhaps she simply needed someone to help distract her. Maybe the madness would fade. She told Darien she needed rest. But it was only an excuse. Amethyst knew Darien was no fool. Still, he let her be, perhaps hoping she would not go on a blood-filled rampage.

Several more weeks passed and finally they landed at Eliha, a large and well-known port on the coast of Tysck. It was miles away from where the house with Stephan had been, but it felt a bit odd to be there regardless.

Amethyst at last emerged from her room, seemingly back to herself in front of her crew. She was giddy, partially from rum. She gazed over her ship briefly and then moved to the edge of the deck, staring over the ocean.

Amethyst felt reckless and liberated. As the *Gargoyle* docked, she noticed that the *Golden Lion* was also present. Its crew were ashore for market goods while Leo remained on the ship. Amethyst instructed her crew to finish the ship and gather supplies while she paid Leo a visit.

Aye, perhaps a distraction was just what she needed. And, she hadn't seen him since she'd escaped from Stephan. Or rather... since he'd helped her escape. It was only right to see him.

Amethyst boarded the *Golden Lion* without fear. Her alliances with Leo had come and gone as far back as she could remember. She moved easily across his main deck and down a few steps to where she knew the captain's quarters were located. Leo's quarters were two joined rooms. One was the equivalent of a study while the other room was Leo's actual quarters.

As soon as she entered the study room, Leo looked up from a small desk, his eyes wide with surprise, but a warm smile filling his lips. "Well, I see ye're back from the dead."

She didn't respond, but rather continued across the room and grasped him in a hug. She smiled warmly. "I've missed you, Leo."

Amethyst felt his hesitation before he returned her hug. She didn't care if she was being forward.

"I've heard the tales already begun of ye defeating some sea beast," Leo said.

Amethyst chuckled. "Yes. And a monster it was. Tore my ship apart. But repairs have been made and the dastardly thing won't bother any more of us sea folk."

"I'm assuming ye're here for supplies then?" Leo asked.

She nodded, breaking their embrace and moving about the space casually. "Have you missed me, Leo?"

She wondered if Leo noticed that she had changed somehow. "Aye," he answered.

Amethyst continued her movement, finally stepping beside him again and trailing a finger up his arm. She pressed her generous chest against him and stood on her tiptoes to whisper in his ear. "No, Leo... have you missed me?" She paused. "I mean, you mustn't have forgotten. After all, you did return my ship to me, acquire my crew, help my escape. Surely you must have thought I would repay you."

Leo seemed to finally understand what she meant. They had once been lovers in the past, though it had never been anything long-lasting for Amethyst. He had accepted it and moved on, which had been fine for her at the time. Now, Amethyst decided she was ready for more too.

She saw the surprise, the desire, the curiosity, and the hesitation all in his eyes. "It was a favor to a friend. Ye were a slave to a tyrant, and there're many of us who woulda seen ye freed," Leo said.

Amethyst was silent a moment, simply staring at him. "Come now, Leo. There must have been a reason you were the one, hmm?" She leaned upward, teasing his lips with her tongue and tracing a finger down his navel to his pants. His breath came short.

Finally, he gave in to her demands. Leo grasped her shoulders, pushing her back against the wall. "Amethyst," he murmured, his tone deeper and rugged. It was not a difficult decision for him to make, she thought. There were no reasons for him to hold back. So he didn't.

# 17

# *Darkness and Light*

*H*ours later, Amethyst awoke with a groan, having passed out after her time with Leo. She looked around, her mind running through all of her recent events. Finally, her gaze fell on the sleeping form of Leo beside her.

They had moved from his study to his quarters, the two rooms connected by a single door leaving no fear of being seen – not that she would have really cared. Amethyst needed to leave and be on her way. She sat up, reaching for her clothes lying not so far away and began to dress.

Leo woke up as she began moving around. Amethyst felt his gaze follow her a moment, then begin to sit up himself. "Ye should stay a while."

She looked at him, wondering what all he was thinking. Certainly he must know what she had been wanting – and that it had been nothing more. Or maybe not. "I can't. It's been too much time off the seas for me and I have much to do."

Leo laid back, releasing a sigh. "Aye." He paused. "But ye'll send word if ye need anythin'?"

Amethyst nodded as she was slipping on her boots. "I need to see what progress my men have made on the Gargoyle. You may accompany me, if you wish."

He stared at the ceiling. "I'll see ye around."

She leaned down, planting a kiss on his forehead before she turned and left.

After that night, Amethyst realized that a distraction had helped only temporarily. The bloodlust still raged beneath the surface after defeating Stephan. Even though weeks had passed... it had not faded at all.

When Amethyst returned to her ship it was late morning. For the time being, her crew continued work on what remaining repairs were needed and were restocking the ship as well as selling what goods they could. Amethyst knew that they would be able to once again set sail within a day or two's time.

Amethyst spied Darien standing at the helm of the ship and watching over the crew. He smiled at her and she waved back, moving quickly toward him. "Good morning, Darien!"

"Good morning, Cap'n," he responded.

Briefly, Amethyst discussed her future goals with Darien. She told him to have her breakfast prepared and brought to her in her quarters. With Stephan behind her, she was going to attempt to regain her old self. The first step was becoming queen of the seas again. She would do as she pleased with no others who would dare oppose her.

After breakfast, Amethyst left her ship once more and went to the market. She spent the day shopping and making a presence. The whole world needed to know that Captain Amethyst and her *Gargoyle* had returned.

What Amethyst didn't realize was all of the talking her crew had already done. Perhaps they couldn't help it. Perhaps they were concerned over their captain's mental state. Perhaps they were glad of her return more than anyone. Perhaps a mixture of all. As they had made repairs, worked on the docks, and shopped for supplies, they had talked with the other pirates, sailors, merchants, and travelers present. At night they drank at the local pubs and even more farfetched tales were spun.

Soon, Amethyst discovered the result of their tales. The story spread, word of Stephan's defeat wildfire on the lips of all associated with the seas. The tale had already become embellished where many believed it was actually a sea monster of some sort that Amethyst and her crew had defeated. Not all knew who Stephan was, but still the tale became widely known, even amongst the merchants and those living ashore.

Amethyst spent the remaining nights at port with Leo. She finally opened up to him and told him the details of her troubles and her battle. Leo seemed both pleased and worried.

As soon as her ship was ready, Amethyst prepared to set sail.

Within her first few weeks back at sea, Amethyst found she was with child, much to her distasteful surprise. But the thought was not so unpleasant as she realized the child was Leo's. She welcomed the child, preferring one with Leo than with the bastard who had taken so much from her.

Her blood thirst continued to lay beneath the surface, suppressed by force. She had to take care of herself.

The baby was born, a boy. He looked almost just like Leo. Amethyst named him Ercio and sent word to Leo of his birth. After then, Amethyst spent much time with Leo and began to enjoy his company. She began to feel herself growing attached, though there was a pull in the back of her mind against it, holding her heart back.

Leo kept her distracted and happy, keeping the bloodlust at bay. Ercio grew swiftly, and she enjoyed watching him play and run about. Yet in her time alone, thoughts began to plague her mind and her sleep. She grew bored with simply spending her days with good food, a bottle of rum, and pleasurable swims in the ocean.

Amethyst began to recount the battle with Stephan in her mind, smiling at the thought of tasting Stephan's blood on her tongue. The thoughts of Stephan also made her blood boil and the resentment and anger which had been buried for so many years began to surface within her, demanding to be heard.

All of that time, pent up, her resentment had not been entirely vanquished in Stephan's defeat. Bloodlust was consuming her mind, and soon she craved it. Any soul which had dared allow her captivity to continue was now present on her mind. Further, there were many who had wronged and continued to wrong her kind. Even after Stephan was no longer living, she knew that fae trafficking continued.

Amethyst's darkest side awakened.

Darien advised her to send Ercio to Leo's care for a time for his best interest and soon, Amethyst led her crew on a blood path.

She began to hunt any individual she could who had participated in the fae trafficking Stephan had pushed across the land, her crew growing stronger and more powerful with each victory. She drank the blood of each captain, and the others she would leave in a pile of rotting corpses, watching them float away with sweet satisfaction.

Soon, her reputation on the seas grew dark and other ships became wary of her, going so far as to steer clear. Her mind was lost to her bloodlust and her rum, all of her anger and resentment which had grown over the years toward Stephan finally being released on her victims.

Her crew knew Amethyst had lost her mind, yet still they remained loyal, seeking to please her and also loving the taste of victory after their battles. They clung to the hope that soon she would come to herself once again.

Several more years passed full of only blood and battle, and finally Amethyst desired to make port for a brief time. With much of the fighting, some of the crew had been lost and she desired to acquire more men. Plus, they needed supplies. Despite her many attacks on other ships, they had hardly pillaged enough. Instead, they had simply wasted the cargo or let it burn for Amethyst's crazed satisfaction.

So, they set sail for port on one of the mainland shores. They came to a well-known cove where breathtaking hills stood over the sea. It was summer, and as soon as those on shore caught sight of her ship, word spread quickly of her presence.

The *Gargoyle* now spread fear and uncertainty in its wake, most knowing of the beautiful yet fearsome captain at its helm. She did not seem to care that her fame was now for fear rather than respect: either way she held the place on the seas which she desired.

They dropped anchor near the docks. With Darien and much of her crew in charge, Amethyst set off with some of her most trusted men to shop the market. Once they had purchased the supplies they needed, Amethyst felt like relaxing in one of the pubs before they had to leave. It was *Skull's Mark*, and it was there they stayed for a meal and some drinks.

# The Gargoyle

For weeks now, similar dreams had plagued Cadell's sleep, and each time, he awoke with a start, drenched in sweat. Today was no exception as he groaned and rolled out of bed. The dream was still vivid in his mind.

*Rain hammered at his face. Through a blur, he could see her. Were those tears or just raindrops running down her cheeks? He tried to scream, but the wind carried his voice away. "No! No!" he yelled. The sea and the storm drowned out his voice. He couldn't help her. The arms of his enemy wrapped around her, the other captain staring back at him with that ever-present smirk. That smug look of victory. Cadell felt the sea swallow his feet, his body. His ship was sinking somewhere behind him. He sank beneath the surface, too weak to hang on.*

Each time, toward the end of the dream, Cadell reached out his hand in a last attempt at fighting the waves trying to swallow him, and then it all slipped into black.

Cadell shook his head to clear his mind and stumbled into the water closet. He bent over the sink and hoped the cold water he splashed on his face would help. He knew the dream was a memory, but despite his efforts, he couldn't remember anything about the events leading up to the moment of his sinking below the surface of the waves.

As he moved about his room, getting ready for the day, he glanced out of the window beside his bed.

Light glimmered off the waves which crashed on the Orlesce coast. Rumbles of carts, shouts of merchants, and the dull conversations of passersby all rose into the air, a reminder of the daily activities happening at Port Drelle, where he lived. He liked it here, where travelers of all kinds were welcome.

As the dream lingered in his mind, Cadell's thoughts drifted to his childhood. As a boy, he remembered long days aboard his father's ship, sailing to and from various ports. A well-known and respected merchant trader, his father had been able to afford him some education. Still, though well-taught, Cadell rarely let it show. What graces he had learned remained in much of his mannerisms, but they were subtle.

When he had grown, he had been able to purchase his own ship with a little help from his father. After a few years as captain of his ship, pirates began their attacks for his merchandise. Cadell and his crew fought back, and he quickly grew a reputation as a fearsome captain not to be trifled with on the seas. Eventually, he discovered it was profitable to trade with pirates, and soon he was a pirate in his own right. However, he still believed in his dignity and had never quite fallen to the cutthroat and merciless nature pirates were known for.

After that was where his memories were a blank.

Since the strange encounter in Tysck amongst the pirate captains, he had decided to focus his efforts on land as a trader in the local markets. He was incredibly grateful to Mikhail, who had truly become someone far more than he ever would have thought when he'd first met him ages ago. Mikhail had helped him to establish himself and get on his feet.

Since then, Cadell had built a reputable name for himself among the locals.

Despite all of that, there was an ever-present feeling of longing. Every time he watched the ships coming in or sailing out yet again, he couldn't shake the desire to board one.

He couldn't deny his yearning to sail as part of a crew once more. Maybe it was just in his blood. He had occasionally asked about it while trading in the market, but it never seemed to pan out for him. Either the captains weren't looking to hire or didn't seem interested. Even the few interviews he had gotten, some with merchant captains and some with pirate captains, didn't feel quite right and he had chosen to remain at port.

A few hours later, all this was still circling his mind as he approached *Skull's Mark.* He approached the bar and sat on one of the tall, round wooden seats. He didn't venture here often, but as it was a popular hangout for pirates, he had a stirring in his gut to be here today. Why was he continuously tormented by the dream of defeat every night? He needed sleep. And he needed answers.

As he waited for the barkeep, Cadell took a moment to watch the few others going about their business. It was early afternoon, and the pub was quiet, though it would grow loud as evening fell and more pirates filtered in and became drunken and animated. Still, there were more than usual present for this time of day, though they paid Cadell little mind. They were all busy in their own affairs.

The main room was dimly lit from the sunlight filtering in through the windows near the entrance. As time went on, candlelit lanterns hanging from poles around the room would be lit by the keep.

"What'll ya have?" The barmaid was a large, rough-looking woman. She could easily have been mistaken for a bartender except for her huge bosom and lack of a beard.

Cadell's gaze turned toward the woman behind the counter. "Get me an ale," he responded gruffly. He hadn't spoken much since he had gotten out of bed.

A roar of laughter exploded from a table across the room and Cadell turned out of curiosity. Around the table were five people: a woman at the head and two men on either side. He noted the skullcap around the woman's head, which was tilted back. Her cap featured a gargoyle's face with two silver daggers crossed behind it.

Cadell turned his full attention on the woman and her group. It was not difficult for him to hear their conversation, even from across the room. Cadell had kept his vampiric abilities to himself since settling at Port Drelle, and he rarely used them. It was better for people to assume he was human. However, he now listened in to the group from where he sat.

He couldn't help himself as he traced over the woman's figure. Her dark eggplant ringlets bounced with her laughter and tumbled down her back. Her ears were long and finely pointed and were pierced in their entirety with many silver hoops. As she laughed, he caught a glimpse of two pointed fangs.

Clearly, she was not human, although the men around her seemed to be. On first instinct, someone might think she were a vampire, although Cadell knew better. From her features, he suspected she was fae, though there was no way he could be completely sure. Still, he'd spent a great deal of his childhood among the fae folk when his father had traded with them. That thought sparked another rush of memories from his youth.

His father often traded in the fae markets. He would run and play with fae children. That was how he had become so close with Akaisha.

He remembered listening to old stories of conquest from fae women, when the fae had struggled against other races and had developed their cruel reputation. They spoke of themselves as superior and carried themselves straight, shoulders back, heads high. Even those on the docks.

Cadell also remembered their roadways had been paved with gemstones and, though he had never been told directly, he remembered rumors that the fae had special access to the magic flowing through the world.

As he continued observing the woman, flashes of that day on the beach a few years before danced across his mind. Could it be? He frowned. This woman seemed so different from the woman he had seen then.

On the beach, the woman who had declared her love had been small, fragile even, and in great distress. If he were honest, it was even a bit blurry in his memory for he had been so confused amidst the explosion of events at the time, that he barely remembered very much at all.

In contrast, this woman seemed fiery, confident, and quite lively. In fact, the very way she carried herself exuded power and a certain air of danger.

Her men all wore dark clothes with short or no sleeves, showing the same insignia as her skull cap branded onto their arms. As she calmed down, almond-shaped eyes opened to reveal golden irises. She tipped her mug to her reddened lips, taking a deep sip and setting it back down on the table. She looked at her clean-shaven companions with a grin.

"My lads," the woman sighed with a chuckle, "you sure know how to make a girl laugh."

"Anything for you, Cap'n," the man sitting on her left responded around a mouthful of food.

"I hope our new crew members will be as good as you all," she said.

*Her crew, eh?* Cadell thought. She was a pirate captain then.

There weren't many female pirate captains that he knew of. Captain Zyara of the *Bloody Rose* was infamous... and Cadell knew she was also human. So, this couldn't be her.

Could it be that this was the famous captain of the *Gargoyle*, he wondered? He had all too often heard the tales from merchants and pirates alike during his trades. The *Gargoyle* was a ship feared on the seas for its captain's reputation. She was known for random fits of bloodlust and a lack of interest in treasure. But she was also reputed as a great captain with a crew that would defend its own with fierce loyalty.

Cadell's attention was brought back to the counter as the barmaid roughly put his ale down. He grabbed the mug without comment and sipped its contents. His focus returned to this female captain. He noted she was dressed in a white pirate's shirt, loose over her shoulders, but it did not fail to outline her distinct womanly figure. She wore dark pants and leather boots that reached halfway up her calves.

After setting the empty mug on the dirty counter, Cadell moved toward the group with the fascinating woman. She intrigued him, this female captain who demanded such a fierce reputation. There was something about her, and he felt a desire to know more. His shadow loomed over them, and he folded his arms across his chest.

"Guess you're the captain of this crew?" Cadell asked, speaking directly to the woman at the table's head.

With Cadell's approach, all merriment ceased, the men's hands automatically going to their sides and the weapons there as they prepared to stand. They stopped only when the woman held up a hand.

When he saw she was listening, Cadell asked, "Ye' don't mind me joining yer crew there, lass, do ye?"

"Ye think ye have what it takes to be a part of the Gargoyle?" she questioned, leaning back slightly and looking up at him. He noticed the way her speech shifted to the common pirate's and sailor's language. He found that intriguing since she had been speaking properly only moments before with her crew members.

Her question confirmed his suspicions. This was indeed the very captain of the *Gargoyle*. Cadell was silent a moment, gazing back at her firmly. He hoped she could tell the answer to her question by his direct approach.

Her gaze traced over his figure briefly, taking in his features. What was she thinking? How did he look to her?

Finally, she turned her gaze toward the table nonchalantly and responded, "Remove the gold and the beard, and perhaps I'll consider ye. Come down to the docks when the sun is just touching the horizon. Someone will be waiting. Ye'll come aboard my ship, convince me that ye should be a part of my crew, and I'll think 'bout hiring ye." She grabbed a bottle of rum from the table and filled the goblet in front of her.

Cadell was a little surprised at her response, and the gold hoops in his ears jingled slightly as he raised a finger to touch them. Perhaps he had caught her at the right moment, or perhaps in the right mood. Perhaps his luck was finally looking up. Whatever the case, he was glad for the chance.

Cadell briefly glanced at the rings on his fingers. He would not be so eager to part with them, but he would do as he must. He had also noticed from his previous observations the clean-shaven faces of her crew, and he was curious, though did not ask. A smirk flickered across his lips, and he gave a slight nod in response. "Alright," he muttered.

He turned to leave, thinking there was nothing left for him to say. Then, he paused and turned back slightly. Cadell glanced at her through the few locks of hair that had escaped the short bundle tied loosely behind his head. "Consider yerself with a new crew member," he said simply. He wanted her to know that he was confident and bold. He didn't wait to see her response.

Cadell left, glad to finally be getting back on the seas, or so he hoped. Yes, everyone knew of the *Gargoyle* and many men tried and failed to become a member of the crew. He'd have better luck, he was sure.

The thud of Cadell's boots as he walked down the docks echoed in the air. There weren't many people here; it was near sundown. Cadell ran a hand through his hair. When he had left *Skull's Mark*, it had been in a short bundle. His hair now hung loosely over his neck, barely long enough for the ends to touch his shoulders; he had cut it along with shaving his beard for his interview. All accessories had also been left behind, except the two signet rings: the one with his father's symbol, and the one with that of the *Reaper's Scythe,* both of which were tucked in his pocket. He let his hand fall to his side. Moving forward, he looked for the woman he had seen previously. His gait was confident, ready for anything.

There was another man standing near one of the lamp posts, hands stuffed in his pockets. It was one of the men from the woman's table. He was tall, and somewhat lean, with defined features. When Cadell approached, the man waiting looked up and smirked. "Good. You can follow instructions." He motioned for Cadell to follow.

Cadell's fingers rose only briefly to touch his now smooth chin.

The man led him along the docks, getting into darker areas, where the ships anchored at port cast looming shadows. The man stopped and went down one of the sides of the dock, heading up a plank.

Especially in the moonlight, the *Gargoyle* looked eerie. It was clearly named for the carved figurehead, grinning wickedly at the town below from the prow of the ship. While it remained as still as stone, the face of a lion, eyes fierce, glared downward, daring any unwanted company to come closer and test fate. Two horns jutted from its brow and sharp teeth gleamed in the pale moonlight as if it might devour any passersby.

As he followed the other man aboard, Cadell couldn't help staring upward at the ship. Aye, it was a beauty. It was a frigate, a ship with two full decks and three square-rigged masts. The hull was deep brown in color and the sails pale. Though raised, he swore he caught a glimpse of pale green and grey as the sea wind caused the sails to ripple.

On first approach, Cadell had not failed to glimpse the dark spaces below the main deck where he knew cannons lay waiting. From what he had been able to see he had counted at least sixteen holes, but he knew there were many more. A slight chill ran down his back as he realized this ship was far more deadly than even the stories about her described.

There were only a few torches lit and some crew members were finishing up their duties. The man Cadell followed led him across the main deck toward the stern where a short stairway led downward, past the gun deck and to the lower deck. This was where all the men's cabins would be. The man went down a couple of steps and spoke quietly with another man who allowed them entrance to a brightly lit room. Cadell paused, and then he moved into the room.

Cadell was shocked when he saw the female captain, sitting in a bolted chair behind a simple wooden desk. A rather burly-looking man held one of her hands, carving at her nails with a small piece of wood that had been flattened and smoothed.

For one, Cadell had expected his interview to be held in the captain's quarters on the deck above this one. Secondly, it was unheard of for a pirate to be given such luxury. Cadell was intrigued, curious, but of course, did not ask. This woman grew more fascinating the more he learned. She definitely hadn't grown up in common life, he thought. It was only a suspicion... but even the arrogant fae he had known as a child were not so privy to being pampered.

As soon as the large man finished tending to the woman's nails, she waved him away. After grabbing a silver goblet with a gargoyle clutching the cup, her eyes focused on him. "Please," she said, "take a seat." She gestured to another chair that faced hers. "What is your name?" she questioned, speaking properly and inspecting him closely. Her voice was silvery, soft, and pleasant.

Cadell looked around the room briefly, memorizing it. Even if this were not the captain's quarters, an assumption he made based on the room's location, he figured he wouldn't get to come here often. If she was like most captains he had spoken to, such a private meeting with the captain had to be for a very specific reason. He wondered what sort of captain he had once been. Still, he nodded, taking the seat. "Cadell. Just Cadell."

He noted her proper speech, which only raised even more questions, and again caused the thoughts of her past to echo in his mind. Aye, she was no commoner. He silently argued with himself whether or not he should respond in kind. He also had learned how to speak well in his childhood but had only done so in interactions with the fae kind. Otherwise, he had always used common language in order to better blend in.

Finally, he asked, "I'm curious if you'll be testing me, or merely asking questions?" He was now quite sure she was fae; that fact alone caused him to want to accommodate her speech. If nothing else, perhaps it might help this interview.

"I'll do whatever I please to deem if you're worthy to be a part of my ship," the woman replied calmly. Despite the softness in her voice, Cadell noticed her shoulders tense briefly when he mentioned his name, though she forcefully relaxed them and sat back. Was she trying to hide it? He silently tucked this piece of information away. Would she have recognized him, he wondered? It was a possibility... from the memories which evaded him. But other than the brief motion, she otherwise seemed to have no recognition. Maybe he had imagined it.

She took another sip of her goblet, beckoning one of the crewmembers over; he started to rub her shoulders and she visibly relaxed, sinking back into her chair.

After a moment of silence, she asked her next question. "So, Cadell, what makes you think that you can be a part of my crew? Why mine, and what stories have you heard of me?" Her eyes gleamed as she asked, a smirk tugging at the edge of her lip. Was she merely recalling a particularly pleasant memory, or was she eager to hear what he had to say? Perhaps both. Her reputation *was* a bloody one.

"Where to start? I could tell of the tales and legends I've heard, that the Gargoyle is run by no common woman. One myth, most intriguing, is of your ship here and a sea monster, at least in the tale. You weren't on the seas for long back then. It was you and a small crew pulled together to man the ship. There are different versions, but they all give the same idea. You, defeating that monster almost single-handedly, your ship almost being sunk to the bottom. Those hideous roars, the crash of the sea. How I'd give anything to have been there..." He trailed off slightly, yet quickly snapped back to attention. "The tale set your reputation."

Amethyst listened as Cadell spoke, remembering everything quite clearly. Her eyes closed as the memory of their encounter with the sea monster came back. She found it amusing that Stephan's defeat had become such an embellished tale where he was made out to be a sea beast.

Amethyst relaxed into her seat as her massage continued, enjoying her glass of rum. This Cadell intrigued her greatly, and she was briefly imagining him being on her crew. He would make a fine addition. He was handsome enough, for one, with his tousled dark hair and piercing black eyes. And with his broad shoulders and strong arms, he looked like he could take a lot of work. She briefly remembered eyeing him at his first approach in the pub. Despite his loose clothing, she had been able to note distinct muscles beneath his shirt.

The room had grown silent for a moment after Cadell finished recounting the tale for her. But not for long. She listened as his voice resumed, her eyes still closed. There was something about his voice that was smooth, calming.

Familiar.

"Well, to answer your question concerning my worthiness for this ship," he said. Cadell was silent for another moment, and she wondered what he was thinking. "I once was a captain myself. Before that," he stopped, "storm," he finished, his voice growing lower with his last word.

Amethyst opened her eyes as he mentioned his days as a captain. "Were you now, Mister Cadell?" She couldn't help but smirk. "It must have been a nasty affair for such a man as yourself to have been stripped of his position?" Amethyst paused, watching for his reaction.

She noted as briefly, his eyes grew darker and his lips curved in a frown at the mention of his little tragedy. "Aye," Cadell muttered, his voice that same low tone it had grown to at the mention of the storm.

Amethyst was silent a moment longer, simply staring at him. Aside from the things he had already mentioned, this very piece of knowledge was what sold him. As a previous captain, he would know his way around at least and would not need to be trained. Besides, she couldn't help thinking there was something about him which she wanted to learn more about.

"Very well," Amethyst stated. "I will hire you on and see how I like you. If I don't, I'll just throw you overboard with a cannonball tied to your feet!" she laughed heartily.

"Now, the rules. I am Captain Amethyst, and nothing more or less to you. No woman is *ever* allowed on my ship. Accept whatever payment you get without complaint and stay clean-shaven at all times. Otherwise..." She paused to rest her chin in her palm as she leaned forward for dramatic effect. "I'll hold you down and shave you myself. If in town, don't bother anyone without my order. I've got a reputation to upkeep. Mutiny equals torture, no gold allowed." She paused again, examining her nails. "Oh, and rules can change without notice. Think you got it?"

"Of course," Cadell said, tapping his head slightly. "So, what're my orders, Captain Amethyst?" She didn't fail to note the smirk tugging at his lips as he spoke her name. He seemed eager.

"First things first, you've got to get a brand," she said.

Amethyst snapped her fingers and the man rubbing her shoulders stopped and exited. A few moments later, he came back with an older man carrying some items, one which included a metal rod with an image formed at the end of it. It was the same as the insignia on her skull cap, the gargoyle with two silver daggers. The older man set up by the fireplace, poking the hot coals and resting the metal on top of it.

"Of course..." Cadell muttered, a scowl crossing his handsome features.

"Where do ye want it? It mus' be visible at all times," the man who would be branding him said as he looked at Cadell expectantly.

As the men prepared to mark Cadell as a member of her crew, Amethyst stood and leaned against the windowsill, watching as fog crept across the water and onto land. She gave a slight hiccup, putting more of her weight on the window.

Despite staring out the window, she listened to everything going on, still very much aware. She heard Cadell release his breath. "My forearm. Where else?" he said.

In the reflection of the window glass, she watched him hold out his arm, glaring at the wall while waiting. As the branding iron seared the mark into his skin, he grunted, though she could tell he did his best not to reveal signs of pain. She smirked slightly to herself. Good.

"Go ahead and shove off," Amethyst commanded sleepily, letting out a wide yawn. She felt so tired all of a sudden. "You'll be under First Mate Darien. He's upstairs. Not hard to miss. He'll give you orders," she told Cadell, setting her goblet down on the windowsill as she moved toward the stairway leading into the room. "As for me, I am retiring to my cabin. Good evening to you." As she started up the stairs, orders could be heard above, and the ship started to sway lightly as they set sail.

'*I guess that means now,*' Cadell thought, watching as the captain left. "G'night... Captain Amethyst," he muttered to her back. He raised his arm, glaring briefly at the still-burning mark on his forearm.

'*Captain Amethyst.*' Her name seemed permanently etched into his mind. There could be no doubt now. This was indeed the same woman who had clung to him so many years before. However, she seemed not only an entirely different person, but she showed no indication of remembering him now.

Besides, despite his inquiries, the other captains had revealed nothing. They had only *insisted* he forget and let it go. Was that what she had done, perhaps?

He resolved to keep it to himself. For now, he must focus on being the best crewmember he could be.

Soon, he left and quickly found the stairs Amethyst had mentioned. After climbing them, Cadell spotted two men speaking together and approached. He wondered if he should uphold the speech he had used with Amethyst or return to the common speech. He had no clue what being on board the *Gargoyle* was like and he figured much of the crew were more common than whatever origins Amethyst came from. "I'm new, an' was told to speak to Darien. Will ye' point me in the right direction?"

The man Cadell had asked grunted, moving from his position and forward toward one of the upper cabins. He knocked on the door. "Sir, there's another new member to tha crew. Cap'n sent him to ya." Cadell simply stood there and waited, arms hanging at his sides. He was eager to sleep and thus felt impatient to get this meeting over with. While he, the newest crewmember, knew the necessity of respecting the first mate, he also knew the hardest part was over.

"The door is unlocked lad. Come on in," a soft voice called out to him.

At the voice, Cadell turned the knob and entered, unsure of whether or not to close the door behind him. He settled on closing it partially and stepped forward.

In the room was a simple study. Behind the desk sat a man with dark navy hair, silver eyes flashing as they looked up. Was that surprise that crossed his features? Cadell wasn't sure if he had imagined it, as the man's face was once more stoic.

"Ah. Mister Cadell. Welcome to the Gargoyle. I am First Mate Darien, as you already know. Let me first say congratulations on making it to the crew. It isn't very often that we hire people on." He was extremely soft-spoken, but just as proper as Amethyst, Cadell noted. He decided then and there he would not speak so commonly on board as a member of the *Gargoyle*'s crew. He had a feeling it might raise his position faster among the rest of the crew.

Cadell glanced around the room briefly before his gaze fell on Darien again. First mate. He was more than he seemed. When Darien congratulated him, Cadell smiled and gave a slight nod. "Yes, so I heard... thanks."

"Your brand is to be visible at all times, but I'm sure you know that from your past as captain of the Reaper's Scythe." Darien looked back down, writing on the paper on his desk with a feather quill.

As Darien spoke again, Cadell blinked, caught off guard at the mention of his ship's name. No, he hadn't missed that look of surprise... and recognition on Darien's face. The *Reaper's Scythe?* He certainly hadn't mentioned the name of his ship to anyone on board.

Finally, Darien stood. "I will give you a small tour of the ship, give you your duties and release you." Darien headed toward the door rather quickly.

Cadell nodded in recognition that he understood and turned, following Darien out the door. "Aye," he muttered. Though he didn't admit it, he was excited about touring the ship, much like a young lad.

The ship was further out to seas now. "Drop anchor!" Darien commanded once they had moved far enough from port. Afterwards, Darien led Cadell around the ship, only showing him the kitchen, the dining room, the washroom, and the cabins, which were situated on the third level of the ship, the lower deck. The first mate finally stopped in front of one of the cabins, opening the door. It was plain inside. Two beds were on opposite sides with two small wardrobes. A desk sat near the window, covered in dust. He pointed to one bed that already had a pair of brown pants and a white sleeveless shirt. Boots and socks lay at the floor.

Cadell silently observed the different rooms and finally his own. He stepped in. It would do. He looked at the clothing. He preferred his own clothes, but he would make good use of them.

"This isn't a required uniform, but rather a small gift. You will be responsible for your own clothes to be washed," Darien stated.

Cadell nodded and muttered a brief, "Aye."

"For now, you do not have a roommate, so enjoy it while it lasts. Your first job will be to polish all weapons. Come to my study tomorrow at dawn and I will tell you where to go," Darien instructed. "Any questions?"

Cadell only shook his head and gave a brief smile. "I'll be fine. Just inform me on anything new such as getting a mate if it happens." He paused. "Suppose I'll see you in the morning." Once Darien left, Cadell closed the door and set about going to bed. He thought about his happiness at finally being out at sea and drifted off to sleep.

The crew of the ship were already busy early the next morning, just as the sun was rising over the watery horizon. Below deck, Cadell had been up an hour or so before sunrise, dressed and prepared for the day. Even so, he had felt no need to move about until closer to dawn. Cadell now easily climbed toward the main deck.

Amethyst was leaning against the rail with a mug in hand. Steam rose over the edge of the mug and he noted a faint, pleasant smile on his captain's lips as she sipped its contents. Her gaze was fixed on the sunrise. Suddenly, her mouth stretched into a wide grin and she began waving at something in the ocean. He saw what she was waving at jump from the ocean surface; it was a family of whales. She then began giggling gleefully.

Cadell was surprised, though slightly amused. He'd heard she was mad, but he'd never really believed it. Even now, he wondered if perhaps she was simply drinking something which made her more carefree. He approached Darien, who was standing near the middle of the deck, eyes on Amethyst and a soft smile on his own lips.

"Mornin'," Cadell said shortly. "What's first?"

Before Darien could respond, Amethyst whirled and moved excitedly toward them, a bounce in her step. "Oh!" she exclaimed, "I missed you yesterday, lovely!" Clearly, she was talking to Darien as she planted a kiss on her first mate's cheek and handed him her mug. "How are you this morning? Have you had breakfast yet?"

Darien shook his head, his smile having widened into a grin. The first mate still was silent.

Cadell was entirely unsure how to react as he watched the two. It seemed Amethyst wanted to leave him as shocked as possible: she grasped Cadell's hand and pulled him toward the side of the ship.

"You must see the whales," she told him excitedly, pointing toward the water as the great creatures emerged and sank beneath the surface. "Aren't they lovely?" the captain asked with a sigh.

Cadell folded his arms and rested his elbows on the side-railing of the ship, watching the whales, and he nodded. "Aye, they are," he said slowly. This was hardly what he had imagined aboard the *Gargoyle*. Maybe she really was mad. Or maybe she was a normal woman behind her bloody reputation. One thing did cause a wave of relief in him: it wasn't all work. They were here to enjoy the sea in all of its pleasures, which satisfied him.

"Oh, yes. They're so lovely. And so friendly!" Amethyst responded and waved a couple more times. Finally, she turned her gaze toward her first mate. "Darien, stop the ship please," she requested.

"Aye, aye, Captain," Darien responded. A bit later the vessel was stopped.

"Thank you, lovely!" Amethyst said as she smiled at him, removing her skullcap. She sat down and took off her boots and socks. "Come look for me in an hour," she said, climbing onto the side of the ship and then diving into the sea.

Darien only laughed, turning back to Cadell. "Are you hungry, Cadell?" he questioned.

Cadell nodded in agreement, glancing at Darien, then out toward the sea once again. "Aye..." he responded, baffled. Despite his confusion, Cadell suddenly felt an attachment to their captain. He desperately wanted to know more about her.

"You'll have to excuse the captain. She likes to go swimming every now and again." Darien watched as Amethyst swam. "Sometimes she acts like a child. But she is certainly not to be taken lightly. She is still this ship's captain and each of us would do anything for her. She deserves whatever she wishes at this point."

"I see," Cadell murmured. Amethyst's antics were good to know, and it was also a good reminder that no matter how laid back everything seemed, he couldn't be too careful.

The first mate sighed. "If you would, join me in my office for a chat and a bit of breakfast before you start working." After shouting orders to the lookout to watch Amethyst, Darien started toward his quarters. They were right beside the captain's quarters, just below the main deck, though they used the same stairway he had first descended before his interview; they stopped on the second level, the gun deck, instead of climbing all the way down.

When they entered Darien's office, a breakfast of steaming food was set out on the first mate's desk, along with two plates and two goblets of juice. "Please, take a seat," Darien said. He took a seat himself followed by a sip of his drink, and finally he looked at Cadell.

Cadell obeyed. Was it their custom to do this with all new recruits? Should he ask Darien about the past, since the first mate had clearly recognized him the day before? "So what did you want to talk about?" he questioned slowly, hiding the fact he was also a bit eager to eat.

"How much do you really know about the captain? I mean, besides her pirate life," Darien asked as he ate a bit of ham.

Cadell drank some of his juice. It was freshly squeezed. At first, he was taken aback at Darien's question, although he now knew why he was not dining with the crew. This must be some sort of assurance he was not here to carry out any devious plots against the captain. He pondered a moment at Darien's question and finally answered slowly. "Very little. From stories and legends, I'm seeing more of it's true than I'd expect, but who wouldn't know of her? She drives one of the fiercest ships at sea."

Cadell paused, taking another sip of his drink and beginning to chew on a biscuit followed by some eggs. "For her personal life, I've heard of a son and her alliance with his father aboard the *Golden Lion*. Met the captain of that ship before. He's a strange lad. Good captain though."

Darien nodded. "Yes, he'll be turning five this year, her son." He paused and seemed to observe Cadell for a moment. At last, Darien spoke clearly. "You know, the *Golden Lion*'s captain was just one of the many men Amethyst has taken to her bed. She can be rather promiscuous." He stabbed his eggs and chewed thoughtfully on them, letting what he had said and all it implied sink in.

Cadell was not really surprised to hear such information about his captain. He'd heard she tended to be a bit like that. But even so, he felt a strange feeling of disappointment as well as jealousy flit through him. He stared at his plate a moment, dismissing the feelings. It wasn't like he had any right to feel jealousy, he reminded himself.

"I hope it goes without saying how you will be expected to respond if she asks," Darien said softly.

Cadell hesitated before giving a slight nod, meeting Darien's eyes and showing he at least understood. "Anything else I should know?"

Darien shook his head.

Before he could stop himself, an unexpected question tumbled from Cadell's mouth. "Tell me... has she ever had one man in her life?"

Darien sighed, appearing as though he were not at all surprised by the question. "Twice. The first is the reason for everything that happened to her in the beginning. Her first ex-husband." Darien paused, as if debating how to word the answer. "He was with her right before she became a pirate. Sometimes I wonder what would've happened to her if I had not been there. No one would've rescued her. He abused her, in more than imaginable ways. In fact, it wasn't until four or five years of being in the open sea for her to even consider bringing a man to her bed. The one she had been with had ruined that experience."

"When she realized that this could be very... fun," Darien continued slowly, seeming to be in thought once more, "she became addicted to the pleasure, like her rum. Of course, she's calmed down over the many years she's been sailing." Darien stopped, eating more of his food.

Cadell nodded slowly, replying only with, "Suppose she owes you a lot then, in a way." He was glad of Darien if he had rescued her from such a man. Cadell glanced off for a moment before turning his attention toward Darien once more.

"The second... well, a tragic tale." Cadell's and Darien's eyes met, briefly, and Cadell felt as though Darien were trying to read him. Finally, the first mate bit into a piece of toast. Apparently, he didn't want to elaborate on this tragic tale. "It wasn't until five years ago, when she met up with the captain of the *Golden Lion*, that she seriously started to consider her relationship with him. Of course, she still has trouble with it, especially when she comes into her season," Darien finished. Afterward, he smiled. "The rest of her story is not mine to tell just yet, and that is enough for now. You still have work to do," he said.

"Aye, I do, and I shouldn't waste too much time talking. But..." He paused again. "What sort of attention does the Gargoyle typically draw?" Cadell needed to know so he'd be prepared for any attacks. Or so he thought.

"It can go either way. Sometimes people come to us, but we go to them as well. Especially when the captain gets into one of her moods," Darien said with a shrug. "I just hope you don't mind killing even without reason sometimes." The first mate took another bite of breakfast. "Anyway, lunch is when the sun is highest, unless otherwise stated. Dinner is announced, usually. We don't care where you eat breakfast and lunch as long as you clean up afterwards. But everyone eats dinner together. Also, you are to report to me when you have completed your tasks or need help. When the alarm bell rings, you drop anything you're doing, and you assemble at the bow of the boat. Understand?" Darien asked, looking intently at Cadell.

Cadell nodded. "Shouldn't be a problem." He didn't want to just up and leave, so he asked, "Should I be off then?"

"Yes, go ahead and go on," Darien stated politely, picking up a piece of an iced pastry. "If you need anything, just ask anyone around the ship and they'll be glad to help you. Don't forget to come to me when you're done so I can assign you another job."

Cadell nodded. "Aye..." He turned, hesitating a moment, then walked out, closing the door behind him. He looked up at the sky that was turning bluer and smiled before moving to the weapons room.

All the weapons lay piled up, dirty and in dire need of cleaning. Polish and cloths lay to the side, patiently waiting for him to use them.

Cadell began working on polishing and cleaning the pile of weapons before him. He hadn't been responsible for polishing in a while, he thought, and yet he had done it in the past enough to know exactly what he was doing. The task wouldn't take too long. Now and then, he glanced off, thinking of the captain.

# Wreckage

Cadell paused from his work and looked out toward the sky. The sun was nearing its high point. He sighed and raised his arm to wipe some sweat off his brow. He was nearly done.

He couldn't help the swell of pride in his work, smiling as he examined the weapons. The freshly cleaned and polished weapons gleamed in the sunlight. Cadell then glanced toward upper deck. It was time to meet once more with Darien.

Cadell jumped as soon as he set foot on the deck; the alarm bell began to ring madly. As he'd been instructed previously, Cadell rushed forward toward the bow of the ship, joined by the rest of the crew who appeared from other areas of the ship. The captain was already present, staring intently through a scope across the waters.

Not so far away was another ship floating without any sense of direction. Its sails were red in color though they were tattered and hung lifelessly. The image of a crouched golden lion was barely visible amongst the shreds of the sails and there appeared to be no life aboard the deck.

A sense of dread took hold of those aboard the *Gargoyle*. Amethyst turned to her crew, her face somber. "Speed the ship up," she barked out loudly, and several men exited and headed below deck. Soon, the ship lurched forward as the vessel began to truly move. She turned back around to look down her scope.

Darien came to Amethyst's side and they began to talk quietly. As soon as the first mate turned away, Darien's eyes met Cadell's.

"Come with me," Darien ordered. "Help me get the plank ready to board." Already they were approaching the other ship rapidly. Amethyst continued to look uneasy and as they drew closer, she grew jittery. The crew were not arming themselves, but their faces were grim.

Cadell looked at Darien, trying to assess his face while following his order. He glanced up at the ship they were quickly approaching and finally noticed the etching on the side of the ship. *'Bloody hell.'* Cadell frowned slightly to himself yet turned back to what he was doing, only sparing another concerned look as they followed Amethyst's next instruction.

"Lower the plank!" Amethyst yelled as soon as the hull was brushing near them. Ropes were tossed overboard from the *Gargoyle* and hooked the other ship, keeping it steady as they dropped anchor. A wave of silence settled over as they finally saw what was on board.

Dead bodies were skewered across the decks, blood staining what seemed every inch of the surface. Amethyst was deathly still, turning paler than the sails above. As soon as the plank lowered, she dashed across it.

The entire crew were in shock. Although all of them had seen such a sight before... this was somehow different. Cadell told himself he had to remember his place on this ship and had to resist the urge to dash across the plank as well. He wasn't captain; he wasn't first mate; he was the newest crewmember. "What happened here?" he muttered darkly under his breath.

A bloody murderous scream like a banshee echoed from somewhere aboard the other ship and Cadell cringed. Darien cursed under his breath. "Men, explore the ship for any survivors," the first mate barked before motioning for Cadell to follow him as he headed across the plank.

Cadell followed Darien as he was commanded. It was strange the way Darien seemed to keep him close, as if under constant scrutiny, or perhaps because he knew more about his previous life as a captain than he let on.

Darien stopped in front of a room in which Amethyst sat. She was sobbing uncontrollably over a bed, one that held the body of a young man with soft brown eyes open wide in shock. A dagger was sticking from his heart, a note pinned to it. This man, Cadell recognized instantly, was none other than the father of Amethyst's son.

This ship was the remains of the *Golden Lion.*

Cadell moved forward after Darien. "Who?" he muttered under his breath '*Could have done this,*' his mind finished for him. Rage swelled, but he waited in the doorway.

"Amethyst," Darien breathed softly, approaching their weeping captain slowly. When he was close enough, the first mate managed to pull her away from the dead body and blood-soaked mattress to hold her tightly in a hug. She clutched onto Darien's shirt, sobbing hysterically.

"Captain," Darien said softly, stroking her hair gently, trying to calm her. Darien looked to Cadell. "Go see what the others have found," he stated firmly, continuing to hold Amethyst.

Cadell only managed a short nod and he turned and left.

On the main deck, the crew were moving among the dead bodies. The man who had met Cadell on the docks the previous day approached him. "We have found Amethyst's son. He... he's still alive, er... half alive, if you can call it half."

The man turned and led Cadell through a maze of dead bodies before reaching their captain's son. The boy was scrawny and there was no way to discern what he truly looked like beneath the cuts and slashes which covered his skin. Blood was caked across his clothes and matted his hair and he lay limply, barely breathing. The sight was awful.

"Help me with the boy?" Cadell asked softly.

He didn't want to take any chances of dropping him and hurting him any worse. As soon as they had the boy safely in Cadell's arms, the others followed as he carried him gently toward the captain and first mate. As soon as they reached them, Cadell spoke, "Captain, we've found your son. He's still alive. Barely, but alive."

"My baby," Amethyst whispered, tearing away from Darien to gently touch her son's face. "Ercio, can you hear me?" she asked softly, tears dripping down her face. She looked up and cried out with a shriek. "Someone get the doctor!"

After making her command clear, Amethyst huddled closer to her son. With gentleness, she lifted her son's arm up and kissed the wounds. As she kissed him, her lips moved in a strange fashion and her eyes glowed.

Cadell did not use his heightened senses to listen to her, but he wondered if she were whispering words of healing in her native tongue. "Please stay alive. For Mommy," she whispered more audibly, her fingers trembling as they touched the boy.

Amethyst glanced up sharply toward Darien. "Leo was bringing him to me." She paused. "The bastard will pay."

All remained silent and glanced toward the door when the doctor came down, also a member of the *Gargoyle*'s crew. The doctor hurriedly rushed toward Ercio's side and touched Amethyst gently. "I don' know if he'll live, Cap'n, but I'll do what I can." He smiled faintly and then made a slight motion toward her son. He needed to get him somewhere safe and comfortable.

Cadell gently passed Ercio, as Amethyst had called him, to another crew member, who followed the doctor.

The doctor paused briefly and glanced back at his captain. "Cap'n, me thinks it'd be best if ye come along, t' be there for him. But that's up to ye." With that he turned and left, accompanying the men who were taking Amethyst's son back across the plank onto the *Gargoyle*.

Darien moved to help Amethyst, but she only pushed him away. "I'll be fine," she whispered, following after the doctor in a stumble.

Darien let out a sigh, then slammed his fist into the nightstand, making the wood shatter. Splinters stuck out from his bloody knuckles, but he paid it no concern. The first mate went over to the dead body and pulled the dagger from it, snatching the already bloodied letter away from the gush of more blood that followed from the blade being extracted.

He scanned over the paper and then cursed and turned towards Cadell, who had been feeling rather helpless. "Help me with the body, Cadell," Darien instructed. His normally soft voice had turned rough and low as he grabbed the arms of the slain pirate captain.

Cadell resisted his own urge to shatter a piece of wood. Instead, he nodded when he was instructed and grasped the man's legs. He helped Darien move the deceased captain.

They set the body down on the main deck, watching as the other bodies were piled up. "Go over there and help finish piling the dead," Darien ordered before turning and heading toward the *Gargoyle*. Cadell wondered if Darien was going to find Amethyst. There was no doubt she needed some support right now.

Amethyst was leaning against the wall, holding herself tightly. She barely heard Darien's entrance as he approached and grasped her firmly. She buried her face in his shirt, trying to hide her sobs. She felt a little stronger as she felt his chin rest firmly against the top of her head.

Behind her, the doctor was working on the boy, caring for his wounds. At first, he had set about cleaning his patient, blood staining red both his rag and the water in his basin as it ran from the body. He had then taken some of Amethyst's blood and given it to the boy. Finally, in the secrecy of the room, his eyes glowed softly as he whispered foreign words while he worked, using magic to help the healing.

The wounds were already beginning to close from the attention Amethyst had given them before as well as the doctor's work now. It helped also that he was now using stitches, particularly on the gashes and larger wounds. The doctor bandaged what he could.

Amethyst was glad her son was unconscious; his body must be in so much pain. With how much blood that had already escaped him, she was amazed and just glad he was even still alive. She silently prayed the doctor's work would be a success.

Time seemed to drag on and on. The doctor was almost done with what he could do. He worked slowly, careful to avoid any mistakes.

At last, he was done. Amethyst heard him step back and sigh. He glanced her and Darien's way, his eyes narrowing a bit and growing soft. "Cap'n, he needs t' rest. After that, we'll need t' give it time." With that, he began to leave the room, his face ashen and solemn.

Now that the blood no longer hid his features, Ercio's face was clearly visible, so calm despite the wounds which would scar. He had dirty blond hair with wisps of soft blue and handsome features despite his young age. His skin was freckled, and its tan color showed long hours in the sun. Once he awoke, Amethyst knew his light brown eyes would further remind her of his now-deceased father.

Amethyst reached out a hand toward him but drew it back. She shouldn't disturb him. She turned to her first mate. "Construct a pallet in here for me. I will stay in here with him until he is better. I want you to burn the ship and set it afloat again. Put... put his body with his crew." She couldn't yet bring herself to say it. Leo was dead. The *Golden Lion* was destroyed.

"He would've wanted a burial at sea, not on land. His spirit would be confined to the shores, just in reach of the waves but never able to touch them. This way his spirit can be free to roam the sea. Afterward, I want you to take us to somewhere where we can all rest in peace."

Darien nodded and hugged her gently before heading out.

Amethyst's son slept peacefully but groaned now and then in his sleep. She knew he needed as much rest and support as possible. She lay down beside her son's bed, tears still dripping down her cheeks as she too drifted off to sleep.

Night had fallen and the crew had been busy since discovering the massacred remains of the *Golden Lion*. As soon as the first mate was seen leaving the sickbay, Cadell heard Darien shouting orders. "Get torches lighted! We're setting the ship on fire and letting it drift!"

The crew moved quickly, obeying orders. Cadell approached Darien, feeling driven to voice some concerns, "How're the captain and her son?" He wasn't sure why he cared so much. He just couldn't shake the feelings lying somewhere within him.

Darien was silent at first, arms folded across his chest as he stared across to the *Golden Lion*'s main deck where the rest of the crew were finishing up with their orders. The first mate finally spared Cadell a brief glance. "The chances of her son surviving are rising, but we are not out of troubled waters yet. How the captain comes out depends on her son," he stated gravely.

Cadell slowly nodded.

As the *Golden Lion* began to burn, Darien spoke once again, "Thank you for your help. You may go to your cabin now. I will expect you in the morning."

Cadell only nodded once more and left.

# Another Dream

Amethyst was burnt badly after a day of being out on the ship. Heedless of whether her lover was in her room or not, she began to strip off her clothes. Leaving a trail of clothing on the floor, she headed into the small washroom attached to her cabin.

The cool water from her tub stung the burns. Amethyst was grateful, however, for the magic which allowed her to bathe even at sea.

Once she finished bathing, Amethyst sprawled across her bed on her stomach. She grabbed a blanket and covered up her lower half. Moving her hair, she exposed her reddened back from the fires of war which continued to rage. Her tipped ears relaxed against her hair, but she was extremely alert. She was waiting for her companion to come in so she could tell him to fetch the lotion and perhaps assist her in putting it on her back. Her eyes flickered closed as she drifted off.

From beyond her door, there was a heavy sigh and a soft curse from a deep voice. Her ears twitched lightly as the door creaked open and the soft thud of boots sounded against the floor as he stepped in. She smiled as he cracked his neck and then sat down on the bed beside her, beginning to squeeze lotion out of the bottle he grabbed from her nightstand.

She didn't even have to ask him.

*His hands were calloused from hard work, but nevertheless, he began to gently rub the lotion into her exposed back. She hissed softly at the feel of the cold lotion against her burns.*

*"Ho, Amethyst, you got it bad this time." Cadell paused, his hands continuing to massage the lotion into her red skin. "How're you feeling," he asked softly. His breath was warm on her ear as he leaned closer.*

*"I hurt," Amethyst muttered, nuzzling into her pillow as her back arched lightly, "but this makes the hurt feel better."*

*They both glanced up at the sound of shouting, clanging swords, and roaring fires that carried in through the window. How much longer was this war going to last? It had been going a while, and though the enemy ships were lessening in number, the list of allies was also growing thin. They'd managed to defeat the enemy ships they had faced so far, but this war seemed endless, and it seemed only a question of how much longer they would last.*

*Amethyst turned her thoughts from the war. Cadell was her strongest ally and the man she had chosen... the one she loved more deeply than any other.*

*"Cadell, you have the softest touch," she murmured approvingly. "I couldn't have asked for better. How are you? I know you got just as burned as I did. In fact, once you're done with me, I'll return the favor. How does that sound?" Amethyst asked, her gaze meeting his as she turned her head.*

*Cadell's mouth curved into a grin. "Mm... ye know that's not true. My hands are only trying to soothe ye. But, I'm glad this makes ye feel better." He leaned down close to her once more, so close his breath tickled her skin, as if to kiss her, and then drew back up. "The returned favor... It sounds alright. Long as ye don't mind."*

*"Maybe the fighting will die down just for a little bit and give us some peace and quiet. I feel as if I haven't slept in days." Amethyst sighed, continuing to enjoy his soothing massage.*

*Cadell turned his gaze toward the window again, frowning as he nodded at her statement. "Aye, I know what ye mean. Ye know Darien and Aurek will keep an eye on things if we wanted to take a break."*

*Amethyst smiled at his suggestion, closing her eyes. "They are such good men."*

*His warmth was soothing as he leaned toward her again. "Do ye want to?" Cadell murmured, implying his unspoken desires.*

*"Can we just... cuddle?" Amethyst asked slowly, opening her golden eyes to meet his dark ones. She looked exhausted and he assumed she wanted to rest.*

*"As ye wish." He paused. "Tell me when ye want me to stop. I could rub ye like this forever." Cadell's smile was full of light-heartedness, despite the raging war outside the cabin.*

*She knew he was trying to lighten the mood given the struggles they had been through lately, and that he hated to see her down even about something small. His hands gently moved down her back and back up again, massaging her. "Just relax," Cadell whispered.*

*He glanced around the room, then toward the bathroom, then finally back at her, "Ye don't really want to cuddle with a dirty pirate do ye?"*

*"I was wondering what that smell was," Amethyst teased with a chuckle.*

*Cadell grinned and shook his head. "Oh, I see. So wenches really don't care for stinky men. Ah, well. It can't be helped." He laughed, his eyes dancing with teasing mischief, and then he stood, tracing a finger gently down her back before he turned, heading to wash.*

*"Hurry so I can return your favor and we can cuddle," she demanded, letting out a large yawn. "Perhaps we can catch a nap together. You make the best pillow."*

*"Aye, aye," he said as he opened the door.*

*Amethyst had become very attached to him over the last year. Already they were bound to each other... yet it had still* taken time for her to really overcome all the damage that had been done in her past. She had finally been able to move on and open her heart once again.

Whenever he put his hands on her, whenever they were close together, even whenever he just walked into the room, her heart always gave a little flutter. Late at night when there was no fighting, she would lie awake and think over that feeling in her heart. This was real love.

Cadell was similar to Amethyst in his thoughts. He had thought she was a fine beauty when he'd first laid eyes on her, but he'd discovered her beauty within as he'd gotten to know her. At first, he'd agreed to an alliance with the threat of upcoming war. But soon, their alliance had grown into much more, and while he understood the scars of her past, even if he didn't know the full extent, he cared deeply for her and strongly desired to earn her truest love.

Cadell stripped and got into the tub, letting the water from the spout above pour over him for a moment. He winced as the water stung his open wounds, yet he let out a sigh and began to wipe down. There were indeed many benefits to being allies with a fae captain, including the magic flowing through her ship.

After he was done bathing, he got out of the tub and dried off with one of Amethyst's fluffy, pale towels. He opened the door to the bathroom, shaking his head slightly and sending a few remaining droplets flying into the air. His usually tousled, dark hair was still wet, and it hung loosely over his broad, strong shoulders, tanned yet red with burns and scars.

As he entered her room again, Cadell saw that Amethyst, while he was in the shower, had gotten up and slipped on one of his shirts. She had once told him she enjoyed his scent and *found it comforting. She was rubbing lotion in her hands and sitting up on the bed.*

*Cadell moved toward the bed. "How is that smell now?" he asked.*

*She leaned over, sniffing his shoulder. "Much better," Amethyst said. "It's not that I don't like stinky pirates, but I just bathed myself and I want to feel clean, if only for an hour."*

*"Of course," he said with a smile.*

*Amethyst talked casually as her hands rested on his burnt skin and began to rub. Her hands, opposite of his, were smooth. "Feel better?" she questioned, her hands going over every inch of his back and shoulders.*

*Cadell closed his eyes and relaxed into her touch. "Aye," Cadell murmured, "Thank you, Amethyst." His words were soft.*

*They fell quiet while she continued massaging his back.*

*After a bit of time, he opened his eyes. He turned and curled his arm loosely about her and rested his head against hers, staring down at the blanket on the bed.*

*She moved closer to him, eyes half-open. "Cadell, what do you want to do after this war is over and we are both alive?" Amethyst whispered.*

*Cadell hesitated a moment when she asked him that. "Guess I hadn't gotten that far... Perhaps we'll put the war behind us and settle together." He gave her a light squeeze as a gesture of a hug, his fingers curling around her own. "What 'bout you?"*

*"I want to be one of the first female pirate captains to ever terrorize the seas," Amethyst stated in an almost dreamy voice. "You'll come along, won't you?" she asked, looking up at him hopefully, her eyes shining in the dim light. "I'll need someone to help me man the ship." She nuzzled under his chin, blinking slowly. "I want to be feared. I want everyone to know that a woman can be just as good a pirate captain as any man," she stated boldly.*

*"Man the ship? I'll come along only to sail beside ye, darling." He chuckled and wrapped his other arm around her.*

*"So, it's a promise then?" he asked gently, staring blankly at the wall. At this point, he didn't even hear the fighting just outside this room. He only heard her and her alone. "I wish ye good luck on yer goal."*

Amethyst woke with a start. Her tanned skin gleamed in the pale moonlight shining in through the window. She blinked sleepily, sitting up and looking momentarily at her son. Her son wasn't on her mind. Cadell was. The war, her heart learning to love again. She racked her brain to try and remember the rest but found she could not. '*Why?*' she thought desperately. What had happened?

Then Amethyst remembered. She had deliberately buried those memories. Yet the spell must be weakening with Cadell being so near to her now. Was it truly mere coincidence that after all this time, he had simply walked back into her life? The tragic story Darien had mentioned to Cadell was his own. She could still feel his hands massaging her back and she jammed a fist in her mouth to keep from crying out and waking her resting son. She had to talk to Cadell. But would he remember? Even if it was only this little bit?

Amethyst slowly stood, looking at the doorway. She didn't want to abandon her son, yet she wanted to talk to Cadell. Needed to talk to him. She stepped outside and grabbed the nearest crewmember, talking to him briefly. She instructed him to remain with her son while she took care of some business. The crewmember went inside to sit with Ercio while she began moving quickly down toward the lower deck and across the ship toward where she knew Cadell's cabin was.

Cadell sat up, staring out of his own window and into the night. He groaned and rubbed his eyes before turning and putting his feet on the floor. He cursed to himself and moved his fingers up to his chin, then away. This dream was different than all the ones he had been having, and he wondered why all of a sudden that specific event had come. He was confused by the torment of his amnesia, but this dream he had hardly hated. Cadell knew there was something heavy just beneath the surface.

But the memories remained a foggy blur.

After this dream, Cadell knew one thing: his loss of memories had been the result of a great war. Because of that war, he lost everything important to him. But he still couldn't remember much of anything. The memories were coming back. Slowly. Cadell desperately wanted to know what had happened.

He sighed and finally rose to his feet. At least one more thing had become clear. Amethyst was the woman in his dreams. Her image was still vivid in his mind. There was no mistaking her face and fae features.

But there was no way she'd remember. Cadell doubted he should ask her.

After all, as Darien had said, she slept with someone new every now and then, being promiscuous. How could she be expected to remember each one? Cadell lazily pulled on his clothes and began to leave his cabin.

As soon as his door closed, he stopped, leaning back against the wood and staring up at the starlit sky. "Amethyst..." he whispered to himself, closing his eyes for a moment. He told himself he must not mention anything. Amethyst was already worked up with her son. His mind still swam with curiosity about why he'd had this specific dream now.

"Cadell." Cadell jumped at the soft whisper of Amethyst's voice. His cheeks grew warm. He shouldn't feel anxious. It's not like she would remember anything.

Cadell pulled himself together. "Yes, Captain?" He began to move toward her, "How's your son doing?"

"He's still sleeping," Amethyst responded.

"Oh," Cadell said.

It was silent a moment except for the gentle waves swishing against the side of the ship. Amethyst was staring at him straight in the eyes, her brows curved in a curious and uncertain way.

Finally, her features settled, and she blurted out, "Have you ever worked with me before? I had the strangest dream, or maybe memory. But we were... together." She shifted on her feet, and as soon as she had spoken, her gaze fell to the floor, hands flying behind her back.

Cadell's gaze fell also, then toward her face again. "So, it wasn't just a dream then," he whispered.

She sucked in her breath at his comment.

"I had the same dream," he explained.

"Will... will you come back with me? To my son's room? I want to talk to you, but I wish not to leave him alone." Her large eyes looked hopeful, yet almost fearing.

Cadell nodded slowly, "Of course."

Amethyst turned and began moving back the way she had come.

Cadell waited a moment before following after her. As he walked, his mind was reeling. He remembered the longing he had had for her before. Vaguely. Perhaps more so from the recent dream than anything. But just this sliver of a memory was nothing. There was no way to suddenly regain everything he had lost. Still, he knew she needed comfort.

What Darien said flitted through his mind.

As soon as they entered her son's room, the other crewmember there left. Amethyst closed the door softly. She moved effortlessly across the room and sat by her son on his bed. As she stroked two fingers through her son's hair, she spoke. "What happened, Cadell? Why did we ever separate?"

He remained near the door, simply giving her space. Cadell was silent at her question. What could he possibly say? Amethyst was clearly an emotional wreck right now. He watched fat tears start to roll down her cheeks and he now noticed the large bags under her eyes.

Was this truly the reputable captain he had heard so much about?

Or perhaps was this merely a side of her the rest of the world never saw? He knew it was also possible she was simply broken for the moment.

Before he could help himself, or even stop to think about it, Cadell half darted across the room, kneeling at her side. He raised a finger and gently wiped the tears from her cheek. Her skin was as soft as her hands had been in the dream.

Finally, Cadell sat down beside her. He glanced toward her son briefly, concerned, yet turned his attention on Amethyst once again. "I don't remember. My only memories aside from this dream are those where my ship sank, my crew with it, and..."

Some fresh memories came rushing back into his head, of the screams and fires and roars of both cannons and storm. Cadell gazed at the wall blankly a moment, then glanced down. He was feeling overwhelmed with the combination of recent events, his memories, or lack thereof, and the emotions toward Amethyst flooding his system.

"When I recovered, after my ship, I couldn't remember anything. I've had only dreams as clues since." Cadell paused. "It's a small world, eh? I tried my luck on land for a while, but deep down I knew I belonged at sea. Yours is the only crew that seemed to fit despite trying several others."

Amethyst was silent again, staring at his chest. She was biting her lip, and her brows shifted. She looked as though something else wanted to escape. But this time she didn't tell him. Instead, she finally met his gaze again and her eyes were shaky. "I'm so sorry, Cadell," was all she could say, her voice breaking and more tears spilling over.

Cadell gulped slightly, still hesitant, before gently wrapping his arms around her shoulders and giving a slight tug. "Amethyst, it's not yer fault." He paused as she sobbed, and finally pulled her to him in a hug.

Amethyst sniffled and finally seemed to relax in his embrace. "I know I've been with other men in the past, but do you think we could try again?" She looked up again, her eyes half-lidded with fatigue. Her arms wrapped around his middle. "I want to try again."

Cadell felt conflicted. Was this really a good idea? Especially now? "Perhaps ye should rest, Captain," he murmured.

Amethyst smiled, and only nodded, continuing to chew on her lip. She looked at her son once more. Finally, with a fluid motion, she slipped toward her pallet. Amethyst tugged at Cadell's hand briefly. He understood her silent question as if she had said it out loud. '*Stay with me tonight?*'

Cadell did not resist and he lay down beside her, curling an arm around her. If nothing else, he hoped she would be able to get some rest.

It wouldn't be long before he knew Darien would come looking for the captain, questioning if she and her son were alright. He wondered how the first mate would react. At least now it also made more sense why Darien seemed to know what he did. But now Cadell was curious if he also remembered only some or more than they thought? To Amethyst, he murmured, "Try to get some rest."

Amethyst nodded again, burrowing close to him. Her body relaxed and her eyes closed. "Thank you... Cadell..." she whispered as she drifted off to sleep.

# Caught

Cadell was right. Darien came in around sunrise, opening the door and peeking in.

By the time Darien came in, Cadell had also drifted off to sleep. He had been extremely relaxed with the warmth of Amethyst against him. Perhaps to Darien, the scene the first mate saw was entirely barbaric and Cadell should be dispatched immediately, seeing as Darien had specifically told him the captain would probably ask him to bed and he must resist her.

Yet, Cadell had felt the circumstances were different than what Darien had mentioned. He and Amethyst were not complete strangers to each other. At least in Cadell's mind, it was justified. Once the door opened, it didn't take Cadell but a few moments before his eyes slowly opened. He had a feeling they were no longer alone. He pushed himself upward and began rubbing his eyes. At last, he glanced toward the door. "Darien!" he said as he jolted himself from the cot and stood. Cadell looked back toward Amethyst.

She jerked in her sleep but did not wake. Darien frowned, then said, "Mister Cadell, if I could speak with you alone." The first mate stepped outside the door frame, waiting for their newest crew member to come outside. Already the sun was starting to rise.

Cadell nodded toward Darien, then leaned close to Amethyst. "I'll be right back," he whispered. Now that his initial shock was gone, calm settled in his chest. Already Cadell was planning his explanation. Still, perhaps he should worry a little. He was the newest crew member on board and facing the first mate.

Cadell stepped outside, blinking in the bright morning sun, and then closed the door behind him. He gazed down for a moment, before looking up, leaning back against the wall and folding his arms across his chest. "I know what you want to say," he said softly, glancing at Darien.

"Very well, I will keep myself short. I just wanted to say that even though I do not like you being with Amethyst after such a short time of knowing her, I accept her decision to be with you. But I will be watching you," Darien said.

Cadell nodded, though was a bit surprised at this response.

"Darien, we remember." Cadell glanced at Darien only briefly. He noted the way Darien's brow rose a moment in surprise, and then a small smile tugged at the corner of his lip. He shrugged and seemed to accept Cadell's statement. It wasn't entirely true, but it seemed enough for now.

Finally, Cadell moved past Darien and back into the room with Amethyst and her son. He needed to prepare for a new day. But he decided to wait until Amethyst woke first.

Amethyst cracked open an eye. "Hmm?" she asked softly, letting out a yawn.

Cadell smiled down at Amethyst, "Sorry to disturb you," he murmured softly. "You just missed Darien. Had to explain a bit." He paused, tracing her tanned arm slowly.

"Oh, well, you're still in one piece, so that's a good thing." She smiled sleepily up at him and shivered lightly at his touch.

Cadell only smiled and nodded slightly. "I guess so." Cadell paused. "Mind if I take a few minutes?" he asked.

"Sure," Amethyst murmured.

"I'll be back," he said. With that, Cadell turned and left.

Just as he had promised, Cadell returned to Ercio's room within a short time of leaving. As he peeked in the door, only Darien was present, sitting calmly on Amethyst's cot from the night before and reading a book. "Pardon, where's Amethyst?" Cadell asked.

"She's bathing," he replied simply.

"Ah," Cadell said, nodding faintly, "I see." He was about to leave when Darien spoke again.

"Were you going to go find her or stay here with Ercio until she comes back?" Darien asked.

Cadell shrugged and stepped in. "I can stay." He moved toward Darien. "I'll watch him." When Darien left, he took his seat and waited patiently for Amethyst to return.

While he waited, Cadell gazed over the sleeping lad's figure. He wondered if when the boy woke, he would give any clues to who the attacker had been.

About an hour later, Amethyst returned. Cadell glanced up at her entrance and noted the way her eyes softened as she met his gaze. "Thank you for watching him, Cadell," she said, leaning against the doorway, hiccupping. Early morning and already tipsy.

"Aye, Captain. He's fine." He mirrored her volume, trying to be reassuring given the emotional instability he could only imagine raged in her.

"Won't you join me for breakfast on the deck? I'll have someone else watch my son for a little bit. I don't like being cramped up in the room. Perhaps we could take a swim. I like swimming. It's fun," Amethyst babbled lightly.

"Sure, starving anyway." Cadell paused, glancing back at her son and then moved toward her. He couldn't help himself as he took in her figure outlined by the glow of the morning sun. Feelings of jealousy flitted through him at the thought of her other numerous lovers. Cadell didn't fail to notice how quickly she seemed to have gotten over the fact that only yesterday they had discovered her most recent lover and his entire crew massacred. Or perhaps that was the reason for her losing herself in her rum this time of day.

The bags under her eyes he had seen the previous night were still present and he could still make out the tear streaks beneath the little bit of powder she had sprinkled on her face.

Maybe she just wanted him to make her feel better.

"So, what's for breakfast, then?" he asked, stepping out on deck and taking in a deep breath.

"I think we're having these scrumptious cakes. They're like bread stuffed with blueberries accompanied by some sweet syrup. They're absolutely wonderful!" Amethyst squealed lightly as she hugged him around the middle before darting off toward their awaiting table.

"Aye, sounds delicious," Cadell said.

They were heading east, and the sun was just rising over the horizon. Amethyst stopped momentarily, looking at the rising orb of fire.

She seemed so carefree for the moment.

"Isn't it beautiful, Cadell?" she asked, then thanked a crew member as he helped her into her seat.

Cadell stopped beside her, following her gaze and watching the sunrise as well. He smiled and nodded.

Amethyst stabbed two of the cakes and piled them on her plate, drenching them in syrup as she began to eat.

"Captain, you mentioned swimming? Today is gorgeous and those waves are calling you." Cadell smiled faintly and took another bite out of one of the cakes he was eating. Perhaps the swim she had suggested was what she really needed.

"You're right, you're right," she nodded with a laugh.

"Amethyst!" At that moment, Darien's voice echoed across the ship, calling his captain.

Amethyst smiled. "I suppose I must go speak with Darien first." With that, she rose and moved across the main deck and down to the gun deck from where Darien had called her.

It was wrong of her to so readily ask for Cadell's comfort. But she didn't care. She could do as she pleased and if having him close calmed her emotions or was a pleasant distraction, all the better.

Darien had moved back to his quarters and as soon as she entered, he gestured for her to close the door.

In her gut, she had known something was coming after they had found the *Golden Lion's* remains. Perhaps it was another reason she had tried to be playful and carefree. To ignore the feeling, and also not to let anyone else on to it. But as always, Darien was in tune. There was a pit of dread she couldn't shake.

And she knew. She must face whatever had been coming.

In the first mate's hands was a bloody piece of paper. She couldn't even begin to describe the look on his face as Darien met her gaze. It was beyond rage. Amethyst blinked, her smile only then falling. "What's wrong?" she asked, a tremor in her voice.

"Read this, Amethyst," Darien growled out.

She snatched it from his hands.

*Amethyst,*

*By now you should have discovered the remains of your precious ally, the Golden Lion. While you have evaded your kind for the last half of your life, if you do not return to Clozza at once, what you saw will be the fate of every last one of your beloved crew.*

Below the writing rested the stamp of the Fae Royal Navy.

As she read it, Amethyst's eyes widened, then narrowed. "How dare they!" she screamed, crumpling the paper in her hand and letting it drop. "What makes them think they can do this to me? I owe them nothing!" She paused, huffing for a moment. "We've got to hurry to Aeoumrese."

"Yes, Captain. I shall get the rowers going immediately." Darien walked toward the door. Before he could even open it, Cadell was stepping in. Amethyst looked between them as the two stared at each other silently. Then Darien said, "You come too. We'll need every helping hand we can get." Afterward, Darien briskly stalked out.

Cadell nodded, though approached Amethyst. "I'm here," he murmured to her. He then turned and quickly followed Darien.

Amethyst looked briefly at Cadell as he came over, smiling lightly. She managed to give him a brief hug before he went back to Darien. She headed toward the main deck, instructing some of the men who were already there that they were getting a move on.

"What's first?" Cadell asked Darien. Cadell's voice had become more dark, somber. Several men swept past Darien and Cadell, heading down below. The ship lurched forward with more speed from the rowers.

"Follow me," Darien ordered, heading to the second deck with the others who had come. There were not many rowers down below, but they made up for the small number in their strength. A drum was magically beating itself to keep the rhythm going. Cadell did as ordered, slowing slightly to observe the drum.

Darien sat on one of the first benches and motioned for Cadell to do the same. Even the first mate was helping. As soon as he placed his hands on the oar, it lit up a brilliant green before settling back down to its normal color.

Cadell took a seat next to Darien, observing the other momentarily, and wishing he could use magic himself. Still, he placed his own hands on the oar, beginning to row manually. The other oars flashed and immediately the ship went faster as they began to row in unison. Aye, the *Gargoyle* truly was full of surprises, Cadell thought.

After some time had passed, Cadell took note of the salty droplets which burned his lips and dripped on his hands. It was sweltering below deck, but no one seemed to mind.

"Darien, what's going on?"

Darien opened his mouth to answer when a powerful explosion boomed and the ship rocked dangerously. "The Fae Navy has started firing!" a crew member yelled from upstairs. Darien cursed, let go of the oar, and ran upstairs.

Cadell hadn't been in this sort of situation before, that he could truly remember. But then again, it was natural; somehow it was still familiar. Cadell continued to row, only glancing at Darien when he left. He wanted to rush above deck also, but he had to obey orders.

Then again, what was more important to him? Obeying orders and staying here, or disobeying orders to do something for Amethyst? He wasn't sure entirely what it was that continuously drew him and his thoughts toward her. And he knew if he did, there was always the chance he'd do something foolish, but he had once been a captain; he was a quick thinker. It was almost instinct what to do. Cadell stopped and quickly made his way above deck.

Men were scattered everywhere, and Darien was demanding to know where the captain was. One man pointed to a form that was huddled on deck, a stronger crew member protectively covering it.

"Get down!" another crew member yelled and more explosions rocked the ship. Several of the men hit the deck, covering their heads before trying to get up once again. Cadell looked briefly around and froze as he finally noticed the myriad of naval ships surrounding the *Gargoyle*.

Everything seemed to calm as a plank was thrown aboard and a male in a white uniform came across, several guards in silver uniforms following. The crew members tensed, getting ready to attack. But the echo of cannons being loaded stopped all movement.

"It wouldn't be very wise to attack me." Fangs glinted from his mouth and two finely pointed ears rested calmly against his head. His skin was fair, far more than Amethyst's, and showed off his sharp facial features. His dark green hair was folded over one side of his head. "Now, bring me Amethyst."

There was some protest, but all knew it was pointless. All attention turned to the grunt of a female. It was Amethyst as she stood up, stumbling slightly. She was bleeding from her arm where a small chunk of wood stuck out of it. She stepped forward, a look beyond hatred on her face. "Zador," she whispered, the sound almost inaudible except for the slight movement of her lips.

Cadell simply stood there, watching, a frown coming over his features, and his gaze fell on his captain as she stepped forward in defiance of whoever the man was. It didn't take long for him to figure it out. The pointed ears and teeth gave him a hint.

Still, Cadell was confident of one thing: this was the *Gargoyle*. She would not be sunk and so easily disposed of as the captain's late lover's ship and crew. Or so he hoped.

"You received our little letter, didn't you, Amethyst?" Zador questioned, a smirk on his face. Flashing blue eyes looked her over.

Amethyst remained quiet.

"You did? Then why didn't you head back?"

Still, she did not respond.

"You owe us nothing? My dear, you have a very large bounty on your very pretty head." Zador seemed to read the unspoken words in her eyes.

Amethyst's gaze, defiant, never wavered.

"You won't go? Too bad. That means we'll have to sink your precious ship and your crew and return you back to your family. A certain hesi is eager to see you again." His smirk widened into a wicked grin. "But, if you do decide to follow through with our orders, then you may keep your ship and crew." His voice was tantalizing, mocking.

At last, fear came into her eyes.

Zador smiled, or rather smirked. "You wouldn't want that, would you?" A pause, "I didn't think so. So, come along, Amethyst, you'll ride with us."

Trembling, she took a step toward him.

"Amethyst, Captain, wait." Cadell's voice was firm, and strong, and perhaps louder than he'd expected, but it didn't faze him. He stepped forward, watching the mysterious man in white. "Just what exactly do you think you're doing?" Cadell asked the male fae leader. "Don't make the mistake of thinking that just because we're pirates we have no loyalty to our captain. We won't let her simply be taken off without a word said or a notion of resistance made." He stopped, staring at Zador. His eyes never changed in intensity and confidence as he chanced a glance toward Amethyst and back at the fae leader.

"Cadell!" Darien hissed, though never moved from his spot. Amethyst looked at Cadell when he spoke, and her eyes narrowed. He wasn't sure. Was she upset with him? Or wondering what he was doing? She trembled and took a semi-step back. What was she thinking?

Her movement was noticed by everyone, the crew especially. Their grips tightened on their weapons, preparing to strike as soon as Amethyst took that second step. It seemed as if they would be taking victory, until the man in white spoke again.

"Hmm. Another lover, Amethyst, dear? Just couldn't stand being alone after I killed your former one? His blood was delicious," Zador said with a laugh. "But think wisely, Amethyst. What do you want to happen? You want your ship and crew to go down, along with your precious son, if he is still alive, and be returned back to your husband? He misses you dearly. Or, you could keep your ship and crew alive and serve under our iist the way it was supposed to be, in whatever war he is planning."

When the male fae leader spoke yet again, Cadell resisted his urge to say anything. How dare this fae male propose such a threat!

Finally, Amethyst opened her mouth to speak. "*Ex-*husband," she corrected. "What will happen after the war?" Her voice was shaking.

It was only then Cadell realized: she was terrified. Was it this fae captain in particular? Or the Fae Navy itself? Was it what this Zador had threatened? He knew she was outnumbered. Was that the cause?

Zador shrugged. "I don't know. Whatever the iist decides to do with you then. I mean, you are still a pirate. Perhaps you will be made to spend the rest of your immortal life in the Fae Navy." He smirked and she tensed.

She looked around, staring directly into each crew member's eyes, searching. Amethyst's eyes locked with Cadell and she licked her dry lips, turning back to the male. "No."

Zador's response came swiftly as her answer still lingered on her lips. "Very well. We will take you by force." And with that, the *Gargoyle* rocked violently as cannonballs hit her from all directions and guards flooded aboard.

The pirates let out a cold-blooded call, rushing forward to meet the enemy. Darien went for Amethyst, trying to shield her as she struggled to defend herself. She was too weak right now. The blasting of cannonballs continued as several crew members yelled. "We're taking on too much water!"

Cadell's mind drifted for a moment in wrath toward Zador. *'This fae lad just doesn't get it,'* he thought. Pirates had no loyalties but to their captain, at least that's always what Cadell had come to believe. It didn't matter what race or creature. Pirates were pirates, free-living rulers of the seas who did as they pleased. They signed allegiances to no one; they served no one; they were feared and hated, but also secretly admired for their ways.

As soon as the fight erupted, Cadell sprang into action, glancing at Amethyst only briefly before Darien was with her. Cadell knew he didn't need to worry; Darien could handle it. He moved forward.

Despite their valiant efforts, the *Gargoyle* was badly outnumbered. She was being hit on all sides from the Fae Navy and whether the pirates liked it or not, the ship was starting to go down. Zador did nothing as he watched from his stance on the plank, ignoring the blood as it splattered on his pristine outfit.

Cadell had a target, and he knew what he wanted to do. He was in no place to order anyone to do anything. He left that to Darien and was pleased to hear him telling the men to load the cannons – about time! Cadell's sword was drawn and he plowed through those who stood in his way. Before long he was reaching his target, dark eyes focused on the man in white, the leader of this Fae Navy fleet.

"Hey! Your fight's with me," Cadell bellowed above the shouting men and exploding cannon fire. His gaze was steady, eyeing his opponent and anticipating what would come next. He circled slightly like an animal, making no lunges or attacks. Yet.

Zador raised a brow lightly as Cadell challenged him. The man's expression was both amused and unaffected. He dismissed a couple of guards to apprehend Cadell while he stepped back. The guards nodded and advanced, holding long pointed swords. "Surrender peacefully," one ordered.

Cadell frowned, a change coming over him. In that moment, he was no longer the pirate who had just joined the

*Gargoyle* and was doing handiwork and speaking respectfully and obediently. His eyes and face had changed to that of determination and something else. He smirked faintly at the two men Zador had sent toward him. "Not in any immortal life," he said, and he swung his sword through the air, adding to the echoes of clanging metal and exploding cannons. Smoke and debris filled the air as parts of the ship exploded. He refused to let this ship fall as his had fallen.

Cadell quickly sliced through both opponents and glared at the man in white. "Send all you want, they will all have the same fate. Draw your weapon and fight, coward." Cadell advanced toward Zador.

The fae navy captain only smirked and motioned for more fae soldiers to apprehend him.

Meanwhile, Amethyst could only stare blankly at the scene before her, not even able to draw her own weapon and fight. Never had she felt so weakened. She barely registered when Darien swept her away to her son's room for some protection. A blend of fury, terror, and grief consumed her.

How had this happened? She had successfully evaded the Fae Navy for years. Ever since her first escape. She had known better than to confront them. At the first notion they were closing in, she had always run. After all, she knew when she was outnumbered and outmatched. Two to one? No problem for her. But surrounded?

It was among pirates and civilians she was feared. But the Fae Navy was one thing she had always run from, and with haste. Yet even now she wanted to stand up and fight back.

Still other thoughts taunted her mind. The *Gargoyle* was going to go down to the murky depths and she would be returned to her ex-husband on the fae mainland.

Briefly, images of her time with her ex-husband began circling in her thoughts. His face was so near to hers as he grasped her and pain resonated along every inch of her body with each of his motions as he forced her to do anything he wanted. The slaps of flesh being impacted echoed in her ears and bruises were etched along her fair skin where his fists pummeled her. Her soft cries and the tears which burned against her cheeks had only caused him to taunt her, grasping her all the more.

No.

She couldn't go back there.

She thought briefly of her son and decided that she had to surrender. For him, for Cadell, for her ship and crew. No matter how powerful she was, she could never outmatch this Navy Fleet.

The *Gargoyle*'s captain fumbled around and finally revealed a trap door. She slipped into the passage below deck which would lead to an opening to the exterior of the hull. Amethyst knew this way she would not be hindered by her crew, who would try and stop her.

Soon, Amethyst reached another opening, blocked by another trapdoor just big enough to crawl through. She opened it up, looking at the water below. She sat there for a moment, trying to figure out what to do to get across. Lo and behold a rope dropped down carelessly from the other ship. Exactly what she needed. She reached out and grabbed the rope, pulling herself toward the opposing ship and then planted her feet against its hull. Finally, Amethyst started climbing her way up. She was weak and struggled with her climb, but she wouldn't let that stop her.

Amethyst gasped for air as her hands clamped onto the side of the ship she was climbing, her chest heaving. Luckily her crew was too engaged in battle to notice their captain scaling the opponent's vessel. However, she did not stay hidden for long on the Fae Navy ship. When she looked up, there were several soldiers staring down at her. They grabbed her hands and not so gently hoisted her aboard. Immediately her hands were bound, and they dragged her to Zador.

"Stop firing," Zador yelled as soon as Amethyst was brought before him. He held her arm roughly, but she did not fight back. Zador's men stopped fighting immediately and the pirates of the *Gargoyle* did as well, clearly wondering why. Amethyst's crew's faces were full of questions as they watched her.

"Put down your weapons," Amethyst ordered with a faded voice. The crew did as she told them. She knew they trusted her judgment. She looked at her first mate. "Darien, make sure they follow orders."

"Aye, aye, Captain," Darien responded with a nod, looking at her intently.

Cadell's voice rang through the silence. "Wait. How can we know our captain won't be slaughtered?"

"I guess you'll just have to trust me, won't you?" Zador sneered back at Cadell.

Amethyst huffed, looking at the man in white. "You won't kill me. You need me too much."

She let a small smirk drift across her face, but it quickly disappeared as his hand made contact with her face. The impact rang out on the two ships and Amethyst's cheek started to turn red and purple. Her eyes were glossy with tears, but she refused to cry.

Zador turned back to the pirates, eyes narrowed. "Anyone else like to talk?" There was silence. "That's what I thought. Men, hook the *Gargoyle* up to our ship. Put the others in the brig. We sail for the mainland."

The fae soldiers, which were fewer in number now thanks to the *Gargoyle* fighting back, immediately put their commanding officer's orders into effect. "You heard him, filthy pirates. To the brig." The soldiers drew their weapons and started to herd the pirates up like cattle towards the bottom of the Fae Navy ship. Amethyst was shoved along with them.

Cadell felt Darien's sharp gaze scrutinizing him as they were marched to the brig. "Do not do something foolish and try to mess with these men, Cadell. As your first mate, you will obey me or so help me," Darien growled.

Cadell's gaze caught Darien's as the first mate spoke to him, and he scowled. "Aye, aye," he retorted. Though he knew Darien was right in every way possible. "I'd pro'lly end up dead if I did," he muttered more softly to himself.

Darien seemed satisfied at the answer.

The brig smelt horribly of death and decay and there were even some long-forgotten bones lying around, a full skeleton in one of the cells. They were split up into four different groups: the crew in one cell, Darien in another, Cadell in his own little cell adjacent to Darien's. and Amethyst also in her own cell across from Cadell's, chains wrapped heavily around her wrists and ankles. As the three most threatening of the prisoners, Amethyst, Cadell and Darien could be guarded more closely if separated from the group. Amethyst sagged against the wall, crying softly.

Cadell angrily slumped back against the side of his little prison. He glared at the opposite side, as if it would somehow mysteriously break if he stared at it long enough in his wrath. He barely even noticed the other things about this place. The smell of rot and death. The decayed skeleton. One thing was certain: for the most part, even if they wouldn't admit it, the rest of the crew were scared and unsure. Who knew what was going to happen from here?

It didn't take long for Cadell to come back to reality and face the fact that being angry wasn't going to help.

But so far, no ideas were coming.

Cadell moved to the far side of his cell, staring around the brig. The cool tip of something sharp on the back of his neck made him freeze. His first instinct: dagger, don't move. A raspy woman's voice whispered from the shadows of the adjacent cell behind him.

"Oy, mind helping me out? You want out, right? Well, I know a way. If you cooperate. Got a dagger? Or even a knife will do."

For a moment, the shock left him a bit dazed, and then he slowly started to pull himself together. He stepped forward, realizing that even if it was a dagger or a knife, there was only so much reach. And why would this person be asking for something she already had? He half-turned, enough to be able to see the girl, and a frown came to his lips. "No, of course not. What's it to you?"

She glared at him, and he could feel her icy blue eyes scrutinizing, watching him. Finally, she hissed, "Liar! Listen, you have to trust me."

"Why? I'm in enough trouble as is without any help from you," Cadell said.

"What if I could help you all escape? What if I'd take all the blame?" she asked.

"We could 'what if' the world away and it wouldn't help. What if you decide to take the escape and run out?" was Cadell's question.

"Are you mad? Who would do a foolish thing like that? This place is full of people who would kill any one person trying to escape! I'm going to need others to even try. Dolt."

She had a point, but he was still hesitant. He frowned. "Wait," he told her, disregarding the fact she couldn't really go anywhere anyway.

Cadell moved back toward Darien's cell. He glanced around briefly, and had to wait a moment, the guard watching him suspiciously. As soon as the guard took his eyes elsewhere, Cadell recognized his moment. "Darien," he whispered. At this point, his eyes didn't even fall on Amethyst. He used the excuse of it hurt too much, which in a way it did. "Sir," he said, biting his tongue.

Darien did not look at him but motioned with a hand that Cadell had his attention.

Cadell spoke quickly, and quietly. "There's a woman in the cell by mine. She says she can get us out."

Cadell waited as Darien remained silent. Finally, the first mate released his breath slowly. He turned his gaze on Cadell sharply. "We will wait until tonight. It will be far easier to pull off whatever it is she has in her head."

Cadell nodded and slowly backed away.

The girl impatiently glared at him across the shadows as he approached her again. "Well?" she asked in her raspy voice, annoyed at the fact he seemed to be ignoring her. Cadell gazed at her full in the face now and said, "We will wait until tonight. I cannot do anything until then."

Now that he was staring fully at her, he was able to take in her features.

She appeared in her mid-twenties. Thick wavy hair curled down past her shoulder blades, hiding most of her huddled frame as it blended with the black of the shadows. The only exception was the two thick streaks of icy blue near the front of her head. Her clothes were like those of a gypsy: puffed out pants and a top that covered her chest and barely clung to her shoulders. An opaque fabric covered her stomach. Her clothing was faded but its color resembled the streaks in her hair. Her nails were long; that must have been what she had stuck against his neck. He wondered how long she had been here.

What Cadell didn't notice at first was the change that came over her features. Her eyes grew a bit wider in shock "C-C-Cadell!" she squeaked.

Cadell's face twisted into a confused frown and he looked at her as if she had two heads.

She let out an exaggerated sigh. "Don't you recognize me a bit, you dolt?"

He continued to look at her in silence, obviously not remembering.

"It's me. Akaisha. Come on, please tell me you didn't forget me. We practically grew up together."

Cadell continued in silence for a moment as her words sunk in and finally, the light came on in his own eyes. He wasn't exactly sure what to say, though. "Aye... aye... I remember. But what happened to you?"

She scowled and only shook her head. "Never mind, I'll tell you later. What's more important is what's happening with you right now. How the hell did you get mixed up with this? I mean, I can't believe you're with Amethyst... again."

Cadell chuckled softly. "Maybe it's fate. Although I'm not sure how you know about that. How do you know Amethyst?" And for that matter, his past with her.

She stared at him blankly and finally gave another exaggerated sigh. "You really don't remember, do you?"

Cadell shook his head. "No. All I've gathered is a foggy dream where my ship is sinking and then I go under."

Akaisha was silent a moment, scrutinizing him. She sat back, trying to get a bit more comfortable, and let out her breath. "Would you like me to tell you?"

Cadell was uncertain. Would he eventually remember on his own? Finally, he nodded slowly. He hoped this might at least pass the time until Darien was ready to try whatever escape plan Akaisha had in mind. And now that he was ready, she began.

Hours passed as Akaisha recounted everything that had happened since Cadell first captained the *Reaper's Scythe.* As she spoke, Cadell sat back, listening intently. He wasn't surprised she knew so much. For one, she made her living being a source of information, and for another, she had always kept up with him in particular, even when he'd tried to keep her out of it. It was just her way.

She was able to share the events up until he had settled in Tysck.

The moon was shining through the cracks around the brig when Akaisha's tale finally drew to an end and she fell silent. She met Cadell's gaze, searching his face for his reaction.

For a moment, he said nothing, still trying to process everything she had shared. Even now knowing all of it, the physical memories were but shadows in his mind.

Cadell glanced over at Amethyst and Darien, curious about what they were thinking. He knew Amethyst and he had remembered some of it on their own, from the dreams before they had been captured.

Finally, Cadell spoke, his throat hoarse from extended silence. "So here we are..." It was strange, as he gazed at Amethyst. He supposed the feeling of the truth had always been present, yet it had never revealed itself, particularly in his dreams.

Amethyst had only listened here and there as Akaisha had recounted the entire tale. She had no interest in this other fae woman whom she vaguely recognized from the past. Amethyst stared straight ahead, lost in her own thoughts and concerns. First, she was remaining constantly alert for a chance to escape. She knew if she couldn't find one, she needed to plan how to get out once they returned to the fae mainland and were presented before the court. She had escaped once before... but it had been much easier back then.

It took Amethyst a moment to realize the bitch was done blabbing about everything and there was a long silence.

She glanced over, her eyes looking over Cadell's figure. The memories were less foggy for her own mind, yet the spell she had cast so many years before was still present, preventing the memories from truly surfacing.

Amethyst wondered if it were really necessary to have all the memories return at all... for either of them. She didn't see how it would be beneficial whatsoever. At least practically. For one, the feelings the memories would bring would probably only prove distracting. And second, if all of the story were true, would she remember Cadell and her love for him only for him to be ripped from her again?

She knew well the ways of her people... Amethyst also knew she wouldn't be able to watch Cadell die, again. If the story was true, and if she remembered it. The thought of Cadell being truly dead this time would be too much for her to bear, she knew.

Yet to a certain extent, she could feel old and buried emotions burning in her chest, crying out to be known. There was a reason she had buried those memories. They simply caused her too much pain. But now? Now it may be different.

Amethyst wondered if her feelings might be her salvation. She couldn't help herself; she moved toward Cadell, separated from him by only these bars. Perhaps it was the spell weakening with his presence, or perhaps it was long forgotten desires within her. Perhaps it was a different kind of spell all on its own. But Amethyst could not help it as she reached through the bars toward him, beckoning for him to draw closer. "Cadell," she murmured.

Cadell was unsure what Amethyst would do next. She was unpredictable after all. As she crouched against the bars and beckoned, he found he couldn't resist. He moved toward her. Both of them seemed drawn to each other.

Cadell wondered if this could have been the answer all along. Was it possible? He could feel an unknown force indicating what to do. It must be the magic. The spell Akaisha had said in the story that Amethyst placed on herself to forget must be weakening. The magic must have sensed Cadell's presence.

As soon as Cadell was within her reach, Amethyst grasped him, pulling him toward her until her lips met his, a whoosh of energy rushing through their bodies at that moment. She gasped, and the two of them were briefly enveloped in light, blinding both Darien and Akaisha for a few seconds until the light faded in a flash.

Cadell felt it as the memories flooded him. The effects that broke Amethyst's spell must have healed his mind. Magic. "Amethyst..." Cadell whispered, reaching up a finger to brush away an eggplant ringlet from her forehead.

She smiled at him.

At last, the memories had returned, each one a flaming brilliance in their minds as if it had all just happened. Had they been normal humans, they probably would have both passed out. But sleep was not currently an option.

Cadell's eyes were bolder, more certain. In truth, after his fall and amnesia, he had not been quite the same though the same man was at the core. A piece of him had been lost, leaving him confused and searching. Now, that was not the case; the same old captain of the *Reaper's Scythe* was fully present.

Cadell was a bit disheartened not to have been part of Stephan's demise, yet there was no changing the past. He could hardly blame Amethyst for tearing Stephan down the way she had after all that he had done to her.

Cadell did, however, find it slightly ironic and perhaps even a little irksome that the punk Mikhail had been the one to help him get back on his feet. Still, perhaps it had been for the best, as they had become closer as a result. Mikhail had found a girl of his own anyway and was no longer hinged on Amethyst.

Yet suddenly tears began to surface in Amethyst's eyes, and uncontrollable sobs escaped her. Had they been brought together now only to be defeated? She looked up to where she knew the Fae Royal Navy was probably discussing bringing her back to the mainland. No doubt anyone who had assisted her would be put to death.

Cadell was a little taken aback by Amethyst's sudden anguish. He reached toward her, grasping her hand.

At the touch of Cadell's hand on hers, Amethyst looked up, staring into Cadell's dark eyes, searching. Her tears came at the thought of what would happen now that she had been abruptly brought home. For all her fierceness in battle, she knew it would do no good, her one ship against the Fae Navy.

Yet hope was still a feeling in her gut. No. They wouldn't be torn apart. Not ever again. Her brows furrowed, and she gained a look of certainty. She then looked toward Akaisha, now remembering the other fae woman had claimed she had some plan to get out.

Amethyst really hated the sight of her. But she had to admit that she had proven quite useful. Amethyst still had the driving instinct of her kind not to trust this other woman. But so far, she somehow felt less aggressive. "Akaisha," she said sharply, still not finding it within herself to be kind to her either, "What are your plans?"

Akaisha glanced at Amethyst, glaring. Amethyst knew the other fae woman had only done anything for Cadell, but whether Akaisha liked it or not, if she was sticking with Cadell, Amethyst came too. "Get me a knife," Akaisha said finally.

There was a brief silence. Amethyst scowled and Darien rolled his eyes and shook his head.

They had all been stripped of weapons. There was no way anyone had a knife on them. Or so she thought.

Cadell always had a small knife which he kept in a place *no one* would ever dare to look for such a thing. It was strapped inside his trousers along his upper thigh. Of course, he had forgotten about it before with all the chaos, but now, his head was definitely clearer. Pulling out the thing, he ignored the look given him by the others and handed it to Akaisha.

Akaisha whispered something under her breath and the knife glowed. Afterward, she used the blade to slice through the latch of the cell door and she was free. Once she was free, she released the other prisoners with her.

As soon as they were free from their cells, it was all they could do not to clamor with excitement. Now, they could take the fae soldiers above by surprise, take back the *Gargoyle*, and sail to freedom.

Amethyst clung to Cadell in a fierce embrace, reveling in the feeling of his arms around her once more. Yet after a few moments, she straightened. They couldn't linger here below deck forever!

As silently as they could, they huddled together. Amethyst ordered the crew into three groups. "Darien, you take your group to the first deck. Cadell, take yours to the second deck. I'll take mine and handle Zador," she whispered.

"Aye, aye," they all said in hushed voices.

They turned around, preparing to move.

Before they could do anything, however, Fae Navy soldiers descended below deck, seizing them. Time was up. One knife was not going to do them much good and even if they tried to gang up, the soldiers had weapons.

One of the fae soldiers stepped forward, his face scrunched as he studied the prisoners' faces. "*Eir,*" he snarled in fae tongue as he grabbed Akaisha's arm. She dropped the knife, its clatter echoing against the floorboards.

Cadell lurched toward the solider but received a swift punch to the stomach. He coughed, snarling at the man as he dragged Akaisha away from the *Gargoyle*'s crew to another part of the ship.

Amethyst's mind briefly went to her son, who was still resting in the sickbay on her ship. She silently prayed he would somehow get away.

The prisoners were brought up to the main deck, Zador peering down at them from the upper deck. They were pulling into the harbor of Ieola Iezril, a common trading market for the fae folk. As they were pushed forward, their eyes met with a brilliant scene.

# Trials

The seas glistened bright blue, white foam crashing on white docks along the shore. The fae lands were some of the most beautiful in all of Aseath. The market near Ieola Iezril bustled with all different kinds of people whose skin, hair, eyes, and clothing varied widely in colors. There were a handful of people allowed to trade with the fae folk and take the products elsewhere to be sold. Those who appeared 'normal' stood out from the others.

The Fae Navy ship quivered lightly as it pulled up to the loading dock. In the distance, Cadell could see high towers and elaborate homes scattered across the landscape. The soldiers pushed the pirates off the ship and onto the docks, making sure to keep them in check.

Amethyst's face was a grimace as she glared forward. Cadell knew she must be angry about returning so abruptly.

From the docks, the pirates were led toward the palace, the market giving way to houses that increased in size and lavishness as they went further inland. The structures towered high into the skies, lined on each edge and pillar with vines and wildflowers.

Cadell had only seen the fae mainland a handful of times when he had been very young. His father had been one of the merchants to trade with the fae people. While his father had traded, Cadell had spent many long days near the sea playing with Akaisha and getting to know her family.

Still, he hardly remembered the details of the fae lands except for the large buildings at the heart which could be seen from afar. Cadell, at first, was rather captivated by the sight. He regained focus as they were forced off the ship and proceeded forward.

For most of the journey, they followed distinctive roads, paved in cobblestone and dotted with various gemstones. Now and then they followed an unknown path through countryside hills. In the distance, dark entrances dotted the hills. They were tunnel entrances leading deep into the earth where gemstones were mined from below.

Amethyst came to an abrupt halt as the two soldiers who were grasping her on either side forced her to do so. She glared up at Zador who, previously walking ahead of them, now stopped and turned. "These rags do not suit you, Amethyst, dear. And certainly not to be in the presence of his and her majesty." He glanced toward the soldiers. "Take her away and prepare her for her trial. Take the others to the prison. And do not let them out of your sight."

Cadell became still as soon as he realized they would be split up. He glanced at Darien but knew there was nothing they could do at the moment. For now, they must comply. Cadell resigned himself to taking in the sights of the city as they began moving through it again.

As the fae were a proud race, with a long history of battles with others and a reputation for bloodlust at times, their land, particularly the great city, flaunted their wealth and their victories. They wanted any outsiders to look on with awe and respect and to never even think of attempting to rise against them.

The streets were surprisingly clear except for a few children who ran about and their mothers who watched them with doting looks on their faces. The city itself was an ornate assembly of buildings and pathways, the pathways made of marble and shaded by large white arches hidden beneath thick layers of vines and foliage.

Trees billowed high into the skies; large branches full of leaves tumbling downward to blend in with the earth. With each change in directions the pathways took, there was a center of sorts in the forks in the road. Tall statues stood as these centers, dressed ornately with solemn looks on their faces.

As the group neared the capital, the pathways condensed, the arches growing closer together and the natural light becoming vaguer. Only a few rays of light shone down through breaks in the treetops. At last, they broke into a large square, the ground covered with pale marble.

The pirates moved forward through the square, pushed by the navy soldiers. Many of the fae people present paused to stare before glancing away and murmuring among themselves. Clearly, it was not often that prisoners were specifically escorted through the square so near the palace. Or perhaps, there was cause for attention. Cadell wasn't sure.

As they moved around the great tree, the group crossed a long, arched bridge, painted deep maroon, under which flowed a steady stream with cattails along its banks. After the bridge was a long stretch of statues, right arms raised with long swords in their hands so that the statues themselves now formed the arches. They were great fae of history, some of them rulers, others leaders of battle, and yet others heroic warriors that had fallen.

Past the statues was a temple, small pillars decorating each corner of the building and a gentle sloping roof with vines curling toward its tip covering whatever lay inside. From there were various other buildings, some houses, shops, and yet more buildings that were perhaps other sorts of business.

The buildings seemed to increase in size until the group stood before a final pathway, this one lined in precious metals. At the pathway's end was a large arched doorway with great pillars of alabaster stone at the farthest corners of the palace. The wall was high and at the very top, a great dome covered much of the building. The dome was surrounded by statues overlooking the edges of the roof.

With a shout from someone above, the gates began to open with a loud creak and the group entered, the gates closing with a thud behind them.

The palace itself featured high ceilings and mostly open space with great pillars as the main support. Inside were fewer walls, though corridors still lined the structure with arches along their sides.

Cadell wasn't able to observe further as they were led to one corner which had a winding stairway down. The stairs were pale in color with gemstones filling the railing. Deep beneath the palace was the prison, which was heavily guarded. In fact, only a small handful of people had ever successfully escaped and even then, only one had evaded recapture.

Once more, the prisoners were put in separate cells. Amethyst was nowhere to be seen and Cadell quietly wondered where they had taken her.

Meanwhile, Amethyst was also thinking of Cadell.

Being very familiar with her homeland, Amethyst knew where he was at the moment, not that it did her any good.

Amethyst was in an upper room in the palace. The room itself appeared as though it hadn't been touched in years. It was her old room.

Dust lay on all the furniture and Amethyst was surprised her parents hadn't taken better care of it. She brushed it aside. Already, maids were busy cleaning the room up and tending to long forsaken details.

Amethyst was sitting in a dark chair and some older fae women were tending to her. At the moment, she was no longer Amethyst, feared captain of the *Gargoyle* on the seas. Rather, she was *mah sieei ueltho* – the royal maiden – Amethyst, still fierce and respected, but this time under the word of her parents, the *iist* and *iieta* – lord and lady – of the fae people.

Amethyst hated her title and all that it entailed. She wished her parents would let her be. She had no interest in being the princess of the fae folk, the priestess of their magic, and the heiress to the throne. It just wasn't her.

Still, despite her silent resistance, she was in no position to argue and had allowed them to return her at least physically.

Her hair was decorated with pale flowers and a string of iolite gems dangled just above her shoulders from her ear lobes. Her lips were painted stark blue and she wore a long silvery dress which snugly hugged her figure and accentuated her curves. Just above her breasts was a diamond-shaped peephole revealing the top of her cleavage and starting at mid-thigh was a slit down her leg revealing her nicely tanned skin. Upon her feet were pale, iolite-decorated slippers.

There was a knock on her doorway and the maids opened the door to reveal a tall man, dressed similarly to General Zador. She glared at this man, her temper still evident. Amethyst may have been forced back into her previous royal *sieei* role, but she still felt rebellious against it. Nevertheless, she rose, moving toward him with grace and accepting his arm.

"It's good to see you again, dearest Amethyst, back where you belong."

"This is not where I belong," was her coy response.

The man escorted her down one of the main corridors toward the high seats where the *iist* and *iieta* were waiting. Though inside her heart raced, she remained collected, refusing to show any weakness.

Her emotions were still trembling from having just regained all of her memories of Cadell, from Leo's massacre, from being stuck in the brig of Zador's ship, and now being thrust back into a place she had thought she wouldn't see again for years to come.

And worst yet, she knew in her gut that she would be forced to deal with the horrid man who had started all of this in the first place. Her ex-husband. The first man to abuse her in countless ways. She tried to swallow back her dread at the thought of him.

As they entered the great room, Amethyst was surprised to see it was only the *iist* and *iieta,* her parents, and a handful of guards holding Cadell and Darien to the side. Normally for a trial, a crowd was present to witness.

Her eyes remained steady. Amethyst could not discern what her parents were thinking; their faces were guarded. Her father, Etan, looked the same as he always had, with cropped golden hair and fierce azure blue eyes, a shade which could not be gained except from fae genes. His jaw was set and his defined features seemed even sharper against the white and pale blue robes cascading down his figure.

Jaspia, her mother had eyes filled with a tangle of emotions. They were a brilliant amber, accented by her burgundy hair. It was as curly as her own, and it was clear where Amethyst got her womanly figure from.

A male voice echoed, citing the prisoners on trial and their crimes. Amethyst assumed her trial had been sped along past any others for its mere priority – being herself.

"On trial, *mah sieei ueltho* Amethyst, for crimes against the *iist* and *iieta,* all the fae people, as well as many members of other races including murder, theft, piracy, and failure to fulfill oaths of responsibility as priestess and host of the fae magic within her."

"On trial also, the mage Darien for protecting and aiding the royal maiden in her escape and assisting in the crimes already mentioned."

"Finally, with them on trial, Sir Cadell for harboring, protecting, and aiding the royal maiden in the aforementioned crimes and furthermore aiding the fae woman, Akaisha, in eluding the Fae Navy from facing her own crimes and responsibilities toward the fae people. Also for partaking in the crimes already mentioned."

"The trial will proceed as the *iist* and *iieta* see fit."

As soon as the announcer was finished, the lord, her father, rose, garments flowing down his tall, strong frame. "The royal maiden shall have a few moments to speak in her defense before we will determine her fate."

Amethyst felt her father's eyes staring into her own more than she saw it. She could sense he was torn between his obligations against her crimes and his joy at seeing her again. Amethyst imagined he was probably just hoping she wouldn't do something to seal her own fate as penalty of death or worse.

For a moment, Amethyst was silent, all eyes on her. She held her head high, shoulders pushed back. Finally, she spoke, her voice resounding in the high ceiling and firm arches. "I request the presence of only one other before I may speak." *'Please, grant me this. May the gods give me strength to go through with it.'*

There was a brief silence. "And why should I grant such a request to any prisoner?" Etan asked.

"This person should face trials for not only directly causing these crimes I am on trial for, but further acting in crime against the entire royal family." Amethyst's tone was bitter.

"And who might such a person be?"

"Merrick." She almost choked on the name as she spat it out, refusing to use his title. Tension spread like fire throughout her body.

Amethyst's father's eyes narrowed as the name was mentioned. It was the name of her ex-husband, whom Etan had selected and given her to in marriage so many years before.

Merrick was a trusted member of the fae people who had been first to inform the *iist* and *iieta* of her escape. As far as anyone had known, Merrick had always been worthy of his status and Amethyst suspected he had fooled everyone into thinking he'd actually grieved at her running.

As if.

Amethyst had never had a chance to explain to her family why she had run. Perhaps they thought it was because it had been a forced, arranged marriage. She itched for them to know the truth.

"Very well," Etan responded finally. He gestured and two guards left as he told them, "Fetch him."

All was still as they waited. Darien and Cadell struggled against the men who held them to the side. Amethyst imagined they desired to be closer to her for comfort and support. Such good men.

At last, footsteps were heard coming up the corridor. It so happened Merrick had been in the palace already. Word had reached him of Amethyst's return, and he had been on his way to investigate.

As he entered the room, Merrick paused as he saw her, his eyes tracing over her figure.

She was disgusted. As soon as he had entered the room, the tension within her became rigid tightness in her muscles. The very sight of him caused her to sweat and feel sick. She choked back the feeling, clenching her fists. *'No weakness,'* she reminded herself again and again.

With a nudge from the guard, Merrick continued forward, standing on the opposite side from where Cadell and Darien were held. Darien stared at him with daggers and fire. Merrick was large for a fae male, well built. He had deep onyx hair and rusty eyes, not quite red, not quite brown. He was quite attractive and held a certain authoritarian and commanding demeanor.

"Speak, Amethyst?" Etan commanded as soon as all were settled.

*'No weakness.'* "This man is not as he seems." At first, her voice was soft. "The crimes which he has committed are crimes also against his and her majesty and are directly responsible for

the actions which I am accused of." Amethyst silently reminded herself why she was putting herself through this. Truly she had never thought she would ever have to see him again.

"You are the one on trial, Amethyst," Etan interrupted her.

"If I may finish?"

He nodded.

"You gave me to this man, but in the belief I would be protected and cared for. Instead, the marriage placed the magic I am responsible for in the wrong hands." Amethyst paused, as a lump swelled in her throat and she swallowed it back.

"He beat me and demanded to use the magic in order to destroy this city and overtake the high seats. He sought to destroy you both, through me, and furthermore through words and physical abuse, sought to subdue me into doing his will to eventually take over the entire fae territories." She forced back tears at the memories and closed her eyes briefly. '*No weakness. No more running.*'

When she opened her eyes, Amethyst glanced toward Cadell. There was no need to fear. Not anymore. Her voice grew bolder, fierce, angry. "In order to escape the horrors I faced, I asked Darien to use the magic of his own kind, though weaker, to help me."

"I was terrified that as my husband, this man would sense it if I used my own magic and would continue to keep me prisoner. I ran to protect not only his and her lordship, but also the magic for which I am responsible and all of the fae people." Amethyst paused only briefly.

"Furthermore, any of those I killed while on the seas were only those who sought to use me in a similar fashion or those who harmed me or anyone else within our people. For months, I had nightmares and felt I could not mentally escape this man, even though physically I had."

"Had it not been for Darien, and Cadell," she continued, gesturing toward them, "I would never have begun to return to my former self. They protected me as true guardians of our magic and our people so that I might heal and someday return." The last part was only partially true; she had never intended to return. But for the salvation of Darien and Cadell, she said it.

"At the time, I couldn't stay. I was certain *he*" - she pointed toward Merrick - "would destroy me. I knew I had to be constantly on the move; on a ship would suit me best." Amethyst had also run and become a captain to prove to herself and all others that she could not be subdued or controlled by anyone, but she left that part out for now. If her parents pressed the matter, she determined to claim it was part of her overcoming the severe trauma Merrick had caused.

The room was silent. Amethyst knew from memories as a child and witnessing other trials that prisoners would often say anything to escape a certain fate. For some, death. For others, perhaps a life in misery rotting in the dungeons below. She knew the *iist* and *iieta* knew this as well.

But Amethyst was their daughter, and this wasn't any common trial. Amethyst silently prayed they would forgive her and her companions on account of Merrick's wrongs, though she knew they were rarely that gracious. Her crimes had still been committed, and much time had passed since she had run away.

"That's a lot to accuse a man of Merrick's status. Do you have proof?" Etan finally broke the silence.

Amethyst had suspected such a question would be asked. She knew if she used a spell to show her memories to all present, Merrick might say she was only creating them to deceive - it was quite within the capabilities of her magic to show false memories from herself.

At last, Amethyst nodded, stepping away slightly from the man who had escorted her and had held her to prevent her escape. Amethyst knew that while Merrick could accuse her of fabricating her own memories, she could not do the same to those of another. It was simply against the laws of their magic. "Darien," she murmured, motioning for him.

Her first mate moved toward her. In her time as Merrick's wife, Darien had been her servant and had witnessed in person much of her abuse. She reached toward him, grasping his hand in one of her own and with her other hand touching his temple. She whispered a spell in her tongue and above them, a great globe of light expanded, an image within it becoming clear.

Again and again, many different scenes played out, ones Amethyst had strived to forget. It was Merrick in all of them. In some, he struck her down until she bled, leaving her in a mess of tears and injuries with Darien coming to tend to her wounds. In others, Merrick forced himself on her, subduing her will and in doing so, taking a little more of her magic for himself.

"Enough," the *iist* finally spoke, his voice barely containing his wrath on witnessing his daughter's abuse for himself. Etan looked toward the man he had trusted for so many years. Merrick's pale face only confirmed Amethyst's accusations.

Still Merrick attempted to redeem himself. "May I speak?"

The *iist* hesitated but then nodded.

"First, and with respect, my lord, how do we know what we have just seen is the truth and not false images planted to accuse me? It is well known a criminal will try to blame others in an attempt to be free, and one so powerful as Amethyst can do more than most."

"In question," Merrick continued, "shall his and her lordship trust in the word of a murderous, bloodthirsty pirate? A fae woman who has gone mad from years at sea? Or will you trust a man known to serve the fae people and his and her majesty for years before and after her escape? If your humble servant had truly sought after such a grand scheme, would I not have found some other way to achieve it in all this time?"

Amethyst suddenly burst forward, a snarl curling on her lips and rage burning in her eyes. She feared her parents might accept his argument. "You! You knew you could never do it without me. Your power could never rival that of the *iist* and *iieta*! You did not attempt any plot because you feared losing the place of power you already had. You waited, hoping I would return so you could subdue me and carry out what you had intended all along! You–"

She stopped only as Darien grasped her, her chest heaving. "Amethyst..." he whispered. Sweat had broken on her brow and she waited, eyes never leaving the vile creature who was her ex-husband.

If there were any lie to save herself, the suspicion of it was erased. Only true anger and suffering could produce such an outburst.

"Silence!" Etan's voice rang through the room and as he stretched out his hand.

*Iieta* Jaspia finally rose and stood beside him.

"This day, as witnessed by those in this court, we sentence you, Merrick, to death by execution for crimes against the iist and ieta, *mah sieei ueltho*, and for plots against the good of all the fae kind. Tonight, when the moon is highest." Etan's voice rang through the room.

The *iist* paused, turning his gaze on Amethyst again.

Amethyst returned his gaze. She could see his conflict. After all, she had still committed countless crimes, most with the penalty of death, and regardless of her reasons, he was still bound by law.

Finally, he spoke. "Your request was granted and your case made. If there is anything further, speak it now." Her father seemed to be giving her just a little more time to defend her actual crimes.

Amethyst faltered only for a brief moment. She had hoped if only slightly that exposing Merrick would cause her parents to change their minds about trying her. At last, her gaze hardened again. She didn't regret anything that she had done, with the exception of her time with Stephan.

Amethyst recognized at this point that her fate was in the iist's hands and if what she had already shown them had not turned things in her favor, she wasn't sure what else would. Finally, she shook her head, keeping her mouth shut.

"Very well." There was a pause, "This trial will be continued after the execution. Tomorrow at dawn. Until then, return the prisoners to their cells."

Amethyst was not sure what that meant was to come, and she struggled as fae guards grasped her. "I can walk myself," she said sharply, shoving her arms from their hands.

They were taken back to the prisons beneath the palace, once more placed in separate cells. This time, Amethyst was placed with the others.

All were silent, though once the guards left, Amethyst began to sob softly to herself, attempting to keep it from the others. She, at last, released the torrent of emotions that had risen at the sight of Merrick and she deeply desired for Cadell to erase the memories of her ex-husband.

All night she was awake, unable to rest with all that was happening. Though deep below the palace, Amethyst knew when Merrick's execution was over, for a sudden feeling of relief swept over her body and mind. No longer would she fear him. Yet the impending verdict from her parents still held a knot in her stomach. What she wouldn't give right now for a bottle of rum!

Amethyst was startled at the jangling of keys unlocking her cell when the guards returned to take her but was surprised when they came only for her and not the others. Her gaze met Darien's and then Cadell's, fear for them and the possibility she might never see them again flashing through her. "No... Darien... Cadell..." she murmured, tears coming to the surface, but she forced them back. Surely fate would grant her something!

She struggled the whole way as the guards took her through the palace, though they surprised her once again as they took her to her father's study instead of the high seats. Amethyst settled, calming as they approached her parents. At last, she stood before them, her face and the stains streaked down her cheeks clearly showing her feelings and exhaustion.

The *iist* was seated at a plain desk, the *iieta* standing quietly beside him. "Leave us," said Etan to the guards.

They did so with haste.

Once they were alone, Etan gestured for Amethyst to sit across from them in a chair similar to the one in her room.

"Amethyst... forgive us for the trial and all you have been through on our account. You know the laws. Over last night, we discussed everything brought to light. While Merrick's death brings some justice, there are still debts to be paid."

"Darien, as your servant, should have brought you back to us in the first place, or as soon as he was able, and reported everything he had witnessed. Rather, for his own freedom, he helped you abandon your people and your duties to them. For that, he must be tried. And this Cadell... while he is not one who answers to us or our kind, he chose to suffer his fate when he aligned himself beside you."

Amethyst's father paused, his eyes studying her face. She was trying to remain as calm as possible.

"However, you are our daughter," the *iist* continued. "It is your rightful place to be a priestess of our magic and the royal maiden for our kind. Because of Merrick's wrongs, and using your status on the seas to fight against the fae trafficking, we've decided you will receive forgiveness for your other crimes."

"But don't take this lightly. For everything, your return to status is gracious. You will go to the temple at midday, and wash in the spring to renew yourself." Etan paused again. "I'm sure you're more than aware of it, but the fae trafficking amongst the pirates has now gotten completely out of control. I've decided to direct the navy to end it once and for all, which will require a war which will begin soon, and you must be ready to direct the magic as well as our people."

Amethyst remained silent as he seemed to finish. She knew he was right that her forgiveness was gracious... but she would rather be sentenced to death than to life back in the palace. She didn't belong here.

"Welcome home, Amethyst." Suddenly, both of her parents' faces were alight.

More silence followed. She was in shock, and completely uncertain how to respond.

"What is your response?" the *iieta* asked, her voice light.

Amethyst had been chewing on her tongue. "I haven't returned by choice and I don't need any favor. If this is my fate, I'd rather stand on trial with my companions for whatever sentence they are given. If you truly wish for my happiness, let us return to the seas. I rule my own life and my ship." She paused. "I have no intentions of aiding you in your bloodthirsty wars." Not that she really had room to talk. Even if it was against the fae trafficking. She had other ideas on how to deal with *that* problem.

Her parents were silent a moment. "You know we can't."

Amethyst's true nature was bold and she had learned to fight for herself. No more would she ever let anyone force her to do anything she didn't want to – and that included her parents.

Instead of biting back her outburst, Amethyst leaped forward, hands landing on the desk. "*Ebba,* you've never considered any of my desires. You chose my husband and you chose my duties without ever asking what I wanted. I never questioned you. But I am not the same and I now know what matters most to me. Please, grant me this one request!"

Jaspia responded swiftly, "Amethyst! You know very well it was fate that predetermined your duties. You were born with the magic." She paused. "Come with me."

Amethyst's eyes remained hard, her golden irises glimmering, and she turned, watching as her mother moved past her. She followed her, knowing she was still bound and there was no use trying to do otherwise.

# Home

$\mathcal{A}$methyst and *Iieta* Jaspia walked through the palace, stepping finally into one corridor that opened into a large courtyard. It was framed by trees, their branches expanding outward and reaching high into the heavens, full of dark green leaves.

In the center was a great fountain on top of which was a statue of a woman, dressed similarly to Amethyst. She was bent downward, one hand tucking her long hair behind her ear, the other hand lightly touching the pool of water in which she stood. Many flowers grew all over the ground surrounded by soft grass and several stones which were scattered across the courtyard.

On the opposite side was a shaded path, almost invisible to anyone who didn't know it was there. They soon came to a doorway made by low-hanging branches, through which was a hidden grove.

A serene pool lay under a steady waterfall with an unseen source high in the stone face behind it. The top of the waterfall was covered by foliage growing beside and over it. The interlocking branches of the trees ensured light only crept in where it could.

Without hesitation, Amethyst and Jaspia moved into the pool, walking through it until they passed beneath the waterfall. Behind it was a large cavern, stalactites and stalagmites hanging from the ceiling and jutting up from the floor. The walls glistened with all manner of precious stones. Great pillars which had been erected rose along the walls and within the cavern was another pool.

A soft glow emitted from the stalagmites and the pool and, as Amethyst moved closer, the glow grew brighter. She had been here before many years ago before she had been given to her ex-husband. She remembered this place well.

Amethyst stopped when Jaspia did, silent. She wasn't a fool. She knew why her mother had brought her here. This was the temple her father had spoken of and she knew the *iieta* meant to invoke the feelings they believed she once had.

But being here, guarding this place, nurturing the magic – it just wasn't her, if it had ever been.

Still, with *Iieta* Jaspia behind her now, Amethyst didn't have much of a choice. She silently burned with frustration. She understood that she really had no room to negotiate. The list of her crimes was a long one and truly she felt that there was no win for her. It was either this sort of prison over her will or a physical prison where her body would rot away.

Finally, Amethyst moved forward. "*Uh shamish...*" she whispered, before touching her finger to the water of the pool. '*Restore me.*' She was enveloped by the light that flew out from it.

Soon, the light faded, and there was a soft glow coming from Amethyst as well. Finally, she turned, facing the *iieta*. "Mother... you know I always wanted to leave here. Even before Merrick, I wanted to explore the world."

Jaspia was silent, staring at her daughter a moment.

There had been times in the past when Amethyst had been able to influence her father's decisions by asking her mother. But that was a long time ago before Amethyst had even come of age.

After all, the fae women were usually suspicious of other women of any kind, even mothers and daughters. And in this case, Amethyst and Jaspia hadn't been around each other in a very long time.

Amethyst hardly thought her mother might move against her. Ultimately, her leaving had probably been better. Within the royal bloodline, relationships usually became tenser if one of the family members was a source. With the duties involved, once a female had come of age, the *iieta* was typically wary of the source wanting to take over.

Of course, it also depended on trust and relationships. If a mother and daughter were particularly close, they would strengthen each other. In Amethyst's case, she felt her mother probably didn't feel a threat from a daughter who wanted nothing to do with any of her duties as a royal maiden.

"We will discuss it further at dinner. Go to your companions for now... but remember your place, and theirs, for the time being," Jaspia said.

Amethyst left and moved quickly back to the prisons beneath the palace. She thought about escaping again. But she knew even trying at this point would be foolish, and probably much more impossible now than when she had so many years before. She put it out of her mind.

As Amethyst approached the cells, Cadell, Darien, and her other crew members imprisoned there looked up, all quite curious. "Nothing's changed so far," she said simply.

Darien knew what she meant immediately, but Cadell's eyes were still searching.

"I am to return to my duties as guardian and priestess. And you will stand trial to determine your fates." Amethyst paused, longing to embrace Darien and Cadell yet knowing she would not be allowed to enter their cells or to release them even temporarily.

Amethyst found it infuriating that, for all her power, she could not be granted what she wanted. Of course, she was quite capable of using her power to take what she wanted by force, if she so desired. She could overtake her parents' position of authority and become the new *iieta*. But then she would truly be tied down to the mainland lest she lose everything altogether and plunge the fae people into chaos.

Also, despite her free spirit, Amethyst hardly wanted the magic to be used in such a terrible way. In her heart, she had always kept it hidden from the outside and protected it from those who would use it darkly.

As she waited, she thought of what she could possibly yet say to persuade them.

Finally, it came time for dinner. Amethyst left the prison, albeit reluctantly, and moved through the palace toward the dining hall. She felt very strange, having become used to the way things had been for her on the seas. Surely, she would suffocate if her parents made her stay.

As she reached the hall, the *iist* and *iieta* were already waiting. "Come, Amethyst, sit."

She obeyed. Amethyst could understand why they were so happy to see her and eager for her to stay. They had no other children and while they would live for a long time yet, they probably wondered who would succeed them. Or perhaps, they desired to have her near so they could use the magic to prolong their reign indefinitely. Amethyst also wondered often why her parents had never had more children, but then she had always been troublesome.

Still, she had been blessed with the magic and she was one of the few fae who could do the necessary duties. But that didn't mean they couldn't find someone else. It was just easier and better for them to use Amethyst, she was certain.

They were eating a full meal, something she hadn't had in a long time, even considering her meals as captain and her time as Stephan's wife. She was quite hungry and though her eating showed her appetite, she was still well-mannered. Perhaps her parents felt once she had eaten, she would be more approachable.

"Amethyst..." Etan began.

She met each of their gazes, though did not feel like any more arguing. Surely, they knew she would find some way to escape again if they did force her stay... eventually.

"While we both understand why you left, and why you never returned, you must know you have a responsibility to your people. You cannot spend the entirety of your life as a hapless vagabond running amuck and wreaking havoc on the seas–"

"And why not?" Amethyst interrupted him. This was her last chance. She felt it. "At least the fae people are respected now. And actually, being on the seas probably worked even better than if I had stayed here to protect the magic. At least two of the sources were separated so they could not be destroyed or overtaken all at once in one place.

"And while I was on the seas, I made a significant impact in preventing our women from being sold into fae trafficking, as you already pointed out. I practically single-handedly disposed of the worst scumbag who was behind the whole thing. If it wasn't for me, our people would certainly be in a worse place. Without me, it will undoubtedly lead to utter chaos and, also as you shared, war. Will you really go to war against the entire world, Ehba? That would result in far more deaths of our own people. I am fully aware of my *responsibilities,* and I have no less fulfilled them on the seas – perhaps even more so!"

Clearly, a meal had made her mind and her tongue sharper. They were silent a moment.

Amethyst's gaze remained firm. She wondered what her parents were thinking. Couldn't they see she didn't belong here?

"My heart belongs on the seas alongside my" – Amethyst paused briefly – "alongside those who would die to protect me," she finished, glancing toward her plate and taking another bite of meat.

Amethyst had to catch herself. She almost said, '*my husband and greatest ally*'. Cadell. She hated the fact that she had allowed anyone else near her. But she had thought he was dead! They hadn't officially married other than their marking bond, but with Stephan gone and her memories returned, she longed more than ever to be with Cadell as his wife, officially in the eyes of the world this time. Sailing side by side.

Instead, her choice of words merely included Darien and all of the men in her crew. She wondered if her parents realized she had meant someone in particular.

"Your arguments are sound, and it's true that many of your actions were against those who would harm you. Let us consider your requests." Etan paused.

Amethyst knew that for the most part, killing and domination were hardly concerns. After all, the fae were a people of conquest and power. She knew the real concern here was the fact she had run away and become a pirate. A lowlife being plucking at the success of others. At least, that's what most pirates did.

"Let's discuss this later." A smile graced Jaspia's face. "For now, let's just enjoy the meal. It is the first time since you left. Tell us of all we have missed, since it has been so long."

The rest of the night they talked and caught up, enjoying their time together for the first time since her return. At last, high moon approached.

"It was pleasant to dine together," the *iist* said. "We will part for tonight. You should be aware that your accomplices' trial will be at dawn. But aside from that, you may sleep in your chambers." Amethyst knew better than to hope there was any chance of freedom though. She knew that even if she was in her own room, it would be heavily guarded.

Amethyst's eyes fell, but she simply nodded and left. Soon, she was in her old room. Once again, she could not sleep. If this continued, she would certainly begin to go into one of her states. Or perhaps being so near the natural magic source in the grove beyond the palace would prevent it for longer.

Rather than going to bed, Amethyst began moving about her room, little waves of nostalgia crashing over her as she sorted through old trinkets and looked at what were once her belongings. At last, she opened her old wardrobe, running her fingers along the silken materials of many dresses, nightgowns, and various other items of clothing. She had certainly been spoiled when she was younger.

She slipped into a plain gown, the shade the softest of greens, and finally lay back on her bed, staring up at her ceiling. This life was no longer hers and she longed to be lying on deck, staring up at the night sky instead with the sound of waves crashing against her ship and lulling her to sleep.

Amethyst awoke with a start, not realizing she had even drifted off. It was not yet dawn though the earliest signs of morning were already creeping through her window.

The trial.

The words pulsed against her brain.

Amethyst groaned and moved to don other clothing, slipping into a different dress than the silver one she had worn the previous day. This dress was the color of topaz with vibrant blue accenting its edges. It draped around her shoulders and curved widely about her neckline. She let her hair fall loosely about her and slipped a simple white lily into the eggplant ringlets.

Finally, Amethyst left the room, moving toward the high seats where she knew the trial would take place.

When she arrived, Cadell, Darien, her parents, her crew, and several others were already present, apparently waiting on her. Amethyst stared at Cadell and Darien, temporarily debating using some sort of spell to cloak all of them and escape right now.

But with the royal guard, there was a slim chance they'd get away. One of the drawbacks of being a magic source was that others of her kind could easily tap into her magic and discern where she was. It was part of why she had constantly stayed on the move all these years to evade the Royal Navy.

Amethyst moved toward the group of people nearest her parents, waiting for the trial to proceed.

Cadell and Darien were brought forward, their crimes in assisting her restated from before when she had been the one on trial.

Amethyst's face was stoic. She knew most of her crew were looking at her right now to figure out what to expect and if they should try anything. '*Ah, their loyalty never wavers,*' she thought pleasantly to herself.

As the *iist* and *iieta* had done with Amethyst, the two on trial were given a chance to speak for themselves.

Darien shook his head. "If I am to die for my actions in protecting her royal maiden, so be it." He was her protector, always.

Cadell was one far more outspoken, typically. He knew the fae were proud people, stubborn, set in their ways, and hell-bent when it came to the things they believed in and cared about – especially concerning possible threats to said things. But he knew one other thing: they appreciated loyalty and respect.

Cadell lowered himself in a semi-bow and met each monarch's gaze. To the fae, avoiding eye contact was a sign of disrespect. Further, it could imply something to hide. "I won't deny my crimes as a pirate. It's what I am and always will be. But know I've always acted in favor of the fae kind and have protected the royal maiden. I've actively sought to assist her in healing many wounds – physical, mental, and emotional."

Amethyst was glad when Cadell referenced Merrick in this. The scum deserved to be loathed, even in death.

It was clear both men showed no remorse, though they apparently did not believe their actions should be considered true crimes either.

Amethyst watched as the *iist* and *iieta* stared between the two of them.

Their faces were steady. Briefly, Jaspia looked at Amethyst. Their eyes locked for a moment. Amethyst silently pleaded Cadell and Darien's cases. Then, the *iieta*'s gaze was back on the two on trial.

Finally, Etan spoke. "Well you have said it yourselves. For your crimes, you will be sentenced to execution on the morrow. Re-" He stopped as Amethyst burst in between her parents and the two on trial.

"Ehba! Don't do this."

The *iist* looked at her and she met his gaze squarely. She could see he was searching her, questioning her silently. "What, Amethyst, should I do, then?"

"Let us swear an oath by our kind. Let us go and live free, and in return, we will return every fae who has been taken." It was true she had already massacred Stephan and some others who had kept the trafficking going. Yet there were still many fae women who were being held far from home, and she had no doubt there were others involved in furthering the trafficking.

And, while it was also true fae women were extremely territorial and she in no way intended to let even one step a single toe aboard her ship, their lives were still valuable and deserving of honor, freedom, and respect. She could only imagine the horrors they were suffering and above all else, she had learned that *no one* deserved to suffer the hell she had lived through. She was certain there was some way to fulfill this oath she was swearing before the court, without allowing them physically aboard her vessel.

"I will put them under the protection of the *Gargoyle* and her crew. The ship has a name not many will trifle with. I'll do all in my power to reunite our people from the seas. Further, we will bind and hand over anyone who dared bother with our kind. Let them suffer the fates they deserve. Ehba, Uhlmse, let this be the way we repay the debts of the crimes, with every fae woman returned."

A faint smirk tugged at the corner of Etan's lip. The *iist* remained silent a moment longer, staring into Amethyst's face.

A further argument dawned on Amethyst. "My responsibilities can still be fulfilled. As a well-respected and feared captain, I can continue to protect our magic and keep threats at bay."

Etan nodded slowly. Apparently, Amethyst had a point. She wondered what had become of her parents discussing her requests.

The *iist* raised a hand and snapped his fingers. A young mage scampered in with a piece of parchment and pen. No words were needed. Etan drew up the oath in the form of a contract and as he extended it toward her, Amethyst stepped forward, signing her name across the bottom.

She glanced at Darien and Cadell and motioned for them to do the same. They each paused a moment. The two men glanced between each other and then at Amethyst.

She knew they must be confused. They had come with the expectations of death sentences. Or worse. And now all of a sudden, they were being granted pardon and even being allowed to return to the seas?

She would fill them in later, after she also found out what her father was really thinking. She knew there must be more.

Finally, Cadell and Darien complied and followed suit in signing the document.

"It is done," said Etan, tucking the contract aside. "Join us, Amethyst. You all must stay tonight, at least."

Amethyst nodded, her eyes still firm as ever. Beneath the luxurious gown and jewelry, the sea captain was the one standing before them. With that, she turned and left, Cadell and Darien following after her.

Amethyst led them down the corridor and proceeded to slump against one of the walls, finally releasing her breath. She never could have imagined this sequence of events. She looked between Cadell and Darien, and finally threw her arms around both of them.

To Amethyst, everything was still surreal.

After the trial, the crew had been released. She couldn't return to the sea without her crew to man the ship, so they spent the day preparing for the next. They gathered supplies in the market and made plans for once they left.

Amethyst paid some men on the docks to make repairs on her ship since the *Gargoyle* had been hooked to one of the Fae Royal Navy ships when they had been captured.

While the crew worked on details, Cadell and Darien stayed in the palace and moved through the gardens. Darien showed him around a bit since Cadell had never before been to this part of the fae territory.

Amethyst, meanwhile, met with her parents as they'd requested.

They finally explained to her why they had agreed during the trial. On one hand, they had felt she still needed consequences and must repay the debt she owed for abandoning this life the way she had so many years before.

But they had decided they could no more dictate her life as they had when she was a child. They could see her abilities to rule, and that she was a woman now.

They had at last decided to use her position on the seas to their advantage. It was a small way she could repay her debts, but they had agreed with her statement during the trial that returning the fae women and fighting against the fae trafficking was a worthy agreement. They hardly wanted to lose her again after so much time and they finally recognized that if they didn't let her return to the seas, they would lose her forever.

At last, night descended, and after eating, Amethyst and her parents parted for the night.

Darien went to one of the rooms down the hall from Amethyst.

Cadell started to follow, but Amethyst beckoned for him to join her. She had longed for his touch through all of this, and now was her chance. As soon as they were alone, she grasped him in a very long kiss.

Cadell gasped, surprised, but not complaining. "Amet–"

"Shh... don't talk," she whispered, pressing her lips into his again. She pulled him to her room, intent on making up for much lost time.

Sometime later, Amethyst lay back on her blankets. Her fatigue was weighing on her and pulling her to a sleep she had not been able to truly enjoy in far too long.

Cadell, however, lay awake, his mind restless. Now that he remembered everything, he longed to regain what he had lost. Of course, his *Reaper* was at the bottom of the sea... but that didn't mean she couldn't be rebuilt. He longed to captain his ship again, sailing beside Amethyst with his own crew... rather than merely as her subordinate.

Finally, he drifted off to sleep, deciding all would be worked out later.

They left early in the morning. After another meal, Amethyst said goodbyes, mostly for her parents' sake. At last, they had been reconciled.

As soon as they boarded the ship, they searched for Ercio... but he was nowhere to be found. He hadn't been anywhere in the prisons – she would have known. "We have to find him," she declared.

After hours of asking on the docks, a young merchant mentioned seeing a lad of Ercio's description aboard another ship sailing from port on the day Amethyst had arrived.

He had escaped.

Amethyst prayed for his safety and swore to find him amidst her journey to restore the trafficked fae women.

Once they were out to sea, Cadell walked up behind Amethyst. She was standing against the edge of the *Gargoyle*, hands grasping the side rail and eyes staring off.

Cadell's hands encircled her arms gently, and he leaned in, his breath tickling her ear in spite of the sea wind that was blowing all around them. "Welcome back, Captain."

# Glossary

The fae language was invented by myself, K. L. Dimago for the world of Aseath. As such, I've included a glossary of terms for your convenience in translating.

While there are only a few phrases used in *Ametrine: Twists of Fate,* the fae language is expanded and explored throughout the series. Enjoy!

*Mah sieei ueltho* – her royal maiden

*Iist* – lord

*Iieta* - lady

*Uh shamish* – restore me

*Eir* – you

Ship Cloaking Spell:
*Ihm mala aalo bh uiiecht miolzam*

*Ksiu hohulha tesc eot oselo heha*

*Osimhum ue Zeszieih, osimhum ue ushy*

*Mlii yh esh aekh eot ueo shohy*

*Ehba* – father

*Uhlmse* – mother

*Hesi* – an earl or member of the nobility

Energy Draining Sword Spell:
*Ilzam ebioh klii ue bieth*

*Blot mah tescohaa bhkish ue*

*Ahsh eot oiy yh ylii bh aeoht*

*Mala ursah oi uish ylii bh!*